AWKWARD ON THE ROCKS

MARCEL FELDMAR

DEAD SKY
PUBLISHING

Paperback ISBN: 9781639511976

eBook ISBN: 9781639512348

Published by Dead Sky Publishing, LLC

Miami Beach, Florida

www.deadskypublishing.com

Cover by Reiko Murakami

Design & Formatting by Apparatus Revolution, LLC

Edited by Anna Kubik and Megan Yundt

Copyedited by Megan Yundt

To my wife, Shelley: My love, my inspiration, my drinking partner.

CONTENTS

1

THE RESURRECTION

I stood on my front porch, feeling the air, holding the phone loosely at my side, staring at the sky. The atmosphere was trying to tell me something. An electric tingle slid across my skin, and I glanced down at the birthmark on my wrist. It was glowing again. It hadn't done that in a couple of years. A storm was coming.

I lifted the phone up, dialed Trevor. Nothing. I stared at the screen while a familiar heavy feeling started sinking down my throat into my chest. No answer. I hung up, but the sense of foreboding stayed with me. A body had been found at the bar I work at, and I was pretty sure I knew who it was.

I needed a drink, but that would have to wait. I was a bartender at The Lost & Found, and I'd also created most of the specialty drinks on the menu. I'm a Mystixologist.

The Lost & Found is stylish, but not fancy. Like one of those hipster Mixology bars, but with a supernatural twist. It's a DarkWaver bar, and I'm one of them. I didn't like to talk about that as my 'powers' are unavailable.

. . .

Every town, every city, has a crossroads and the Lost & Found was built on Vancouver's very own X marks the spot. Our drinks could push you towards whatever eternal damnation or guiding light you believed in. That's where I was last night. Before my entire world had crashed and burned through an unwanted phone call.

My shift had ended, and I was sitting with my drink, rubbing my left wrist. Moving my thumb around the triangular birthmark that tied me to the DarkWave.

Technically, I'm a Fire Elemental.

In reality, I'm an alcoholic.

Sometimes I work, sometimes I drink, sometimes drinking is work. And sometimes work interrupts my drinking. So, I was sitting at the bar with drink number two, watching Dabriel mix up a batch of Lucifer's Last Call for the end of the night. She was one of the other bartenders, but she was also my friend. We'd spend hours pairing ingredients and working out descriptions while talking about anything and everything. I was about to ask what her plans were after work when my phone buzzed distractingly.

I hated phones.

I answered quickly hoping to get it over with and get back to my Ezekiel's Wheel (a sort of biblical tiki drink, one of the good ones.)

"Yeah. Thomas here."

"Um...Thomas Dante? Awkward?" It was a man, a very anxious man.

I almost dropped the phone.

Only two people ever called me Awkward, an unwieldy nickname, and as far as I knew both were dead. My father, may he still be drinking with the angels, and a shape-shifting bastard named Nick Noir.

"Who is this?" I asked, as I drained the rest of my drink.

"Nick..."

I could feel the liquid get stuck in my throat, leaving barely enough room to breathe.

"Now that's the definition of an Awkward silence. C'mon, don't you have anything to say to your favorite shifter?"

"You're dead..." I felt a tightness inside; one I didn't want to deal with. I hung up.

Staring at the phone in my hand, I whispered, "You're dead."

Dabriel was looking at me from the other side of the bar, I made a pleading gesture while pointing to my now empty glass. She shot me a quick smile as she started on a drink. I turned my phone off and leaned back only to be startled upright by a hand on my shoulder.

"Dante!"

"Slone," I smiled. Trevor Slone, the owner of the Lost & Found.

He gave me another pat on the shoulder as he sat on the stool next to me. "What are you getting?" he asked, eyeing Dabriel as she casually spun a barspoon.

"Bartender's choice," I shrugged.

At the Lost & Found, the bartenders will never tell you what to drink, but they do provide hints. You don't want to find yourself on their bad side. They could lead you on an alcoholic path towards misery without breaking an ice cube. I've seen them do it. I completely trusted Dabriel's palate and expertise. Naberius, the other bartender, was Dabriel's brother. I wasn't so sure about him.

"Sweet or sour?" Dabriel asked.

"Not too sweet, but not too strong, either. Maybe...like springtime with a touch of summer."

She pulled a quick sleight of hand motion so I couldn't follow along. She placed the finished product in front of me, her two hands on either side of the highball glass as if daring me to drink. I accepted the challenge.

It was gin based with strong essence of Juniper, but there was a slight lemon pepper sweetness smoothing it out and brightening the drink at the same time.

I took a sip, "Like fresh cut grass."

"Wait for it," Dabriel said.

Then it hit, a slow build of spice. Not too hot, but a curling burn on my taste buds.

"That's the summer," she grinned.

"Amazing. What is it?" I asked.

"I call it the Resurrection. It strengthens the soul," that was all she gave me. Some recipes were hers alone.

No matter what I asked for or what mood I was in, Dabriel would find the right mix to fit. Trevor Slone, however, wasn't one for suggestions. "I'll stick to the Mephistos."

Dabriel wrinkled her nose. "Are you sure you don't want to try what Thomas is having?"

Trevor squinted at the bottles behind the bar, pretending he didn't know what was there, "Nah," he glanced up at Dabriel. "Thanks, though."

She narrowed her eyes and wiped down the counter, "Fine. It's your soul."

Mephisto's Waltz was one of the bad drinks. The bad drinks taste the best. All souls are born into this world perfectly balanced. The choices you make on your way towards death tip those scales. The drinks we make can add weight to either side. My cocktail added light, while Trevor's added dark.

THIS, of course, was the easy explanation. There's more to each drink, and rules to each mix. Those in the industry had to be in the know, and that's why Dabriel wasn't happy with Trevor's order. Dabriel begrudgingly started the pour; I knew what the look on her face meant. It meant she was getting really annoyed. I also knew Trevor wasn't being difficult on purpose.

Since I started working at the Lost & Found I've noticed that Trevor couldn't stick to the good drinks and ignore the bad. He kept a balance going. I'd tried a few Mephistos in the past. They're nice. The kiss of the Gin hits with a little Whiskey slap, and a hidden rush of sweet rises and fades against a dangerous whisper of absinthe. It's not a powerful concoction, but it does give you a little psychedelic head rush that pushed your consciousness about a day into the future. There are those who think precognition is a good thing, but it isn't.

Trevor had been drinking this mix for a week, and I was sort of hoping he'd switch it up soon. Last week he was ordering Holy Grails. Those were all light. Like a day at the spa in a glass, it just gave you a nice glow. And unlike the Mephisto, which left you with a sharp headache and the desire to knock back another drink, the Grail just faded away softly.

"You okay, Trevor?" I asked.

"Yeah. Tired."

Trevor's not big on conversation, but we've spent so much time together that a few words can hold a lot of meaning. I knew "tired" meant that he was unhappy but didn't want to talk about it. I gave it another shot.

"How many drinks have you had tonight?" I asked.

He answered with his eyes closed, "Too many…"

"Alright, my friend. Try not to have too many more. You don't want to be on Dabriel's bad side," I could tell this wasn't the night for a heart-to-heart. "I'm out. But here's to the night," I lifted my glass, and we solemnly cheered as Dabriel leant against the bar, watching us.

I finished my drink, gave Trevor a nod and Dabriel a backwards wave. It was time to go home. I walked down Cordova Street towards my car, thinking about coffee, got in my car, did a slow exhale, and turned my phone back on to dial the most recent number.

I had no idea what I was going to say. I almost died because of that man. I killed because of that man…I killed that man.

I listened to his phone ring. No answer.

It rang for so long I started wondering about what sort of voice mail one was supposed to leave for a dead shapeshifter. I didn't get far with it, though. The ringing stopped.

"Nick?" I queried.

The response was hesitant, the voice familiar, "Thomas…I didn't think I'd hear from you."

I clenched my teeth. I was surprised at how hard it was to not yell. I took a deep breath.

"I didn't think I would either, but here we are. Just tell me what you want."

"Well, this is going to sound strange," he said. "But I was wondering if you could help me find an old book."

"Strange is you calling me in the first place. I'm not really the best person to ask about missing books."

He laughed, quick and nervous. "It was one of your father's books."

That shut me up for a second. "What are you talking about?"

"I know you probably don't want to hear this, but I was going to buy a few books from your father before the..."

"Before you killed him?" my voice came out tight and cold.

"I had nothing to do with that. I was there, but I didn't kill anyone."

My chest felt like solid rock, but I needed to follow this though, at least to figure out why Nick was still alive.

"What book are you looking for?" I asked, shaking off the hits of memory and emotion and biting the words off between clenched teeth.

My father had been the owner of an extensive library dedicated to the world of the DarkWavers, including some very rare books on Mystixology. His own writings were full of information dealing with the ties between different ingredients for cocktails and the unseen world surrounding us.

I HAD STUDIED HIS RECIPES, and through them I'd learned how to see things that shouldn't be seen. Recipes for drinks to amaze your taste buds and open your eyes as well. I ended up knowing more than I wanted about the things living in the shadows.

I also learned how to help people get out of those shadows.

Not my parents, though.

"Look Awkward..."

"Don't call me that," I snapped.

"Okay, whatever, Thomas. I'd rather not discuss this over the phone. I'm probably being paranoid, but can we meet in person? I'm willing to pay you for your services."

Perhaps I felt it might bring some good karma around, perhaps I was a glutton for punishment. I didn't really have the closure I needed after my parents died, I hadn't even been on speaking terms with my father, but family was family.

"How about tomorrow night? Do you know where the Four Calendar Café is?"

He did. He could be there around eight.

I hung up, feeling dizzy. Thinking too much about it would drive me crazy.

Crazier.

It was time to lie down, turn the lights off, and pretend to sleep.

THE PRETENSE BECAME the real thing around five in the morning, only for the phone to wake me with its evil buzz an hour later. I answered out of habit, and angrily, "Someone better be dead."

"Thomas. Can you meet me at the Lost & Found?" It was a woman, but as opposed to Dabriel's smooth tones, this voice was sharp-edged and wouldn't take no for an answer.

I believe in coincidence, up to a point, but having both Nick Noir and Agent Jessica Fervor call me in a space of less than twenty-four hours was no coincidence.

Something was brewing.

"Well, hello Jessica," I said, all sweetness and flowers, "I am doing wonderfully well. And you?"

"A body, burnt to a crisp, turned up at the Lost & Found. How do you think I'm doing? I need you to get your ass over here."

"What?"

"Listen, Thomas, now's not the time. There's an extra-dead Dark-Waver at the bar where you work. And a missing book of recipes that, according to your unctuous bartender, Naberius, is priceless. You were here last night. I need answers before the VPD asks too many questions."

"I'll be there in an hour," I hung up. I stood still for a few seconds, just breathing in the air. It was going to start raining soon. I could taste it.

I sat at my old Mahogany desk, leaned back, reached down to pull the bottle of Final Angel Bourbon from the bottom drawer, and took a swig.

Then I took another.

Between Nick Noir, Jessica, my parents, and the whiskey in front of me, the only things I had that were solid were old photographs, torn letters, and fragments of a broken heart.

2
INTRA INCENDIUM

I stood on my porch clutching my phone and wishing the drink had been stronger. It was for the best, though. If I was going to face Jessica it would be better to be sober and try to not let her see what a joke my life was. I started learning the best way to mix drinks long before I'd learned the best way to drink them. Still don't have that part down. My parents had been amazing mystixologists. Amazing enough to attract the attention of the Agentia Obscura. As a teenager that piqued my interest more than living life behind a bar; so, I dove into the DarkWave and learned all I could. It paid off. The Agentia officially hired me when I hit nineteen—old enough to drink; old enough to mix. Mystixologists are sort of like bartenders, but that's like saying you're a magician because you pull crap out of hats for children. This is closer to saying you're a magician because you can pull a demon out of the darkness. It's one of those jobs that can only be done by DarkWavers.

The last time I'd heard Jessica's voice she had been refusing to come back up to my apartment. There was a fast hug, a stain of tears on my shoulder, and she was gone. Vanished into the rain while I was caught in the sudden crash of a breaking heart looking like John Cusack on a bad day. And now she was back.

Jessica Fervor, ace agent of the obscure. Now that, maybe unfortunately, bothered me more than a possible homicide at the bar.

Well, no. That's a little dramatic. It's just that when I last left our intrepid agent, she was choosing truth over love. She chose the rules of the Agentia over a relationship with me.

I tried calling Dabriel. I locked the door with a phone pressed between my head and shoulder, annoyed by the lack of an answer. She was probably otherwise occupied, but still, it was me calling. I grumbled as I headed for my car. I needed to get to the bar, but I needed more coffee first. Especially if I was about to see Jessica again. Alcohol keeps me steady, but coffee keeps me sane. Didn't have time to go through the brewing ritual again, but there was nothing wrong with a café stop on the way.

I arrived holding a large mocha and a slightly bad attitude, but that started to dissipate when I saw Jessica. She attempted a smile, but I could tell she wasn't happy. I knew it wasn't me, this time.

"Hey Jess," I said, softly.

She nodded, looked at me, and then quickly away. Her attempt at keeping a professional cool didn't seem to be working…

She hadn't changed much. Other than the length of her auburn hair and a new shade of lipstick she looked almost the same. Small details that clashed with my memories.

She motioned for me to follow, and we moved towards a concrete bench situated outside the front door. Usually crowded with smokers, today it was us and a pigeon looking for a handout. We sat, startling the bird, and she smiled. This time it felt real…

"How've you been, Thom?" she asked as we sat down.

"I've been all right. You know, the usual," I jabbed my thumb towards the wall behind us. "Working, drinking."

She gave me a distracted nod, "That's good."

I knew she was thinking about what had happened inside; finding the remains of a crispy fried ghoul at a Crossroads bar is not a good thing. But if we were doing small talk, I could play.

"Why'd you come back?"

All right, so maybe I couldn't.

Jessica gave a quiet laugh, "Still going straight for the throat, I see."

"Ok, never mind," I paused. "What happened here?"

She stared up at the sky for a few seconds before answering me. I knew whatever happened was really bothering her. Not only because she called me, but through her unusual lack of conversation, the way she was sitting on the bench, almost turned away from me. The glances towards the ground, like she didn't want to make eye contact for very long. I used to be so comfortable around her. Even when things got bad between us, it wasn't like this. . .

"The fire started somewhere around three in the morning. The VPD got here first and cleared the area for the Identification Officer," Jessica explained. "They found a few things that led them to call the Agentia, so now we have jurisdiction. But I can't really tell you more than that. We're still waiting on an ID for the body."

The shock of seeing Jessica again started wearing off. The Lost & Found had seen its share of strangeness, drunken brawls, hauntings, noise complaints, and poltergeist activity. But as far as I knew, never a murder. And it had never actually been shut down before.

"Shut down?" I shook my head. "This is definitely not good."

"I know, but that's all Gilles told me when he called. Dead Dark-Waver, missing book, Lost & Found. The Agents are pretty much done down here. They got here close to four a.m. I've been here since five. Still, you can't go in until he gets here."

I didn't hear a word Jessica said after the name Gilles escaped her lips.

"Gilles? Gilles Deuxcoeurs? You're still working with him?" I asked, eyes wide.

"Don't start," Jessica let out a slow breath, pausing before speaking again. "He called me a couple of weeks ago. I've been working with the Toronto branch of the Agency since I left..."

"Me."

"Vancouver," She glared. "He needed my help with this case."

. . .

I CLENCHED MY TEETH. I owed Gilles a lot, but after the inferno at the Riddle House our relationship went sour. Meanwhile, I glanced at Jessica, I had my suspicions they'd been involved on more than a professional level, but I hadn't talked to Gilles in years, and I wasn't looking forward to breaking that streak. Everyone seemed to think he was smooth and suave; I thought he was smarmy. Whatever it was; Jessica had fallen for it.

"We aren't sure about all the players, yet, but there's a chance it involves a shapeshifter, so he wanted me on board..." Jessica explained. "I almost didn't come, but I still need some sort of closure," she paused, struggling with the memory, "I left Vancouver after Nick attacked me," her eyes shone with a hint of sorrow. "I had to get on with my life, and I couldn't do it here. Too many memories. But when Deuxcoeurs called I knew I had to come back. It sounds stupid, but I guess I'm thinking if I can find another shapeshifter at least some of this will be put to rest."

I'm an idiot. I didn't like Gilles, but I didn't like seeing Jessica upset either.

"I understand. I...it took a long time before I could go out and deal with people. Working here has helped."

"Listen, Thom, there's more," Jessica sounded worried, "I think this involves you, and I mean more than the fact that you work here."

"How do you mean?" I asked, knowing I probably didn't want an answer.

"I don't want this to be weird, and I do want your help, but the fire...I'm sorry, but it reminds me of...you know," she went quiet.

Oh.

I tried to lighten the mood, "So how is our favorite Batcaver?"

It was a general term I liked to use when referring to the wonderful Agentia Obscura. Mainly because of the tongue in cheek gothic noir flair, but mostly because Gilles hated it.

DarkWavers are made up of, basically, immortals, shapeshifters, elementals, psychics and sorcerers. Almost all unnatural denizens of the world fall into one of those categories. For example, vampires are immortals, werewolves are shapeshifters, and Voudou falls under sorcery. This isn't set in stone; it's more of a loose guideline defining the roles, hierarchies, and laws making up the Waver world. Both Gilles and Jessica fall under the psychic umbrella. Jess has slight empath abilities, while Gilles has a very specific type of mental capability that can be used to convince the NoWavers that the strange thing they just saw was really something normal.

GENERALLY, DarkWavers have half a soul. There are some exceptions. The NewWavers are those who have recently become, through curse or bite, part of the DarkWave clan. The dead ones: zombies, wraiths, all your favorite ghosts and demons are NextWavers. Usually, soulless. Normal humans are blessed with full souls, and we call them, fondly, NoWavers. Then there are the ones you don't want to mess with. The ColdWavers. Sort of like the "great old ones".

Jessica shot over an annoyed look, "Gilles is fine. You'll have a chance to catch up with him soon enough."

"Great," I deadpanned. "So, how long have you been here?" I asked.

"About a week."

"And you didn't call me until today?" I tried to sound casual, but it didn't work.

"Look, you know how I can get when I'm working. A bit…"

"Obsessed?" I interrupted.

"Absorbed. "She glared at me. "You know this isn't the ideal spot for me to be in either, Thom."

She stopped as her phone rang. A ringtone I recognized instantly. "Buffy The Vampire Slayer?"

"It seemed fitting," she shrugged and answered. "Gilles?"

She nodded a few times, then put her phone away, "He's almost here. We're okay to go in."

I stood up, thinking about walking into my home away from home and having it tarnished by a charcoaled body. I already felt on edge, and this wasn't helping. A few lines of yellow tape and a couple of cops stood by the door. Jessica handed me a pair of gloves and shoe covers, flashed her credentials, and the cops moved aside. I took a moment, and a deep breath. I'd seen some messed up scenes before, but it had been a while, and this was my home. The bar was brightly lit by high intensity lights. Everything was visible, the cracks on the wall, the paint chipping on the ceiling, the stains on the floor. I knew the Agentia had already been here, as the Vancouver Police didn't have the same type of equipment. The Batcavers worked on a higher budget. That's another thing I didn't like about Gilles. His paycheck.

AS WE WALKED towards the bar I forgot about Gilles. All I could think about was the smell. Burnt flesh and hair. A horrible combination of beef fried with battery acid and a side of sulfur. It wasn't as bad as it could've been. It must have been quite the stench a few hours ago.

It was obvious where the fire had hit. The body had been removed, but the charred wood remained. A crisscrossed patch of black scarred the floorboards at the foot of the bar. It looked as if that's where the damage had started, and then lines of seared wood radiated outwards towards the bar and nearby tables. There didn't seem to be a pattern, just a layer of destruction across the hardwood floors. I started to move to the other side of the bar, while Jessica looked around the room. The velvet drapes lining the corners had been torn and pulled off the walls, about half of the liquor bottles had been smashed, and almost all the taxidermy had been thrown across the room. Jessica held a hand up.

"Wait here," she ordered. "I'm going to check out the office, I'll be right back. Please, try to not touch anything. You don't do this anymore, remember?"

I GAVE A SLIGHT NON-COMMITTAL SHRUG, and she turned and moved back towards the office. I waited a second and then walked over to the other side of the bar, trying to see if anything seemed out of place. The fire hadn't reached this side of the bar, which seemed very strange. But bottles had been smashed, and the cash register was open and empty. Then a flash of green caught my eye. The CD player was still on, and the lights were flashing on the display. I knelt, something was stuck in the tray, but then quickly stood up as I heard someone come into the room.

"Don't drink all the evidence," sneered a voice behind me.

"If it isn't Liaison Officer Gilles Deuxcoeurs," I replied.

I hadn't seen him since Jessica left; I hadn't spoken to him for longer. We were never friends, didn't like to be called acquaintances, and we'd worked together enough to know we'd rather not work together.

"Dante," he curtly replied, the faintest hint of a French-Canadian accent pushing the vowels in the wrong direction. "And it's Operations Director now."

"They promoted you?" I asked, wide eyed with fake surprise. I hated to admit it; but Gilles Deuxcoeurs was excellent at his job. He was obviously also good at getting dressed. Suited up like a man in black, he was spiffy for a special agent.

"Nice shoes," I gestured to his Kenneth Coles. Black, spotless. "Pay for those yourself?"

"We don't need to start off on the wrong foot, Dante."

"Foot," I chuckled.

He sighed, "Look, no jokes. This is serious. We've got a fire that seemed to skip a large section of the bar, a dead DarkWaver, and a missing book."

"The Intoxicantata," I nodded.

THE INTOXICANTATA WAS one of the Lost & Found's prized possessions. Trevor usually kept it locked up, but I had seen it a couple of times at the bar. Opened under Trevor's supervision when we needed to track down an obscure recipe or two. "It's usually in the safe in the office."

"It's not there now. The unfriendly bartender says it's one of the owner's prized possessions," Gilles said.

"Naberius. That's Dabriel's brother."

"That's good to know. And the book. Is it worth killing for?" Gilles asked.

"I guess that would depend upon who wanted it," I said, "Have you talked anyone else who works here?"

"Just the two bartenders, Dabriel and Naberius," Gilles paused, "We haven't sorted out the ID of the deceased, but the owner, Trevor, has not been answering his phone."

"Do you think..."

"We wait for the evidence. You know that," Gilles said shortly, then gave me a stern look, "And where were you at three am?"

I stared at him for a second, "Really?"

"Look Dante, you were here at some point last night. I'm just doing my job."

"When I left, Dabriel and Trevor were still here. But you knew that already," I turned my back to Gilles and pointed down towards the CD player, "But here's something you didn't know. You might want to look."

"You're still a suspect, so stop playing detective," Gilles snapped. "That's not your job anymore," Begrudgingly he moved around the bar to see what I was talking about.

Slipping on a pair of gloves he bent down and tried to eject the disc. The CD player finally opened with a clicking whirr and a squeezed groan of metal and plastic.

Gilles straightened up, the disc between his fingers. "This isn't for music. Possibly digital files. But then why would it be in a CD player?"

"Could have been a last-minute hiding place," I pointed out.

"Play nice," Jessica said, walking up behind us.

"We are," I smiled sweetly, "I'm just giving Deuxcoeurs a little refresher course in detection."

Gilles curled his lip in a sneer.

Sometimes it's the little things.

Gilles turned to Jessica, "I think I can read it if it hasn't been scratched up too much. I'll have to take it back to the office."

"Where's the body?" I asked.

"Back at our offices with the Medical Examiner," Gilles said. "We should head over there after this. You could join us if you want."

"What I want is to know why I'm here. Jessica called, so I came, but other than the fact that I work here, I'm not sure why you need me," I wondered out loud.

"I wouldn't say we need you, Dante, but you were here last night. And there's the fire, as well as the traces of alcohol on the floor, the walls, and the victim."

"It's a bar," I noted.

"Obviously. No surprises there," Gilles ignored my tone. "But I need to know if one of the drinks could have done this. You know the ingredients, and you know more about mystixology than anyone at the agency," Gilles explained. "You also know the Wavers who hang out here, and you must admit there's a similarity between the fire here and the one that hit the Riddle House. The way it emanated outward, the way it didn't destroy everything, but what it did touch...it decimated. And, well, you used to be a good investigator."

"Emphasis on the used to. I don't do this anymore," I countered.

Jessica stood across from me on the other side of the bar. "Thom, listen. Not only do you have a stronger connection to the elements than I do, but maybe because of the drinks you've mixed, or just that bartender's intuition, you sometimes see things the rest of us don't. When we used to work together, I wouldn't have been able to find most of the things I did without your help."

"Without my help you wouldn't have ended up in the hospital," I muttered.

Gilles narrowed his eyes, turned to Jessica, "Jess, could you give us a minute?"

She smiled, a little longer than she should have, I thought, and walked away. He waited until she got outside and then turned to me.

"Look, Dante, I know you got into trouble a while back with the Triple Alliance, and your powers aren't what they used to be, but we all need to work with what we have. I also know Jessica doesn't know anything about it, and I'm fine with keeping it that way. Thing is, we need you here now. But even if you don't help us, you'd better stick around."

"Are you saying I'm a suspect?" I asked, stunned.

Gilles buttoned his jacket, "I'm saying this isn't your first fire, or your first dead DarkWaver."

I knew it was going to come up at some point. "Alright, so I've got a past, but it's not my present."

Gilles sighed, rubbing his forehead. "Okay, look. You're not a suspect, and we need your help, but there is something going on here that involves you. Maybe you don't know what it is, but you know how the NoWavers work. They want things tied up in nice little packages. The local cops are going to be asking questions, but we have jurisdiction. Work with us and I can get them to go easy on you."

"Don't do me any favors."

"I'm not doing this for you, Dante, it's for Jess," he nodded towards Jessica who was walking back in.

"Right...don't leave town. I know the drill," I also knew Gilles was right. This was a crime scene, but the NoWavers would treat it differently than the Agentia.

We know who they are, they don't know who we are. That was Gilles' area of expertise, making sure they didn't find out about us. The Triple Alliance was created to keep the peace between our worlds, the core being made up of DarkWavers, NoWavers and ColdWavers. The ColdWavers being the wild card, but in order to maintain balance, they had to be included.

I don't think any of us had ever met a ColdWaver, although I had felt the presence of one at my hearing...it was like being touched by a moment of darkness.

"Dante," Gilles glared at me.

I shook off the memory, "What?"

"We want your help, but if it's too much to ask you can go home. I can come by with questions for you later," Gilles looked over at Jessica, then back at me, "Honestly, I still have my suspicions, but Jessica trusts you. And yeah, Jess is right. You'll probably see things we'd miss."

He held up the disc as an example.

"Ah, that was just luck. You're not that bad."

"Just don't tell me it's some kind of spontaneous combustion curse."

"I don't know yet, Deuxcoeurs," I said. "It was either a curse, a potion, or Dabriel really messed up one of her flaming cocktails. Maybe she put too much whiskey in a Blue Blazer or something. Only thing is Dabriel doesn't mess up her drinks."

"So, are you going to help?" Jessica asked, standing next to Gilles.

"I don't know. I need some air. Clear my head. The smell in here is getting to me."

I really wanted a cigarette, but I couldn't allow myself to smoke one. I had a silver tin holding three cigarettes, and it had been holding them for almost two years now. I knew they wouldn't taste good, but taste wasn't what I needed. Besides, I hadn't quit, I'd stopped. There's a difference.

I WALKED OUTSIDE, stared at the clouds unfurling in the sky as if they were going to spell out some answers. I wanted to help Jessica, but I'd already promised to meet Nick. I had to focus on that first. The cold air, sparked with fresh rain, helped clear my head. I closed my eyes and pictured the scene inside the bar. It could have been spontaneous combustion, and I could be working the X-Files, but it wasn't and I'm not. It could have been a curse, but I had a feeling Gilles was on to something. I was willing to bet it was connected to a drink. Especially if you combined that with the missing Intoxicantata. I tried calling Dabriel again. Still no answer. This was not normal, and not good. I tried Trevor. Answering machine. This was even worse. It wasn't unusual for Dabriel to not answer, but Trevor was usually reachable. I left a message. If someone was using the Lost & Found's recipes to do things like this, he should know about it.

"Any luck?" Gilles asked over my shoulder, startling me.

"No," I turned sharply, glared at him. "Have you been able to find Trevor?"

"No," Gilles pulled out a cigarette, offered me one, shrugged when I declined. He lit it and took a long drag.

"Okay, walk me through this."

Gilles flicked his cigarette, ashing the ground. "Dabriel found the body. She said she'd left after Trevor, the owner, right?"

I nodded.

"She'd made it halfway home but turned back to make sure she'd locked up. Evidently the two of you had been trying out some recipes, and she was a little distracted?"

"Just a little fun, she wasn't drinking though," I added.

Gilles continued, "She didn't see anyone, but a car passed her right before she pulled into the parking lot. It was raining hard so she couldn't see any details. The door had been forced open. But the book…The Intoxicantata. It's a list of your drinks?"

"It's a list of drinks," I corrected. "We rarely use them. Some of the recipes in there can do some serious damage if they fell into the wrong hands."

"I think the wrong hands have what they want, and I need to figure out who those hands belong to. Who was the last person to use that book?"

"I don't know. Dabriel didn't have it out last night, so maybe Naberius?"

Gilles narrowed his eyes and dropped his cigarette, grinding it into the asphalt with the heel of his shoe as Jessica joined us, "Anything else you might want to add?"

I shrugged, "I think the book wasn't the only thing the suspect was after. There was one body, a missing book, and the disc we found, right?"

"Yeah, so? What are you getting at?" Gilles questioned.

"I figure someone broke in to steal the book, but someone else tried to hide the disc. So, that must be connected. The body is either the burglar, and we need to find Trevor, or…"

"Or Trevor is dead," Gilles finished for me.

I could feel an uncomfortable tightness in my chest, and an unwanted emotion building up behind my eyes.

"We don't know that yet," Jessica interjected. "He could have been taken, which isn't good, but it would mean he's still alive."

I was pretty sure that wasn't the case, but it was nice of Jessica to try and make me feel better.

"Is there a chance it wasn't a person? One of the DarkWavers conjuring something up, like a fire spirit or demon or something like that?" Gilles asked.

"I doubt it," I said, "A demon would have done more damage, and they aren't usually summoned for petty larceny."

"I hate magic," Gilles grumbled.

"Maybe you should get another job, then."

"Maybe you should try being sober for more than an hour."

Jessica stepped between us, "Boys."

I could smell her perfume. I had to take a couple of steps back. Jessica stared at me, wondering.

"Just a little dizzy," I lied.

"Maybe you should go home," Gilles said.

"Come on, we can figure this out. Someone's dead, and magic or no, we need to figure who it is, and why."

Gilles crossed his arms and gave a tight nod, "Yeah, I can agree with that."

"And is there any way you can send someone to check on Dabriel? I haven't been able to get a hold of her, or Trevor."

"I'll send a car to Dabriel's, and there's a BOLO out for Trevor."

"That's better," Jessica said, moving between me and Gilles. She put a hand on his shoulder. "We can figure this out faster if we're all working together. And Thom, you're sure it's not demons?"

"Seriously, fire demons don't do things this small. Plus, the alcohol…" I looked back at the bar. "It's a curse or a cocktail, and I'm betting on the cocktail."

I remembered a recipe for a drink called the Intra Incendium. It was either in The Intoxicantata, or in one of the few notebooks my parents had kept at home. I'd never made it, but it referenced fire. I had a few other ideas on what might cause a flame-on moment, but I wasn't ready to commit myself to those sorts of mixes.

I started thinking out loud.

Partly trying to sort it out but mostly to keep my mind busy.

"I KNOW the Demon Adramelech wouldn't bother with the Lost & Found. If he did, there wouldn't be anything left. The Drunken Abbott and Kill City both dabble with Mystixology, but the Abbott is low class and Kill City is straight up Voudou. I hope we're not treading on Voudou territory, though, because if Ogoun is involved, that would be bad."

"Why?" Jessica asked. She wasn't looking at me but hurriedly typing notes on her phone.

"The Lost & Found is a Crossroads Bar. And I'm not talking goddamn Eric Clapton; I'm talking full on Robert Johnson. Not like literal Heaven and Hell, but a place where you can choose good or evil. The bar is a gateway, and our drinks can open those doors. It's a very powerful place to be," I explained, "When most people think of the Crossroads, they think about the Devil buying souls, but there's more than Christian iconography here. Crossroads appear all over the world, in almost every religion. Including Voudou."

"Right, okay. And Ogoun is the patron Loa of fire and war, which connects to the fire," Gilles pointed out.

Jessica laughed, a little nervously. "Voodoo. That's just fantastic."

Gilles looked worried. "You're saying the Lost & Found was the site of a Voudou ritual? Would Legba be involved?"

"If we're talking crossroads, we could be talking Legba," I admitted.

"And that would be bad news," Gilles explained. "Not only is he one of the Tricksters, but he's also in charge of opening and closing doors. And I don't mean physical doors."

I nodded, "I hope it wasn't, but we're looking at all the options, right?"

"Well, other than alcohol, there were no traces of any accelerants, and no ritualistic evidence," Gilles paused. "And the Drunken Abbott?"

"It's a possibility, but most of the people who work there are seriously a few olives short of a martini," I said, "What worries me is if a recipe from the Intoxicantata caused the fire, there might be similar incidents in the near future."

"You don't think the killer got what they wanted?" Jessica asked.

"I think they got what they wanted from the Lost & Found, but I don't think it's over. You don't mess with these drinks unless you're going to use them. If you don't get the book back, there will be more deaths."

Jessica frowned, "If *we* don't get the book back."

"I don't do this anymore, Jess," I found myself unable to meet her gaze.

She answered me with a loud silence.

I shuffled my feet.

"Look," I pointed out. "There are hundreds of flame touched recipes out there, and God knows how many are listed in the book. I know my way around a drink or two but the last time I set someone on fire with a cocktail was never, so I don't have any specifics for you. And if I ever figure out how to get my own personal pyrotechnics going, you'll be the first to know."

"Look Dante, I don't know why, but the Agentia is willing to put you on payroll for this," Gilles said abruptly, surprising me. "But that means you're going to have to work with us."

Jessica sighed, "Gilles, could I have a few minutes alone with Thom?"

Gilles visibly softened for a second, then walked up to me, matching my six feet and raising it two inches. "If I find out you're involved in this I'm hand delivering you to the Alliance. And if you find any leads, you'd better keep me in the loop. Get me?"

Unflinching, I stared right back at Gilles. He was slightly intimidating, but I wasn't going to let him know. "I get you. And if you get in my way, the Alliance won't save you."

"Screw you," Gilles said. He wrinkled his nose and stomped towards his car.

"Will you at least investigate some recipes? Find something to help us understand what could cause this?" Jessica asked.

"I'll try."

"Can you give me a time frame?"

"I'll know when I know," I squeezed my forehead with my hand, trying to stave off an approaching migraine. "This isn't lower level magic here. I'll do my best, but I can't promise anything."

"Dante!" Gilles yelled from his car, "Jess!"

He waved us over. He stood there, hands on his hips, watching us walk towards him with a steely gaze.

My wrist pulsed. He knew who had died.

"Who was it Deuxcoeurs?"

He paused a second before answering, "Trevor Slone."

3
BRIMSTONE ROCK

"Are you alright?" Jessica asked.

"No."

I went to my car, ignoring Jessica who was telling me not to leave. I wasn't, yet, but I needed a drink and the bar wasn't open. I grabbed my flask, turned on my heels and walked towards the bar. I glanced at Jessica as I passed but didn't say anything. She gave me that arms crossed, head tilted you're being a jerk kind of glare, and I responded with an "I know" kind of look. I didn't have many friends in this world, and with Trevor gone it was close to none. I heard Gilles drive off as I continued towards the Lost & Found and walked back inside.

The smell from the fire still wafted like graveyard perfume through the room but the silence unnerved me the most. How could they think I had anything to do with this? I sat at the stool on the far end of the bar and took a long swig from the steel container. It was the seat where Trevor always sat. This sucked. Another hit of liquor. Another sharp cut in my chest. I hadn't been expecting this hurt. I turned around on my barstool, back to the bar, looking across the floor and remembering how it used to be; Dabriel dancing to Screamin' Jay Hawkins while moving between tables picking up empty glasses, Trevor sitting at the piano trying to decide between starting another song or finishing another drink, Naberius glowering at customers, and me. Just trying to mix the perfect drink.

There was a smell of Autumn that always seemed to float through the air, and I could never tell if it was from the candles that Dabriel would sometimes burn or the cinnamon that Naberius loved to add to almost everything. The lit was always dim, like October, but at the same time the reflections hitting off the mirrors behind the bar sent shards of springtime through the room. And when Trevor did play, it would be something perfect and unexpected. And now that song is over. My eyes closed for a second, to let the memory go. I reached up and touched the amulet hanging around my neck on a thin black wax wire chain. A gift from my mother. It was warm and felt like sadness. An amulet that's only power was to focus the power of the one who wore it. So, for me, it's only power was sentimentality. My connection to the elements had been cut, leaving only a birthmark that felt like a scar.

I started mixing drinks at my parents' bar. A lifetime ago. Growing up watching alcohol pours and DarkWavers drink wasn't quite a normal childhood, but it wasn't a bad one. I was a fast learner and by the time I turned eighteen I could mix up a Brimstone Rock that could literally make smoke come out your ears.

Now it's all coming full circle, and I don't know if it's one I want to be stuck inside. The first time I met Gilles, the first time I met Jessica, the first time I met Nick Noir…

It was Liaison Officer Gilles Deuxcoeurs who had given me my first assignment; figuring out what was causing the patrons of Code Blue, a Goth club on Commercial Drive, to start craving real blood. Gilles was building a new team, so that's when I was introduced to Jessica. One of the Agentia's field agents. She was smart, beautiful, and so not afraid of ghosts. She could also get information I couldn't.

Gilles was the lead investigator, and the three of us quickly solidified as a strong team, and outside of that, Jessica and I became great friends. That led to dating and slowly, a more solid relationship. It seemed perfect; and for a couple of years, it was. Until another case led us back to Code Blue. But this time it was bigger than a blood lust cocktail; it was straight up selling souls. Together we connected the dots, which ended up forming an arrow pointing directly at a shape-shifting rock 'n' roll singer with the stage name of Nick Noir.

It all came to an end during a fiery showdown at the bar my parents owned. The bar I grew up in. The Riddle House. Nick Noir wanted to use my parents as leverage, and he had Jessica's sister as well. That was what started the divide between me and Gilles and Jessica. Sometimes the rules aren't as solid when your family is threatened.

Perhaps things would have gone a little smoother if I'd been a little older, a little wiser, but I wasn't. I was turning the heat up on the term hot-headed, so when I showed up, things turned bad real fast. I wasn't sure what to expect, but I wasn't expecting a ferocious wolf. I had my elemental powers, but I didn't have the best control over them. I don't know what happened. It was a blur of fur and fire, and I blacked out. Lost in some fear filled adrenalin fueled elemental frenzy.

By the time Gilles arrived I was passed out by the door and Nick Noir had escaped. I don't know what would have happened if it hadn't been for Gilles. He managed to drag me out of there in time. I made it. No one else did.

I ended up at Vancouver General Hospital; as did Jessica. Supposedly she'd been attacked by a wild animal. I knew it had been Nick Noir. Unfortunately, Gilles hadn't seen the wolf, or the fire start, so he had to come at it from a different angle, and that angle was pointing towards me. Especially because by the time the Fire Department arrived at the Riddle House, the fire had been extinguished. Burnt itself out. Nothing was left other than strange, charred markings across the walls and some of the floors, and the bodies, still smoldering. Gilles knew about my Elemental blood, so I was connected to the fire.

. . .

THAT'S the first time I ever had to directly face the Triple Alliance. A sort of Supreme Court for the Waver world. When you deal with magic, you've got to follow a strict set of guidelines. The supernatural cannot be known by the natural. It doesn't work. There are rules and regulations, policies and procedures, and I had failed to comply. While like the normal structures of law and order, the consequences were usually a little more severe. I was placed under Alliance Eye, Magic-Watch. But that was the least of my problems. I was lost. I was destroyed. I was without a family, and without friends. Jessica couldn't deal with it, and she didn't want to deal with me. It was my fault that she was in the hospital, my fault her sister was dead. And she was angry. She left me, and I left the Agentia. Gave up everything but the drinking and a desire for revenge. Even though it was my fault, I still blamed Nick Noir for creating the situation. It took me two years to find him, but I did. In a dingy dive of a pool hall in Quebec City. Two years spent learning about shapeshifters and how to kill them. Silver bullets can work and waiting until they're in their original form always works. If they know you're coming, it's a hard form to hit.

Nick didn't know I was coming.

It was quick, and I probably should have been more careful, but I wasn't thinking about consequences. And there were consequences. I made my way back to Vancouver feeling like I'd accomplished something but hating myself for it. I thought it might appease my guilt, but it only made the gnawing hole inside me darker. I was still the one at fault. I tried to make things better with Jessica, but she wasn't having it. She didn't just leave me, she left Vancouver. I thought I'd covered my tracks, but the Agentia could follow an invisible man through a blackout. They didn't bring me in, though. They brought me in front of the Triple Alliance. It was time for judgment to come down. My elemental powers were rendered useless. Under the Alliance's orders, I had a dampening curse placed upon me. I had the abilities, but I couldn't use them. It was a punishment known as Reoite Corraich. Frozen Anger.

After that, anything that connected me to magic would be thoroughly scrutinized. Paranormal Parole. I didn't care, I had nothing to do, and I felt as if I'd lost part of my soul. Nowhere to go, no one to see.

That's when I discovered the Lost & Found, and that's how I met Trevor. Due to the conditions of my punishment, I could work with magic but could only do it under the supervision of a licensed practitioner. That was Trevor, and it was a perfect match. The bar became a new home, and he became like a second father, but more than that, a friend.

I felt happy for the first time in years, hanging out and drinking, chatting, creating. Surrounded by oddities and obscurities from around the world. Taxidermy ranging from Jackalopes and FeeJee Mermaids to squirrels and foxes. Bats and butterflies hang in the corners alongside masks and mystical charms. As the decorations were, the clientele could be even stranger.

I'd found my place.

"THOMAS?"

Jessica was standing in the doorway, framed in a soft grey light.

"Hey," I looked at the empty flask in my hand.

Jessica came and sat next to me; I wasn't alone. It made me almost forget the sadness.

Almost.

Jessica knew me, but she didn't know everything. Gilles had been right; I'd never told her about my second major infraction. She knew about the fire, but I'd never told her about what happened to Nick Noir. How I'd killed a DarkWaver.

It had been a case of an eye for an eye, but those cases are never treated lightly or forgotten. Too many strikes and I'm out. And out means dead.

"It is strange seeing you again, Thom. I know we need to talk about things, but it'll have to wait until we're finished with this case," she shook her head. "I'm still trying to deal with working alongside Gilles again."

"Yeah," I managed a smile, "That's gotta be rough."

Jessica gave me a nudge, “He’s not that bad. If you two could ever have a decent conversation…”

“If you’d really wanted to stay out of this you could have. You know Gilles has other Batcavers to work with.”

Jessica thought about it, “I know, you’re right. But I had to do this. I did want to see you again, but there’s more to it. It’s about this case. You don’t know the whole story, and now, neither do we. Until now, we were working under the assumption that it didn’t involve elementals. And this bar? Come on, Thomas. You know it can’t be coincidence.”

“Yeah, I get that,” I said. “But am I seriously a suspect?”

“I don’t think so, but Gille might need a little more convincing.”

We walked back outside, the remaining agents putting the yellow and black crime scene tape back up behind us. She gave me a familiar mischievous smile. “And besides, how are you going to solve any mysteries without me?”

I gave her a fake look of shock, she laughed.

“You are going to have to give me background on this case,” I noted.

“Thom?” she started, still chuckling. For a second it felt good to be standing there.

“What?” I asked.

“When you said you might not be able to figure out how to work this cocktail of fire…”

“Yeah?” I stretched the word out.

“You know how to do it, don’t you?”

I winced.

“Jess, with this magic,” I said. “Knowing how to do something is completely different than doing it. I want to keep what’s left of my soul intact.”

“But sometimes sacrifices must be made to do the right thing. I know what those decisions are like. I know it’s difficult,” she said, turning around to look back at the bar.

I turned to look with her, “Difficult is an understatement.”

She was right about the fire drink. But if I mixed the wrong one, things could end up going badly for me, and even worse for this investigation.

EVERY BIT of magic costs something, and a soul, while intangible, is finite. It doesn't mean you turn evil and grow a goatee, but you do lose pieces of your humanity.

"Jess, I'm serious. Even working at the Lost & Found affects me, and if I start handling magics powerful enough for this," I pointed towards the bar, "I could end up so far into the dark side even my shadow would seem bright."

She looked disappointed. "I'm not asking you to go around setting people on fire, Thom. If we can figure out how, we'll be closer to who. Look, this investigation is happening with or without you. I'd prefer to do it with you, but I understand if you're not up to it."

"Reverse psychology? Really?" But it worked. Maybe there was a way around it. Maybe if I worked out what was needed for the drink, I wouldn't have to make it. I would have to be careful, though. It wouldn't look good if I was found working on dark spells.

"Remember, Gilles is going to be asking everyone questions. Everyone," Jessica said. "So please don't take it personally. You know the Agentia likes to make sure all the t's are crossed."

"Great," I'm not a math genius but I know one drink plus one death multiplied by fire equals a whole bunch of questions. I need to come up with the right answers.

I let out a tight sigh, "Look, I'll see what I can come up with."

If I could, I would, and Jessica knew I wouldn't let her down without good reason.

Jessica smiled, "Thanks. That's better than nothing."

I shoved my hands in my pockets and waited for a random breath of wind to push my hair back; dramatic and forlorn. It didn't happen. Either way, I had another possible source of income to meet up with. "Alright, we'll talk later. You going to be okay?"

She nodded. "I'll be fine. Gilles will be back soon, and it looks like I'm going to have to make a few 'no comments.'"

She motioned towards the street. There was a line of reporters forming against the 'Do Not Cross' barrier being patrolled by members of Vancouver's finest. I smiled and gave Jessica a quick, slightly awkward, hug.

I didn't look back as I walked towards my car. The wind finally decided to arrive, bringing a light haze of rain with it. I opened the door, sat down, and started the engine. I had a book to find. I glanced back at Jessica, visible in the rearview mirror.

And a drink to make.

4
HOLY GRAIL

I drove through the rain, distracted. Otherwise, I would have noticed I was being followed. My wrist was throbbing a steady but dull pulse. There was a power behind it, one I couldn't access. I hadn't heard anything for years, but I knew the Triple Alliance were still watching me. Once their eyes were on you, they were always on you. I rarely thought about it anymore, but with Trevor's death and the Agentia asking questions, I knew they'd hear about it from Gilles. If they hadn't already. Still, I thought as tightened my grip on the steering wheel and my knuckles whitened, I didn't really care. I didn't kill Trevor, but someone did, and they would pay. Besides, if Nick Noir was alive, then I'd have been punished for nothing, and the Alliance would not be happy about that mistake. I felt a sliver of anger wedge underneath my grief.

I pulled up and parked across the street from the Four Calendar Café. I hadn't seen the burgundy Lincoln Continental behind me, so when it pulled in front of me, I was a little surprised. I was even more surprised when someone stepped out of the Continental and started towards me. He made me look like I needed to lose some weight, and I knew I didn't. His legs sliced through the air as he walked, and I wondered how many people he had accidently cut with his elbows.

His shoes were a deep red suede, and sharp. His face was even sharper, reminding me of a starving hawk with glassy black eyes. I got out of my car, watching him, and turned to move in the opposite direction, where I almost ran into a woman.

Where the man reminded me of a hawk, the woman had more foxlike features. A soft face and slightly pointed ears peeked out from under dark orange hair. Her eyes, green with flecks of hazel, pierced through me in direct opposition to the wide smile on her orange lipsticked mouth.

I was not in the mood for this.

"Excuse me, did I park in the wrong place?" I asked. I looked over at the café, judging its distance and my speed.

"We only want to talk," said the Fox as the Hawk moved swiftly and silently behind me. Fox gestured towards the Continental.

"We can talk in the café, I'm buying," I quipped.

"We can talk in the car," Hawk sneered, opening his coat to reveal a gun.

Fox smiled softly, "Kurtis, Mister Dante is our guest, not our prisoner," she turned to me, all sweetness. "Please don't be alarmed by Kurtis's abrupt manner. I'm sure we startled you, but it was not our intent. I would have approached you at the Lost & Found, but I did not want to interrupt your reunion with the lovely Ms. Fervor."

She'd done her homework, but what did she want? Hawk stayed behind me as the woman moved into the back seat, motioning for me to follow. "Please, Mister Dante. I know the Agentia Obscura is looking for the Intoxicantata, and they're willing to pay for your help. But I can pay you more."

AND SUDDENLY, I was following in my father's footsteps. Becoming Vancouver's most wanted librarian. A path I never really wanted to take. I didn't know if I could trust the fox and hawk. Probably not, but I wasn't exactly able to argue. Kurtis the hawk breathed behind me as the fox lady quietly waited for a response.

"Much more," she added.

"Why not," I muttered. Besides, the rain had started, and I didn't have an umbrella. I slid into the back seat next to the woman, and Kurtis closed the door behind me. He got into the front seat, and the car doors locked. Not my first bad decision, but I hoped it wasn't my last.

The car smelled faintly of white musk, but I couldn't quite pinpoint the source of the scent. Fox extended her hand, "Please, let's start over. Allow me to introduce myself. My name is Murmur, and our driver is Kurtis."

I gave Kurtis a worried half smile, but his cold eyes gave me no comfort as they studied me in the rear-view mirror. "I hope this isn't going to take too long; I have a scheduled meeting soon. You know, when you make plans with someone instead of forcing them into the back of a car?"

Murmur gave me a look that held nothing but menace. Kurtis, on the other hand, just let his face slip into a grin, which was more unnerving. He looked like someone who could slit your throat then calmly sit and sip a martini as blood flowed out of your body.

I felt Murmur's eyes against me like a blade between my ribs and waited for her to start the conversation.

"Thomas Dante," Murmur said, pleased with herself, "Tell me, what does an esteemed Mystixologist like yourself know about the Intoxicantata?"

"I wouldn't exactly say esteemed," I replied. "Obscure is a better word," I peered out the window, the rain was coming down harder. I tried to change the subject. "Thank the gods you got here when you did. I don't have an umbrella, and it's looking quite dreadful outside."

Kurtis coughed sharply and glanced back at me; I smirked, leaned back and folded my arms across my chest.

Murmur kicked the back of the driver's seat, annoyed. "Kurtis. Enough," then she turned and shot my name through a sneer, "Mister Dante. Things would go better if you appreciated the gravity of your predicament. We are willing to pay for your services. You don't want to hear your other options."

Sometimes the money isn't worth anything when the people

you're working for could kill you faster than a check could clear, but that's when you have to hear them out.

"Well, I'm curious, of course," I told her. "But I can't promise anything. I'm working for the good guys."

Murmur laughed out loud. It wasn't a pleasant laugh. It was a Disney villainess on acid kind of laugh. I made a mental note to not make her laugh again.

"Good, bad, it's all relative. This book is very important to us. I am sure you know why, so I don't have to explain. We know it was last seen at the Lost & Found, and that it was part of your father's extensive collection."

THAT ANSWERED one of my questions. Nick Noir was looking for the same book. But did he find it? Was he at the bar last night? If I made my meeting, we'd have things to talk about.

"Okay, I know the book."

Of course, I knew the book, and I knew my father had left it to the Lost & Found. I didn't know why everyone wanted it. "But you've got to understand why I don't want to talk to you. I rarely find employment opportunities during a kidnapping."

"I apologize. Like I said before, it was not my intent to alarm you. We are prepared to offer you two thousand dollars a day for as long as it takes."

I tried, but failed, to hold back a look of 'damn that's a lot of money'.

"Seriously?"

"Listen to me, Mister Dante. You must act with discretion. There are others who want the book, but if you work for me, I expect your loyalties to be undivided," she pulled an envelope out from the back of the car seat and handed it to me, "I need you to find it."

I wondered if they knew Nick Noir, but bringing up his name was probably not a good idea.

"I'll definitely give this some serious thought, Ms.…ah…Murmur,"

I returned the envelope, maybe a little more hesitantly than I meant to. "And what is your employer's name?"

"That's information you don't need right now."

"Well, all right then. Perhaps I can get in touch with you tomorrow?"

Murmur squinted at me with either displeasure or distrust, I couldn't tell. "Perhaps I'm not offering enough?" She looked out the window for a second, as if contemplating an important decision, then back at me. "What if I doubled it?"

"I'd still have to think about it," I said. "I don't work for crooks."

"I'm going to try to not be insulted by that comment, Mister Dante," she said holding a tight threat between syllables. "I am not in the business of forcing people to take my money, but I will give you another day to think about it."

Murmur moved closer to me until I was pressed tight between her and the angularity of the Hawk man. "If you do not want to work for me, so be it. But if you are working against me, things could get unpleasant. For you and those you align yourself with."

"Is that a threat?" I asked calmly, even though I was starting to feel a little more than nervous. These people had information, money, and weapons. All I had was a few drinks.

"No, Mister Dante," she whispered. "It's a promise. I hope you accept my offer, but if you get in my way, I will not hesitate to get you out of my way."

"If I see you coming, I'll step aside."

She just smiled.

I KNEW I had to be careful. I also knew I didn't want to endanger Jessica. If I could slide through this without hurting anyone, I'd be ahead. "We'll talk, Murmur. Later. Right now, all I want is to get out of this car."

She looked at me, I didn't look away. "Don't do anything you'll regret. You're familiar with magic. I'll let you in on a secret. If you ever cross me, not even death can protect you."

I continued with my attempts at nonchalance, "Alright, I get the point. You really need to relax."

This time the laugh was light, "Well said, Mister Dante. I hope I will be able to."

Kurtis opened the door and stepped out while Murmur turned to look straight ahead.

"Goodbye, Mister Dante."

"I'd say it's been a pleasure, but I don't think it was."

KURTIS SNEERED at me through the window as they drove away. I pulled my collar up against the rain. The anger had solidified, pushing away both sorrow and fear. Angry I'd been kidnapped, angry I had no idea where this magical book was, and angry no one had bothered to call and see if I was all right. I stopped on the corner. I was upset Dabriel hadn't checked in. Worried. There had been plenty of time for her to get a hold of me. But speaking of time, I might make it to my meeting with Nick. If not, I'd at least be able to get a nice hot cup of coffee.

I needed a coffee. And I needed to talk to my bartending friends. Maybe I could kill all these birds with one shot…I also wanted to make sure Dabriel was okay. And maybe see if either of them had made any interesting drinks recently.

Our drinks are like magic potions, but with alcohol. Cocktails to produce a wide variety of effects connected to a world most people refuse to see. Every Mystixological cocktail, every spell, every potion used, is built on a triangle. A triangle that can break without balanced parts. You can add flavors, increase, or decrease quantities, but each drink is basically a variation on 'The Father, The Son, and The Holy Spirit', with the spirit being alcohol. Then it's bound and directed by its description. There is, of course, the flip side to that trinity. 'Lucifer, Lilith, and the Lost Leader'. You can guess which way those drinks go.

. . .

For example, the Holy Grail. At the Lost & Found it's a drink that combines gin, Green Chartreuse, vermouth and some bitters. Described as a cocktail where every sip adds a distant echo of holy blood to the thread lines of the soul. For a NoWaver, that's just poetic nonsense describing a bright and clear drink mixing the juniper of the gin and the more citrus hits of the Chartreuse. For a Waver, however, it alludes to a powerful push towards the lighter side of the other world. The light and dark should always be in balance, so these drinks are perfect after you've done something that needs a little alcoholic atonement.

I'm great at the descriptions, but Dabriel is a master of the mix. A mixologist creates drinks with flavor profiles that can fill your senses, while a Mystixologist creates drinks that will affect your soul.

5
COFFEE TALK

There was always someone at the Four Calendar, but it was never crowded. During the evenings it was speckled with after-hours refugees from the waterlogged night. Streetwise kids with no desire to head home, or no home to head to. A safe place for angst ridden teens and a good place for great coffee. I took my jacket off, giving it a quick shake by the door. I didn't see any familiar faces, but then again, Nick was a shapeshifter. I looked around suspiciously. I'd already killed him; I probably shouldn't trust him. No one even gave me a second glance, so I figured he was running even later than I was. I'd give it one coffee before switching to find Dabriel mode. I wasn't in the mood for waiting.

I walked up to the counter and found an empty stool at the end. I let myself relax a little bit. The Four Calendar is a regular café. The employees are mostly normal, as are the customers. I don't mean boring normal; I mean normal people. Regular ones. That's what Mori wanted, a regular non-wave place. We'd met years ago, during my long nights of wakefulness trying to work on different recipes. She didn't have any Waver powers, but she was aware of their existence, and it had been nice to find someone normal I could confide in.

"Thomas?" She practically jumped over the counter to give me a hug, her arms wrapped around my waist, squeezing the breath out of me.

"If it isn't the wonderful Mori Shai," I said, turning to face her. "My favorite barista."

"It's so good to see you," she said, shifting back into a stoic steadiness before standing back to look me over. "What's wrong?"

"You always know how I'm feeling," I sighed.

"I know how everyone's feeling," she pulled her hair, midnight black with emerald-green highlights, back into a ponytail, gave me another hug, and moved back behind the counter. "Years of playing the ever-attentive coffee-shop girl. I also know what you want to drink."

"You always know what my insomnia wants," I said, as she pushed a triple shot mocha towards me.

"Who needs sleep?"

I looked up at her over my coffee. My angel of caffeination.

"What is it, Thomas?" She asked quietly, starting on a drink for another customer.

"Trevor. He's gone."

"Gone?" Mori stopped mid-pour.

My eyes moved back down to the cup in front of me, "Dead."

"Thomas, I'm so sorry. Do you know..."

"Nothing. Not yet," I passed the coffee cup back and forth between my hands, "But I'm going to figure it out."

Mori nodded, placed a hand on mine, "I know you will."

Before I could respond, the door behind me opened and I felt a distinct shift in the room's temperature. A siren wailed in the distance, but underneath that the sound of the rain was a constant rhythmic patter. I tilted my head slightly but didn't turn. Mori's face was unreadable, but her shoulders and neck had stiffened. The birthmark on my wrist felt strangely tight, as if it was pulling my skin into a knot.

"Mori?" I asked quietly.

She allowed herself to smile; just briefly. "It's okay. I can handle this."

"What?"

"It's a Bruxsa. Maybe...part human though."

That made me turn, but I kept my cool.

"What does she want?" I whispered.

Mori shrugged, "Coffee?"

The woman took a deep breath and moved towards the counter and sat a couple of seats down from me. She looked a little nervous. She had a soft face, smoothed by wrinkles, and framed by long pepper grey hair. Her eyes, though disarmingly lined with decades of smiles, were a stormy grey, and sharper than stone.

Without looking up she scanned the menu placed in front of her hurriedly, as if in a rush to find something good, or in a hurry to get a drink. It seemed as if no real thought was put into it, as she placed her finger halfway down the page and showed it to Mori.

"I'll have this one. It's good right?"

"If you like lavender," Mori replied with a noncommittal wave of the hand. "It is a great choice for a rainy day waiting to happen."

I leaned back, trying to act casual. I wanted to get a lay of the land without looking as if I was eavesdropping. It didn't seem like the right time to interrupt.

Her head snapped towards me; grey eyes flashing obsidian as grabbed on to mine.

"Can I help you?"

I shook my head and gave her a warm smile, as if we'd been friends for years. Sometimes friendliness disarms a lot faster than animosity.

"Is this your first time here?" I asked, swiveling the stool to face my new friend. "The drinks, these ingredients...so fresh and vivid, don't you think?"

The older woman nodded but still held me with a distrustful gaze.

"The coffee is great, but you must be careful if you're thinking about drinking here often. It can get addictive."

She looked back at the menu, speaking in hushed tones, "I've been here a few times, although I wouldn't say I'm a regular."

I saw Mori watching us with a look that bordered on dangerous. Her eyes holding warning signs.

"You look familiar to me, though, but not from here," the Bruxsa slid a little closer to me, "You are a regular somewhere else, are you not?"

"Maybe at the Lost & Found," I said casually.

"Yes, that's the place. With the special drinks and the books of magic."

Suddenly things started to feel very wrong. A sharp pain shot through my wrist, as if a sliver of electricity had been driven into my birthmark. I can focus on my birthmark for slight bursts of energy, sometimes, but it's never powerful. Maybe small breaths of heat. Or if I push all my thoughts together hard enough, I can create a tiny flame. Like lighting a sad match with my mind. What having this birthmark, this bloodline, does do, however, is connect me to the raw magics of the Wave. And this creature sitting next to me had some raw magics.

"What do you want?" I questioned.

She returned my query with an innocent smile, "I'm just here for some answers."

Something occurred to me "Did Nick send you?"

"Nick?" She stopped and smiled again. She was very good at that movement. I almost didn't hear her words, as I was distracted by the shape of her lips.

"No. Nick won't be joining us today."

I saw Mori give me a look as she placed the woman's order in front of her but gave her a quick 'I'm okay' gesture and she moved back down the bar.

I got another flash of a grin, "I've done my research. You used to work with the Agentia. It's probably not a good idea to openly discuss why you…left…but suffice it to say, you ended up at the Lost & Found. Oh, and that it's possible you've been convinced to take up your previous job as detective of the obscure."

I liked that. I'd never heard it put that way before, but it wasn't quite accurate. "I don't think any final decision has been made…"

"I have heard that perhaps that's not quite true. Which is why I'm here. I think we might be able to help each other."

I finished my coffee and motioned for another. "How can I help you?"

"You can tell me where Dabriel is."

I gave her a slight eyebrow rise, "And how can you help me?"

"I can tell you where the book is."

"And Nick Noir?"

"If you find the book, you'll find Nick."

I was interested, but suspicious, "Nick is supposed to meet me here."

"But he's not here." The Bruxsa smiled, "So where is Dabriel?"

"I don't know. I haven't heard from her since the fire."

The Bruxsa's eyes narrowed, "Shame."

"How do you know Dabriel?" I inquired.

"She never talks about me, does she," a quiet sigh, "we were once… very close. But she has kept something of mine and I need it back."

"What is it?" I asked. "If I see her, I'll relay the message."

THE BRUXSA'S demeanor changed from sunshine to storm in a matter of seconds, her smile shifted into a sharp sneer. "I'll tell her myself. You don't need to know."

The door opened and closed a couple of times, as the few customers who had been in the café abruptly left, sensing trouble and not wanting to be part of it. The Bruxsa let her fingers slide across the smooth countertop, and the slightest trail of smoke curled up from beneath her turquoise fingernails. Mori was suddenly standing across from her, both hands on the counter, her look sharp but her tone soft and steady, as if trying to calm a wild animal.

"I think you should leave," she said, through clenched teeth.

She blew me a little kiss as she stood up. It felt like I'd been stung by an icicle.

"Not good," I muttered, as she left without a word.

"Another day, another lost soul," Mori muttered.

"What do you think that was about?" I asked.

"Not sure," Mori hesitated. "But the Bruxsa love having all the secrets, and I know you have a few of those."

The door started to close behind the Bruxsa, but before it could, two new customers entered. Only neither of us thought they were proper customers.

"I might need some help with these ones," Mori said under her breath while retaining her barista's grin. I turned.

"Great," I muttered under my breath.

As if an unexpected Bruxsa encounter wasn't enough, suddenly the café was playing host to a couple of what looked like hammered businessmen. They moved straight towards me.

I tilted my head slightly, squinting to see if I could place it. There was something off about them. It wasn't their square-toed shoes, but those didn't help. One of them, looking like a Pierce Brosnan rip-off, stood right next to me and slapped the counter with an open palm, "Two Red Eyes."

I caught a whiff of something that made me almost retch. I covered my nose with the back of my hand and looked at Mori. She returned my look and nodded. It was like an invisible cloud of rotten eggs and old sardines. My eyes were starting to water.

"Asmodi," I whispered, as Mori leant in towards me with her fingers pinching his nostrils shut. "Bet they know our Bruxsa."

Asmodi, demons under the banner of Asmodeus, were all about seduction and lies. Not as sexual as Incubi, but sort of related in terms of evil intent.

Fake Pierce gave Mori a wink before turning towards me, "What say you tell us what our friend wanted to know?"

"Don't worry about it, Thomas," Mori said as I stood up.

"I don't think I have a choice, Mori."

The offending Asmodi laughed, "You always have a choice, bub. Live or die, right?"

"Look pal," I held my hands up in front of me, apologetically, "You don't have to go back to hell, but you can't stay here."

Wannabe Pierce answered with a sly grin, "Hey, we're not looking for trouble, just answers," He glanced back at Mori, who was standing behind the bar with her arms crossed.

"Maybe a new friend as well?"

"Not here," I gestured over my shoulder towards the door.

"We got nowhere else to go," Fake Pierce said. His friend moved, slightly wavering, towards me. Now I had two rejects from Satan's Modeling School for Men making moves. Now the trick wasn't how to get them out; the trick was to get them out without breaking anything. I caught a flash of pointed teeth from the one closest to me, and a shadow of the short horns pushing out above their eyebrows. Whatever illusion they had been projecting was starting to fade.

"Thomas?" Mori said. She'd come out from behind the bar and walked towards me.

"Nah, I got this."

Fake Pierce found that funny. His mistake. I moved behind him with a surprise arm lock and held him between myself and the other demon. "This can go any way you like, but perhaps leaving would be the best way."

He started to struggle, but I knew I could handle it for a couple of minutes. Besides, thanks to the triple-shot Mori had made, I could feel a little caffeinated electricity shooting through my veins. And then something happened. I'm not sure what the trigger was, the caffeine, the adrenalin, or the danger, but I started to feel a familiar prickling sensation around my wrist. I felt the heat, so did the Asmodi. His eyes widened; his jaw dropped.

"You're elemental," he said in a shocked whisper.

I was as surprised as he was, but I wasn't about to let him know that. I let him go, pushing him towards his friend. They stood, ready to fight or flee. I don't think anybody knew what was going to happen.

Then there was the sound of shattering glass and Mori was standing next to me with a broken bottle held as a weapon, syrup still dripping from its jagged edges.

"Let's all just take it easy and maybe we can all get what we want and go about our business," I said reassuringly. Mori just glared and crouched down. Intense and fearless. Her crazed expression convinced him.

"We want Dabriel. What do you want?" he growled.

"Where's the book?"

"I don't know what you're talking about."

I started to move my hands together, acting as if I was going to create some elemental ball of power, while Mori took another step forwards, brandishing her weapon of sticky broken glass. "Wrong answer. You don't want to start a fight with us."

The demon paused, calculating.

"It's not worth it. We'll find her before he does," the other creature whispered.

"Blundertown. Christophe has it."

Blundertown Books. I'd been going to Blundertown Books since I'd started drinking at the Lost & Found. It was a ten-minute walk away. The owner was Christophe Grey. He was British, he was extremely well read, and he was a DarkWaver. An eccentric one.

Christophe was an immortal who pretended he was a vampire. He didn't drink blood; he did drink a lot of wine. He enjoyed being a dark and brooding creature of the night. Sometimes he'd waltz around the bookstore wearing a cape.

"Just go," I said, pointing at the door.

"I won't forget this," Fake Pierce grumbled.

"That's okay, I will," I smirked.

Mori cheered as the business demons left. I gave a quick bow and moved back to finish my coffee; relieved. I could fight, but I didn't like to. I looked over at Mori, "thanks."

"De nada," she responded. "So, I guess you're going to visit a bookstore?"

I nodded, "But not yet. I'm thinking it might be a trap. Also, it sounds like Dabriel might be in trouble, and I'd like to find her before the Bruxsa does."

6
MONK'S DREAM

Dabriel still wasn't answering her phone. I tried Naberius, not that I wanted to talk to him, but if anyone knew where she was, he would. But he wasn't answering either. I didn't want to call Jessica yet, not until I'd learned more about what was going on with Nick Noir, and the book everyone seemed to want. And speaking of Nick…

I dialed. No answer. No message. He should be here by now.

Maybe it was time for the inevitable alcohol collision. I glanced around the café. It had been empty when the demons were playing around, thankfully, but now there were some customers. A couple sat against the wall, arguing over lattes and a flower cloth tabletop. Bites of conversation tied together too tight. I tried to pick up floating sentences, but my mind was stuck on static and all I got was noise. I couldn't tell from where I sat if they were both Ghouls, or only one of them. Either way, it was strange.

I sent an eyebrowed question towards Mori, who was shadowed behind coffee steam. She waved me over and poured something in a mug and placed it in front of me.

"Drink it. You'll need it."

I took a sip, no questions asked.

For a second everything was perfect. The touch of perfect foam, a buzz of cinnamon, the slightest aroma of honey as the coffee touches my lips. I let the warmth fill me and the caffeine start to clear the soft blur in my mind. It was almost as if Mori could do with coffee what I did with alcohol. Except as far as I knew, her talents were all natural. I stared, frowning, into my cup as if it was some sort of caffeinated crystal ball. I wished I could understand the language of coffee because I knew there were secrets within the steam. Secrets to show me the right way to go. Destination caught somewhere between the broken lines and the blind spot. But coffee was not my magic. Alcohol was.

I GAVE a discreet look over my shoulder towards the Ghouls. They weren't causing trouble, but the fact they were in the Café wasn't good. There had been an unspoken truce between NoWavers and DarkWavers for decades. In Vancouver it had been reasonably quiet since the riots of 2011, but that wasn't entirely their fault. They like to incite but rarely participated. Once Jessica shared her suspicions about the Great Fire of 1886. Everyone loves a good conspiracy theory, especially Jessica. She thought it had a slight supernatural beginning, but again—no proof.

BUT THIS RECENT influx of Wavers; the Bruxsa and the Asmodi at the Lost & Found, the Ghouls, the fire, the missing DarkWaver book. It seemed coffee wasn't the only thing brewing.

I sat for a second, looking over my notes, tapping my pen distractedly on the word Legba. Was Voudou at play? I really hoped not.

I was mentally playing with puzzle pieces made up of fire, Voudou, and cocktails, when a man who'd been standing in the shadows walked past me towards the street. Expensive suit, and he wore it well —as in 'I've killed men with a letter opener and didn't get a drop of blood on me' kind of well. He barely glanced at me as he pushed past, but his steel eyes seemed to grab at my insides, and I was left with a dark sense of worry. I wanted to run after him, ask who he was, what was going to happen, and where he got his shoes. I started to stand, but Mori distracted me.

"What's up?" she asked.

"Nothing," I paused, "Do you know the man who just left?"

Mori squinted, "No, why?"

"I just got the strange feeling…" I trailed off, looking towards the empty doorway.

"I wouldn't worry about it; people are all annoying sometimes," Mori said, as she blew a lock of hair out of her eyes and gave me a look of fake annoyance which switched to real when another customer intruded.

She sighed, "Especially when they're in my café. Too many goddamn tired people. I need a real job."

I smiled, not really paying attention, as she walked away ranting about how she hates people who don't know the difference between "latte" and "au lait". I wanted to talk to her about Jessica, about Dabriel, about Trevor, but I knew I should wait until she was alone. We should be sitting alone with whiskey in front of us, not in a public place. Not everyone knew about the Wavers, and most people never will.

Another customer appeared, so after saying good-night I was out like a light. Just one more cup of coffee, another drift into the night.

I stood outside of the café. The rain had stopped, but I could tell by my throbbing wrist that it would probably start up again soon. It was either that or something very bad was about to happen. I flashed back on the incident with the Asmodi, something was changing within me, with my powers. Ever since the 'freeze', my elemental powers had been in tune with the weather, the natural elements around me, but it had stopped giving me that special little spider-sense that it used to give me. Until recently. I checked the time. It was late, but not bartender late. I tried Dabriel again. This time she answered.

"Hey, where've you been? I was getting worried. Thought you skipped town or something," I said. "Are you okay?"

"I'm sorry, I know. I should have called. It's just been so…"

"Crazy?" I finished.

"Yeah," Dabriel said. "Between the cops and the Agentia I've had no time to process this. You know the drill, all that don't leave town stuff, I've been scattered."

"I get it," I sighed, "Listen, Dabriel. We need to talk. There's something going on and it's bigger than just the fire…"

"Yeah, I kinda figured. The Agentia wants me in for more questioning," Dabriel paused, "We'll be able to open the bar back up again soon, right?"

"I don't know."

"Trevor must be going crazy," Dabriel gave a slight laugh.

"Dabriel," I said softly, "He's… Trevor's gone. He was caught in the fire."

Silence.

"Dab?"

"You're wrong," she whispered. "He can't be…"

"I'm sorry," I didn't want to shift gears, but I had to get some answers. "Look, we're trying to figure this out."

"We? Are you playing detective again? I thought you gave that up." Dabriel sounded surprised.

"Evidently not," I said. "Look, there's a Bruxsa looking for you, along with two unpleasant demons, and there's a connection to the Intoxicantata."

"Bruxsa?" Dabriel repeated sharply. "What did she tell you?"

"Nothing, really," suddenly I thought it might be better to not share everything. "Just that you knew each other and was willing to trade the whereabouts of the book for your location."

"What did you tell her?" Dabriel sounded nervous.

"Nothing. I didn't know where you were," this wasn't going like I thought it would. "I still don't know where you are."

"The Intoxicantata. Do you know where it is?" Dabriel asked quickly.

Maybe too quickly?

"What's going on, Dabriel?" I asked. "Who's this Bruxsa, and why is she looking for you?"

"I'll tell you later. We'll have a drink soon."

"Wait..." Too late, she'd hung up, and she didn't answer when I redialed. I had more questions, no answers, but I was glad Dabriel was alright, even though I knew she was hiding something. Still no sign of Nick. I tried the Lost & Found, sort of expecting no answer, but I got one. It was Naberius.

"What are you doing there? The bar's not open yet, is it?"

"No," Naberius said. I could hear the clink of glass in the background. "They've cleared behind the bar, but they've still got the main room, and the office closed off, so I'm just trying to clean up some of this mess."

"Listen, strange question, but do you know about Dabriel and the Bruxsa?" I asked.

He paused, coughed, spoke, "what is that, some sort of Goth band?"

"Seriously," I said, annoyed, "the Bruxsa?"

"Not on the phone. Come to the bar. We can talk here."

"I need to find someone..." I started but Naberius interrupted.

"No. Meet me at the bar," he hung up, and I sighed.

WHEN I GOT to the Lost & Found one officer was stationed outside the door and another inside. I could tell by the lack of expression and bad dress shoes it was Agentia and not VPD. Naberius was already there. The unhappy bartender.

Naberius lined up three shot glasses as I sat down across from him, then poured a swift stream across from a flask.

"BYOB, for now," he mumbled

"Who else did you invite?"

I got no answer, just an expressionless stare as he poured three whiskey shots. Straight up, no magic. I looked at him, and he just looked back, giving me nothing, a soft red glow of neon from the sign in the window echoing on his face. He raised a glass; I played along and raised the one in front of me.

"To Trevor," he said quietly.

Dammit. I nodded. Shots knocked back, and Naberius moved the third to the side. Spirits for the spirit.

"Have you talked to Dabriel since this happened?" I asked, breathing through the burn of the whiskey.

He shook his head, "No, but I'm not surprised. I need to come clean with you, Dante."

"Another shot first?" I asked. "I'm not sure if one's going to be enough."

I realized I should also concentrate on what was around me. I was at the Lost & Found, ground zero, so was there anything different, anything else missing, and were there any leads on what cocktail lit Trevor on fire. The emptiness of the room was haunting. I'd been there before after closing, but it felt different. It felt like we were doing something we weren't supposed to but mixed in with a heavy sadness.

I leant forwards over the bar. "So, what do you need to tell me?"

He shook his head slowly, "You're right. Another shot first."

"On the rocks?" I asked.

Naberius poured. Just two this time.

"So, what are we drinking to?" I asked

"Forgotten days."

Strange toast, but I nodded and repeated. Ritual is ritual.

"Done. So why are we here?"

Naberius moved his glass back and forth between his hands, "About a month ago, after I'd closed the bar, Christophe..."

"From Blundertown?"

"Yeah, him," Naberius finished his drink and poured himself another before continuing. "He came in like some dark shadow. He was at the doorway, then at the bar before I could even blink, looking for Trevor. He was pretty intense, whispering about how some things should not be shared and some secrets should be sacred. You know how some people get really quiet when they get angry? Well, this dude got so quiet he was scary. I tried to mellow him out. Offered him a drink, but he just waved me away and sort of lingered in the corner.

Finally, Trevor came out of the back office, and the two of them went through to the Blind Pig."

"So, what did he want?" I asked. I hadn't heard Naberius talk this much in years. It was almost exciting.

"Evidently our missing book belonged to Christophe?"

"The Intoxicantata? That was my father's. He gave it to Trevor."

"That's what I thought, too," Naberius said. "But Christophe did not agree. At all."

"So, what happened?" I leaned forward, my hands pressing down on the bar.

"Well, I didn't mean to eavesdrop…"

"Right," I smirked.

Naberius glared, "but I wanted to make sure Trevor was okay. He's not the toughest guy around, and Christophe has some crazy strength," I nodded as he continued, "I didn't get all of it, but from what I gathered Blundertown has been losing money for years, and Christophe wanted the book back so he could sell it. I guess priceless doesn't mean priceless, as the sale would save the bookstore."

"But obviously, Trevor kept the book," I said, "and Christophe just left?"

"Yeah. He was not happy about it," Naberius said. "He said it wasn't over. Did that whole 'I'll be back' thing. He was mad."

"Mad enough to come back and kill?" I asked.

"No, I don't think so. Stealing the book, sure. But fire? That's not Christophe's thing. But listen, Trevor was planning on buying Blundertown out from under Christophe."

"What?" I'd heard nothing about that.

"Yeah, he was going to join forces with Kill City and open a new place, where Blundertown is located. Create a Voudou DarkWave super bar."

"With Marinette? Seriously?"

Naberius nodded. I couldn't believe Trevor would be planning something like that without telling me.

"Okay, so listen. What if there were two people involved? What if Christophe took the book, but someone else started the fire?" I asked, but there was no response. Naberius wasn't paying attention to me, but something behind me.

He leant in close, "Dante," he whispered. "We've got company."

Not knowing what to expect, my shoulders knotted up and I wrapped a hand around the glass in front of me. I tried to remember what descriptions would work with the Monk's Dream to give it a something extra, but I couldn't. I made a silent note to do more remembering in the future. I could, however, still use the glass as a weapon. I saw a broken reflection in the bottle covered mirror behind the bar and caught a familiar scent.

"We've got to stop meeting like this, Jessica," I said without turning. "People are going to think you still like me."

The reflection stopped.

"You're still using the same perfume," I said, gesturing to the seat next to me. "Have a seat."

She sat, and I smiled. I did miss her. I knew we couldn't start again, not now, but it was hard to ignore history. I still think about her more than I should. Our too brief time together. Work was great, but the time after work. Long café nights that led to longer nights. Long drunken nights that led to longer days. Doing nothing was never as good as it was when I was doing nothing with her. I wish I could have said more. Told her more, but that's my thing. I never tell you anything until you're too far away to hear.

I shook it off and gave her a quick smile. She had on a pair of black Converse with silver stars, tight black jeans, and a black hoodie over a skull print shirt.

"New uniform?" I asked, she didn't laugh.

"Can you manage another round?" She asked Naberius, while pointing at his flask.

"How'd you know we were here?" I asked. "The bar isn't open, and it's not like you were in the neighborhood."

She gave a little half smile and shrug as Naberius placed the cocktail in front of her. "I have my methods, remember?"

I nodded, "All too well. Who'd you seduce this time?"

"Thomas," she admonished, "You're still hung up on that?"

Naberius gave me a smile, "I'd like to hear this story…"

"No, you wouldn't," I snapped.

"Thomas and I have a little history," Jessica explained, "But we're good now. I think?"

I ignored the question and waited.

Jessica gave me a dirty look, "I knew you'd be coming back here at some point, and I know how to pull off a stakeout. I thought maybe we could work closer together on this?"

Naberius shot me a quick wink.

"Not what she meant, Naberius."

Jessica gave me an exaggerated pout and then laughed. "Still the same oversensitive Tommy."

"Look, now's not the time to get into that. We're good. Right now, okay, we can share information, but not all of it, conflict of interest and all. I have other clients," I said.

"Not when you're working for the Agentia," Jessica countered.

"Ah, I'm going to go and…ah…play some piano," Naberius excused himself.

Jessica watched him leave then turned back to me, "You need to focus on the fire, Thom. Trevor's murder. The book is part of that, I'm sure, but the death of a DarkWaver? That needs to be your priority."

"You really want to look good for Gilles, don't you."

"That's uncalled for, Thom," she sounded mad.

"Like you said, I know you too well," I pointed out.

"Just give me something solid," she leant back in her seat and narrowed her eyes, "Or is that still too difficult for you to manage?"

"Talk about uncalled for," I shook my head, "C'mon Jess. You left me. Let's leave it at that and move on."

She looked at me with a sharp laugh and raised eyebrows, "I left you? Is that how you remember it?"

"Okay, doesn't matter right now. You want to work together? Fine. But we don't need to revisit the past. Okay?"

She looked over towards Naberius, who was paying very close attention to the sheet music. I knew she didn't want to let it go, but I also knew she wanted me to get my work done. I watched as she twirled a lock of her hair between two fingers.

She knew I was attracted to her. She also knew how to use that against me. She used it against a lot of people. I appreciated her style, but I didn't always enjoy her methods.

Thing was, I knew if I upset her, I'd upset Gilles—and he could make sure I'd never work for the Batcavers again. I was starting to feel like that was a bridge I shouldn't burn.

"All right, Thomas," Jessica let her hand fall on my arm. "A trade. I tell you what I've got, you tell me who you're working for."

"Not a good idea, Jess," This was going to be difficult.

She faked a pout, "The fire. Have you determined what caused it? Was it a drink or was it something darker?"

"It wasn't a demon, if that's what you mean," I responded.

"So...Voudou? A cocktail?" Jessica threw her hands up in an exaggerated question, "A Voudou cocktail?"

I looked towards the piano, trying to catch Naberius' attention. He made a point of not looking at me, but his fingers drifted into something that sounded vaguely spy themed.

"Dammit, I can't do this," I told her.

"Have you been questioned by the police yet?" Jessica asked.

I looked at her, curious. I knew Gilles wanted to talk to me, but I figured the VPD would find their way to me at some point as well. And they'd ask questions the Agentia wouldn't want me to answer. "No," I said.

"Well, listen. If you give me what I want, I'll make sure the police don't bother you."

"And how are you going to do that?"

"I have my connections."

"Gilles, right?" I asked suspiciously.

"Don't worry about who, or how. Help me out, I'll help you out. Simple as that," before I could respond, Jessica stood up and held out her hand, "think about it. We'll talk soon."

"C'mon, a hug at least," I said, standing up as well.

She nodded, moved in for a hug, and then kissed my cheek before stepping away. Her lips felt too much like I'd remembered them feeling.

She moved towards the door and turned before leaving to hit me with *a look*. I sat down, feeling like I'd been punched in the chest.

Naberius returned, figuring it was safe. He sat next to me; I let out a sigh and finished my drink. "She's going to get everything I know out of me, isn't she?" I asked.

"Yeah," Naberius said, looking back at the door. "Probably."

"I wish I could talk to Dabriel about the cause of the fire" I said. "I know she has a few recipes up her tailored sleeves."

"She's not here," Naberius said.

"Yeah, thanks."

Naberius looked up at me "Look, remember what I said about Blundertown. I don't know if it is connected, but somebody should talk to Christophe. I just don't know if we should involve the Agentia at this point."

"Why not?" I asked.

"What if I'm wrong? Christophe's been a good friend to this bar, and I don't want him being looked at for murder if he only took a book. You should check it out first."

"Me?"

"Dante, I know we haven't always gotten along, and I have no idea how you were at your previous detective job or whatever, but you are a good bartender and as far as cocktails go, you're great at figuring things out. You know the mix is only part of it. Without the ingredients the drink is nothing, and you've always been on top of the game as far as putting the right parts together."

I WAS surprised at that but pleased as well. Naberius and Dabriel were both superb Mystixologists, and I had no idea that my efforts had been noticed, let alone appreciated. Part of the reason my father had taken to the Awkward tag when I started mixing was the fact that while I could gather all the ingredients, the effects of my mixes didn't always hit as they were supposed to. Supposedly it's because of my elemental blood. It's Wild Magic. Chaotic. If I'm not paying attention, I can add unwanted energy to my cocktails. It took a lot of concentration to balance that out, the intent and the impact. Things had gotten a little smoother with the mixes since I had my powers dampened, but still, I was surprised Naberius had taken notice.

"Thanks for that, Naberius," I looked around, "So how are you feeling about opening up without Trevor?"

"I mean, the city needs this bar, right?" He said.

"Yeah. It'll be alright. We'll figure this out," I told Naberius. "C'mon, let's go. I was going to work on some drinks, but I think I'll leave it for later."

We walked outside, the agent at the door gave us a nod. Naberius shook my hand, turned up the collar on his coat, and disappeared around a corner, heading for somewhere. I watched him go, wondering if maybe I'd been wrong about him. It's not like I didn't trust him, but...yeah...I didn't trust him. At least, not yet. He did seem like he was being honest with me, though.

IT WAS TOO late to call Dabriel, though I did need to talk to her, but it wasn't too late to check out the scene around Blundertown Books. I knew Gilles was going to start pushing me for answers soon, and he wasn't going to be an easy person to avoid. I'd have to try, though. Especially since it seemed as if my ex-girlfriend might attempt to seduce information out of me. That was something I hadn't been expecting and wasn't sure I wanted. I had to focus on the priorities. Figure out who had mixed that goddamned fire drink and prove it wasn't me.

First though, there were a few things I had to grab at home, and I needed some caffeine. Or even better, a caffeinated cocktail. Blundertown was closed, but there were ways around that. I just had to find the right person to ask the right questions, and I'd have to be very careful doing it. While I wasn't planning on throwing any dark magics, any kind of summoning was frowned upon by the Triple Alliance.

7

SLIGHT QUERY

I got home and went right to work. I started a pot of coffee brewing, and got out the cream, and my special cinnamon liqueur. A couple of shots of Cinnasomnia would help me avoid sleep for at least another day or two. A little of the stuff goes a long way. Besides, I knew my limits. Didn't always pay attention to them, but I knew them. Mixing caffeine and alcohol wasn't always the best way to go, but if you get the balance right it can sharpen the mind and relax the body. While the coffee dripped, I gathered a few things for my secret mission: flashlight, Swiss army knife, a couple of pens, a notebook, phone, orange bitters, a bag of ashes, a small can of pineapple juice, and a flask of rum. I shoved it all into my leather messenger bag along with my small black bartender's bag which held a cocktail shaker, a bar spoon, a muddler, and a small bar whisk. Be prepared.

When there was enough coffee for two shots, I downed two quick ones, grabbed my keys, locked up and walked to my car. An old 1970 flat black Corona fondly known as Black Sunshine. I should give her a better name, but I've been too busy for a rechristening.

I made my way to Blundertown. A fantastic shop, but it's the kind of place you can't find unless you know about it, and unless you've been there, you probably haven't heard of it. It's on 4th avenue but not facing the street. Bad for business, but good because their books aren't for everyone. Thing about Waver places is that some are okay for everyone, like the Lost & Found or the Four Calendar Café. NoWavers and DarkWavers can enjoy the same drinks and not get too involved in the magiks that might be swirling around in the mix. You don't have to be a chef to enjoy a fantastic soufflé, but Christophe's bookstore was a totally different matter. It was full-on DarkWaver lore, and the normal people would not understand.

WHEN I ARRIVED, the street was quiet. Not much around other than small neighborhood shops. I parked around the corner and walked to the narrow space between buildings leading to the side entrance.

The path was laid out with broken stones in varying shapes and sizes surrounded by moss. Privacy shrubs on one side, an ivy-covered wall on the other, and I felt like I was entering a secret forest instead of a closed bookstore. I stopped at the door. It was cold, the air smelled like rain, but there was none falling. The weather was strange.

I made my way around the entire building, casing the joint. There were no lights on inside, but a dim bulb glowed at the back, over the trash cans and a pile of empty boxes in the driveway. At the far end of the lot there was an iron gate surrounded by hydrangea bushes leading into the alleyway.

Everything was locked up, but I'd expected as much. Breaking and entering wasn't on my agenda for the evening. It wasn't something I really enjoyed doing, and when the place in question was owned by a vampire, even a fake one, it was something I liked to do even less.

On the other hand, the windows were within reach. I paced. Should I? Shouldn't I? I shouldn't. I walked back to the driveway and as I passed the boxes I stopped.

I'd assumed they were empty boxes of books, but they were from a local liquor distributor. One had held bottles of rum; one had been full of whiskey. One was stamped with Russian letters, probably vodka, and then two empty cases of wine. It seemed as if someone had already started moving in with the liquor.

I could feel my insides start to battle against the shots of Cinnasomnia. Sometimes it was a smooth hit, but not tonight. Because I was already exhausted, the liquid had more to fight against. I had sunk down, back against the iron gate, facing the bookstore. The sky still threatened rain, while the moon, cut in half, pushed a dull glow through the shifting grey.

I stood up slowly. I had questions to ask, and I might be able to get answers, but I needed to ask them while it was still dry. Rain was an elementally charged liquid and would throw off any mix that didn't include it. All the elements were very specific ingredients. Much more than the base alcohols used. I also needed to ask my questions while I was near the bookstore. This mix doesn't work from a distance. Location is everything.

I rummaged through my bag. Shaker, rum, juice, bitters, and a pinch of ashes. I focused on the shaking, which most people don't realize is as important as the ingredients. I poured the mix into the glass, set the shaker down, and scraped a little cement off the ground to sprinkle it over the drink.

The description of the drink is an incantation, and the recipe, the spell. But it's not only about the mix; it's knowing what the mix is for. Some drinks need blood, some call for sweat, and some for tears. Thankfully this was a light cocktail. Easy on the soul, so no need for the heavy stuff. I gave it a quick stir with my finger. The specks of asphalt floated in the mix, glinting charcoal shimmers in the night. I took a deep breath, the final ingredient, shut my eyes tight, and blew into the glass before taking a small sip.

The taste left a little to be desired, and I made a note to myself, less ash, and maybe a different orange for the bitters. This is partly magic and partly chemistry with an alchemical twist. There's an almost infinite number of combinations, and each one has a different effect. Sometimes the differences are too small to be noticed, but they're always there. I have to get everything right to get what I want, and if I get a couple of things wrong, I could be in trouble.

The name of the drink is essential. You must know what it's for and who it's for. I needed answers. So, I built a Slight Query. The stronger it is, the longer it lasts. Right now, it's about quick answers. That's where the ashes come in.

I swirled the remainder of the drink around in the glass and concentrated on the question. Where is Christophe? I pushed it through the drink. A quiet extension of thought. Thankfully, the dead are almost always thirsty.

I WAITED for what felt like an hour, but it was only a few minutes. A little circle of clouds shimmered between the top of the building and the edge of the moon, then stretched like a helium balloon losing altitude. The circle looked like it was pulling the sky towards me before it snapped into a flash of starlight. Silence, then a figure stood before me. A translucent shadow of a man. Hair spiked and blonde, a silver suit, probably what he was wearing when he died, only now it really sparkled. The clouds had broken up slightly and the moonlight shone right through him. Not quite a ghost, but a Wisp. Somewhere between a soul and a spirit.

If there was something here, I needed to know, the dead man would point me in the right direction. This is Dead Magic, and I really should not be using it.

Dead answers weren't always the easiest to understand, as not being alive prevented you from seeing certain shades of reality, but interpretations were possible.

"Who are you to call on me?" the figure whispered.

"You can't have my name, yet. Right now, I'm just the bartender. I have something for you," I showed him the drink. "In exchange for answers."

"For me?" he laughed delightedly. His voice was little shreds of sound. "Do you have any idea how long it's been since I had a drink?"

Floating down in front of the glass, the Wisp moved his finger in a circular motion above the rim. I was glad I'd already finished half the drink. The remaining half was for the Wisp, but he needed me to drink it

"Whenever you're ready," he gave me a big smile, which didn't quite have the desired effect, as you could see right through it.

I braced myself for the possession. It flickered in the moonlight, vanished, and reformed right behind me. "Cheers," the Wisp whispered in my ear.

"Cheers," I said, raising the remaining half of the drink.

EVERYTHING WENT BLACK.

Do you know what it feels like to have a dead man inside of you? It feels like you've died. No life flashes, no sound, no light. Nothing. It feels like an eternity of oblivion tied up within a shadow that swallows your soul and spits it out empty and shaking back into yourself.

And then it's over.

I didn't open my eyes; they were already open. It was like someone turned on the light of the world and I was in it again. Holding an empty glass.

The Wisp flickered happily in front of me.

"That was fantastic," it grinned. "A little heavy on the ash and I've had better rum, but for the time and place? Couldn't have been better."

"Glad you enjoyed. Now it's your turn."

The wisp chuckled, "Of course. Who was it again?" He glanced back at the bookstore and gave me a look that felt strangely solid. "You are going to give me the name, right? I need the name," his words moved whiskey smooth.

"Yeah. Christophe Grey."

The wisp spun in a tight circle, "I know that name," he seemed extremely pleased with himself, "I remember."

He spun some more. I was getting dizzy watching.

"There are things you don't know about him," the wisp said.

I tried to focus on his face, it wasn't easy. "No, I know. He's immortal, thinks he's a vampire."

"That's not what I meant," still spinning.

I looked through him, "What do you mean? Where is he?"

"He was not born a DarkWaver, but I know much more than that," the wisp said.

"What else?" I asked. "Something about the book?"

"I'll show you," foolish me, I thought he was going to tell me.

His hand stretched out, fingers extending like tendrils into my forehead. It felt like brain freeze multiplied by a thousand. I could feel my eyes shiver and my skin tremble with some sort of electricity. The wisp's eyes, for a second, turned as solid and as white as the moon.

I didn't hear words, I felt them. I saw the shape of what he was telling me.

I saw the Intoxicantata. I saw Trevor holding it, he was with Marinette, Christophe, and a man I didn't recognize, his face in shadow. The vision shifted to Dabriel holding the book. Naberius stood behind her, the look on his face a strange sadness. He was whispering something as Dabriel made a quick crisscrossing gesture over the cover with the index finger of her left hand. There was a flash of silver light, like electric ice, and the book was sealed. A latticework of spider-web thin threads surrounding it.

"They're doing Dead Magic," my voice trembled. "What's going on?"

"I don't know," said the voice in my mind. "Looks like a binding is being placed on the book. All I have is information."

There was a shiver through my brain and the vision vanished.

"Wait," I spun around, looking for the wisp.

It floated in front of me, "I am Zee. We have shared spirits; my name is safe with you."

"Okay, Zee," I asked, attempting to remain calm, "You can call me Thom. But I need more. Where is Christophe now? And the book? And who was that man?"

"Christophe is no longer the owner of this store..."

"I knew that. What else? Who bought the store?"

"I couldn't get that or where Christophe is. I tried, but something's blocking my inquiries. Something very strong," he paused for a second, his colors shifting from pale to paler, "Maybe ColdWavers?"

"I hope not," I shuddered and pushed it aside. The ColdWavers were mysterious beings that were somehow beyond good and evil. Beyond morality. And that was a dangerous force to mess with.

"Dabriel and Naberius. Zee, how are they involved?" I asked.

"They know how to unlock the book. One last thing, about Christophe. The thing you don't know. He's not your friend. He's dangerous."

"That's just great," a dangerous immortal. Not what I wanted to be worrying about. "The Lost & Found…Zee, who killed Trevor?"

"I don't know. Too many questions, not enough to drink. Maybe next time," he gave me a smile only a dead man can give and then his body, transparent, stretched out above me. A slick sliver, a mercury lined membrane, and a shift into darkness, and he was gone.

I sighed. I shouldn't have expected anything different.

Alone again, and more confused than before. I had to figure out who bought the store and track down Christophe. I'd have to ask Dabriel and Naberius more questions.

Like why they'd been using Dead Magic and why hadn't either of them come clean about the book. There was a connection between the Lost & Found, Christophe, and my father's books. I understood the importance of secrets, but not if you're keeping them from someone who's trying to help you. Then the wonderful psycho twins. Murmur and creepy guy. They wanted the Intoxicantata as well, but why?

I GATHERED the scattering of objects on the ground and placed everything back in my bag. I felt like I'd been drinking for days. The dead can take a lot out of you.

I walked towards the street, and as I moved past the hydrangeas everything started to feel a little dreamlike. My hands were shaking. There was no one else around; no cars, no pedestrians, no witnesses. Just the beginning of what felt like an endless emptiness of night.

It was too late to call anyone, too early to go anywhere. I decided to wander, clear my head. I turned down Macdonald Street figuring I could go through Tatlow Park.

I walked blind and uncaring, swerving, side walking. Almost

getting hit with the jitters, but not like shaky hands, more like shaky mind. I sensed some strange reaction pushing down heavy on my soul. Maybe a bottle of whiskey could make all of it go away, but all I had was a shot of rum. Headlights cut across my shadow with a spin of car tires. My first thought was they've found me. But I didn't know who they were. I didn't even have time to run. The car, an old olive green Chevelle, stopped right next to me. The driver gave me a quick glance, then smiled. It was an empty smile but holding a noticeable state of urgency. I felt like I should've recognized him, but I didn't. I also felt like he was someone I shouldn't trust, but at the same time I didn't think I should run. At least not yet.

"Thomas Dante."

Not a question. I didn't nod. Adrenalin built up in my chest, getting ready to push me off in the opposite direction.

"Get in," the face was in shadows, but the voice was smooth, strong.

"Who are you?" I asked.

"Earnest," he said curtly.

"That doesn't really help."

"It's about the book."

"Somehow, I'm not surprised."

"Look..." He raised his hands; used one to pull open his jacket, "No weapons, no worries. I don't want to cause any problems; I only want to talk." He paused for a second, "Come on, I'll buy you a coffee."

I knew it could be a bad idea, but I could use some coffee...

8
VISION THING

There's a twenty-four-hour diner up on Granville Street called Komakino. Never crowded, always weird. It looks like the kind of restaurant David Lynch would have created if he'd reached into an old dream of mine and pulled out a red velvet diner with seedy lounge décor and shoved it into a surreal roadside attraction. "So, why are we here?" I asked.

"Because Komakino caters to a very small group of dedicated regulars. Anything we say will not leave this room. Trevor Slone and I used to come here all the time."

"You knew Trevor?"

He nodded, "It was shocking to hear he had passed."

There was something very familiar about this guy. He was well dressed, wearing a superbly cut black suit, black hair speckled with white, and if it hadn't been for his eyes, I would have thought he was some European fashionista. His eyes were the flattest, deadest, shade of grey. The waitress came over with two coffees and two shots of whiskey. "We're going to need a couple more of these," I said, holding up a shot. I looked at the man across from me. "So, who are you, how do you know my name, and what do you want?"

I watched him stare through the smoke-stained glass as he sat across from me. His eyes scraped across the view, and he spoke,

"Earnest. Earnest Caan," the way he said his name I was expecting some sort of Frau Blücher lightning flash, but all I got was another mysterious smile. He continued to speak, without looking at me. "You are here because I need your help."

"You need my help? Why does everyone suddenly need my help? I can't even help myself these days."

When he turned his eyes on me, out of the emptiness came a glint of the sharpest silver. Like a blade. Waiting.

I'd seen that look before when I'd been brought before the Triple Alliance. It wasn't as simple as a practiced expression; it was a talent. Was Earnest Caan one of them? What did they want with me now? I hadn't done anything recently. Unless it was the Wisp? Using ashes for a summoning was Dead Magic territory, and I knew I wasn't supposed to play there.

Earnest's hands absently ripped apart an empty book of matches. "You are working on the wrong side of this."

"Wrong side?" I shot back, "as far as I know, I'm helping to find a missing book and a murderer."

Earnest turned to me, "You don't know the whole story."

"So, what is the whole story?" I asked.

He leaned forwards and I caught a whiff of smoke. Not the nice autumnal scent of burning leaves and quiet fires, but of faded cigars and smoldering oak.

"There are many stories," he whispered in that stained breath. "You need to focus on the right one. Everyone wants to find the missing book. Me included. But your story is different. It shouldn't be about an old book; it should be about creating a new one. A better one. Cocktails for kings…"

I WAS CONFUSED. "Look, I don't know who you think I am, or what I can do, but I'm not a bartender for hire," I said, a little angrily.

Earnest sneered, "Don't play the idiot, Dante. I know exactly who you are. I know the Lost & Found is next to useless without The Intoxicantata. But you need more than a recipe to make a drink work. You know how to read the recipes; I want to create a better place. A place where all our dreams come true. So yes, the book would help, but it's the drinks I want."

Think Thomas…I may be closer to a drunk than a detective, but the skills are there.

I had a flash of the vision I'd experienced with Zee. Earnest was the one I hadn't recognized. This wasn't about the bar…

"It's about the location," I narrowed my eyes, "You want to own the Crossroads."

"I knew you were clever. Yes. Why bother with a balance when you can have it all?

THE LOST & Found is on the tip of a supernatural iceberg. There's so much underneath. This is big, Dante. This is a once in a lifetime…" Earnest paused and looked straight at me, "No. A once in an eternity opportunity. The cocktail bar at the end of the Universe. A place where you don't need to worry about good, or evil. A place where you could live forever, a place with the power to create an opening between worlds, and I will be the one holding the door open. Forget about a bar where you can drink a little magic, and you'll make it into heaven. Why go anywhere at all?"

"And all it will cost is your soul, right?"

Earnest gave me a crooked little half smile, "The souls will help, yes. But since Trevor refused to sell to me, I'm going to have to find another way to put his bar out of business. That's why I'm buying Blundertown Books."

"You?"

He nodded, "But I need the right clientele. That's where you come in."

So, Earnest wanted the Intoxicantata, and the Lost & Found. Which meant he probably didn't want anyone else to have them. "Did you kill Trevor?" Hell with subtlety.

That made him laugh, "Me? No. I'm still not sure it wasn't you. You could take the recipes in the Intoxicantata further than anyone I know. Listen, the Lost & Found is holding you back. Without Trevor in the way, who knows what you could accomplish."

"You're accusing me? You think I flambéed one of my best friends?" The thin sheet of anger was starting to thicken.

Earnest shrugged dismissively, "Whatever, I'm not here to talk about what you did or didn't do. I'm here to talk about what you are going to do. Still, I appreciate the negative press the fire generated. Anything to help shut that place down is a good thing."

My outrage finally surpassed the anxiety I'd been feeling. I didn't care if the person across from me might have some impressive powers, I didn't care if I was arguing with a member of the Triple Alliance or a well-dressed thug. I finished my drink and set it down slowly.

"I'm not going to work with you."

Earnest placed his hands on the table and sat up straight. "You're not seeing the big picture. You aren't listening. You have a talent, Dante. Only I can make that shine."

I didn't care who this asshole was, he was pushing me a little too hard. He thought he knew me, but he didn't. To assume I would hurt Trevor in any way made me see flashes of red. If he pushed me any further, I could see myself hitting him. Not the best plan, but sometimes it couldn't be helped.

Earnest stood up. He was a little more intimidating when he wasn't seated; taller and much more muscular than me. I hadn't noticed initially, as he hadn't been as angry before, but his fitted suit looked ready to bust at the seams. And his shoes. I recognized his shoes.

"You were at the Café, weren't you? You've been following me."

"Following you? Dante, I've been watching you since the fire at the Riddle House," Earnest said. Earnest took a couple of steps forwards, his dead sharp eyes piercing through me, and spoke in one of the most menacing whispers I'd ever heard. "Thomas Dante. I am the one who placed the Reoite Corraich upon you. I am the only one who can take it away."

"You?" The anger was getting hard. Sharp.

Earnest ignored my outburst. "You need to calm down. I'm here as a friend. I do not have to leave as one. I am asking you to join me in a venture that could benefit the entire human race. You are still under the watch of the Triple Alliance, your elemental powers are still bound, and your recent queries of the dead have broken one of the Waver Laws. Any further infractions could lead to a cursed death, or possibly even worse, a cursed life. You would do well to remember this. The fact you are now involved in Trevor's death won't help your case."

I'd been in tight situations before, but to have this proclamation of doom delivered by a dead eyed trader of souls in a surreal diner was extremely nerve wracking. The verdicts of the Alliance were derived from the magic of the Great Cold Ones, and that was powerful magic. I held my breath for a second, my eyes focusing on the whiskey in front of me.

I didn't like being threatened. I thought about what I needed to turn the drink in front of me into a weapon. I could concoct a quick Dark Codladh with the ashes in my bag and the coffee. It wouldn't hurt, but it would leave Earnest caught between a deep sleep and a coma long enough for me get a decent distance away. There were a few cocktails you didn't need to drink for them to work, and the Codladh variation was one of them.

I decided against it, though, because it really wouldn't look good on my record. Fighting fire with fire was one thing, but using magics against the Triple Alliance was another altogether. I had to keep my cool. Let reason prevail.

"Earnest, the Wisp supplied specific information in exchange for payment. I didn't break any of your laws. I asked, it answered. No other information was shared, and no secrets went beyond us."

Earnest attempted a pleasant smile but ended up with a lopsided grin. "That's fine, Dante. But remember I'm willing to help you out if you are willing to help me," he straightened his suit jacket and sat back down.

"Are you trying to blackmail me?" I didn't want him to sense my fear, but I was afraid. I had kept my nose clean since the incident with Nick Noir, other than a few random concoctions here and there, but Earnest had the power to make my life extremely difficult.

"Don't think of it like that," Earnest said with a slight shrug. "It's more along the lines of working together for the time being."

"All I want is to find out what happened at the Lost & Found and track down a missing book. Honest jobs and honest money," I said, "I don't need to work for you."

"Need to have to. Sometimes it makes a difference," Earnest muttered.

I was starting to really dislike this man. "Earnest, I'm not doing this. And I have a feeling your peers won't see things the same way you do. So, if you want to gather the court and make your case, go for it. It'll only take a month or so to get everyone in the same place, and I won't mind explaining your plan to open the Crossroads and take on the balance of people's souls for payment. Maybe they'll take your word over mine, but is it worth the time and effort?"

Earnest looked like he wanted to bite my head off, and I wondered if I was doing the right thing. He spit the words out, "You won't say anything about this to anyone. Nobody will believe you."

He gulped down the rest of his whiskey and set the shot glass down firmly. I breathed a silent sigh of relief, feeling like I'd side-stepped a very uncomfortable episode.

"Well, I guess that's all we have to talk about," I stood up with a little salute, "until we meet again."

Earnest's arm shot out and grabbed my wrist, "we aren't done, Dante."

My mind started spinning. Earnest worked for the Alliance, but this was off the record. I was pretty sure his plan would break more of his Waver Laws than I ever had. So maybe I could get away with certain things. This wasn't going to be reported which meant I had less to worry about. Earnest had threatened me, scared me, and annoyed the hell out of me. Now he was physically assaulting me. I wasn't sure if it was the right decision. I didn't care. I took a step back and swung hard with my free arm. My fist connected with the side of his head. I probably hurt my hand more than his face, but he let go of me. He looked at me, wide-eyed, mouth open. Neither of us could believe what I had done.

I stood my ground, "I don't like being grabbed, or told what to do."

Earnest's jaw clenched; his neck veins pulsed. "You hit me?"

"I could've done a lot worse," I said. "You might be Alliance, but here you're just a bully in an empty diner."

He was furious, but he understood. He also wanted to hit me back. To his credit, and my relief, he didn't. He did give me a glass cutting glare, "You have no idea, Dante, what kind of enemy I can be."

"I'm guessing one that'll still take care of the bill," I intoned. I was wary, thinking he might still strike back. If he did, I wouldn't get out in one piece. It looked like he was going to let it go.

"There's a dead DarkWaver, Dante. Charred beyond recognition at the Lost & Found. Perhaps you weren't involved, but I think you were. When the Alliance takes the investigation over from the Agentia things are going to get much more complicated for you," Earnest said as he lifted a hand to his face. His lip curled when his fingers came away stained with a little blood. "Even if you haven't used your powers since the Riddle House, Dante, you still have them. The bindings placed upon you don't take them away, they just hold them inside. I think you're clever enough to figure out how to remove them."

"Just because I know how to do something doesn't mean I'm going to do it. I'm not a criminal," I said. But I could see how the shots were being lined up, and they were leading straight to me. Not only did I have my elemental birthmark, but I also had a working knowledge of Mystixology, and because of that, I'd learned a few descriptive curses. Sometimes you needed a Malediction or two. I knew I was on the DarkWave watch list, so of course they were looking at me as a possible cause of Trevor's death. I hoped Jessica wasn't going to be as easily swayed as the Alliance.

"You've got to be kidding me," I said, incredulous. "I can barely heat up a cup of coffee. I'm not going to break Alliance parole. There's no way I could've pulled off a fire like that."

Earnest puffed his chest out as if he was about to blow my whole house down. "Don't play innocent little bartender with me, Dante. Curse or cocktail, you know how to put it together. Being an elemental runs in your family, and it's a strong line. One of the strongest I've ever encountered. But it doesn't matter. When they find out how you did it, the Alliance will come down on you, hard, and you won't make any more drinks for anyone."

"Is that a threat?" I asked. I struggled to keep my voice from wavering. What did he know about my family? "Look, it wasn't me, and I'm going to prove it. I'm going to find out who it was, even if it was you," I stood up and Earnest looked at me as if I was even crazier than he was, "and I'm not going to help you."

"Very well, I tried," he said, standing as well. He held out a card, "in case you change your mind."

"Okay," I took it. "Now what? I'm not going to let anything happen to the Lost & Found."

"Admirable, but sometimes you can't stop progress. Things change Dante, remember that. Things always change."

The way he said it sliced cold through my bones. I didn't really know who Earnest was, or what he was capable of.

"Don't worry, I'm not going to hurt you. Right now, I can't afford it," he paused, rubbed his forehead. "I had hoped this would go a different way, but still—don't try to stop me, or the next time we meet will not be as pleasant."

"I can't imagine how it could be," I smiled.

Earnest threw some money on the table and left.

I GOT a taxi back to my car, still parked near Blundertown books. I thought about going ahead with my original plan for a second, find my way inside and search for some answers, but realized it was probably a bad time to attempt anything tied to the Magics. That included messing with wannabe vampires. Moving forward I'd have to be very careful. I hadn't realized how close The Triple Alliance had been watching me, and now Earnest was waiting for me to make a mistake. I suppose it was foolish of me to think what had happened with Nick Noir would've been forgotten by those high and mighty keepers of the law. I didn't have a choice at the time, though. Maybe I shouldn't have used a curse, but if I'd tried to fight without any tricks up my sleeve, I wouldn't be here now. I didn't win because of talent, but out of pure desperation. Either way, I was still tied to the killing of a shapeshifter and that's not something anyone gets away with. In the meantime, I should probably get my hands dirty with more mixes that could start the fire at the Lost & Found.

With Earnest and the Alliance watching me it would be tricky. If I recreated what caused the DarkWaver to go all barbecue at the Lost & Found, they might use that to jump on my case like a last supper. I knew whoever did it would have needed more than a recipe. Directions aren't enough. They would have had to know the proper techniques as well. So that pretty much ruled out your average bartender. There weren't many people who fit that description in this city.

I could feel myself fading though. I might have to give myself at least a couple of hours of sleep, or a stronger hit of the Cinnasomnia.

It would be nice to get a little help on this, though. Especially with Dabriel. It seems I might have let her get too close. After recent events it felt like she'd moved up past Naberius on my list of suspects. Which means it's possible I'd been wrong about him. I'd call him in the morning. As far as the missing book went, that was something I'd need to do on my own.

I wasn't about to let either Jessica or Gilles know about Earnest, not yet. Gilles could very well choose to go with a member of the Triple Alliance over believing me. With Jessica, well, maybe because I wasn't sure if she trusted me. Maybe because I wasn't sure if I trusted her.

. . .

When I stood in front of the bookstore, I lit one of my three cigarettes. It felt good.

By the time I got home it was lighter, but still dark enough for too many shadows. I felt as if someone, or something, had been watching me since I'd left Komakino. I was tired but wired. Sleep was not happening. Research was out; I couldn't concentrate with my head doing the synaptic shuffle. So, I was left with drinking. Practical research. I figured I'd need a few new cocktails in my arsenal. My home is basically the second floor of an old house off Commercial Drive near Salsbury Park with access to the attic. It's too small to be an actual room, but it's a great place to sit and mix drinks. I felt very comfortable in my place even though the walls seemed to whisper strange things on occasion. Sometimes I wondered if I might have ghosts, but as far as I knew I was only hearing the effects of time. I've done some decorating, working around the strange hieroglyphics caused by cracks in the paint, and tried to keep the place in decent condition. It's a little shanty, but it's my home and we get along.

I heard a sound. It wasn't the walls. I turned to see my wayward alley cat, Dr. Sax, staring at me. He was a skinny little Tabby with matted fur. It was mostly black but held thick stripes of orange. He had some whiteness around the face and paws.

Dr. Sax sat on the kitchen counter; head slightly tilted as if scolding me for being home so late. He pushed back on his front legs, stretching out his spine; and seemed to wink at me.

"What is it?" I asked.

He stretched again and paced around the sink delicately balancing on the stainless-steel edge.

"You want a bath?" I walked over, curious, then surprised. Dr. Sax stopped and jumped into the sink. Moving closer I saw what looked like a spider or a bug; but it was a button. And it wasn't mine. I picked it up, much to the annoyance of the cat, and rolled it around in the palm of my hand. There was a small black anchor engraved upon it.

I paced a few circles around the apartment, button in hand. Something was off. I noticed a few books had been knocked off the pull-up stairs attached to the attic entrance. I stood in front of the makeshift shelves feeling a little uneasy while Dr. Sax watched with an expression falling between bored and curious. I closed my eyes and focused on my other senses. I couldn't hear anyone moving around up there, but I did notice a strange scent that wasn't coffee, old cat food, and the remnants of a sage and cedar incense mix.

White musk.

I remembered my earlier encounter with the mysterious fox woman, Murmur. I softly placed a foot on the bottom stair. Dr. Sax gave me a disdainful flip of the tail and casually walked back into the kitchen. "Thanks for your help," I muttered and moved up into darkness. There was a small circular window upstairs facing the street, but it wouldn't be enough to illuminate the waiting shadows.

I smelled a faint breath of nicotine, a whisper of lilac, and I knew who it was before I made it to the light switch. "Dabriel?"

She grinned, "You're home."

"What are you doing in my attic? And how did you get in?" I asked.

She fidgeted with the lid of the whiskey bottle in her hands, "I have my ways."

I flicked the lights on. A soft light emanated from two vintage emerald glass globes hanging from the ceiling. I walked towards my makeshift bar. My attic looked like a crazy cross between a tiki bar and a shipwreck, but it was sanctuary. "And why?"

"Sit down," Dabriel said abruptly.

I did as she asked. I knew better than to argue with her. The scent of White Musk still bothered me, but I filed it away for later.

She placed two full glasses on the counter, "Just sit. A drink won't kill you."

"It might," I offered.

"This is serious, Thomas."

"Ah...okay," I said, floundering. I sat, absently stirred the drink, took a sniff, and asked again, "Why are you here?"

She smiled slowly, or at least her eyes did. "Drink. It's not your average Voodoo Sunrise."

"C'mon, Dabriel. After what happened at the bar? You go missing and then show up, uninvited, at my place? Should I call the Agentia?"

"No need to involve them. I'm here to help. We need to figure this out, together," Dabriel said. "What happened to Trevor was horrible."

I tried to stay stoic, figure out what her game plan was, without giving away mine. "Yes, but still, why here?"

Not that I really had one yet.

Dabriel waved my question aside and pushed the drink closer to me, "Have a drink, it'll do your soul good."

She stepped back and waited. I took a sip. She was right. It was amazing.

"Naberius has been acting very strange, and I know it has to do with what happened at the bar," she said, scratching the back of her neck.

Okay, so who's playing who here? I thought.

Another sip, pause, and I looked straight at her, "I know we've been working together for a while, Dab, but you and Naberius have been doing this a lot longer. Are you really saying this was him? Why would he do this now?"

"I need to show you something..."

She reached out and touched my arm. I felt an electric shock run all the way up it and hit my chest.

"What was that?"

"Side effect of the Vision Thing. I've been drinking them for a couple of months now, and the other day I was hit with a big one."

I GAVE HER A WORRIED LOOK, Vision Things were one of the more powerful shots, but not one of the better shots. If one played it right, drinks at the Lost & Found could take you on a cocktail trip to heaven, or you could end up going in the other direction. The problem was if you had to choose between an Angel Wing in a martini glass with a mini-marshmallow garnish or a Sin Kiss, which comes on the rocks and on fire, which would you go for?

All the drinks that fell on the dark side were usually a little more enticing. But it's up to the drinker. Usually.

"You have to be careful with those, Dabriel."

"I know what I'm doing Dante," she glared, "Anyway, I had a vision. Certain people hold certain energies, and some of them are triggers for my abilities. But what I saw was almost dream-like. There was a book floating above the bar at the Lost & Found, on fire. Behind the flames a figure appeared with a sort of triple-spiral symbol above its head and took the book. The fire stayed behind."

I raised my hand as if in a classroom. "Wait, you know who took the Intoxicantata?"

She gave me a serious look, eyes unwavering. "Possibly, yes. The visions aren't literal, but symbolic."

"Dabriel," I said. "If I knew who had the book, I would've told the police or figured out a way to get it back myself. You know you're a suspect too, though. You've been avoiding everybody. Why didn't you tell this to Gilles and clear your name?"

"Because a vision isn't proof, and I don't exactly have the cleanest past," Dabriel said, crossing her arms, "Look, it doesn't matter. We both have secrets, Dante, the point is I need more proof. And the symbol, the spirals? It was a Triskelion."

"The symbol of the Alliance?" I thought about it, "Do you know someone named Earnest Caan?"

Dabriel's green eyes glimmered slightly and shifted into emerald. "So, you've met the rebel alliance. You didn't bow down before him? I'm impressed."

"We had a little…disagreement," I said. "What do you know about him?"

"He's a sneaky one. His abilities allow him to be very easily forgotten. A nice trick if you use it well. The fact you remember him says a lot about your own abilities."

"So, it was him?"

Dabriel sighed. "I don't know. That's what I need to find out."

"You want to form an alliance against the Alliance?"

She raised a perfectly curved eyebrow.

"Sorry, but is that why you're here?"

Dabriel nodded. I wasn't sure if I could or should trust her, but it felt like playing along was my best move. "So, what's your plan?"

She motioned towards the shelves behind her, "I know you've been studying and practicing your mixes, but I think you might need to learn a few more recipes."

I didn't say anything. I grabbed the cocktail in front of me and knocked it back. "Okay. Show me."

9
BULLEIT THE BLUE SKY

I figured a little extra firepower couldn't hurt, and I might as well learn something. If I was going to go up against Earnest I'd need some new tricks, and if Nick Noir really was back from the dead, I'd need some strong drinks.

I made a sweeping gesture, "My bar is yours."

I knew a lot about making drinks, but watching Dabriel move around my bar I realized she was right up there with me.

"You've been holding back," I said, impressed, as she poured me a pretty decent Magus Martini."

"Not really," She smiled, getting in the flow. "It's just at the bar; our customers dictate our drinks. But what if we moved it to the reverse? There isn't always time to sit down with an angry demon and offer it a cocktail, so you need to be able to mix for the situation."

She showed me some concoctions for drinking, some for spitting, and some for flinging. Even a martini variation you could use like holy water. Of course, I'd have to run pretty fast after throwing a drink in the devil's face, but I was willing to try.

Dabriel really knew her potions, and alchemy never tasted so good.

"Okay, so you can mix a decent Magus Martini," I said, pretending I wasn't impressed.

"You can do better?" She winked.

"Maybe..."

The main ingredients of a solid cocktail are spirit, sweet, and bitter. That's the hardline base. Everything you add after that pulls the drink and the drinker in different directions. It's also important to use the right name and the right description. That's what seals the deal. It's like the Rule of Threes, the Holy Trinity, or the third time's the charm. But these threes can get you intoxicated. I organized my bottles for a second. There were so many delicate details. Add an extra drop of bitters to the wrong kind of rum and you might get a Fire Twist instead of a Fire Split. Similar flavors, but one will burn going in, the other will burn coming out. And it's not only the name that's important, either. It's about flavor, it's about proportions, it's about the purpose.

"Brimstone Rock," Dabriel gave a satisfied nod, "Good. That's not an easy one."

I gave a dismissive shrug, "No big deal, what else you got?"

Dabriel looked around, "Seeing as you've got this place decorated Tiki style, I was thinking maybe an Aloha Lover. I think you could use a little love in your life."

"No thanks," I said, "Skip the love potion."

"Come on, you've got to start somewhere," she said. "Learn the love and I'll give you something to help you fight."

"Seems like a problem waiting to happen," I muttered.

"Fine," Dabriel narrowed her eyes, "All right, my dear. Watch. Learn."

She pulled a few bottles off the shelves and started stirring, shaking, and swizzling. My attic became a flurry of alcohol. With "normal" cocktails there are usually three ingredients. Dabriel was mixing drinks with at least six.

I was amazed at her techniques and knowledge. I'd never seen her mix like that at the bar. She gave me a quick wink and moved back to the mix. Was I wrong about her?

"Let's try a nice little hex," she said, spinning a bottle in her hand. "Not quite a beauty spell, maybe more like a handsome spell. Not that you need one. You can use it for a little charm when you feel out of place."

The cocktail, which Dabriel called The Jack Risen; was basically a Jack Rose. Two parts Applejack, one part lime juice, and a little Grenadine.

"Now we build on that," She explained. "A little Pernod for the mind, almond bitters for the body, and a touch of honey for the soul."

"Nice. Deceptively simple," I said.

Cocktails can get much more complicated, but the simple ones can be harder to get right. Dabriel's Jack Risen tasted only slightly different than the original cocktail. The best ones are the ones that don't stand out. Most people couldn't tell the difference between a Bloody Mary and a Crimson Jezebel if they drowned in it.

"Will this make me irresistible to women?" I asked, squinting at the Jack Risen.

Dabriel snorted. "You wish. No, this only gives you an aura of stylishness. So, bottoms up?"

"Oh no, not right now," I held my hand up. "The last thing I need is for you to fall in love with me."

Dabriel looked at me in fake shock, then burst out laughing. "Right. Whatever. Let's put this aside and start on something to use in a fight."

She grabbed an empty Mason jar and poured the Jack Risen into it, labelling it with a quick scribble of Sharpie on masking tape. She reached for the Bulleit.

"Ah, that'll make for a nice hit but are you sure you don't want the Angel's Envy?" I asked.

"Depends on the strength, right?" Dabriel said. "Angel's is a bit more ethereal, Maker's is a bit rougher, while Four Roses would be stealthier."

I nodded, feeling a little flushed from the warmth of the attic and the alcohol,"Makes sense."

Dabriel continued without missing a beat, as I moved to open a window.

"With this one the name is super important. Like Number One with a Bulleit, a Silver Bulleit, or a Bulleit's Kiss."

"And this is what, Bulleit with my name on it?"

She groaned, "No. A little more subtlety is needed here. Bulleit the Blue Sky. Do you have any Maple bitters?"

"Maple? To add smoothness to your moves?"

"At least your drinks are better than your jokes," Dabriel snorted.

I dug out a barely used tincture of maple. I gathered the other ingredients as she listed them; spiced rum, blue curacao, pineapple juice and Bénédictine.

"Go for it," I said, stepping back with my hands on my hips.

She lined everything up and started measuring and pouring into the shaker.

"So…what do you know about Trevor wanting to buy Blundertown?" I asked, casually.

Dabriel almost spilled a scoop of ice cubes, "You know about that?"

"I do now," I told her. "Naberius…"

"Of course he did," Dabriel shook her head. "Dude cannot keep his mouth shut."

She gave me a sharp sideways look, having recovered and added the ice, "What else did he tell you?"

"Just that Marinette was involved, and that Christophe wouldn't kill Trevor."

Dabriel was silent for a second, stirring the mix with a long copper bar spoon.

"No," she whispered. "He wouldn't."

A switch seemed to flip, and she stood up straight, giving me a big smile before looking into the shaker, "Done. Unless you want a little extra punch. Then you can add a little spit."

I decided to go with the flow and counted on my fingers, "That would make seven ingredients, right?"

Dabriel nodded, "The rule of threes is more metaphorical than literal. Mind, body, and soul, remember? You don't have to use an equal number of ingredients if the pyramid is balanced."

"Okay, I'm getting that. I've always stuck to the standard triangle. But if it's for fighting, blood might work better than spit?" I asked. There's magic inside all of us, and it doesn't matter if it's blood, sweat, or tears. Sometimes it's skin or hair, other times you'll need pieces of the world around you. Dreams, light, wind. Everything can be used if you know how.

"You would think that blood would be good. If it's yours, no. That'll weaken you and shift the energy from the drink to the one fighting. If you want to make it stronger, you will need to find a way to add your enemy's blood," she said.

And all that was left was the binding. That's where I usually shined. It's in the name, the description, the energy used to activate the mix. You can't haphazardly throw ingredients together and call it a drink. That lets the curse fly free or fall flat. You need to tie it to yourself, or to someone else. Otherwise, it's a match waiting to be lit. A drink waiting to be drunk. A car waiting for a crash.

"Remember, energy comes from two places. Inside or outside. For this concoction, we concentrate on what's within. If we were dealing with external forces, you'd have to know where to go. Where the right places are. They aren't as obvious as you might think," Dabriel pulled her hair back into a tight ponytail and shook the mix in the silver canister. "The energy inside is stronger, but harder to tap into. Most people can feel emotions but it's rare to find someone who can harness and use it properly. Anger isn't only hitting something; love isn't simply kissing someone. You can use everything, nervousness, anxiousness, or arousal…if you put it in the right place."

Dabriel placed two martini glasses in front of me. I poured slowly, as she whispered something Latin sounding.

"What are you saying?" I asked.

"Potestas in caelo. Power in the sky," she only met my eyes a moment, then looked away.

"You don't need Latin, though, right?" I'd learned a little, but my descriptors were mostly English, though I could pull of the occasional French or Spanish flair if needed.

"No, but it can add a nice weight. Other languages work as well, depending on the drink."

"Then it's ready?" I asked.

"Almost. This one needs to be lit up."

"Right," I found a lighter.

She smiled, "Not literally. This is for a fight. We've named it, we've mixed it, but to turn this one on you need to find the will and strength within you and really taste the drink. Smell it. Breathe it in and find the description. Then place anger within it."

I put the glass to my lips and started to tilt my head back.

"A taste!"

I stopped, then touched the liquid to my lips for a hint of the flavor. I thought about fighting, about anger, about bullets flying. I thought about my fists like hammers, about what happened to Jessica, about my parents and Trevor, and Nick Noir. A jagged shape of hate grew in my chest, pushing at my ribs.

Dabriel smiled, "Good. Form it, then let it out. Describe the drink while filling it with what's inside. That is the last ingredient. The final addition."

I held the anger and the drink. I let the taste inspire words in my mind, behind my tongue. Bulleit the Blue Sky. I thought about the drink, the fight, the victory.

It's not about fighting, it's about rising, it's about facing your fear, it's about winning. There it was. The description.

I spoke slowly with my eyes closed, "The glow of the bourbon wraps around your heart like a tropical touched fire, strengthened by the bond between rum and juice, while the slight lingering of the Bénédictine provides staying power for your soul. And it's all balanced by a boxer's ballet of maple. From a butterfly to a bee... Bulleit the Blue Sky."

"Perfect," Dabriel whispered.

The drinks in front of us seemed to glow for a split second. I felt drained, empty of all emotion. No anger, no fear, no strength. It had all gone into the drink. I almost slipped off the bar stool. I drew a couple of deep breaths to fight off a silvery blackness circling the edges of my sight.

"Are you alright?" Dabriel asked, reaching out to steady me. "That shouldn't have happened."

"I'm fine. Tired, that's all," I stood up and grabbed another Mason jar for the drink.

Dabriel stepped back, nodding appreciatively. "Good. And that was a great description. Menu worthy."

"I'm learning," I said happily, feeling a little tipsy from all the taste testing.

"Listen, I don't know what your plans are, but I know that the Agentia wants you to help them," Dabriel said. "Detective Deuxcoeurs kind of alluded to that when he was questioning me. I also know that Jessica is working this case as well, and from what you've told me that relationship was a bit of a mess."

"Yeah?" I gave her a quizzical look.

"Well, I don't know if that's the right move," Dabriel moved around the bar and sat next to me. "You left all of that for a reason, so why go back now?"

"It's Trevor, Dabriel," I closed my eyes, took a deep breath. "Look, we've shared a lot of the past couple of years, but we really don't know each other that well. What happened with Jessica, that's in the past. I don't think there's anything there. But I need to help figure this out because I owe it to Trevor."

"Okay, but I think there's more to this than what it looks like. Something else," she leans forward; brow furrowed, "Someone else?"

"I'm not sure what you mean…" I answer, fidgeting with the cold mason jar in my hands.

"I feel this bad energy in the air. It's not just the Triple Alliance, either. It's all tied together with threads you shouldn't be pulling. Too much power."

I stood up, slightly unsteady, "I don't feel too good."

Dabriel stands and nods, "Okay, let's talk later. You probably just need to sleep this off. I'll let myself out."

I went downstairs without looking back and fell on top of my bed. Dr. Sax was waiting for me, curled up halfway underneath a pillow. He opened one eye slowly to make sure he wasn't going to be disturbed then shut it again.

I tried to focus on what I'd need to do tomorrow before I drifted away. Figure out what was going on between Dabriel and Naberius, try to take on with Earnest Caan, and find a book for the Agentia. And besides the mysterious Murmur, Marinette, a Voudou queen who was not someone to be trifled with, was involved, as was Nick Noir. A person I thought I'd killed.

And I really needed to figure out who'd killed Trevor before all lies led to me. The fact I couldn't even light a match with my powers wouldn't make a difference if I didn't provide the Agentia with options. I'm the token fire elemental, so I'm the one that's going to get burned.

10
ÉLAN VITAL

When the phone rang, I was still in bed. "What?" I whispered. It felt like my voice was still sleeping.

"Thomas," it was Jessica. She sounded angry. "Tell me what you've got."

I sat up, rubbed my eyes. I needed coffee. Or more sleep.

"Thomas."

I wasn't going to get more sleep.

"I'm working on it," I said. I didn't want to mention who I'd been working on it with. Dabriel didn't need to be more of the Agentia inquisition than she already was. "Can I call you back? Just waking up."

There was a second of silence. I could picture the look of displeasure she was probably holding on the other end of the line. "Thom, you have no idea how important this is. I need something better than 'working on it.' If I don't get some answers, I'm out of a job."

I swung my legs out of bed and sat on the edge of the mattress, staring at the floor, head in my hands. I rarely got hangovers anymore, but last night...I hadn't had a night with that many drinks in years.

"Calm down, Jess. It's not like there's a straight line to follow here. I'm doing the best I can."

"Do it better," she said sharply.

"Hold on, you're getting too upset. You are not going to get fired over this. What's really going on? Is it Gilles?" I knew Deuxcoeurs and Jessica had a history, more of a history than I wanted to admit.

"Gilles has nothing to do with this. He's in the same spot I am," I heard a fumbling sound, maybe a lighter flick, and a deep breath. She was smoking. That was always a bad sign. "I'm sorry Thom, I don't mean to take it out on you. I'm on the edge of desperate and I need answers. Who did it, why was it done, what kind of magic was used. Was it a curse? Was Voudou involved? I can't go on guesses. I need facts."

"Jess," I said calmly, "I think you're overreacting a bit. Seriously, what's going on? Is there something you haven't told me?"

I heard her take a deep breath, "Look, if you can't give me something solid there's going to be a hell of a mess to clean up. This case is moving up the chain and people aren't happy about it. The Agentia heads are on our case, hard, and the Alliance is getting all hot under their mystical collars. This is bigger than a murder in a bar, Thom."

I knew Jessica wanted something solid, but she was acting very strange. I mean, I was hesitant about bringing Nick Noir into the mix, but she was definitely hiding something.

"Okay, what aren't you telling me, Jess? Bigger than a murder? What, exactly, is this case about?"

Jessica was silent, another long exhale. I could picture the smoke pushing out in a thin steady stream. "Someone has been stealing DarkWaver books. Ancient tomes, Manuscripts, Atlases, and Almanacs. Two weeks ago, the Maledictionary was taken from Alliance headquarters."

"Books? Jess… do you know about Blundertown Books?"

"Yeah. That's what brought us here. If the Intoxicantata hadn't been at the Lost & Found…"

"I wouldn't have seen you."

"Right," she said abruptly.

"But you did, and now there's a murder, but the books are still missing, and you don't know why," I stood up and moved towards the kitchen.

"Thom, there's some dark shit going down. The Agentia is worried that either someone is gathering power to use against us, or even worse, collecting these books to sell. And if they are sold outside of our Waver world…"

"Bad shit will happen," I finished. "Alright. I'll give you a solid lead on the Lost & Found murder, and probably some info on the missing book, later today. I'll follow up on the Voudou side and then probably hit Blundertown to track down the owner, Christophe Grey."

"I've got some people to locate as well," Jessica informed.

"Who else is missing?" I asked, suddenly feeling anxious.

"Your friendly neighborhood bartenders. Naberius was supposed to come down to the office, but he never showed. Gilles can't get a hold of Dabriel either."

"I might be able to ferret him out, and I just saw Dabriel last night…"

"What?" Jessica sputtered. "What did she say? She's been avoiding us, and that makes her look a little guilty. I'm just not sure of what, yet. And you should know better, Thom. Besides, you're making a bad habit of being the last person to see people. That does not look good on you, and I know Gilles is not going to be happy about that."

I snorted, "Gilles is rarely happy about anything."

"Don't be a dick, Thom. We're in this together so we might as well attempt to be pleasant about it. Or at least polite. Gilles is on your side, Thom," Jess reassured. "It's just that questions have been raised about the extent of your involvement. You're in deep, so you need to stay clean. Something I know you are not good at doing."

"I'm not the same guy you used to know, Jess," I countered.

Jessica sighed "I'll believe that when I see it. Besides, if you get into trouble with Gilles, I won't be able to get you out. You're the wizard of alcohol, and this murder happened in the bar where you work. Everyone associated is under suspicion, and so far, none of you are being too cooperative. You've been given a little leeway because you're helping us. But if this gets any bigger the Alliance is going to start throwing their weight around and that's going to affect all of us. Gilles does not want that to happen. He's been on this since the beginning, and you know how the Alliance tends to take over."

"And here I didn't think he cared," I said.

"Come on, I'm trying to help. The Alliance has a big problem with DarkWavers killing DarkWavers, and you do not want to be in their line of sight any more than you already are."

"Jess, don't worry about me. I can take care of myself. I know what I'm doing, and I'll get you some answers."

"All right Thom. I trust you. I do," There was a slight pause, and then, "Be careful."

"I will. And can we…" I was going to ask if we could meet up, maybe for drinks, "Jess?" Too late. She'd hung up. I was about to call back but was distracted by a peripheral shine in the hallway by the front door.

It was a small charm, attached to a thin silver chain and taped to a piece of paper. It had been slipped through the mailbox. Scrawled on the paper was a little message.

SOMETHING TO HELP YOU FOCUS. Wear it.

Ethanol, always. -Dabriel

It was a line, double crossed, with small circles on each point. A couple of quick searches and I discovered it was a representation of the alcohol molecule. Ethanol in silver. Couldn't hurt, so I put it around my neck before I went to search out the source of a quizzical meowing.

I arrived in the kitchen to find Dr. Sax casually sitting in the kitchen sink. He wanted breakfast. I wanted coffee. There wasn't any. I rummaged around in the cabinets and soon Dr. Sax was happily licking his paws while I rinsed out his dish. I wished I'd remembered the coffee beans last time I was at Four Calendar. Which reminded me, I should hit the café before I venture towards Kill City. I wasn't looking forward to talking to Marinette alone, so it was part procrastination, but also part need for caffeine.

. . .

I'D TOLD Jessica I'd check the Voudou angle, and if you're talking Voudou, Kill City was the place to start. Still, Walking into Kill City and asking a bunch of stupid questions wasn't going to go over well. I didn't think there would be a fight, but I'd asked wrong questions before.

Which also meant I probably shouldn't go empty handed either. I have a very small collection of cursed objects. Most of them wouldn't be very helpful, but there was my bar spoon. Not only did it stir like silk, but with a whispered phrase and a quick spin in the hand it became the sharpest spoon you've ever seen. Another phrase, another spin; and it was as heavy as a baseball bat. It was part of a matching set. The other one was behind the bar at the Lost & Found. I slid the spoon into a hidden pocket in my jacket then filled two small flasks with the drinks I'd worked on earlier. One for strength and one for sentiment. Who knows, sometimes a little love can go a long way. A few charms never hurt, either. I moved back into the bedroom and lifted a thin leather bracelet out of a black box on the dresser. It had a silver bullet attached to it, and I clasped it around my wrist. It was the first gift I'd ever received from Jessica. I had the charm from Dabriel around my neck, next to the Egyptian amulet from my mother. I stood still for a second and held it in my hand, the symbol of Khet. I could feel the soft metal warm up. I missed her.

"Mom…" I whispered, then shook off the remembrance and looked around. I grabbed some ashes and put them in a small Ziploc bag. I was glad I had a lot of pockets to choose from, if I could remember which pocket carried what. I was kind of underequipped if things went bad, but maybe I'd be all right. No sense in starting a war when all you want is a couple of answers.

I knew the Loa probably would see me as a mere trifle; an amateur. Beneath their notice. That could work in my favor, especially if causing me harm would attract the attention of the NoWavers. The Loa were, on paper, part of the Waver realm, but they tended to work in their own little spiritual clique and had an amicable agreement of 'stay out of each other's way' with the other clans.

"I bet you wish you could come with me, don't you?" I grinned at Dr. Sax. He gave me a slightly annoyed look and went back to licking his paws. I shrugged and went to my car. My phone rang as I was opening the door. I glanced at the caller ID, decided to answer.

"Hello, Deuxcoeurs."

"Dante," His voice was soft but solid. "We need to talk."

I thought about it, let out a slow exhale. He was right. And without Jessica around. Besides, I might need some back up…

"How do you feel about a trip to the Voudou underground?"

"Kill City?"

"Yeah," I affirmed. "Meet me at the Four Calendar Café, and we can go together?

"Yeah. Fine."

When I got there, Gilles was waiting for me. A quick coffee grab, a smile for Mori, and then into Black Sunshine. I wanted to get to Kill City before it got crowded. Crowds were bad, but Voudou crowds were especially bad. I wasn't sure who, or what, we'd find there, but I was hoping it would be one of the more helpful clans. A friendly Loa can be dangerous, but a mean one is even worse. And I knew Gilles had done some studying of this particular religion, so I was pretty sure he knew more about Voudou than I did.

Gilles gave me a tight smile as he slid into the passenger side. "I'm not completely on board with this, but I'll do my best to make sure you don't screw up too much."

"Thanks," I gave him a sideways glance as we pulled away and started down the street. "So…what did you want to talk to me about?"

Gilles stared down into the cup between his hands, "I know it's not easy seeing me again, and it's gotta be hard seeing Jessica, but I just wanted you to know that I didn't want it to go down like it did after the Riddle House."

I wasn't sure how to respond to that. I concentrated on the road.

I don't hate driving; I hate other drivers. They might not like me much, either, but I'm okay with that. If they aren't going too fast, they're going too slow, and that's even worse. I shouldn't let it get to me, especially since my temperamental little Corona isn't good for high speed, or angry driving. It's been fixed a few too many times and is now dangerously close to giving up the ghost. Today though, today I was driving fast. Not angry fast, anxious fast. And that's a different kind of speed.

"There's no need to kill us before we get to the club," Gilles pointed out. I nodded, but didn't slow down.

"As long as nothing kills us when we get there. We aren't far," I shot my passenger a quick grin.

"Dante, look. I'm serious. I know what happened was messed up, and I know it wasn't your fault..."

"Wait, what?" I almost slammed on the brakes but didn't. "You turned me into the Alliance. You got in between me and Jessica..."

"You got it all wrong," he sat back, arms stretched out and pushing against the dashboard. His jaw clenched tight against my acceleration.

"So, what's right?"

"We were a great team. You know we were," Gilles sighed, "but you had a target on your back, so I had to take you out of the equation."

"What?" I slowed down, pulled over towards the curb. I couldn't have this conversation and drive at the same time.

"I should have told you sooner, but Jessica doesn't know about this either. As long as you had your powers, you were in danger. I turned you in to the Alliance because without your powers, you wouldn't be a threat."

"A threat to who?"

"That's where the problem lies," Gilles shook his head, "I don't know. Your parents, and other Elementals were being targeted. The Alliance kept it on a need-to-know basis, and I couldn't tell you, but I could protect you."

"By taking my powers away?" I said incredulously.

"Yeah," Gilles looked at me, held my gaze. "I had to get you out of that whole scene. I owed it to your parents. I know this is a lot, and it's why I needed to talk to you. But right now, since we've got this other thing going on, maybe we should deal with Kill City first?"

"Right," I shook my head. "And Jessica isn't in danger?"

Gilles smiled, "No more than she usually is."

"Right," I pulled out and continued driving towards our destination. "But this isn't over."

"I know," Gilles intoned.

"Fantastic," I kept my eyes on the road. "So, Voudou…there's no reason for anything to go wrong at the bar, is there?"

"Not really, unless you ask the wrong questions, or one of the tricksters show up, or if there's a few unruly spirits in the place," Gilles counted the problems off on her fingers.

"So, tread carefully. Got it. If any big baddies come out to play, I can hide behind you," I glanced at him as we waited for a light to change.

"Sure, Dante. Besides, I brought protection."

"For the sexy ghosts, right?" I tried making a joke.

All I got in return was a roll of the eyes.

"Gilles…"

"Yeah?"

I narrowed my eyes. "Are you two messing around?"

"Messing around?" Gilles exclaimed, as I made a swift lane change. "Dammit, Dante, you really need to do this now?"

"No, but…I mean, yeah," I sighed. "It's Jess."

"I care a lot about Jessica, Dante. I know you do too, but she's very important to me," Gilles shifted a little towards me. "Can we talk about this later?"

"Why?" I asked, my hands tightening on the steering wheel.

"Because you need to focus on the task at hand, Dante. And that means you need to focus on one thing. We're about to enter possible hostile territory, and if your heart isn't focused, your soul won't be, or your mind. You know as well as I do those three things need to be in harmony, and right now there is no harmony. This is dissonance, and the spirits we might encounter here thrive on dissonance."

"Fine."

. . .

WHEN WE ARRIVED at Kill City it looked closed, but it always looked closed. An abandoned warehouse on the corner, except for the neon sign. Solid brick walls painted black on the sides and splattered thick with swaths of electric blue, pale yellow, and little explosions of amaranth red on the front. The flicker of neon struggled against the slowly lowering sun as we parked across the street.

"All right, what'cha got?" I asked.

Gilles smiled and opened his black leather messenger bag. He pulled out a small bottle with a black and crimson label inscribed with the words April Skies. "This one's for you. I haven't forgotten about your coffee obsession. Save it for a special occasion."

I studied the bottle. Sixteen ounces of cold brewed coffee.

"I thought you might find it useful for some of your recipes. I'll tell you more about it later."

"Thanks."

He nodded before diving back into the bag, coming up with a small rectangular mirror about two inches long, and two plastic bottles, each holding about four ounces of liquid. One clear and one amber. I opened the colorful one first, it looked thick. I put my nose up to it then jerked my head away.

"Aww, what the hell is that? Smells like rotten fish in old mayonnaise," I tried to wipe the putrid stench out of my nostrils with the back of my hand, but that only pushed the odor farther inside.

"Asafetida," Gilles said with a laugh. He placed the bottles back in his bag.

"More like fetid ass," I grimaced. "What would you use that for?"

"It's used to protect you from demons or bind those demons to you. It also works with the occasional Voudou curse," Gilles explained.

"That might come in handy. And the other one?" I asked, not ready to smell it.

"Holy water. I know it doesn't work on everything, but it's sort of a standard stop evil ingredient, right?"

"Anything else?" I whispered, starting to feel a little worried.

He shrugged, "A Mojo Bag, a cross, and a Vévé. Thought I should cover all the bases. Shall we go inside?"

I nodded, holding up a finger, "One second."

I dug in my messenger bag and pulled out the flask holding the Jack Risen cocktail I'd made. "It never hurts to be extra charming, right?" I said with a wink and took a swig. "This is like handsome in a bottle."

"If that's the way you want to play it," Gilles shrugged and reached for the door. He stopped just before he touched it, and turned to look at me, taking a step back.

"What's up?" I asked.

"Yeah, if things go south, you'll get out, right?"

"We'll get out," I replied.

"We're going to have to be careful in here," Gilles muttered. "While the Loa cannot read your mind, they can possess you. Usually not without an invitation, but sometimes they don't need one."

"Fantastic."

WE WALKED in and stopped to let our eyes adjust to the darkness and our ears to the music. I'd expected something a little more rock 'n' roll, but it turned out to be more like sad carnival songs. Dark and discordant, but somehow slightly playful. Like a midnight lullaby.

I'd also been expecting more people. A large crowd would have been bad but being the only ones in there was probably worse. A woman stood behind the bar at the far end of the room. I recognized her. It was Murmur. I looked around, but there was no sign of her hawk-faced partner in crime. "I know her," I whispered to Gilles.

"Of course you do," he whispered back.

We started towards the bar.

Before we'd even taken two steps a man appeared from the shadows. When I say man, I mean beast. This guy was huge. The tattoo glaring at us from his right bicep as he placed himself in front of us was a lion entangled within the coils of a monstrous python, and it was bigger than my head. His left arm didn't hold any animals, but was covered in an inked mess of vines, thorns, barbed wire, and script.

I tried to give him a smile saying something like 'Please don't hit me, I'm actually a really nice guy', but I'm afraid all I managed was a sickly quiver.

"You are open, right?" I stammered.

He gave me a look of absolute boredom and pointed at our bags. "On the floor."

We put them down and he gestured for me to raise my arms. He checked me quickly and looked a little surprised when he found a bar spoon in my jacket, but he wasn't worried. He confiscated my Swiss Army knife and examined the charms around my neck.

Evidently not threatened by alcohol or ancient Egyptian symbols, he motioned for me to step back and went through my bag. He studied all three of my flasks and glared at the cold brewed coffee and slightly dented can of pineapple juice.

"You can't make drinks in our bar."

I nodded, "I wasn't going to, but I like being prepared."

"For what?" he growled.

"I get thirsty," I told him.

He narrowed his eyes, then shrugged, "Don't open them in here."

He held up my bag of ashes.

"I'm holding those for a friend," I said nervously.

"You get these back when you leave," He pocketed the ashes and shoved my bag back at me before turning his attention towards Gilles. He smiled politely and let the doorman pat him down. An eyebrow was raised as Gilles' badge was discovered, but other than a wrinkling of the nose at the little black velvet mojo bag, we passed our inspections. He held the mojo bag in front of him like a dead skunk, silently shook his head and pointed to the door.

Gilles obliged, leaving the bag outside, and slipped me a quick wink when he returned. Clever, he wanted it outside. We might not be safe in here, but his mojo would keep any additional dangers from joining us.

Still, it didn't leave us with many options. If anything unexpected happened, we'd have to think fast. Fortunately, the big bad bouncer didn't confiscate everything. I had the coffee, my bar spoon, the Holy Water, the stinky stuff, and a couple of charms.

He led us silently to the bar, and we sat where he told us to sit. As he moved back into the shadows by the doorway Murmur walked over. In the Kill City light her skin shone with an otherworldly crimson glow, and her fox-colored hair fell long and straight over her shoulders, almost to her waist. She looked slightly annoyed by our presence but gave me a knowing nod. "Nice of you to visit, Mr. Dante. Is this visit business or pleasure?"

I gave her what I hoped was a charming smile, "Perhaps both. Do you have a cocktail menu handy?"

She blinked, seemingly surprised by my question. Then she looked away and looked back again. Her confusion swiftly vanished behind a bright laugh, "Of course."

"I can tell the drink is working," Gilles smirked. "Because you are not a good flirt."

"Not now," I hissed as Murmur returned with a couple of drink menus.

"Whatever you like," she slid them across the bar, "On the house."

I looked at her, winked, "Thanks."

"So, you wish to speak to the Invisibles?" She asked.

I looked at her, confused, but Gilles nudged my arm, "She means the Loa. It's another name for them. Invisibles, or mystères."

Murmur gave Gilles an impressed look, "Correct. You are here, so we offer you a drink. An offering of peace. If you mean no harm, no harm will come to you." She looked at me, her blue eyes glistening.

The Jack Risen cocktail must be working. like a charm.

"Well, in that case, I'll have..." I ran my finger down the menu in front of us. Where the Lost & Found played on the good and evil tip, Kill City went straight for life and death. From the obvious; Death in the Afternoon, and the Elixir of Life, to the not so obvious. "An Elysian Field for me. Gilles?"

"I'll try the Élan Vital," Gilles said.

Murmur gave a quick twitch of a smile and pulled her hair back in a tight ponytail. In a matter of seconds, I had a Collins glass filled to the rim in front of me while Gilles received a Coupe glass topped with a soft white foam that seemed to shimmer in the light. I took a quick whiff and caught hints of Chartreuse and Orgeat.

We each took a sip and then looked at each other.

"Amazing," Gilles said.

The balance of the cocktails was phenomenal, and we said as much. Murmur looked pleased. "Miss Marinette will be down in a few minutes," she said with a genuine smile.

I must have looked a little worried because Gilles reached over put his hand on my shoulder. "We're good, Dante. Just like old times, remember."

"Sure. Old times," I repeated, rubbing my neck, "Only we weren't dealing with Voudou vibes back then."

And then Marinette appeared. She glided towards us, shining in a way that simultaneously attracted and repelled the darkness in the room. Wisps of cloth from her long black dress trailed behind her like feathers. Her arms were bare, flowing like shadows against the fabric of what she was wearing, and what she was wearing was stunning.

Marinette wore a low-cut dress revealing a neckline that could make Count Dracula swoon, and the slit up the side revealed just the right amount of thigh. Thighs that pointed down to black suede ankle boots. Beauty in simplicity. No frills and a fit that killed.

When she stood in front of us a golden light seemed to shine out of her eyes. Her hair fell perfectly over her shoulders and down her back in tight dreadlocks, each adorned with midnight blue beads. Her skin, her face, was so smooth it was almost impossible to not touch it. I sat on my hands. She was tall, taller than me, and slender. I wasn't quite sure where to look, and Gilles was trying to not look at the same places. She was breathtaking, and she was smiling at me.

"Mister Dante," she bowed her head. "It has been…a long time. Welcome."

Seemed alright so far. I stood up to greet her. "Miss Marinette," I bowed in return.

She smiled. The sparkle in her eyes caught in my throat. Then she turned to Gilles, "And you. I'm told you are with the Agentia, but I'm afraid I don't know your name."

"Deuxcoeurs," he stuttered, "Ah...Gilles Deuxcoeurs."

Marinette gently picked a non-existent speck of dust off Gilles' jacket with a smooth gesture, "But you know who I am."

Gilles nodded.

Marinette laughed. There was a sound hidden in that laugh, though the laughter itself was wonderful. A sound of something that wasn't right. But it ended with a feline purr that was uncomfortably arousing. Everything about her made me feel strangely hungry. Even her shoes were seductive.

"Well, Thomas Dante," she placed a hand on my shoulder, "I see you are enjoying Murmur's talents, but drinks are not the reason you are here."

I struggled to breathe as her hand moved to my neck. Her fingers touched my skin with the coldest shock. She lingered on the silver Vévé, then with a little shrug she walked around to the other side of the bar. Dismissing Murmur with a wave she prepared another round then stood with her hands on the counter. Waiting.

I took a sip, thinking about what to say. I knew there was a connection here with the Lost & Found; The book, Trevor, and Blundertown Books, but I also knew I needed to approach this delicately. "Why did you send Kurtis and Murmur after me?"

Or I could be direct.

Her eyes narrowed, "What do you mean, after you? I sent them to pick up the Intoxicantata from the Lost & Found. Trevor had promised it to me, and I was collecting. They returned empty handed. Evidently my book had been stolen."

"They didn't tell you anything else?" I tried to hide my surprise but failed.

"What happened," Marinette demanded, eyes flashing.

"Well," I explained calmly. "The Intoxicantata is still missing. There was a fire, and a DarkWaver died. There was no reason to suspect your involvement, but questions have been raised regarding the possibility of Voudou. I wanted to cross that possibility off my list. Your employees, Kurtis and Murmur, took it upon themselves to force me into the back of a car and attempt to bribe me with a large sum of money."

Marinette's glare cut through me. "Who died? And where is my book?"

I debated skipping over some details, but I knew Marinette would learn the truth. It would be worse for me later if she found out I hadn't told her everything, "Trevor. He was caught in the fire."

MARINETTE'S SMILE vanished like sunlight behind a thundercloud. Her eyes flashed gold, and before either of us could move she leant over the bar and grabbed both of our arms by the wrists. Vice like. Her hair moved like snakes across her head and her lips curled back showing a row of perfect teeth. A couple of them a little sharper than they should've been.

I pushed myself backwards with my feet against the bar. The weight of my body broke her hold, and I fell back onto the floor. There was blood on my wrist from where her fingernails had sunk into flesh. Marinette released her hold on Gilles and crawled over the bar towards me.

She was almost on top of me. "You did this," she hissed. "You are the fire elemental. You destroyed the Riddle House, and now you've killed Trevor."

Gilles ran towards the door, but he wasn't leaving. He was making sure our bouncer friend wouldn't join in. I didn't have time to explain myself to Marinette, I barely had enough time to protect myself. I pulled the bar spoon out of my pocket, whispered quick, flipped it, and as Marinette fell on top of me the sharp handle cut right through her. It pierced her dress, slid between her ribs. She screamed and fell back against the bar. I expected to see blood everywhere, but there was nothing. The spoon was still in my hand. Sticky, but not red.

I turned towards Gilles. He had retrieved his pouch from outside and secured a boundary between us and the big angry bouncer who stood by the door, glaring. His muscles flexing like angry redwoods. Marinette had recovered from her pain and surprise. She pulled herself up and moved towards me. She looked furious, but there was something else going on. Her mouth had widened, her teeth extended, her nose almost beaklike in a tight curl over her lips. Her skin, covered with what I had assumed were faint tattoos, was pulsating. Lines of ink-like veins spiraled around her arms and legs and her neck twisted almost full circle to take in the entire room before focusing back on me.

"I was ready to forgive you for what happened at the Riddle House, but I was not going to forget," she snarled. "And now you take Trevor?"

I pushed myself back, scuttling towards Gilles, but in the time it took to think about a breath she had grabbed my left ankle and swung me around. She let go of me like a human shot-put and I crashed at Gilles' feet. The wind was knocked out of me, and I lay gasping as my world crashed into nightmare. Turns out the stories I'd heard about Marinette being a Loa of power and violence were true; a now very frightening looking creature was walking towards us. Steady and determined.

"Give me your wrist," Gilles whispered. I held my arm out and he tore the bullet off my bracelet and doused it with Asafetida, "Hit her with this." He handed the bullet back to me and placed the Vévé and the mirror on the floor.

"What?" I asked, confused.

"Your spoon," he hissed.

Of course. The bar spoon could take on the weight of a baseball bat, and a silver bullet charm was still a bullet. I quickly pulled out the flask of Bulleit the Blue Sky. Another five steps and Marinette would be upon us. I swallowed back a shot tasting of bourbon and maple, and hoped I'd mixed it correctly. I whispered the words my parents had taught me when they gave me the spoons. "Trom, troime." Which was basically saying heavy in Irish. The bar spoon gained weight in my hand. I could hear Gilles murmuring something as well, "Open the gates, open the gates…"

I didn't think. I tossed the bullet up and swung the spoon. There was a blue spark, a crack like the sound of a bone breaking, and the bullet flew as if it had been fired from a gun. It looked as if it hit her right below the ribs, but it didn't stop. The bullet went right through her, burying itself in the edge of the bar. This time there was blood. Almost black.

Marinette screamed louder and more horrendously than before, and fell to her knees, her arms tight around her stomach and sides. Her hair whipped around her head like a nest of cobras.

"What are you?" I croaked, finally managing to stand.

Gilles stood beside me and whispered an answer, "She is Marinette Bwa Chech. She is Petro, evil, and very dangerous. She's tied to the werewolves as well, which is why the silver bullet had some effect. But there's more…"

I watched as Marinette tried to stand. Her face had become even more birdlike. It was rounder, larger, and she didn't remind me of a bird, but an owl. A scarred and featherless owl. Her mouth had opened far too wide, and I knew I'd be having nightmares about owls with teeth for months to come. Her dress had torn, but the beauty it had hidden earlier was gone. The thick ink twisted like wires around her arms had started to tie themselves together, pushing out of her back. They were coming out of her shoulder blades, tying into loose skeletal wings. I knew we were in trouble if those wings solidified.

Her slender shape was now hunched and twisted. Her breasts were sagging beneath her dress, and her eyes were shifting into unblinking moons of amber.

We had slowed her down, but we hadn't done any serious damage. She stood up as straight as she could manage. Her limbs had shortened, her fingers curled into sharp talons, and her face held only malice. Gilles and I stood together. He held on tight to his bottle of Holy Water while I had my bar spoon brandished out before me like a stainless-steel magic wand.

"Marinette, listen, please. I know it's a shock, but I didn't do this. Not the fire, not Trevor. He was like a father to me; I'd never hurt him."

Marinette continued towards us.

I glanced at Gilles, took a deep breath, and turned back towards Marinette, raising my hands, "Look, I'm just trying to find out what happened to Trevor, I only wanted to ask some questions."

A guttural caw emanated from her quivering throat. Gilles grabbed my arm and pulled me behind her. He held the mirror and the Vévé in the palm of her hand, open so Marinette could see. "I will call him again, and he is almost here. Can you feel him?"

Marinette paused; her head gave a bird-like twitch.

"I know you don't want him here, but I will finish the call," Gilles promised.

I knew he was talking about Legba, and I hoped he knew what she was doing. Bringing the trickster god of the Crossroads into play could open a few gates too many.

The woman owl creature snarled, as much as a beak could snarl, and stopped. Her head tilted back and forth, eyes shooting between me, Gilles, and the objects in his hand.

I slowly moved backwards, inching my way towards the doorway. Every movement hurt. I knew I was going to have a nice bruise on my back from where I'd hit the ground, and I was bleeding slightly from somewhere on my head.

"Trevor and I were going to be together, and now he's gone. And it's your fault," Marinette croaked. She was trying to regain her composure. Nobody really wanted to continue the fight, at least for the time being. Marinette stood up straighter, her flailing dreadlocks calmed into gentle shudders, and her skeletal wings drained back into the markings on her arms. She pointed a quivering talon of a finger at me, "If you take one of mine, I take one of yours."

"Marinette," I took a step forwards, dropped the spoon, and held my hands out in a peaceful gesture, "Again, I did not harm Trevor. I'm trying to figure this out. I came here for your help."

"You don't walk into a bar like this carrying weapons like that," she pointed to the bullet still embedded in the bar, "when you're innocent."

How did I suddenly become the bad guy here? The Agentia were suspicious of me, I had a feeling Jessica didn't trust me, and Marinette saw me as the villain. Marinette's owl-like eyes continued to pierce me, and I wondered what she was seeing. I could feel an invisible force pushing at my forehead, as if trying to drill into my brain. I believed in the power of possession, and that belief was what she was using against me.

"I'm not holding anything now," I said.

"He is," Marinette pointed at Gilles. "If he puts the Vévé away, and releases Rodrick, then perhaps we can talk."

Gilles gave his answer with a slight nod. I turned back to Marinette, "How do I know you won't try anything once our defenses are down?"

Marinette smiled a very unpleasant smile, her teeth still far too sharp in her mouth. "I swear on the leg of Ti-Jean-Pied-Sec that you will not come to any harm at this time."

I gave Gilles a quizzical look.

"Her husband," he whispered.

"And your rather large friend back there?"

"Rodrick will do as I say," Her voice had regained its smoothness, though it still fell on a frightening edge. Gilles put the mirror and the Vévé in her pocket and moved towards the door. She cautiously shuffled a foot across the sulfur mix that drew a line between us and the bouncer. It was hard to tell, but Rodrick looked slightly embarrassed as he walked towards the bar. He crossed his arms and stood behind Marinette until she whispered something. He nodded and vanished into a room at the back of the bar, leaving the items he had taken from us on a table.

I could tell Marinette still didn't trust us; her eyes never wavered from mine. I was shaking, but I hoped it wasn't noticeable. She was at a halfway point between who she had been and who she had become, but the changes were still happening.

Her face and head returned to a normal shape, her mouth curled into a perfect smile, and her eyes dropped back into a slight amber shine. Her talons once again became fingers, and she slid her hands down her sides, pushing off the tattered remains of her dress. The place where the silver bullet had entered her had already healed, only a small circular scar remained. I could also see everything else, and the hideous image of who she had been moments ago was erased by the vision of perfect skin; the curves and turns of her legs, her hips. The rounded smoothness of her breasts.

I glanced away uncomfortably, then looked back to focus on her face. She was smiling, but there was no happiness there. She turned and walked slowly back to the bar unconcerned with the state of her dress and what it was no longer covering. With a studied indifference she pulled bottles off the shelf.

"Another drink," she said, waving her hand over a bluish liquid before pouring it into three martini glasses. The liquid started to glow like her eyes had earlier.

Gilles and I stood at the bar, eyeing the drinks nervously. He gave me a sideways look and raised a quizzical eyebrow, tilting his head towards the bar. I shrugged and picked up the glass and held it to my nose. I picked up some floral notes, a very delicate scent.

I slowly swirled it as Rodrick reappeared carrying a scarlet dress. Marinette turned her back to us and slipped into the dress, making the act of clothing herself even more sensual than her previous state of undress.

She turned and raised her glass, "A truce. Drink. There is no harm in this, it's Kanzo Blue. A healing elixir. I keep my promises, as I hope you do."

We drank, and I could feel a warmth spread through my body immediately, my blood vibrated. "I realize you have lost as much, possibly more than I have, so maybe you understand why my emotions run a little wild," Marinette said, watching me carefully. "But you are a bartender, yes? What has pulled you back into investigating occurrences in our DarkWaver world?"

"You are correct, Marinette. My parents died at the Riddle House, and the Lost & Found became a home for me. I am going to protect that home," I looked at Gilles, took a deep breath, and came clean. "The thing is there's someone else involved in this. I should have told you earlier, Gilles, but I didn't want to upset Jessica…but Nick Noir is back."

"What?" Gilles and Marinette exclaimed, almost in unison.

"I know. I should have told you. He's not dead," I scratched the back of my neck, slightly awkwardly. "He wants the Intoxicantata as well. So, if Nick Noir is back, then we both have unfinished business to take care of. We can work together."

Marinette glared. "Where is he?"

"I don't know. Perhaps if we share resources, we can find him"

"Perhaps," Marinette sneered.

"Really?" Gilles hissed, turning to look at me.

"I know, I'm sorry. But let me tell Jess, okay?" I pleaded.

"Your funeral," Gilles said.

"Enough," Marinette barked. "What is it you want to know?"

"First," I asked. "Who was Trevor to you? I've known him for a long time, and we shared a lot of stories, but he never mentioned working with you."

"We were keeping things quiet, for now. A plan to join forces and open another bar that would combine our different ways of doing things. He was very talented and very clever. We were working close, and I think we both felt we might get even closer…if we'd had more time," Marinette paused; her voice wavered a bit. "We started this even though we knew there were others against it. Obviously, you didn't know, but your co-workers, I think they had some idea, and they were not happy."

"Naberius? Dabriel?" I asked.

"Yes. Naberius," she spit his name out, as if distasteful. "He was against it."

"Do you think he had something to do with this?"

Marinette's eyes narrowed and her mouth shaped into a sneer that could cut flesh. "Him? He wouldn't dare cross me."

"Is there someone who would do this to purposefully antagonize or hurt you?" I asked.

She stretched out a finger, and the nail elongated into a sharp claw.

She scratched a small circle into the top of the bar, and then crossed it out with an X. "None who would want to stay among the living."

"Right. I'll keep that in mind," I said. "And the Intoxicantata? You said it was yours? Seems as if everyone has a claim to that book."

She retracted her talon, stood up straight, and took a deep breath. "It is mine. Trevor was giving it to me as part of the deal to open the new establishment."

"Do you know who has it now?" I asked.

"No. But I will get it back," her eyes shot another flash of that unnerving light as she looked at us. "If you wish to help, I would start by finding Nicholas Noir. Of course, he might not be able to help you if I find him first."

"You need to be careful, Marinette," I warned. "The Alliance are very interested in this case."

Marinette leant forwards again, scratching spirals into the countertop. "Why are you telling me this?"

"Because I don't want any bad blood here," I said. "We can help each other. And maybe you'll keep your friends Kurtis and Murmur away from me?"

"Perhaps they are not my friends. I will deal with them. You, on the other hand, are safe. For now," Marinette warned.

It sounded like a threat, but I wasn't sure how immediate of a threat. I didn't feel strong enough to stand, let alone fend off an angry Loa, but I couldn't let her see that. I felt beneath the bar and found the bullet.

"I know you could hurt me, but not without a fight. I may not be as strong as you, but I still have some strength…and some magic," I said, as I dug at the charm with my fingernails.

I pried it out and placed it on the bar, focusing a stare at Marinette. It was difficult. I'd seen what she could become. I took a breath and spoke in a low tone.

"Listen, I'm not stupid enough to think I could defeat you, but I do know if you start something you won't walk away easily, and this place of yours would definitely sustain some heavy damage."

Marinette's arm shot out; her hand wrapped around my throat.

"You threaten me? In my bar? I don't doubt your powers, but I am not helpless, and I am hungry. I have suffered pain and indignity at your hands, and I could easily suffer more if it meant ripping your head off and drinking the last of your life from the hole between your shoulders."

Marinette held my gaze harder than her steel-like fingers held my throat. I tried to gasp but couldn't. I reached my fingers around hers, attempting to pry them from my neck. I could hear my heartbeat pulsing in my ears. A few seconds passed without a breath, then she released me.

"I said you were safe. You have my word. Don't make me regret giving it," she said bitterly as I gasped for air.

"I won't," I sputtered. "We won't. All we want is to find the book and figure out who's been setting DarkWavers on fire."

Marinette turned her back to us and slowly exhaled, staring up at the ceiling. It seemed as if her fire had slightly faded. When she spoke again her voice was soft, almost tired. She turned to face us again. "Find Nicholas. He will know."

She paused, her eyes lowered to my shoulder, where I could feel my muscles throbbing. Her gaze wandered up to my head, but she wasn't making eye contact. I put a finger to my forehead. It came away sticky with red. A serpent-like tongue flickered out of Marinette's mouth and along her lips.

"You had better leave now," Marinette muttered. "I told you I was hungry."

We swiftly turned and walked towards the door, picking our items up from a table. Rodrick reappeared and held the door open, staring at us with lightning shaped hatred. I looked back towards the bar, the Loa stood statue still, but a strange fragility fluttered beneath her dark beauty. For all her power she was still defenseless against her own appetites.

"Don't come back, unless you have the one who killed Trevor," the frailness had vanished, leaving only ice, "Because if you come back empty handed, I will take your soul."

Murmur appeared from the back of the room, but she wasn't

alone. She was leading Kurtis, his arms tied behind her back. They walked towards Marinette and stopped at her side. Murmur jerked the man to a standstill and Marinette gave the slightest nod. The blindfold was removed, and Kurtis looked around wildly as Murmur slid off his coat. Marinette moved behind the trembling man, whispering. Her eyes remained on mine. I knew we should have already been out the door, but we were hypnotized by the scene. Gilles stood next to me; he looked slightly paler than usual. I realized this was for our benefit. A warning, a promise. Marinette's hair started writhing, as it had before. Dreadlocks like tentacles wrapped around the man's pale throat. He said nothing but looked imploringly towards us. Marinette's tongue flickered out again, touching just below his ear. It was almost erotic in a horrific sort of way.

Kurtis closed his eyes. His breath escaped in quick little gasps. Murmur moved away, watching us instead of the scene unfolding next to her. Marinette ran her hands, once again thinning into talons, over Kurtis' chest. His shirt fell into tatters, exposing chest, stomach, hips. His head fell back, and his body pushed into Marinette's arms. His skin was red and beaded with sweat, and there were slight droplets of blood glistening from where her sharp claws had nicked him.

He looked up for a second, eyes caught in a mixture of arousal and surrender, then collapsed as Marinette's teeth pushed and pierced into the shallow skin that stretched behind his collarbone. Still unconscious, Kurtis' body started shuddering uncontrollably. Marinette wasn't feeding on him; she was becoming him. Fingers slid up his sides; down his arms, holding them outstretched and pushing into skin and veins. Marinette's shadow moved out of her body and entered the man. Changing him until Kurtis' shape was a limp and bloody doppelganger of the creature holding him. A woman becoming an owl becoming a man becoming an owl, and the sound… the sound was nauseating. A birdlike caterwauling that stretched outwards in pure anguish. Gilles and I turned and ran towards the car.

"What the hell was that?" I mumbled, feeling faint.

"That was a possession," Gilles said. His voice sounded as pale as his face. "Marinette is one with the owl and those she mounts take on her form."

We sat in the car, cold and shaking, as if there was nothing but winter around us. Gilles lit a cigarette and offered one to me. I was tempted, but no. We knew we should leave, but we weren't sure where to go. I was also feeling a little too shaky to drive.

A few minutes later, probably five, though it felt like a hundred, there was a sharp rapping on the window next to me. I almost jumped into the back seat. It was Murmur. She motioned for me to roll down the window and gave me a flirtatious eyebrow rise and a sly little grin as if we hadn't witnessed a full blown Voudou possession in the middle of a bar. She handed me a card. It had Nick Noir's name and a phone number written underneath. On the other side it had her name and number. "Marinette can't know. About either number."

"How did you get this?" I asked.

"Christophe owed me a favor," she replied.

"Christophe? Where is he? I need to talk to him," I said, tapping the card.

"That I don't know," Murmur replied with a shrug.

"Why are you helping us?" I asked, a little suspiciously. "Doesn't your boss want to find Nick Noir as well?"

"Yes, but if she finds him, she'll kill him, and that would be very bad for business."

"Marinette just killed Kurtis…" I started.

"He's not dead, he just wishes he was. Let's just say the next time he's asked to get something for the Mystères he will not return empty handed."

"And are you going to be safe in there?"

"Me? Yes. That was meant as a warning to me. One you should also pay attention to. For Kurtis, it was just sadistic punishment. I'll be fine as long as I'm careful. I'm helping you, but my loyalties remain with Marinette, and she knows that. If I can protect her, I will. Besides, now you owe me a favor," Murmur said in a seductive purr before backing away and blowing me a kiss. Gilles rolled his eyes as Murmur spun on her heels and disappeared back into the darkness of Kill City.

We sat in the car, still shivering, though no longer from the cold. He ran a hand through his hair, "Okay, I don't need to experience that again."

I drummed my fingers on the steering wheel, thinking.

"Nick Noir?" Gilles asked.

"Maybe over drinks?" I asked. "Is the Lost & Found clear?"

"Not open for business, but we're done with the main bar."

Even though it was now home to a few bad memories, it was the most comfortable place I knew.

"Let's do it."

Gilles nodded.

I also wanted to talk to Dabriel and Naberius. Not that I thought I'd get as much from Naberius as I had last time we talked. I didn't know if they'd be at the bar, but maybe I could get them to meet us there. I also wished things felt better between me and Jessica. I also wished I'd stayed in bed. I shook it off and looked at Gilles. He'd done good back there. He used to be a good friend, and right now I could use a good friend. I hoped being my friend wasn't going to end up being something he'd regret.

11
MONKEY'S MIRROR

We sat quietly for a second in the car. Tiredness hit like a hard crash. I held up Nick's phone number, "Maybe before the drinks?"

"Probably a good idea," Gilles nodded.

He answered the phone on the first ring.

"Thomas."

"You didn't show up at the Café," I reminded him.

A moment of silence and then a shuffling of paper, and some fumbling noises muffled through the phone. A scratching, a kind of hiss, and a heavy breath. A cigarette.

"Yeah," He finally mumbled. "I went but you were busy, so I didn't go in."

"The demon brothers?"

"Yeah."

"Thanks for the help," I muttered. "So, can we talk?"

"No," Nick grunted.

"I understand you don't want to talk to me, but it's about Trevor…"

Nick interrupted, "I meant not over the phone. The bookstore. Blundertown. Half an hour."

"Does Christophe know?" I asked.

Silence again, but this time it was because Nick had hung up.

"What did he say?" Gilles asked.

"He wants to talk. At Blundertown."

Gilles tapped his fingers on the dashboard and nodded, "Do you trust him?"

"No, but I need answers," I said. "I'll drop you off at the bar and meet you there after I talk to Mister Noir."

"Oh no. You aren't doing this alone," Gilles glared.

"Look, he's not going to talk at all if you're there, and maybe you can find Naberius or Dabriel, get them to talk. Just give me like an hour," I bargained.

"You're probably right," he said. "But one hour and I'm storming the bookstore." He pointed at me, I nodded.

We drove to the Lost & Found, and I let him out. He reached into his coat pocket and pulled out his little bottle of Holy Water, "Just in case."

"Thanks," I said, and looked up at him, "I mean it Gilles, Thanks."

He nodded, then turned and walked towards the bar. I sat for a second, wondering if I'd made the right decision. Probably not.

I checked my bag. I still had a little of the handsome juice, and maybe a shot or two of the strength left. I figured it might help right now, as my head was pounding, and it felt as if my ribs were broken. Or at the very least, badly bruised. On the plus side, I wasn't bleeding anymore.

STILL WONDERING if going alone was the right move, I took a swig of the Bulleit the Blue Sky and made my way to the bookstore. Like the last time I found myself outside of Blundertown, the lights were off, and the place looked deserted. This time, however, the door was unlocked. I entered slowly, reaching for the light switch. It wasn't working. Looking around, I realized someone had removed all the lightbulbs. There was a little light coming through the dust caked windows, but not much. I also noticed the piles of books and boxes against the far wall, and shelves filling up with bottles of liquor. It wasn't a bookstore anymore, but it still smelled like one. I coughed through the mustiness and whispered, "Nick?"

"Dante," the voice crept out from the back of the room. "Lock the door behind you and meet me in the office."

I heard the scratch of a match. A flare of light appeared against a shadowed profile, then became a glowing eye in the dark. "I didn't think you'd show."

"I didn't think I would, either."

I took a breath, tightened my fists, and walked into the back room. A small desk lamp flicked on and there he was. The man I'd killed. He looked the same, but his eyes, once sharp and evil, were bloodshot and tired. His hair, black and scattered with white, was cut short but shaggy. A cigarette was pulled from thin dry lips and held by shaking yellowed fingers. He used to look like a suave vampire, now he looked like a dead junkie. Pale skin, thin arms, an old Misfits t-shirt covered in cigarette burns. Tight black jeans frayed at the ankles over a pair of faded Red Converse. He didn't look any older, but he did look frightened. Not of me, but of something. He was chewing on his lower lip and his eyes darted back and forth between me and the doorway. He exhaled a stream of smoke and leant forwards over the desk.

"It's been a long time, Dante."

I sat across from him, "Nick Noir. What the hell happened to you? I didn't think I'd ever see you again. Especially after I killed you."

"Yeah, well…that wasn't me then, right?" He giggled to himself, which was a little disconcerting, then stopped and crushed his cigarette out on the desk. "But I guess it makes no matter now. People are dead and we might join them sooner than expected."

"What people?" I demanded. "Other than Trevor?"

"Yeah, Trevor. That really sucks," Nick scratched at the back of his head. "There will be more, though."

"Where's Christophe, Nick?" I asked.

Nick started a slow smile, "He's gone."

I sat up straight, "Gone? Do you mean dead?"

This time the giggle wasn't held back. "Christophe? He was dead long before you met him. And yes, he's still dead. But you of all people should know that doesn't always exclude you from taking part in things."

Nick pulled another cigarette out of the pack lying on the desk and grinned at it as if they were sharing some secret joke at my expense. I had no idea what happened to Nicholas Noir, but whatever it was had pushed him a little closer to crazy.

He leaned back in the chair. Nick had always been a jerk, but never quite like this. But I had more important things to worry about.

"Alright, be that way," I said, annoyed, "Why does Marinette want you dead?"

That got his attention.

"How do you know that?" he demanded.

"How do you think I got your number?"

"Oh crap," he muttered. He stood up and walked to the window. "If I answer your questions, will you tell her you couldn't find me?"

"Depends on whether or not I like your answers."

"Fair enough," Nick scratched his head, turned around. "You're an all-right guy. I'm sorry things got a little sketchy in the past. It wasn't my fault."

"Not your fault?" I stared at him, incredulous. "You were fronting an illegal blood drive out of an underground Goth club right under the noses of the DarkWavers. And that night at the Riddle House? Dammit, Nick. Both Jessica and I were hurt bad, and it's your fault my parents are dead. I hunted you down, it took me forever, but I found you and I killed you. Because of you I lost my job, because of you I lost Jessica, because of you my life consists of insomnia and alcohol. It's because of you I'm under Waver probation, and for all I know it's because of you I'm going to die alone," I was fuming, and ready to kill again. "And you're sorry?"

. . .

Nick raised a shaking hand, "I understand what it looks like, and dude, that's horrible. But it wasn't me. I know we had a falling out, but I'm not that bad. Yes, I was working out of Code Blue but only getting the blood mix. I had nothing to do with pushing souls. I was supplying a necessary service for some of the club's thirstier regulars. It's not good business to be known as a bar where you get your blood drained. Christophe was the lead man. He's so into the Vamps, you know. He was planning to expand. Take control of The Riddle House, Kill City, probably others. I was going to be his partner, but when he started talking about Kill City, I was out. I'm fine with making money, but there are certain lines you don't cross. Like the ones around a Voodoo Queen. Thing is, someone set me up. I was on the line for a lot of damage, and I knew there was more coming. When the Riddle House fire hit, I got out. Disappeared. Then the book showed up at the Lost & Found, and I need that to get back into the game. That book is leverage, man."

"And that's why you came out of hiding. Called me..." I said. "So, you've been keeping tabs on the bar?"

Nick coughed and moved back to the desk, rummaging around in the drawers. "Nah, no tabs. But those kinds of books attract a lot of attention. I need to protect myself, and those pages will help me do that," he muttered.

"You weren't at the Riddle House?" I asked, feeling adrenalin shift and mix with a slight shake of shock. There was someone else responsible? After all these years, there was someone else out there who had ruined my life? And not only that, but ...

"So, who the hell did I kill, Nick?" I shouted, and moved to the desk, slamming my hands down on it. "Who did I kill?"

"I don't know, man," Nick looked up at me, eyes wide. "I was out by then. I was gone. The Riddle house spooked me, dude."

"Dammit!" I was ready to either beat this shapeshifter into a pulp, run riot in some meteoric burst of anger and depression, or get completely hammered. I figured alcohol was the better choice. That way I could leave here and do a nice harmless slide into quiet depression and not have to answer to the Alliance. Not going through that again.

After the way it ended at the Riddle House, my life crashing down like a pile of bricks…not again.

I stood up, took a step back. Nick pulled a bottle and two shot glasses out from a drawer. Poured. "Straight up, no magic," He whispered, pushing a shot towards me.

I took it, finished it.

"And Marinette?" I asked. "Was she involved?" I could feel my body quivering. Exhausted and confused, and angry.

"With the fire?" Nick shook his head, "Nah, not her style. I don't know who it was. Had to have been someone with connections, and money. Hiring a Shift like this wouldn't be cheap. Marinette and I have history. But I don't trust her people. I'm not ready to show my face there, not till I have protection. I still don't know who framed me. And I'm thinking maybe you…don't want me dead quite as much?" He gave me a hopeful look, eyes wide, eyebrows raised in question. That would explain why he was so nervous, hiding from everyone, not knowing who was after him. But why here?

"And you're here now," I took a leap, "Because you and Christophe were partners?"

"We were. A long time ago," Nick sighed, "But he doesn't know I'm here. I'm thinking he might be the one who set me up, but either way, he's got something else going on."

I thought about it for a second, "So why…"

"Why'd I come back?"

I nodded.

"Honestly, I'm tired. Tired of hiding," Nick gave the doorway behind me another glance, "I was hoping to find some kind of leverage here, something I could use to keep myself alive. I don't know. Maybe I did?" Nick handed me a stained and crumpled piece of paper from his pocket. It was a photocopied page covered in illegible scribbles around a scratchy illustration of an elaborately carved punch bowl. There were a series of heads on the side with ape-like features. A list followed underneath in fine calligraphy; black spiraling letters and slight Ralph Steadman styled splatters. And underneath that, a couple of short paragraphs.

I recognized it immediately. "A recipe. From the Intoxicantata," I studied it for a few seconds, trying to read the printing between the inked scratches. All I could make out were a couple of words. "Eadem maneat?"

"You know Latin?" Nick asked.

"A little," I looked up at him, "A couple of phrases, but I don't know what this means, exactly. Something about the same?"

"Yeah. Pretty close. I think this is what caused the Shifter you killed to become my frozen doppelganger. It means 'remain the same'. The name of the drink is under the picture, but someone tried to cover it up. To rename it and claim it as their own."

I held the paper up so the light slid off it at an angle and could still barely make out the letters. "The Monkey's Middle?"

Nick laughed, "Mirror."

"The Monkey's Mirror?"

Nick squinted at me, "Didn't your dad teach you about this book?"

"Some, but the Intoxicantata was one heavy volume. There were chapters we never got to. He taught me a lot of mixes, but there's no way he could have covered all of them."

Nick nodded. "So, the recipe isn't familiar? How'd you know it was copied from the book?"

I pushed the paper back towards Nick.

"It's the format. The pages are unmistakable. The style of calligraphy, the layout of the illustration over the description, the ink splatters..." I ran a hand through my hair. "The book vanished on the night Trevor died," I eyed Nick warily, "But you know that."

"Hey, I know nothing. Trevor was a good guy, but he didn't know I was around. Besides, after he started spending all his free time with Marinette there was no way I'd come out of hiding. That lady scares the hell out of me," Nick got up and paced. He was acting like a caged animal. He grabbed the paper from the Intoxicantata and shook it at me, "Listen, if the book is missing, we have to find it."

I nodded distractedly; a text buzzed my attention away. It was Gilles.

-you good? -

-fine be there soon - bringing a friend-

There was a textual pause. Gilles was thinking about it. I glanced up at Nick, who wasn't paying attention. He stared out the window, muttering. Another buzz.

-NN?-

-yes-

-your call-

I stood up, "Right. Let's get a drink, and you can tell me why we need this book."

Nick sat back down; he was shaking. "These aren't drinks, you idiot. You know that don't you?"

"I know," I nodded. "They're curses."

"That's right, and this one here," he stabbed at the paper with his finger, "This is the one keeping shifters from shifting. And why is it here? Because fucking Christophe is selling the pages."

I was getting angry. "Right now, I don't really care about Christophe. I'm trying to track down the book and find out who killed Trevor. I'm trying to not think about how I've already killed you, and how I shouldn't try to kill you again."

"Okay, okay. Take it easy. I get it," Nick raised his hands, "But it has to be connected."

"I know Christophe might not be the straightest arrow around, but he wouldn't go out of his way to kill DarkWavers and sell curses," I pointed out.

"You don't know Christophe," Nick glared at me, "He was great at being the charming bookseller, but I've seen his other side. The darker side. Living forever changes you, Dante. He has this page, so he's involved."

"Fine," I motioned towards the door, "Come on, I need to clear my head, and staying here isn't going to help."

We started out, Nick shuffling behind me. "You're going to protect me?" He asked quietly.

"You mean I'm not the only one who wanted you dead?" I said in feigned surprise.

Nick laughed nervously, "I'm not hiding out here because I want to. I know things, things you need to know. But I can't tell you because that leaves me with no leverage. Besides, once you know, they'll want you dead as well."

"Aren't you the considerate one," I said, "Come on. Let's go."

WE WALKED TOWARDS MY CAR. I was trying to stay cool, but I wasn't sure if I had any forgiveness left to offer. Nick walked beside me, hunched over, muttering something about curses, but I wasn't really paying attention.

I'd just noticed a familiar Lincoln Continental parked on the street. I could see my old friend Kurtis in the driver's seat, but he hadn't seen us yet. I stopped.

"Change of plans. I think someone else is interested in checking out the bookstore..." I pointed towards the Lincoln.

Nick looked worried. "I think they're here for me."

"I think we can lose them. Get to the car, fast. Okay?"

Nick gave me a quick nod, and we ran, crouched down, to my car. Still unseen, I started her up. "Hold on."

I TOOK off without looking to see if we'd been made. I turned at the end of the block, then at the next street I swerved around a corner between a yellow and a red light. There was a little screech and wobble as a back tire bumped over the curb. A pedestrian gave me the finger, and I sent back a distracted smile and a thumbs up before slamming back down on the gas. The car let out a thick puff of black smoke, like an oily cough, and shuddered slightly. I ignored it and pressed the pedal down a little further. I leant forwards and looked up at the sky through the dirt scratched window. The clouds were thick, and the sun didn't have too far to go before it would be gone. There was a storm coming.

"They're following us," Nick said, glancing at the side-view mirror.

"Yeah, I know. That's why I'm driving fast."

"Fast is fine," Nick commented. "Careless is bad. Besides, you don't want to add the cops to this parade."

"I won't," I said, shifting quickly between the brakes and the gas to get around the sudden appearance of a bicyclist. "I'll lose them, and then I think you might need to slip back into your shadows for a bit."

Nick didn't say anything, but grimaced as I pulled a fast swerve around a slow Prius. I shifted quick between the brakes and the gas to get around the sudden appearance of a bicyclist. Nick sat up, pushing his hands against the dashboard.

"Awkward, can I ask you something?"

"Don't call me that," I muttered, tightening my hands around the wheel.

A pick-up truck overflowing with newspapers shifted lanes without signaling and to avoid a collision I had to speed past it in the bus lane and cut back in front of it before speeding through a four-way stop.

"Asshat!" I spat out the window but left it at that. No time for road rage.

"Right, sorry," Nick gave me a sideways look. "I was actually curious about you and Jessica."

"Seriously?" I took my eyes off the road for a second to give him my best look of disbelief. "We are being chased by the psychotic minions of an angry Voudou Queen and searching for a book of alcoholic curses that may be in the hands of a wannabe vampire..."

"No, I get that, Dante. I just..."

"I mean right now," I held up a finger, "we are on our way to a bar where one of my closest friends was burnt to a crisp, there is a member of the Agentia is waiting for us, and the Triple Alliance is waiting for me to make another mistake, and you want to know about my dating habits?"

"Right," Nick nodded, tight lipped. "Later."

I glanced in the rearview mirror. I'd gotten far enough ahead of Lincoln to make a few adjustments in direction. Hopefully they wouldn't pick up on the trail until I'd had a chance to fill Gilles in. These clowns might mess with me, but they weren't about to take on the Agentia.

"Is that good enough for you?" I shot a side glance at Nick. "Not following us anymore."

I really needed a drink.

"Good enough for me," Nick replied. "And nice avoiding the subject..."

"Thanks."

"Look, I'm sorry about what happened to you. To both of you. I made some mistakes, and I know we weren't exactly on the same side back then, but I respected you guys," Nick shrugged. "That fire. Both fires—I had nothing to do with them..."

I felt my shoulder blades tighten; my neck suddenly pressed into ache. "Nick. I'm here, we're talking. But let's leave Jessica out of this, okay?"

Nick nodded quietly. "Right, sorry. I'm just..."

"Don't worry about it. Just drop it. We need to get to the bar," I leaned back in the seat, stretching my arms straight against the steering wheel, "I should have stayed in bed."

"You alright?"

I glanced in the rearview mirror, slammed on the brakes, took a hard right down a side street then floored the gas. "Fine."

I was fine.

I'd missed this.

I ran everything through my head, trying to figure out what the answers were. Trying to figure out the right questions.

On top of the obvious, like what was I going to do with Nick, there were two things weighing heavy on my mind. One, where was Christophe, and two, who had killed Trevor.

Okay, three things...I really wanted a cigarette.

Finding the book moved to first place while playing 'who's the killer' settled into second. I figured I'd let Gilles, and his band of Batcavers work on the murder mystery. If there were pages from the Intoxicantata floating around, and someone angling to use it in another bar, the Agentia Obscura could be faced with a whole lot of supernatural cover-ups real soon.

I should talk to Jessica as well, but I wasn't ready to reintroduce her to my current companion quite yet.

I knew we had to figure out who threw the fireball special as well. How they did it, and why. And I knew the book was the key. We were a couple of minutes away from the Lost & Found. I called Gilles.

"What's going on?" Gilles asked. "You're not coming? I thought you were going to bring a friend."

"Yeah, me too," I pulled into a driveway, turned around, and changed course. Time to head for home.

I glanced at Nick. He was staring out the window. "Didn't quite work out."

"What happened?" he asked, worried. "You didn't…"

I gave a short laugh, "Kill him?"

Now Nick was paying attention.

"I thought about it, but no. Hell, I didn't even kill him the first time."

"Tell me what happened," Gilles said.

"Marinette's cronies were waiting for us at the bookstore. We gave them the slip, but I think going to the bar is a bad idea for us right now. I think you and Jessica should concentrate on the fire, and I'll work on finding the book. And Gilles?" I said.

"Yeah?"

"Keep her safe."

Gilles was silent for a few seconds, "Is that all?"

"No," I said. "Someone's been selling pages of the Intoxicantata, and I have a feeling that some of the answers I'm looking for might get me killed. That being said, if you need me, I'll be at home."

"Copy that, Dante. Jessica will be fine," Gilles promised. "And you may not believe me, but I'm here to help."

"Thanks. I'll keep that in mind," I said appreciatively.

. . .

I PULLED up in front of my house, head pounding. A migraine was the last thing I needed.

"You coming in?" I asked Nick. He sat in the car, not saying anything.

"Nick?"

"Yeah. For a bit. You have anything to drink?" He laughed and followed me up the stairs.

Once inside, I stood behind my bar and looked around for my stash of headache removers. I saw a bottle of Death's Door Gin first and decided to mix up some hair of the dog instead. Corpse Reviver style, but with a twist. Some do the Bloody Mary, some work with scotch or whiskey, but I'm not a big fan of Tabasco sauce. And while I wish I could knock back the gin fizzes like Jim Morrison, egg whites aren't my thing either.

I realized I might need some solid food. I hadn't really eaten anything recently other than a stale muffin I'd grabbed from the café. I pointed Nick towards the kitchen, told him to make a couple of sandwiches while I set up my ingredients; the gin already in front of me, a fresh lemon from the small fridge, a clean shaker and the flask containing the Bulleit the Blue Sky.

I found my bottle of Lillet Blanc, then Cointreau, and a dusty bottle of Berger absinthe. I had a few varieties of the faerie juice, but if I only needed a couple of drops, I stuck to the good stuff. Then my own addition, a touch of garlic. Not enough to notice, but it balanced out the spirit and the soul. I grabbed a cocktail glass, then it's shake, rinse, discard, strain, garnish. I dropped in a Luxardo cherry, popped a couple of aspirin, and downed it. The Corpse Reviver is normally a sipping drink, but I needed this to hit fast. As I let the effects of my off-the-cuff cocktail wash over me my dizziness faded into a slow buzz. I wondered if I should invest in something a little more down to earth in case of future battles. I mean, who in the hell brings a gun to a magic fight?

"Nick?"

No answer.

I went down to the kitchen, but it was empty except for a confused looking cat, a haphazardly made sandwich, and a note saying, 'Thanks. I'll be in touch. -NN'

"Dammit," I balled up the paper in a fist, grabbed the food, and went back upstairs.

The clouds in my head were slightly dissipating but my body felt like it could collapse any second. At least my mind seemed to be pulling out of a tailspin. I started sorting bottles and flipping through my stack of notebooks. I'd start on the quest for curse-filled volumes later. Now it was time to figure out how Trevor was set on fire.

12
COCKTAIL MOLOTOVIA

I mixed for the rest of the night, but it wasn't easy. I felt like I was making solid progress, but there was a problem. Alcohol. I was sipping and tasting and measuring and tasting again. I was making sure that the more harmful portions were set aside for controlled experimentations, but as the hours moved, so did my vision. If I couldn't figure something out quick, I'd be passed out and smelling like a liquor store. I jotted notes down, did calculations based on ounces and dashes, and scrawled strange combinations across papers spread out in front of me.

Thankfully I have a greater tolerance for liquor than most. The people who could drink me under the table were few and far between, and most of them had the added benefit of being a little more than alive.

Still, even I had limits. I ended up on the couch with a pizza crust on my chest, a cat at my feet, and a notebook open over my face. My concoctions had resulted in some answers, but not the right ones. Fireball wouldn't get hot enough: Pepper Vodka didn't have the lasting power, Tabasco Tequila pushed the wrong sort of emotions, and my Spiced Rum was very nice but not for this problem. It did however help me come up with a drink that could help the next time I found myself face to face with a Loa.

I dubbed it the One-Eyed Dog, a smooth mix of spiced rum, a nice dark rum from Guyana, brandy, citrus, and a mix of special bitters. It also seemed to focus my attention, which had been slipping between shots.

WHEN I CAME TO, it was almost three in the afternoon. I rolled over, the notebook fell onto the floor, and I fell on top of it. The cat had absconded with the pizza crust. I ended up staring down at the recipe I'd created earlier. I'd circled Rum 151, and I realized I shouldn't be looking for a flavor for the Fire Curse cocktail. I should be looking for a specific ingredient, maybe something with Rum or Grand Marnier. I started coffee brewing, placed a bowl of food on the kitchen floor for the absent Dr. Sax, and renewed my search. I skimmed through books and web pages, looking for liquors and mixes that might fit. After I had stumbled on a variation of a Molotov Cocktail, not the incendiary weapon but the less harmful drink version, it clicked.

The Molotov, the drinkable one, consisted of Vodka for the alcohol, parfait amour for paraffin, lemon juice for gasoline, and black Sambuca for the tar. The variation I found buried in one of my father's notebooks, could leave someone looking like the bodies at the Lost & Found. One problem—there was no way I could test it. Partly because I didn't want to make a barbecue out of anyone and partly because some of the ingredients were amazingly hard to find.

That meant either I had the wrong ingredients, or the killer had managed to find a few bottles of impossible. I called Gilles, who told me to meet him and Jessica at the Lost & Found. I knew I probably smelled like a distillery and looked worse, but I didn't bother changing. Just grabbed my bag and a shot of One-Eyed Dog for the road.

The bar was still closed, but Naberius was behind the bar like usual. I wondered what would happen once the place was open for business, if the bad press would be a problem. DarkWavers tend to avoid places where they might end up dead, and no one knew if Trevor had been targeted because of who he was or where he was.

He gave me a quick wave when I walked in then continued shuffling bottles around on the shelves behind the bar.

I started towards him when I heard my name. I turned and saw Jessica seated in a booth by the wall. There was no sign of Deuxcoeurs. I sat down; she gave me a curt nod.

"Gilles is out back. I'll get the drinks. What do you want?"

"Corpse Reviver. I need a good kick start."

She got up and walked over to the bar. I could tell there was something wrong, and it wasn't just her being upset with me.

Jessica returned and set the drinks down. "Okay, let's talk."

I shot a quick grin, trying to lighten the mood. "Now's not the time to get romantic."

"Shut it, cocktail boy."

"Sorry..."

She glared and slid my drink across the table. "Remember the disc we found here?"

I nodded.

"It held a list of bars across North America with pictures and files detailing menus and bartenders. In Vancouver it listed this one, Kill City, and the Drunken Abbott," She told me.

If you drew lines connecting the dots of drinking establishments and filled them in with recipes from the Intoxicantata, you'd end up with a big mess shaped like one of the more inebriated circles of hell. Especially if the Drunken Abbott was one of them.

Walking into the Drunken Abbott was like walking into a bathroom at a train station, only there were no trains, they served beer, you could usually find a table to sit at, and the bathrooms weren't as clean. Between the stains on the walls and the crunch and stick of endless spills and remnants of broken bottles on the floors, the place looked like a constant crime scene.

"They've been making some mighty fancy drinks recently, and that place is definitely not fancy."

I listened, but I was having trouble following. My body ached, my headache had returned with full force, and my nerves were cracking whips across my stomach.

I closed my eyes against a pulse of an impending migraine, took a sip of my Corpse Reviver, and tried to not think about it. The thickness of anise flavor rolled around on my tongue.

"Are you alright, Thom?"

"I made a few too many drinks last night trying to figure this fire curse out," I spoke quietly, "I came close a couple of times but not close enough."

Jessica knocked back half of her martini and pointed at me, glass still in her hand. "Don't tell me it can't be done. I've seen too much to believe that."

"Don't get all fired up," I winked. "Let me finish."

Her stare hit me harder than alcohol ever could. It was still unnerving.

"Okay, Thom. Finish," She whispered.

I took a deep breath and put my glass down. "It all ties into the book. That's where these drinks are coming from."

"So, it was death by cocktail," A voice said behind me.

I turned to see Gilles standing, arms crossed. Looking unimpressed.

"Yeah, I'm pretty sure…"

He moved to sit down next to Jessica, across from me. "There's something you're not telling me."

I held up a finger, "Hold on."

Gilles looked at Jessica, she gave him a shrug.

I continued, "The Intoxicantata could cause some mayhem if you were to make the drinks without taking precautions and serve them without proper descriptions. The good news, I guess, is I found a possible fire recipe. Bad news is the ingredients are a little hard to find."

"How hard?" Gilles asked.

"Five thousand dollars hard."

Jessica said nothing. She finished her drink and went back to the bar. She returned with another round, took a sip, and nodded. "Continue."

"I'm talking original ingredients here. It could be made with modern equivalents, but it would lack the same power. The drink is known as the Cocktail Molotovia, it contains stuff like the Café Bénédictine and the Kina Lillet."

"Lillet" Gilles repeated, "That sounds familiar."

"You're a James Bond fan, I bet," I said. "The Kina Lillet is one of the ingredients for the Vesper Martini, a drink favored by Ian Fleming, who brought it into the story for Casino Royale."

"That's kinda cool," Jessica confessed.

"And then the Bénédictine was originally created as a medicinal elixir in the early 1500's, and that version is long gone, but it was recreated in the 1800's by Alexandre Le Grand, who used the connection to the Monks as a successful marketing strategy. So, the whiskey called for can go up to three thousand a bottle. I figure you could add another couple thousand to track everything down. Combine these original parts with a solid knowledge of Mystixology and you've got yourself a focused little fireball."

"So, our killer has access to thousand-dollar bottles of whiskey and he's wasting it on people in dive bars?" Gilles asked.

I shrugged, "I'm saying if you want to make this drink hardcore old school style, you'd have to be rich and well connected. The same effects can be had using different brands and some clever substitutions, but you'd have to know exactly what would work and what wouldn't. Top shelf brands react differently than the cheap stuff. I could make a similar drink for maybe two hundred bucks, but it would leave traces of the mix and more scorching on the floor. If I'm right, whoever pulled this off was using the good stuff."

"I'll bet with some help from Research we could figure out who might have access to the ingredients for this millionaire's Molotov." Jessica's eyes narrowed.

I swirled the liquid in my glass. "It's possible. My best guess on the

Whiskey is Port Winestain thirty-year-old. It comes from a Scottish distillery which closed in the early eighties. There are very few people who'd have it, and fewer who'd waste it in a mix. Although it would go great if you were serving a top-notch Rusty Nail."

"Right, Scotch and Drambuie," Gilles noted. "One of Dean Martin's favorites."

"So, we're looking for a rebellious Rat Packer with a taste for top shelf?" Jessica questioned.

I laughed. "I doubt it, but you never know. The thing is you need to follow the money. The money gets the alcohol, and after that comes the knowledge. You've got to know what's going to work."

"Right," Gilles said. "It feels like we might be caught in the middle of a Mystixological turf war."

I nodded and leant back in my seat. I didn't want to worry Jessica, but something was feeling a bit off. Maybe it was partly because Naberius hadn't exactly been skimping on the alcohol.

"Yeah, some recipes can set your soul on fire, and some could move that flame towards a more physical plane. Still, you'd have to know the right order for the ingredients. And the directions were usually on the obscure side. Secrets written down still must be secret. But if you knew how to kill a DarkWaver, you should know how to read a recipe," I said.

"Fantastic," Jessica pushed her hair back from her face. "Do you think it was a competing bar? Marinette could do something like this, right? She's well connected to both booze and money," Jessica asked.

"I doubt it," I said, then slowly moved forwards, resting my elbows on the table.

Jessica paused, "Thom, you do not look good."

I felt an earthquake building between skull and skin. "Yeah, headache. And it wasn't Marinette. She has her own way of dealing with people. She wants the book, but this is not how she would get it."

"Thomas," Jessica's eyes narrowed, "Did you go to Kill City?"

I nodded.

"Are you insane?"

She was mad, and worried.

"I was careful. Besides, I didn't go alone. I had Gilles with me."

Gilles gave Jessica a sheepish grin.

"Gilles? How could you…why would you put him into danger? Dammit, Thomas," Jessica put a hand to her forehead in exasperation, "Doesn't matter. Neither of you should be going up against Marinette."

"I know. I know," I said, apologetically.

She softened a little. "What did you learn?"

"I learned Marinette was trying to go into business with Trevor and…"

I guess I had to tell her. I never told Jessica I hunted down and killed a man, as far as she knew Nick Noir had vanished. She wasn't going to like the fact that he was back.

"And I found Nick Noir," I said, wincing.

"What? Are you serious?" Jessica stared at me in shock.

"Jess, we need to be smart about this. Marinette and her goons know Nick's back, and Nick is tied up with this whole Blundertown Books mess. He knows about the Intoxicantata, and possibly where it is. Marinette wants the Intoxicantata as well, so they're not the ones using it for the fires. But they might try to get Nick to share his secrets, and they won't be as nice as us. So, we need to get to him first."

"I thought you had him," Gilles said quietly.

"I did," I shrugged, "But he left."

Jessica stared up at the ceiling for a second, then looked back at me. "Okay, we'll get him. But the fire was because of the book? Trevor was killed for it?"

"I don't know if the fire was meant to kill him or not. It could've been a message meant for whoever Trevor was working with, but it wasn't from Kill City."

"Great," Jessica said. "And not only are we witnessing the start of the cocktail wars, but fucking Nick Noir is also back in town, and reading is suddenly all the rage," she could shatter the glass in her hand with her glare.

"We'll find him. I think you should talk to him. He might be able to clear up a few things. I don't think he's an innocent bystander, but he isn't to blame for… the incident."

She looked at me as if I'd gone completely crazy "Sure, I'll go have a nice cuppa with the man who ripped my body apart. If he hasn't already been killed by someone who may or may not be working for the goddamm Voodoo Queen."

She pressed her fingers against her side, feeling her scars. I had mine as well. "It wasn't him."

"What?" She froze.

"According to Nick he was framed."

Jessica's eyes darkened. "But I can't talk to him, because you let him wander off?"

She finished her drink and slammed the glass down on the table.

Gilles put a hand on her shoulder, "We'll get him. I'll keep an agent watching Kill City, and we'll stake out the bookstore as well."

Jessica pressed her lips together in a tight smile and locked eyes with me. "It's like you don't realize what you're playing around with here," She paused and scrutinized my face, "What's going on with you?"

"Nothing," I objected but then realized I should go with the truth. "Well, there might be something else."

"What," she demanded.

"About Nick. After he, you know…"

Jessica gave me a slow nod, "Yes?"

"I hunted him down, Jessica. I hunted him down, and then I killed him. Only, now it turns out it wasn't him," I felt my chest start to shudder. I looked up pleadingly at Jessica, who was watching me with wide eyes and an open mouth. I wasn't going to start crying. Not in the middle of the fucking Lost & Found. I closed my eyes and whispered my anguished question.

"Who the hell did I kill, Jessica? Who did I kill?"

I tried to say more but my tongue felt too thick to move. The bar started changing color, and the table felt like a wet sponge under my elbows. I looked at Jessica, thought about apologizing, thought about kissing her, thought about all the things I should say, but there seemed to be two of her, and I couldn't decide which one to focus on.

Jessica stood up. "Thomas, what's wrong with you?"

I figured it would be better to lie on the floor until one of her went away. "Why are there invisible bricks falling on my head?" I asked. But before she could answer, some all-consuming darkness took me away.

13
CAFÉ VÉRITÉ

My eyes opened and I wasn't sure where I was. Someplace fuzzy. Music throbbed in time to the pounding in my head, then I realized it was my head beating to the music's rhythms. Slowly the volume lowered into a quiet melodic hum. I took a slow look around; I was laid out on the velvety red couch in the back room of the Lost & Found. I tried to prop myself up on shaky elbows and look around. That didn't work and I fell back onto the couch.

"Easy now," a voice said, and a hand dropped a cold cloth on my forehead. It was Dabriel.

The shape of her face moved in a soft blur above me. It looked like she was smiling.

"What happened?" I muttered, "Where's Jessica?"

"She left," Dabriel said, pushing me back down.

"Gilles?"

"Said something about Kill City. Seriously, Dante. Trying to figure out what happened here is messing you up."

"Only doing my job," I said.

"This isn't your job anymore," she admonished, "You shouldn't be involved in this."

I looked up at her, "Job. Yeah, where'd you come from? Naberius was here. You weren't..."

"I arrived after you passed out. I'm a person of interest, not supposed to leave town, but it's okay for me to be here. Naberius went home."

Dabriel poured a shot of Angel's Envy. "Here's your medicine, although I would suggest taking it slowly."

I poured the liquid down my throat and handed back the empty glass. I swung my legs off the couch. "What happened? Did Naberius put something in my drink?"

Dabriel looked surprised, "I don't think so, I mean he's not your biggest fan, but I don't think he'd ruin a cocktail to get you to shut up. Although it was nice while it lasted," she laughed.

"I need to get home, recuperate in my own bed. I need to check in with Jessica."

"Don't be an idiot, Dante. The bar's closed, we're the only ones here, and there's no way you're going to be able to make it home alone. We'll leave your car here. It'll be okay."

I shrugged and smiled. It felt nice to not care. The air felt soft, and I was almost worried about what had happened, but not quite. I hadn't had that much to drink, but my head felt like some kind of floaty thing and worries weren't entering into my headspace.

When we got back to my place Dabriel helped me up the stairs and inside. Dr. Sax ran up to greet us but disappeared as soon as he saw I wasn't alone.

Dabriel helped me to the living room, "Stop talking and rest," she said. "I'll see you soon."

I nodded weakly as my phone buzzed. Dabriel took a few steps back and stood in the doorway as I answered. "Hello?"

"It's Nick."

"Nick?" I asked. My brain wasn't spinning fast enough, or it was spinning, but in the wrong direction.

"You okay? You don't sound too good."

"Yes, no. Not really..." I wondered if I'd been drugged, or if someone was working some bad Mojo. "Do you know anything about Voudou curses?"

Nick muffled a cough into the receiver; he wasn't sounding good either. "No. We need to talk."

"Okay...where'd you go? Did Marinette..."

"No. Wasn't her. Look, I've got to go, they'll be looking for me," he whispered quickly. "Later. Tomorrow night. Your place."

He coughed again. He was either heading towards death or stuck in an underground cave. Or both.

"What time?" No answer. He'd already hung up.

"Dabriel?" I called out but got no response. She must've slipped out while I was on the phone.

I lay back on the couch thinking there was something I had forgotten. Was it about tonight? Something I had to do?

"Brain dead idiot," I chided myself. Even with the alcohol and the lumps on my head I was having more trouble remembering things than I should.

"Christophe," I muttered. I needed to track him down. Maybe I should wait until after sunrise. I made it into the bedroom after heating up a wet towel for my head and forcing myself to drink some water with a couple of 222's.

I heard my phone buzz again, but I was already drifting off and it didn't matter.

A warmth enveloped me in dreams until something rudely shook me awake. I sat up, head spinning, and Dr. Sax leapt off me with a hiss. It was evening, but I couldn't tell if I had slept for hours or days.

A glance at the clock by the bed told me it was eight pm. I'd slept the whole day away. Probably needed it, though my head still felt like a velvet brick had been shoved inside of it. And a slow stumble into the bathroom then to the living room to look at my phone told me Dabriel had called. Back to the kitchen and coffee, with a little extra twist, to put a dampener around the hammers in my head. Café Vérité on the rocks.

I called Dabriel, she answered on the first ring.

"Hey, I kinda slept in. You called earlier?"

"Right," Dabriel said sharply, "It was nothing."

I could hear voices in the background. Muffled, but it was a man and a woman. Possibly arguing.

"Are you okay?" I asked.

"Everything's fine."

Something was wrong.

"Dabriel. Do you need help?" I asked.

There was a muffled silence and some mumbling. She'd covered the phone with her hand and was talking to someone.

"Dab?" I said, getting worried.

There was an abrupt cough, and she was there again. "No, everything's fine. Listen, I was thinking about the Intoxicantata and realized that there weas someone else wanting it. Not sure who, but it was a man, low voice. I think he wanted it more than Christophe. He'd been calling the bar a lot a couple of weeks ago."

"Really?" I asked. "Trevor never mentioned it."

I remembered the vision I had, the mystery man…

"Yeah, you know how he was, though," there was a pause, and a muffled sound. "Always a bit distracted. Anyhow, I have to go right now, but we can talk tomorrow."

And that was that.

Confused, I sat on the couch and threw my phone next to me, waking Dr. Sax. He gave a soft growl before curling into a tight ball on my legs. At least someone was fine going back to bed.

14
ON THE ROCKS

I watched Dr. Sax sleep and twitch. It had started raining. September was officially in full swing. Nothing but a blur of winter and fall until March.

I could hear sirens outside; it never failed. Even in a city as used to rain as this one there were always accidents whenever the water started falling. And it was coming down hard. I moved Dr. Sax and stood up, still feeling a little weak. I steadied myself with the edge of the couch. I should probably eat something, as I couldn't remember the last time I had a solid meal.

I could hear something in the attic. It sounded as if the windows up there were being attacked by an army of water pistols.

I moved towards the attic stairs, wondering if maybe I'd been drinking too much recently. Alcohol was poison and dealing with poisonous magic leaves stains on your soul even if you know what you're doing. That's where I can get in trouble. Most Wavers are cursed, leaving only a portion of the soul to worry about. No soul, no stain. I was a rare exception, Waver by blood only.

My soul was intact.

I tried to balance the good spirits with the bad ones, like Trevor used to do at the Lost & Found, only he was stricter about staying in the middle of the road than I was. I usually tried to keep the good drinks at the forefront, which made me think I might have been doing something wrong.

The hallway was illuminated by a flash. The lights flickered and went off. I felt my way into the kitchen as the windows shook slightly against a clap of thunder to see if all the power was off.

The lights flashed on again, and Dr. Sax leapt into the hallway, and stopped. Eyes gleaming like midnight lasers and tail quivering like a snake charmed cobra, he stared at the attic stairs.

"Okay, I'm going," I muttered. Now not really wanting to.

Before I could, though, there was a knock at the door. Either Nick was early, or it was someone else. I grabbed my bar spoon from my bag in the living room and peered through the peephole.

Nobody there.

I opened the door and stepped out. A strange fog had fallen over the neighborhood, tinged yellow by the glow of streetlights. The electricity from the storm still hung in the air like a sharp edge vibrating around everything.

Dr. Sax leapt between my legs and disappeared into the night as I was hit by a blast of icy wind. This was not normal weather. I looked in the direction the cat had run but saw nothing other than a rustle of leaves and a couple of starlings flying up towards the telephone wires above. Only shadows and imagination on these streets, I thought to myself. And another rustle...

"Hello?" I called out, quietly.

I noticed a shadow falling against the gnarled autumn touched tree in my front yard and took a few steps towards it. The shadow turned, and I realized who it was.

Jessica Fervor was getting out of car holding a dark red umbrella. She wore a shiny black neon raincoat that ended a few inches above her knees, she turned to watch the cat run across the street.

"What are you doing here, Jess? Checking up on me?" I asked and gave her a slight pout. "You left me at the bar."

"And I'm sure that wasn't the first time someone's done that," She smirked. "Besides, I figured you were in good hands with Dabriel, and hey, I'm here now"

She walked up the stairs towards me, "Making sure you're alright."

"I'm fine."

I glanced around, "So where's your partner at?" I asked, hoping the answer was somewhere far away.

"Working. I think he's staking out Kill City. Carefully," Jessica added, noticing my worried glance. "You haven't been making things you shouldn't be making, have you?"

"Jess, you asked me to make things I'm not supposed to make, remember?" I said, then changed the subject. "So, do you still have me on your list of suspects?"

Jessica shook her head, "Me? No. And I think Gilles is okay with you as well, at least as far as this case is concerned. Not so sure how he feels about you on a personal level..."

"I think we're good," I said. "He cares about you, Jess, and he knows I do too."

"Thomas," Jessica said quietly.

"I know, not the time," I muttered.

We stood on the porch for a second, silent.

"Thom," Jessica said. "The good thing is that the Agentia isn't as concerned about your involvement. Especially thanks to your friend Naberius."

I looked over, confused. "Naberius?"

"Yeah. He's gone missing, and according to Dabriel, he took a couple of valuable bottles from the bar with him. He's their main suspect now, so you have a little more room to maneuver," she held up a finger, "But you're not off the hook completely."

"Understood," I said. "Dabriel was here earlier, and she didn't say anything about it..."

"What?" Jessica said, alarmed. "After Gilles and I left?"

"Yeah," I nodded, "and then she called, saying she thinks Marinette might be our best suspect. But something was off. She might be in trouble."

"I think she *is* trouble, Thom," Jessica said, her brows furrowing,

"But I'll have someone go by the bar, and her place. There's definitely something strange going on."

"Even the weather is getting in on the strange action," I pointed out.

There was an ominous glow pushing over the trees in the distance, the light of the city awake against the night and sending a thick yellow stain across the gathering clouds. The wind had picked up as well, leaves spinning down the street and branches waving as they passed.

"This isn't good, Jess," I stopped, "Wait, did you hear that?"

"What?"

"Shhh…"

It was like a distant whisper in the air.

WE BOTH SLOWLY TURNED FULL circle, it was getting louder. Finally, we looked up. It was birds. They were having a showdown even against the storm clouds.

The starlings moved between branches, swooping upwards into the air, spiraling around above us, then spinning back into the trees. We stood quietly, watching them, almost hypnotized.

"It's so…dark," Jessica whispered, not sure how else to describe it. It was hypnotic.

I nodded beside her, "And kind of beautiful."

Jessica grabbed my arm and hissed my name, "Thom, look."

The spell of the Starlings was broken as she pointed towards the trees. Although the fog still obscured our vision, we could both make out a man standing in a walkway, between the trees and hedges on the other side of the road.

He was dressed in black, cat burglar style, but the clothes, sweater, and jeans, were torn and scratched. I instinctively stepped in front of Jessica. The man tilted his head slowly and took a step towards us. Jessica moved up next to me and slowly reached for her gun.

I reached out and put my hand on her arm, "Let's go back to the house," I whispered, but before either of us could move there was a sharp curling shriek and a nightmarish crash and flutter in the trees behind the stranger.

"The birds..." Jessica whispered, but it wasn't the Starlings. Two screaming owls swooped down in a menacing spiral of feathers and fury, sliding between outstretched branches. Their wide eyes focused on the man in black beneath them. He turned away from us and started to run down the street, but the owls were flying in too close.

Talons scraping through the air, catching on the man's clothes as he covered his face. He started waving his arms wildly, shouting obscenities, and for a second it seemed as if he was driving the creatures away. The owls stretched their wings out and glided across the street, turning, and curving up above us, before pushing themselves into the sky.

The owls soared until they were shadows against the clouds. The man, jacket torn, stepped cautiously back out into the street. Then the sound came again. The high sharp screeching followed by a push against the air, a rhythm of feathers against wind, and the man in black shouted again and started running down the street. Towards us. The birds of prey swooped down and circled around the man as he ran. Diving in, claws outstretched, beaks trying to tear at head and hair. He screamed again, but it was no longer shouts of anger, but of pure fear. And as he passed, I thought I recognized him.

"Christophe?" I called out, but he didn't, or couldn't, respond.

He ran past us, arms swinging around wild and rapid, trying to fend off the owls as if they were a swarm of bees. I could hear his breath scraping and shallow as he passed, but before I could focus on his features Jessica pushed me out of the way of the following birds. I caught a glimpse of a dirty face, scratched, and covered in flecks of blood and mud. Tufts of white, almost silver hair stuck out from under his wool cap. His jacket was torn, but it seemed as if he was protected by a thick black sweater underneath, and his boots seemed thick and sturdy, but I noticed they were both untied, and the laces seemed to be slightly tripping him up.

He didn't look up but ran down the street towards a busier intersection. I heard Jessica gasp, but at the last second the man turned down the corner at the end of the block. The owls followed, screeching.

"What the hell was that?" Jessica looked down the now empty street, shaking her head.

"Not sure, but it wasn't good. We should go in."

"You know that's not my style," Jessica turned and started walking towards the corner where the man had turned. "You coming with?" She called out over her shoulder.

I knew I should, I knew I didn't really want to, and I knew Nick could be showing up at my door any second. I started walking with her down the street. "Just to the corner, but maybe you should call Gilles."

"Or an ambulance. C'mon."

The fog slowly thickened behind us. We weren't even a block away from my place, but the mist had already almost obscured the entire structure. It rolled across the ground, swaying and swirling. I felt like if we stood still long enough it would swallow us whole.

"Wait, off to the side..." Jessica stopped abruptly, sensing something.

I felt a shiver; a shudder fell over me and I touched the charm around my neck. Quick comfort. Jessica was a few steps ahead of me, moving towards the edge of the grass on the other side of the street. I ran to catch up with her, almost feeling like I'd trip over the thick tendrils of fog. The sky was gone, and all I could see was a dull grey mist hanging heavy and sliding around us as we moved across the street.

"Strange weather," Jessica muttered, "I don't like it."

"I don't know about strange, but definitely creepy."

There was a soft padded crunch in the underbrush next to me. I jumped and Jessica laughed as a slightly annoyed looking cat casually slinked out of the bushes, pausing to scratch the side of its face against an exposed branch before taking a few steps towards me. It stopped and sat in the street, away from the bushes but just out of my reach.

"Oh go home, Sax," I whispered.

I was also starting to feel as if it might be a good idea for me to get home as well. The cat turned and ran back towards home and out of the corner of my eye I saw something falling to the ground. Jessica had already turned, so she didn't catch it. A feather: about 26 centimeters long, mostly white, with half a soft orange mixed with patches of a dark shadowy grey. It spiraled down in a soft slow-motion blur, and I felt as if it was spinning my vision into a surreal dream. I picked it up and put it in my pocket without saying anything and we moved silently through the still thickening fog towards the end of the street. The silence surrounding us still reverberated with the occasional echo of a now distant screech.

"Owls aren't supposed to act like that. Not with people. There aren't any nests around here, so they weren't being protective. They were being…angry. They don't do that with people," Jessica said.

"Maybe it's the weather?" I mumbled. "But there's nothing out here. We should go back."

I was feeling strange; half-awake and slightly dazed. I closed my eyes for a second, this dream should be over. It was time to wake up. There was a pushing on the back of my mind, a pressure on the back of my neck, the top of my spine. Like a memory struggling to push through. Like a warning. It was something about the feather. The owls. The mysterious man. But the feeling was about something else. Something that was connecting all of it. It was as if I had a thread in my hands that could pull each thing together, but the thread had snapped, and now I was left holding nothing.

"It's like the fog is too thick to think through," I said to myself.

"Like pea soup, right?" Jessica said, not really paying attention. She stared up at the trees as we walked. "Maybe the starlings that spooked the owls and that man, maybe homeless, was in the wrong place at the wrong time."

"Maybe, but whoever it was, I don't think he's coming back."

"But you said he looked like Christophe, right?"

I nodded.

"I'm going to head over to Blundertown Books and tell Gilles to meet me there. We can talk later, right?"

"Yeah, I'm around," My problem with Nick Noir showing up had just solved itself.

When I got back inside, I made a beeline for the bar. I needed a little smoothing of the edges.

A strange shadow moving past the window, behind the curtains, distracted me. It could have been Nick, he was a shapeshifter, but it still didn't seem right.

Someone knocked on the front door and I must've jumped a meter into the air.

I peered out. It was Nick.

"Sorry I'm late. It's a mess out there."

Nick moved into the hallway, shaking something out of his hair, he looked up and saw my confusion. "There's a full-on hailstorm. It's insane. Coming down straight through all the fog."

"Did you see anyone else out there?" I asked, stepping towards the door.

"Anyone else? In this weather? No. There's not another soul out there…" Nick stopped and turned to look outside with me.

I moved towards the steps then came to a full stop. My hand on the edge of the banister, my mouth open. I'd never seen anything like it.

There was a miniature meteor shower of frozen water cutting through the deep mist, creating a carpet of ice on the ground below. It covered the lawn and the walkway up to the street, where it vanished into darkness.

We stood together for a second, then moved back inside.

"I'm not sure if I'm imagining things or not, but just to be safe I think we should move up into the attic."

Nick gave a quick shrug, "Sure."

Until I knew what it was, I wasn't sure if I could fight it. I ran up the stairs ahead of Nick and peered outside. The fog had thickened and all I could see were cool swirls of yellowish grey, occasionally cut into splinters of smoke by flailing shadows of windblown branches. I stood still; a hand pressed against the glass.

"So, who exactly are we hiding from?" Nick asked from behind me.

I told him about the man and the owls, and how it kind of looked like Christophe. His face went white.

"Nick?"

"It's Marinette. The Owls. That's what I needed to talk to you about. I don't know what happened, but she's cleaning house. There's going to be a few more people missing soon, and that's going to include us if we're not careful," Nick moved across the attic towards the small window and peered outside. "I also think we're going to see some snow."

"Not a chance, not yet," I said.

"Oh, I could be wrong, Dante, but I doubt it. Perhaps the fog will keep it at a distance for a while, but the fog isn't always the safest..." Nick stopped and flashed a slightly crazed smile. "Regardless, there will be snow."

"Ok, what were you saying about Marinette?"

"Right," He hadn't moved at all, and slowly shifted his gaze towards me. "You know about Marinette and Trevor, right?"

"Buying the bookstore."

"Yeah, but thing is, you're in the will to get the Lost & Found if Trevor dies. So, you're in danger from a few different directions."

It took a second for Nick's words to sink in, but when they did, I staggered back and sat down on the makeshift couch. "Wait, what?"

"You didn't know?" Nick asked, visibly surprised.

I shook my head. "No idea. But then, that means I really was a suspect, if the Agentia knew. Gilles must have really pulled some strings to make sure I wasn't taken in."

"Must be nice to have friends," Nick said, a slight sarcastic tone slipping in. "Still, you need to watch your back and get that book back."

"Do you know who has it?"

"Christophe had it, but I don't know where he is or where he stashed it. If it was him getting chased by owls, I'm willing to bet Marinette will have it before the night's over. Look, I'm getting a bit nervous. I should go. So be careful. Especially if the owls are out."

I looked at Nick and felt my heart stop for a second; caught between icy slivers of fear. For the first time I noticed that Nick's eyes seemed almost unnaturally bright, shining like silver, in contrast to the creases and lines that fell like a map of a hard life across his skin.

He turned without saying anything and moved towards the stairs when we heard a crash from downstairs. I grabbed Nick's shoulder and put a silencing finger to my lips. Crouching down, I leaned forwards and peered down into the dark hallway, letting my eyes adjust. There was a little light coming in from the street, and then a shadow passed by, moving from the kitchen into the living room.

I heard a soft growl.

"Nick?"

"Yeah, I heard it. Not a shapeshifter," Nick crouched down next to me, "Something else."

We both stood up and moved back towards the window. I grabbed the mason jar holding the remnants of my Bulleit the Blue Sky and passed it to Nick. "Drink. It'll help your strength."

He nodded and gulped the liquid down, almost choking when the aftertaste hit. "Not one of your best, but thanks," he sputtered.

"We should pull up the staircase," I said.

I hadn't tried it in years, so I hoped it still worked.

"Nick, give me a hand."

He moved to stand next to me and I handed him the end of a rope attached to the bottom stair.

"Pull as hard as you can," I stood behind him, and we played a game of tug-o-war with the most stubborn staircase in Canada. "Pull."

"I'm pulling," His voice was strained.

"Wait," I grabbed his arm, seeing a small shape appear below. Dr. Sax leapt on the bottom stair and ran up to join us.

We resumed our struggle. The strength potion and adrenalin finally kicking in and working in our favor. With a stubborn wooden groan, the stairs lifted. We probably weren't completely out of danger, but we'd gained a little time to come up with a plan. Were we going to fight or flee. I sat on the floor, slightly out of breath. Nick moved back to the bar and started mixing a drink. Vodka and not much else. "What's that going to do?" I asked.

"Hopefully help me relax," he gave a little chuckle, "Want one?"

"No thanks. Not until I know what we're up against."

I moved to the attic window and slowly opened it, letting the weather drift into the room. I peered out, but the night was still impenetrable. And the coldness I felt was as if the entire room had suddenly filled with ice and it all condensed into a small circle fitting perfectly into my chest. This wasn't being afraid of the dark, or of things that go bump in the night. This was a deep soul shattering terror, and it was moving deeper. My breath caught as I noticed something on the windowsill. A splattering of blood. Watered down crimson drops, diluted by melting hail and rainwater. And sticking out, jagged and ratted, from the corner of the window frame, a large feather. Grey and spotted, like the owls.

15
PAINKILLER

I stared at the attic floor, pretending I had X-ray vision. I was scared, but I wasn't a coward.

"We need to figure out what's down there," I said.

"We? No. I didn't come here for whatever that is."

I attempted to push the staircase down, but it was stuck. I stomped on it, but it didn't budge.

"Nick, Help?" I turned, and Nick wasn't behind me. He was heading towards the window. "What are you doing?"

"I think it's time for me to go, but I ain't going down that way. I can't take any chances here. We'll talk later, yeah?"

He proceeded to climb out the window. It was a jump to the apple tree growing on my lawn, but the branches were sturdy. While he ran, I grabbed my makeshift portable liquor cabinet: A small black leather bag containing a handful of bartender's tools and a mix of assorted miniatures for a variety of situations.

The great thing about magical creatures is the consistency in their weaknesses. Like how a silver bullet is painful to werewolves regardless of their ancestry, garlic annoys most vampires, asphodel will get the ghosts out, and the white clover flower can be used to protect yourself against snakes.

So, I just needed to figure out what I was up against. I'd just have to use the same route Nick took and then try to sneak inside. Unfortunately, I didn't seem to be as agile. I lowered myself and let go, misjudging the distance and landing on my back. Thankfully not on my bag, I thought, as I lay on the grass, wind knocked out of me. Black fuzzy spots floated across my vision, but I had to move. I didn't have time to wallow in the pain, at least not until I had figured out what was in my house…carefully.

I got to the front door, slowly opened it, and then stopped in my tracks.

"Naberius?"

"Thom…Thomas…h-help."

Naberius took two steps towards me, and then collapsed to the floor, blood spreading through his shirt. I ran to his side, and he slowly pushed himself up to a sitting position, one hand pressed to his side. "Just…flesh wound. M'okay."

"Okay? You're bleeding and your face is a shade of green I've never seen before. What was it…where is it?"

"Outside," Naberius mumbled. "Too fast. Made it in through the back…"

I ran to the bathroom and grabbed a washcloth, some bandages, and a glass of water. "Let me clean it up a bit."

I managed to get Naberius to the couch after doing some makeshift first aid and then went for the good stuff.

Painkiller, my way. Typical ingredients are dark rum, pineapple juice, orange juice and cream of coconut, but for this I also add a clove, a pinch of chili pepper, and a slow chanted word along with a quick stir. This version should not be blended unless you want the pain relief to include a few hours of sleep.

"Drink this," I insisted, back at Naberius' side.

He took a sip, made a face, "S'orrible."

"It gets better, and it'll get you better," I promised. "Finish it."

He did and nodded a thank you.

"What happened?"

"Lost & F..." Naberius was having trouble speaking, his words slowing, "Foun...Dab..."

"Dab? Dabriel?"

"Hm, yeah..." and Naberius was out cold.

HE WAS STILL BREATHING, his pulse felt okay, but maybe the Painkiller was meant to be shaken, not stirred. Always get that one mixed up. I had no idea how long the drinks were going to last, but it was going to be at least a couple of hours.

That's when I heard the growling sound again.

But this time it was louder, and outside. Coming around the living room towards the front door. Did I lock it?

I left Naberius on the couch, and checked the doors, back and front. Locked. The attic stairs were up and stuck, so it looked like I was as well. Stuck, that is.

I had to prepare for the worst on the main floor. And, I realized, my car was still at the Lost & Found. I might need some help... Jessica was on her Owl Quest. That meant... "Gilles."

"Dante?"

"Yeah. Are you busy? I'm at home with Naberius. He's been, I don't know, bitten? It's possible something happened at the Lost & Found. And I think there's something big bad and maybe wolfy prowling around outside my place."

"I'll be right there..." a pause, "well, twenty minutes."

I LOOKED over towards the slightly snoring Naberius. At least he didn't seem to be in pain. Slowly I made my way to the living room window and cracked it open so I could get a clear view of the front of the house.

The hail was still coming down. It was the strangest weather I'd ever seen. The thick fog swirling around the iced onslaught was weird, but even weirder was the sound. Or the lack of sound. The thick fog seemed to act as a dampener, causing the hail to fall soundlessly in front of me and cover the world.

I pushed back against a sudden shiver. It was getting colder. I knew the fog would have to vanish, but the hail might transform into snow. Either way, it was going to be a very strange night.

Closing the window, I moved back to the couch and tried to rouse Naberius. Outside the wind had picked up, sending the hail harder against the windows. Like fingers tapping. A hundred fingers rapping, trying to find a way in. I sat. legs up, arms resting over my knees. I knew I was freaking myself out more than I should, letting my imagination go, but I could swear there was a rhythm to the noise. A Morse code in the rattle of hail on glass. I wondered if Christophe was the one who had been attacked by the owls, and if Jessica was alright.

She wasn't answering her phone, but that wasn't necessarily a bad thing. It was something I'd need to revisit, though. I jumped off the couch and grabbed my jacket off the chair before moving back to the window. Nothing but a flurry of darkness between silver pebbles of ice. As I fumbled with the jacket zipper, I touched the two charms hanging there. The one from Dabriel tied to alcohol, the other tied to fire and my family. My mother had given it to me to help channel the elemental powers within. I traced its curves almost absent mindedly and felt myself going into almost a trance as I gazed into the darkness behind the glass. The charm was almost perfectly smooth, feeling like water that's been hardened. Not like ice, but softer. Like solid water. But there was weight to it, a strange kind of weight. It felt like history. As if there were memories, or stories, held within the metal. And it was cold.

I felt an almost electric shock and pulled my hand away, my skin almost white from the chill. The glass rattled as if it was excited that I was near it. I touched the window gently. Just the tips of my fingers. And then the fear hit.

It crawled over my entire body and left me holding my breath, staring unblinking out the window even though there was nothing to see. My chest felt tight and the cold in my hand was now covering my entire body.

I tried to calm down, but the hail against the window shifted into a flurried patter. Like a thousand wings. And the owls from earlier screamed across my memory. Then they receded into the distance only to be replaced by the face of the man who'd been attacked, only now he was staring at me, screaming. His face floating right outside of the window in front of me. I threw myself backwards, stumbling towards the couch behind me. And then the face was gone, leaving only two glowing eyes, red and surrounded by fog and hail.

And then they were gone as well.

Slowly the fear slid away into uneasiness and the threat of a headache. I sat on the edge of the bed and scanned the room, hands gripping the cushions. Nothing had changed. Everything was as it should be, where it should be. All in my mind.

The headache was a reality, moving around to the back of my neck and slowly the fear started seeping in through the window alongside the cold. The rattle and tap of ice on glass had started feeling hypnotic. Trying to push my thoughts towards something as cold and dark as whatever might be waiting outside. But at the same time, it seemed to be calling me, pulling at me...come outside come outside come out...C'mon. Shake it off, man.

Maybe a drink. A good drink. Something strong and empowering. Something warm and comforting...and then suddenly all I could see was the man screaming as the owls attacked, and the splatter of blood on the floor where Naberius had fallen, and the growling outside... what if he'd doubled back, avoided Jessica, attacked Naberius. What if it was the same thing.

What if he had been outside, but had found a way in. What if he had found a way into the attic, as I'd found a way out...

And then a scrape came from outside the window. Like someone was trying to enter. The sound broke the hold of the fear, and I moved. I moved into the kitchen, straight to the alcohol. I grabbed a bottle of rum and some bitters and turned on the lamp in the corner. It threw a soft glow of comfort across the room. Everything falling back into a safe whisper as the light kicked the shadows out of all the corners leaving only the storm and the wind.

That I could handle.

Then the lights started to dim, and the house suddenly went dark. The terror leapt at me. Faster and harder than the last time, gripping and clawing through me. I wanted to get to the fuse box, but I couldn't move. I had a sudden thought that if I turned the light on again it would only get worse. my fists tightened as the storm outside pushed against the window. A scratch, a clawing, and then, everything outside suddenly stopped. A silence like timelessness, a thick hush like the deepest winter. Then like a heartbeat, like the terror squeezing my heart, like a last breath before death, there was a dull thud and a scream of shattering glass.

I jumped and ran towards the front door but tripped over the edge of the carpet in the hall. My head hit the floor, and everything started to spiral into a whirlpool of red and dark. I couldn't tell if I was shouting, or even making a sound, as the floor had begun to feel like an ocean, and I was too scared to swim.

There was a banging at the door, and a voice. A shout. Shadows were surrounding me, and I flailed about blindly. Couldn't let them get me…

And then I heard his voice.

It was Gilles, at the front door.

Finally.

And everything went black.

GILLES WAS KNEELING over me as my eyes slid open. I had to warn him, "Don't know, but there's something…"

I saw a shadow fly past behind him, moving towards the den on the other side of the hall.

"There!" I pointed, adrenalin kicking me to alert.

Gilles turned on his heels, followed by a crash coming from the living room. "What the hell was that?"

"I think that might have been Naberius. He's in the living room. We need to get out. And I know Naberius isn't moving too fast yet." I stood and moved back into the kitchen. "Maybe I can mix something. Can you sneak up and try to get Naberius back here?"

"I'll try..."

"Be careful."

Gilles vanished around the corner, and I studied my options. The classics I had covered. Gin, Vodka, Whiskey, Rum. But I was pretty sure I'd need something with a twist, and my lemons were dry. I opened the fridge, shifted a few bottles and wilting vegetables around, digging deeper into the fridge than I'd been in months, and found an ancient bottle of Burnt Crown lager and an even older bottle of vinegar. There was a thin layer of liquid left. That's something. Gilles reappeared, supporting a droopy and shuffling Naberius.

"Where is it?" I asked.

"Is in your den."

"What is it?"

"Dangerous," Gilles said, "We should go."

"I know, but really..."

"It's some kind of wolf. That's all I got."

"Okay, maybe a werewolf? Can we make it out the front? What's it doing?" I asked.

Gilles glared at me, "Maybe, no, and I think it's looking for something."

Naberius coughed, raising his head slightly, "Dabriel..."

I nodded absentmindedly, going through all my bottles of bitters.

"What are you doing, Dante? We need to get out before it decides that it's looking for us."

"Or we can make it leave..."

"I don't think we should let that thing roam the neighborhood," Gilles said.

Naberius laughed, "Good doggy."

I looked at Naberius, and I knew what I needed to do, "But we could get it to take a nap."

I didn't like killing things, especially anything supernatural, because those actions stayed on your permanent record. Besides, Wolf creatures were rarely true evil, and in human form, for the most part, they weren't dangerous.

"I need to get a look at this thing."

I crept towards the hallway and slowly peeked around the corner. The lights were off, but the room was slightly illuminated by a yellowish glow from the streetlamps outside. The shadow drifting across my window earlier held very little in common with the thing in my den.

It was about seven feet high, standing on its hind legs. A thick fur covered its entire body, matted black and grey, and stinking like a wet dog. It shifted slightly and moved out of the shadows for a second, letting me see something I wasn't ready to see.

There's a type of wolf, mostly found in the Slavic culture, known as the Wilkołak. Very similar to the North American werewolf, but usually much more intelligent when in its wolfen shape, and therefore, much more dangerous. That's what was currently in my den, tearing apart my bookshelf. I almost gasped out loud, then slammed my hand across my mouth and leaned back into the hallway, pressing myself against the wall. There was a sharp grunt, a snarl, and I heard the creature move closer to where I stood frozen. I moved back a couple of steps and realized I could see it's reflection in the windows. Just a looming shape, a shadow, and almost glowing crimson eyes.

Behind me I heard Gilles whispering for me to get back, and then before I could take another step, it was in front of me.

The eyes were huge. Like sharp red gemstones, cutting through me, flecked with black and gold. Its face was mostly wolfen but elongated. Long tangled and matted grey and dirty white fur covering its entire body, which was impressive and frightening when on two legs, but when it fell forward towards me to take up an attack stance on all four legs, it was pure terror.

Its mouth cracked open and curled into a hungry sneer, and it took one horrifyingly silent step towards me. I was frozen, seeing only sharp teeth, drool, and the end of my life inching closer. If I could have moved, I would have screamed, but all I could push out of my throat was a strangled gasp. Then someone grabbed me by the back of my shirt and pulled me back down the hallway towards the kitchen.

"Gilles?"

"We're out, Dante. Move."

I turned and the two of us sprinted for the back door.

I managed to blurt out a confused question as someone else ran past me towards the creature, "Who?"

Still running, Gilles in front of me, I turned to look back. It was Naberius, somehow having roused himself out of a near comatose state, and he was leaping towards the wolf, arms outstretched. The two of them tumbled back into the den as I stumbled down the back stairs and as the kitchen door closed behind me, Gilles grabbed me again and swung me around to the side of the house.

"Naberius…" I panted, "We have to help…"

"Not our help, mine. You stay here. You're not looking too good, Dante. Besides, right now Naberius has a slight edge," Gilles said, "He had a pepper shot?"

"Great," Naberius had a little pre-shift shot he'd take on occasion, as a little pick-up for long nights. A shot of vodka, rimmed with salt and pepper, and an eyelash.

Not a favorite.

"Hey," Gilles said, holding a small brown bag up in front of me, "I'm supposed to give these to you."

"Coffee beans?" I asked peering into the bag, confused.

"Coffee beans," he confirmed. "From your friend Mori. Said they packed an extra punch."

I took the bag, and then suddenly felt a little dizzy. I struggled to stand but fell back against the wall. "What's wrong with me?" I muttered, trying to clear my head by shaking it.

Gilles put a hand on my shoulder, and it felt way too heavy, "I'm going in, I called for reinforcements, you stay here."

I nodded, "Painkiller. There's a glass by the couch. That's what knocked Naberius out. If you can get that thing to drink it, we should be good."

"Right," Gilles snorted. "Just give the wolfbeast a cocktail, and then we can all go hang out at the bar."

Before I could respond, Gilles had turned and gone back inside. I slid down to the ground, feeling the light around me grow dim and shaking with spots of static.

"Can't stay here," I grumbled to myself, and then I remembered the bag in my hand.

I stood and made my way to the top of the back stairs and peered into the kitchen. It was a mess. There was a huge crash, some shouts and something or someone hitting the walls, and it sounded like a bunch of kids slam dancing in my living room.

I threw a couple of beans into my mouth and chewed, hoping it wasn't going to react in a bad way. I opened the door, walked into my kitchen, and moved straight into a head rush like a brick wall brain freeze.

I felt incredible. I strode down the hall, turned the corner, and ran straight into Gilles, who was backing up while holding a gun that was pointing at a very large wolf moving towards us with a mouth full of very large teeth.

"Move very slow, Dante," Gilles whispered. "Back and slow."

I took a few steps back, "Naberius?"

"Out your window. I think he's okay."

"Did you grab the drink?" I whispered.

"Still in the living room."

"Great," I shifted a little, "Okay, "I've got an idea."

I started walking backwards towards the kitchen. The creature's head stopped and turned deadly wolf eyes in my direction. Its brow furrowed and its lip curled back into a sneer showing even more dangerous teeth.

"Dante," Gilles hissed, "Stop."

"I can do this. Just distract it?"

"What? You're kidding."

I caught a movement out of the corner of my eye. Through a window in the living room. It was Naberius.

"Gilles…"

"I saw."

There was a sound of glass shattering in the den, and Naberius shouting to us, "Step back boys, it's gonna get loud."

"Dammit," Gilles said, moving back and pushing me into the kitchen.

The wolf head turned towards Naberius, who was moving into the hallway behind it. He held a hand up, holding some of the coffee beans from Gilles. He shot me a tight smile, moved his arm back, while uttering a phrase in French, and shot again.

"Serrer les dents," he growled. Bite the Bullet. And the beans flew at the creature like, well, like bullets. The beans hit the wolf-thing's chest with enough force to send it backwards with a screeching wail of anguish.

Naberius ran back outside through the front door, and howling in pain, the monster limped after him. I heard Naberius shouting at the thing, and I knew he'd given me the time I need.

"What are you doing, Dante?" Gilles barked, "We need to go."

"Not yet," I hesitated. "Time to bring in some refreshments."

"You mean reinforcements?"

"Either way," I turned my head towards Gilles, "I'm going Kamikaze."

"What?"

"Actually," I grinned as I moved towards the fridge, "A reverse Kamikaze."

THE THING about reverse cocktails isn't the taste, it's the effects. It's the difference between saying come here and go away. With the Kamikaze I wanted to turn the inherent 'Divine Wind' in the opposite direction.

Shaker out, then lime juice followed by orange liqueur. Some vodka, and ice in last. It was my 'Cognitive Kamikaze'. Instead of attacking the creature perhaps I could cause the creature to attack itself.

I moved to the kitchen and poured my reverse-a-kazi into a shot glass. I filled another with rum because I was going to need a little help with my recipe. It wasn't following normal protocol, asking the dead for mixing tips, but I didn't care. Dead mixes always carried an extra punch. And I knew Zee, the Wisp I spoke to at Blundertown, would have something good. I pulled the Ziploc of ashes from my bag and sprinkled some on the rum, held Zee's name in my mind, and a question. How can I stop a ravenous wolf-creature? And down the hatch it went.

A whisper of a wind and Zee was smiling at me.

"That was fast, you must be thirsty," I said.

"I'm always thirsty," Zee snickered behind me. I turned but he was gone.

"Zee?" I whispered.

There was an angry swear from the hallway. I poked my head out and saw where Zee had vanished to. He was floating right in front of a very annoyed looking Gilles. "What the hell is this?"

"That's Zee. I'll explain later. Zee, get in here."

He grinned, as much as nothingness can grin, "Who's this handsome super-spy, Tommy?"

I rolled my eyes, "That is Gilles Deuxcoeurs, Zee. And Gilles, meet Zee. Now heel."

Zee reappeared beside me. "What's up?"

"Giant frightening wolf creature."

"Sounds dangerous."

"I know, so I need your help on the reverse Kamikaze."

"What do you have?" Zee asked.

I told him. "What do I need?" I asked impatiently.

The final twist was a swirl instead of a shake. A fast counterclockwise spin. And then the description.

"DANTE," Naberius ran into the kitchen. "It's coming back. There's something about it..."

"What is?" Zee asked, then vanished and reappeared a few seconds later. "Tommy, there's a goddamn wolf demon crawling up your stairs."

"That's what I said," I grumbled, lining up some glasses. "Wolf creature," From the sound of it I didn't have a lot of time. "Naberius, get out. Back yard."

He started to say something, changed his mind, nodded and left. I had my back to the hallway, but Gilles stood right behind me, gun at the ready.

"I only have one shot, Dante."

"That's fine. I have two."

"It's coming." Zee whispered.

"Dante," Gilles hissed. I turned and the enormous wolf was pushing through the front door. Drool and blood dripping from its mouth, claws out and scraping the wood floors.

"Look out," Zee blurted.

Gilles started to move, but it was too late. The wolf leapt into the kitchen and caught Gilles' ankles with its paw. He fell backwards, his gun sliding back across the floor.

"Dammit!"

"Gilles!" I took a step forward and was hit by the stench of the beast. Like a wet dog covered in thick metallic dirt and sulfur.

I struggled to focus on the glass I was holding, and on the power of the drink. closing my eyes, I spit into the glass and forced my power into the liquid while reciting the spell of description.

"The Reverse Kamikaze. It brings the Divine Wind at your back straight into the center of your chest. The hit of lime stains your mind until the outside wants to go back inside."

I opened my eyes and saw that not only was Gilles bleeding and passed out on the kitchen floor, but he was also inches away from far too many teeth.

I threw the Kamikaze mix with a sharp battle-cry at the creature, and it hit the thing square on its triangular nose. As soon as the liquid touched its fur there was a bright flash. A brilliant flare of sickly orange day-glow light enveloped the monster as the drink dripped down its matted face mixing with skin and spittle.

"Dante?" Gilles was coming to, "What's happening? I can't move."

The wolf was whimpering now, backing up into the hallway, and then snarling, and turning slowly around, as if it was getting angry with itself.

"C'mon Gilles, time to go," I helped him up, and we started moving to the back door. "Zee? What's happening?"

The wolf's massive head had turned to stare at its tail, its tail moved back and forth like a whip.

"Actually, I'm not sure. Never done this to a wolf before. This could be good, or bad. Either way, I'm out," Zee said. He gave me a faded salute and started to shimmer into nothingness. "If you need anything else, get better rum," And he was gone.

The wolf spun in a circle, like a dog chasing its own tail, only more ferocious, and far more frightening. Every now and then it would manage to scratch itself, or tear a bit of fur out, but through it all, as if it knew I was the one who had caused this to happen, it would focus a sharp red eye on me and snarl, saliva dripping from its blood speckled lips.

"Gilles," I pulled at him as he stood slowly, "We need to get out of here. The drink is going to wear off sooner than later," I said, even though all I wanted was to lie down and throw up, not necessarily in that order.

WE MOVED AS FAST as we could out the back door, the wolf spinning like a Tasmanian devil in my living room. I was not looking forward to the clean-up, but at least I was alive and able to do it.

We limped into the back yard and circled around to the front of the house as the sound of glass breaking and things falling off shattered shelves followed us.

I heard sirens in the distance, "about time."

"Yeah," Gilles muttered, "I called for back-up, but we need to get to the Lost & Found. I think someone's cleaning house, and it sounds like Dabriel could be in danger."

"Okay, but you're driving. My car is still at the bar."

"Drive? Yeah, I think I can," Gilles mumbled.

"Okay. Naberius?" I asked. "You okay?"

"Yeah, I can do it," He said as the clouds broke and the rain started again.

We got into Gilles' car and drove towards the Lost & Found. Slightly scraped, wet, and shaken.

16
CORPSE CANDLE

I called Jessica as we walked. She was thankful we'd gotten out but didn't seem too pleased that we'd stayed to fight. She was even less happy to hear the extremely shortened version of what had happened.

"Supernatural chaos at my house. Werewolf attack. We're okay, place is a mess. Gilles called the Agentia, but the VPD are most likely on their way, as well as the fire department. We're heading to the bar."

Jessica said there had been nothing at the bookstore, and she'd meet us in a few. She also told me I was being a reckless idiot. I kind of agreed with her. I mean, we'd kind of left a wounded werewolf in my living room.

"Gilles, the Agentia can clean this up?"

"Your house? No," Gilles said, "But anything connected to the wolf or your cocktails? Yeah. They've concealed worse in the past."

"Thanks."

Naberius moaned and shifted in the back seat. He looked bad. The caffeine adrenalin must be wearing off. He was bleeding from wounds on his arms and his face was scratched and bruised.

"Maybe I should drop him off at the hospital?" I asked Gilles.

Naberius grabbed the back of the seat, "No, the wolf..."

"What?" Gilles demanded.

Naberius sat back slowly with his eyes closed, "Tell the Agents to not hurt her."

"Her?" I snapped, turning around to look at him.

"That was Dabriel."

Before Gilles or I could say anything else, Naberius bent forwards in his seat, clutching at his stomach. "Hurts."

"Breathe slow," I said, "Do you need to go to the hospital?"

Naberius looked up at me, "No, the bar. I can fix this."

"Okay," I paused, "Dabriel is a werewolf."

Naberius nodded. "She's not usually this violent, though. There's something off. I couldn't tell at first because the scent was off. Something must be causing the change. Maybe what I'm feeling is similar?" Naberius stopped, his face contorted in pain.

"This is bad," I said, "What if there's something in what we drank? My alcohol?"

"Let's just get to the bar and figure it out there," Gilles said quietly.

We drove in silence. Tires on wet cement and quiet moans from Naberius.

"I don't know what's wrong with him," I said to Gilles, "But I've been feeling a bit off as well."

Gilles gave me a quick glance before looking back to the street, "You said Dabriel was at your house earlier?"

"Yeah – but she wouldn't have dosed herself..." I stopped. "But Nick was there."

"You can't trust Nick Noir, Dante," Gilles said grimly. "I don't care if he's been blessed by the pope himself, he's not a good guy."

"Yeah, maybe...thinking about it now, my last drink was more draining than it should've been afterwards," I said, thinking about it. "Like a hard crash instead of a slow come down."

A look of concern fell over Gilles' face, "What if there are additional side-effects?"

"I don't feel anything worse coming on, so I hope it's just the energy drain," I said.

"Okay. I'll have one of my agents check your alcohol, see if they can find anything."

We arrived at the Lost & Found and I helped Naberius out of the car. Gilles gestured for us to be quiet and motioned that he was going to circle around to the back.

I nodded and looked around. Thankfully my Corona was parked where I'd left it.

"Dante?" Naberius whispered. "Where are we?" His face was pallid and beaded with sweat.

"Right outside the Lost & Found," I told him. I hoped whatever was wrong wasn't doing any permanent damage. If there had been something wrong with the alcohol, it was causing a slightly different reaction in all of us.

"Hey, Naberius. You and Dabriel. Does this mean you're like her?"

He sat down on the curb, and I sat next to him. He was shaking, but his breathing was steady. "Yeah, but just on our father's side. My mother was a NoWaver, hers wasn't."

"You're a werewolf?" I sputtered, staring incredulously at Naberius. "How did I not know this?"

Naberius gave me a condescending look as he measured out a few shots of whiskey. "The monsters inside are usually very well hidden. You should know that by now."

IT SEEMED like the storm might be heading back in our direction: wind whipped across the street carrying a spray of rain. The clouds were heavy above but looming much heavier on the horizon and scattering the skies with slashes of light and rumble. It wasn't going to be an easy drive back to Jessica's place.

"Let me make sure Gilles is okay. If the bar is clean, you'll be able to lie down in the back room."

He agreed and we started toward the door.

"You shouldn't be here," a voice said behind me.

I spun around to check the street—nobody. My hands went for my pockets to check for weapons. I had a few bottles, a couple of loose coffee beans, and I had my bar spoon. And I had a feeling that wasn't going to be enough.

I turned and saw Naberius was sitting by the front door of the Lost & Found. I'd heard nothing from Gilles. I needed to get into the bar, but not before I found out who was out here. I scanned the street, looking for the speaker, and called out. "Where should I be?"

I saw a shadow of someone, but I couldn't tell if it was male or female. Whoever it was stepped a little closer, but instead of being illuminated by the streetlight it only became a brighter shade of grey. The wind around me felt suddenly colder.

"You should be dead," the voice sneered. Now I knew it was a man. But I had no idea what kind of man. The voice was distorted, as if covered in a layer of static. "Let me reassure you that the fact you are not, is only temporary."

"If you wanted to kill me, you should have sent a bigger wolf," It was a shot in the dark, but it hit.

The man snarled and was suddenly about five meters closer to me, and somehow, he managed to remain obscured in darkness. I was able to make out something strange. He was wearing a bandolier full of tiny liquor bottles. And I thought my stash of miniatures was impressive. He had a goddamn Borracho belt.

"If she doesn't make it out of this, I will destroy you," his voice held a familiar accent, but I was pretty sure sticking around would be a bad idea.

Still, I was curious, and that pushed me closer. I tried to stare deeper into the darkness. Nothing changed, until I remembered something. I had the remnants of a Corpse Candle in my bag. Never let your leftovers go to waste, especially when they're good drinks. Without taking my eyes off the shifting grayness, I found the vial and finished it off.

"What was that?" The clouded man asked quickly.

"A little vision enhancer," I said. Another step forward.

The darkness stepped back in surprise, "You aren't supposed to do that," he whispered.

"You aren't supposed to play with werewolves."

The shape continued moving away from me. It raised a dark arm and pointed. Not at me, but behind me. He was whispering words I couldn't quite make out, but I did hear what seemed to be a British accent.

"If the wolves don't get you, perhaps the bats will..." The shadow said before pulling a bottle from its belt. The shadow drank some of the liquid, then before I could react, he splashed me with the remainder. "And as this begins, you shall find your end."

This man, or whatever it was, had power; probably more than I had. And I still didn't know what I had done.

"Why are you doing this? I don't even know who you are."

"All you need to know is that you are in my way, and there's only one way to fix that."

I looked towards the bar, hoping Naberius had made it inside, or Gilles had made it out, but he was still sitting on the ground. His head in his hands and his back against a wall. Before I could get back to him, a high-pitched whine reverberating on the outermost edge of my hearing pierced through me, followed by a goose-bump raising sound of what could only be described as a multitude of harsh whispers cutting through shadows. The sound broke and multiplied, while each whisper cut closer. It was coming from above, through the rain, through the clouds. I turned to look up and saw a black shape shifting in the sky. A black shape that split into many and then flew into thousands. I realized what it was and turned, yelling at Naberius.

"Get up!" I yelled, "Get inside!

It was a swarm of bats. Heading straight for me. The sky seemed to be turning coal black, and a mass of wings seemed to be covering my beloved Corona and moving like a wave through the air towards us.

I turned and ran towards Naberius, pushing towards the Lost & Found as the bats started to overtake and surround us.

"I think this is where I say goodbye," the shadow called after me. "If things were different, we could have made a good team."

Right there I almost recognized the voice, but I was distracted by the incoming wings of death and didn't have time to follow my thoughts. I moved as fast as I could towards Gilles. The rain had started again, which seemed to disorient the swarm for a second. A second that probably saved our lives. There was a screech of tires and Jessica swerved around the corner in a very familiar Lincoln. Someone in the passenger side…It was Murmur.

Jessica was flashing lights and honking the horn, completely disorienting and breaking up the cloud of bats as she raced towards us across the parking lot.

My body tensed up, ready for a crash, but instead, there was a harsh screech of brakes, and car doors slamming.

I cracked open my eyes to see Jessica and Murmur running towards us.

"Where's Gilles?" Jessica shouted.

"In the bar!" I pointed.

"Let's get in there," she ordered.

I GRABBED Naberius and pulled him towards the door. Jessica was ahead of me, and Murmur was behind me. I turned to look, and she had stopped. She was standing, legs akimbo, with her back to us and facing the bats.

"What are you doing?" I yelled.

She stood steady, silent, one arm pointed towards the incoming creatures, the other was stretching towards me. She held a vial in each hand.

"Naberius, follow Jess," I gave him a light push and turned back towards Murmur.

"Take these. I've got the bats held for at least ten seconds."

"That many?" I remarked wryly but grabbed the vials and ran towards the bar. Behind me I heard Murmur start chanting; "aóratos aéras aéras aóratos…"

Jessica and Naberius were at the door, but neither of them were going inside. They were both staring at me…past me. I turned around.

It was if there was an invisible wall between Murmur and the bats, but I could already see the barrier weakening. Bits and points of bat ears and wings were getting closer, pushing through an invisible viscous air.

"Murmur! Come on, run!"

She started backing towards us, still chanting. Once she got close to me, she instructed me to draw a line with the liquids in my hands.

I opened the vials and poured them out on to the ground. Murmur stood next to me, both arms still stretched out towards the bats.

"Skiá Fóvos Fotiá," she shouted.

The liquid hissed and sputtered, as if the ground was heated, and a thick smoke rose. A deep red glow appeared and started pulsating and forming a line between us and the bats. The smoke thickened and moved outwards, getting darker as it blanketed the area. If I squinted, I could barely make out what seemed to be a cyclone of bats spiraling, unable to break through the smoke. The reddish liquid on the ground shifted, small waves growing and spreading out underneath the whirling dervish until all of blackness was aglow with a scarlet shimmer. Then the scarlet became red, and the red became flames flickering like two thousand matches lit on the skin of the snake.

"Guys!" Jessica yelled behind us. "Come on."

I couldn't tear my eyes away from the spectacle of the writhing mass before me, in the sky and on the ground. Steam billowing from the tortured mass as the rain started to fall even harder. And it looked like the whole mess was about to explode onto my car.

I pointed towards the flames which were being sucked up from the ground and seemingly being swallowed by the bats, making their entire bodies look as if they were made of bubbling lava. There was a horrible hissing sound that grew into a high-pitched wail. All four of us covered our ears as the wail became a scream, the scream became a choking sound, and the choke became a rumble.

My eyes widened, "What the hell is happening?"

The whirlwind of bats pushed together into a black pulsating ball. A ball with two thousand wings and two thousand eyes, and it started spinning. As if it was putting itself out, the fiery red faded, and the smoke dissipated. And then it started growing.

The entire mass convulsed once and then burst. It was like a meteor shower of burning bat bits, but as they hit the ground around us, I realized it wasn't what it had seemed. The flesh, or whatever it was, dissolved and left bits of sickly green flesh. Not human, or animal. These bats had been pulled out of some sick imagination. Created to destroy us.

"Get in here, now," Jessica commanded, holding the door open, and we obeyed.

I pulled Naberius inside with me and Murmur followed, and Jessica slammed the door behind her once we were all inside.

"That's not gonna be easy to clean up," Naberius muttered.

"What the hell did you do that for?" I glared at Murmur as I leant against the bar.

She was crouched against the wall, next to Naberius, who was seated and cradling his head in his hands.

"Right. Like it was on purpose. I did the best I could under the circumstances. Had to use Ouzo for this, and my Greek is a little rusty. Could be worse though," She said, catching her breath.

"Could it?" I nodded towards Jessica, who was slowly making her way towards the back of the bar, her gun drawn.

Murmur nodded, "Probably. Should we follow her?"

"Until you figure out what to do with the bat ball outside, yeah."

"Me?"

"Yeah. You made it, you fix it."

"Will you two shut up," Jessica hissed from ahead of us.

We nodded and made our way to where she crouched, peering around a table.

"So now what?" I asked.

"It's Gilles. He's not alone," Jessica said, looking at me.

I glanced quickly above the seats and saw Gilles and another man with his back to us sitting in a booth at the far end of the bar.

"What should we do?" I whispered to Jessica.

"You should join us," A voice said, followed by a quiet but disdainful laugh.

Three of us moved up to the booth, letting Naberius remain where he was, and were greeted by a curt nod from Gilles, who looked either angry or annoyed. Hard to tell with him. He always looked annoyed. I stood and looked at Gilles' companion as Jessica and Murmur slid in next to Gilles.

"Earnest," I stated.

He gave me a tight-lipped smile, face shadowed under the brim of a cautiously tilted fedora. "Still messing with supernatural creatures that should not be messed with, are we? As if getting rid of a few DarkWavers wasn't enough, you also managed to create a Caldrius Vespertilio."

"I don't know what you think happened out there," I took a step backwards, pointed towards the door. "But whatever those were, they were attacking us. It was self-defense."

"Us? All I saw were those creatures being destroyed and tortured by magiks you created," Earnest retorted. "Plus, touches of a fire that seems to be similar to the ones you've been using to destroy DarkWavers."

"Come on. We both know that thing was called here by someone else, and as far as I know, in the ever-vigilant eyes of your law, I'm within my rights to defend myself against the creations regardless of the creator," I countered, trying to hide a sudden wave of exhaustion from Earnest.

Earnest Caan stood up as well, taking a step towards me. He gave me a look colder than the fire I had recently walked through and spat on the ground in front of me.

"Don't you dare speak to me of The Laws," he said. "I was here, prepared to play nice, but since you are obviously unwilling to help me, I'm using this latest infraction to make a claim against you. The Alliance will decide if your excuse is good enough."

He moved closer until I could smell his breath. Old mint and leather. His eyes were a nose away from mine. "And if it's your word against mine, your words are nothing."

The last thing I needed to deal with was the Alliance trying to place me in some supernatural drunk tank.

"Really?" I gave him a cool and collected look. "You think I'm going to play the bad guy here when you're the one trying to get your hands on the Crossroads? I'm still not going to help you. I've got bigger problems here, and if you're involved, I swear you'll be the one going down."

"Dante, stop it," Gilles hissed from the booth behind Earnest, but I couldn't.

"You should listen to the Agent. I've taken him off this case, so that means you're off too," Earnest cracked a grin that looked like it wanted to eat me alive. "And as for the Alliance? You'll need to give them more than a pretty speech, son. You'll need proof, and that's something you don't have. Some pissant making a living as a magic bartender isn't going to convince anyone otherwise."

"You got one problem, though," I challenged.

"Yeah? And what's that?" Earnest asked suspiciously.

"I have a witness," I pointed towards Murmur in the booth behind him.

"Today you have a witness. Who knows what you will have tomorrow," Earnest sneered, turned to give Gilles a nod, and then pushed past me to leave out the front door.

"Did he just threaten me?" Murmur asked.

"He definitely threatened you," Jessica said.

I sat down and felt slightly sick to my stomach. I didn't know if it was from something mystical or from Earnest. Either way, it didn't matter. The Alliance would come, and I'd be judged. It might help my case if I could find Christophe. If I could get him to speak on my behalf, I might be able to convince the Alliance that Earnest was planning on taking over the Lost & Found. It might not be enough, but it would shift the spotlight. I also knew if I could track down our mysterious bat master, I'd be able to prove I was the victim in this most recent assault.

"Earnest won't do anything," Gilles reassured Murmur. "I know how these guys operate. You'll just have to keep clear of him, if possible."

"And you let him take you off our case?" Jessica asked, staring at Gilles.

"I let him take us off one case. Trevor's death is evidently an Alliance matter, seeing as it was in a Waver bar. But..." Gilles paused for effect, "We still have a book to find, and if our book thief is also a murderer, so be it."

"I need a drink," I mumbled. "Anyone else?"

Everyone nodded.

I gave a wry smile and walked over to the bar. It still felt strange to be in the empty bar. I looked over at the piano in the corner and got hit by a flashback of another time. The music a soft dark lounge, playing melodic in the background thanks to Trevor. He sat at the piano, lost in his music. Naberius was busy wiping down tables and Dabriel was behind the counter.

"Dante."

I shook my head, the vision cleared, and Naberius was standing in front of me, "I said I'll take a shot."

"Oh, sorry. Zoning out. You feeling better?"

Naberius gave me a strange look, "Better than completely horrible."

Murmur came over from the table and joined us. A soft whisper, "Everything good?"

"As good as it can be. We're alive," I answered. "Thanks. And why are you here?"

"Right. It's Kurtis. I think he's up to something. And I'm worried Marinette could get hurt."

I glanced back at the booth where Jessica and Gilles were still talking. "Okay, don't tell the others about this, and I'll see what I can find out. In the meantime, what'll it be?"

"Something to take the edge off," Naberius said, rubbing the back of his neck.

Murmur looked back at the table, smiled, and placed an order. "Make it a round of Drunken Boats, and don't skimp on the Absinthe."

I set my bag on the counter, pulled out some of the bitters that had helpful healing properties, and started to mix some drinks. Gilles and Jessica joined us at the bar and for a second, I could pretend nothing was wrong. There were people in the bar, old friends and new. And all the evil in the world was outside of the walls that surrounded us. And maybe it would stay out there.

I emptied my pockets, placing the coffee beans on a napkin, and started gathering a few little bottles from under the counter.

"Stocking up?" Murmur asked.

"Yeah. I have no idea what's coming next, but something will."

"I know you guys have no reason to trust me; I get that," Murmur shifted an empty glass back and forth between her hands. "And I am still on Marinette's side. She's very complicated, and a very amazing person. But I don't trust Kurtis, and I think there are forces at work that affect all of us, and I'm here to help."

Our conversation moved from fire curses to exploding bats, to owls that hid in the shadows. Then after drinking a couple of strange concoctions courtesy of Naberius, we started really talking.

Murmur was trying to figure out what direction to take with her alcohol and Gilles was trying to stare through a glass of whiskey. Jessica was trying to relax after a long day of dealing with crazy bat demons and I was learning new things about my bartending friend. One of the things I learned was that Naberius wasn't as much of a douchebag as he pretended to be.

"I need to keep everyone at some sort of distance," he explained, "Because I can't afford to let my darkness hurt anyone."

"Does Gilles know about your…lineage?" I asked Naberius.

He didn't.

"Are you serious?" Gilles burst out.

"Serious as a silver bullet," Naberius replied.

Gilles slowly turned towards me, "Did you know about this?"

"I just learned recently," I explained.

"Is he a good one?" Gilles asked, eyeing Naberius suspiciously.

"No," Murmur laughed. "He makes a lot of mistakes."

I snorted, "And you should be extra nice to him around the full moon."

"Alright, enough with the comedy routine," Gilles said abruptly. "Right now, we have more important things to worry about. Dante, you need to find somewhere else to stay. Your place is a complete mess and a crime scene. I know you didn't trash your own house, but I have some questions."

"Ask away, but I still don't have all the answers."

"All right. First question," Gilles leant forwards, elbows on the bar. "What happened to Naberius, was he drugged?"

"I think I might be able to answer that one," Murmur replied, looking at one of the bottles of bitters I'd pulled out from my bag. She held it up and studied it curiously. "I think something has altered the composition of your liquids."

"Wait, really?" I asked, confused. "But they seemed to work exactly as they were supposed to."

"Are you sure?" She opened the tiny bottle and turned upside down on her finger, then placed her finger on her tongue.

"Was that smart?" Naberius asked.

"Smarter than using them in a drink, evidently. I know how things are supposed to taste," she gave him a narrow-eyed glare and continued.

"And?" Gilles asked impatiently.

Murmur gave Gilles a stare harder than the one she'd just given Naberius, "And someone's added wolfsbane, or, more likely, a derivative of it. It didn't seem to affect Thomas as much, but it hit Naberius and Dabriel."

"I have been feeling a little drained recently," I muttered. I was slightly relieved to learn it wasn't because I'd been drinking too much.

"So, who messed with it? And were the wolf twins targeted?"

Murmur shrugged, "Don't know, but I'll bet whoever did this knows a lot about Botanicals and is also not going to make it easy to track them down."

"Dabriel's going to be all right, yeah?" Naberius asked, looking up at Murmur.

She leaned over and placed the back of her hand against his forehead and gave him a soft smile, "Seeing as you're getting better, I'm pretty sure she'll recover as well."

"Do you know where she'd go if she was in trouble?" Gilles demanded.

"I don't know. She hasn't been confiding in me recently. She was super upset by the fire, but that's understandable. I thought I'd give her some space. I didn't know she was going to go all crazy Waver on us."

Gilles stood up, "I'm calling this in. We need to find her. Did she take the book? Kill Trevor?"

Naberius looked up, "Seriously, I don't know. Not after what happened tonight. She might have. Dabriel thought she was in line to inherit the Lost & Found and believed the Intoxicantata was part of that deal. I know Trevor had talked about that, but when Dante the golden boy came back, Trevor changed everything. Dabriel's whole attitude changed. You never saw her when she wasn't working, but trust me, she was not happy. I tried to stay out of it, but she's still like family."

"That's why she's trying to kill me?" I asked.

"She didn't want you dead, Dante. This wolfsbane, or whatever it was, pushed her in that direction. She'll come out of it," Naberius said. "This place, you know how special it is. And even Alliance law can't break the chain of ownership. Marinette and her clan wanted it too, but she was settling for a merger after the bookstore went under. Thing is, Dabriel just wanted it all for herself, so that kind of put Dante in the middle of the bar wars."

"And you didn't say anything until now?" I asked, annoyed.

"I didn't think it would come to this. Honestly. If I'd known, I'd have told you," Naberius shrugged and moved around to my side of the bar and lined up a couple of shot glasses. "I just want to make drinks, Dante. If you're the boss at the Lost & Found, I'm cool with that. You can have the power and responsibility that goes along with it."

"Great. That clears everything up," I said, moving around to sit on one of the bar stools. I was lying. It didn't. "Was Dabriel's mother a NoWaver like yours?"

Naberius shook his head, "No. Her mother was Elemental."

"So maybe that's why the two of you had different reactions to the mix?"

"It's possible," Naberius conceded.

I absently went through my bag, placing everything on the bar, while thinking about what Naberius had said. Naberius watched me and then crouched down behind the bar for a second. He reappeared with a handful of small amber bottles. He placed them in front of me.

"These might come in handy. I don't know what's coming next, but I have a feeling it won't be good."

I examined the bottles. Unscrewing each dropper lid and wafting the contents towards my nose. Six bottles, six distinctly powerful, yet strangely subtle fragrances. I tried to make out the label,

"Ardentness Ardere?"

"This is the good stuff," Naberius said.

I WAS CURIOUS. Naberius hadn't been this nice to me in, well, ever. I inhaled the breath of each bottle; Coffee, Grapefruit, Cherry…and it wasn't simply cherry. It was like perfectly ripe fruit fresh off the tree during the best day of a childhood summer. All the scents were like that. The bottles held more than the obvious fragrance; they held the power of memory as well. Each bottle unlocked a vivid image from my past. Black pepper took me straight to one of my first nights at the Lost & Found, when Dabriel showed me how to make a Marigold Mary. It's almost identical to a traditional Bloody Mary but using only yellow heirlooms and a touch of Galliano, with pepper on the rim alongside infused vodka.

The orange bitters were warm and filled with a citrus flashback, and then I opened the last one. Atmosphere Absenta. The first hint was anise, but it was quickly surrounded by a light fennel drift and mint stained aroma. I was suddenly lost in a vision from ten years earlier. Staying up all night with Jessica after we'd tracked down a haunter in the old Woodward's building. It had been an exhausting couple of days, so we decided to celebrate at a little obscure after-hours bar off Marine Drive. It was called Oversoul. It's not there anymore, but it was a beautiful little bar. We had a couple of perfectly made Death in The Afternoons, even though it felt more like death after midnight. Two drinks turned into six, the night turned into morning, and we walked out of the bar like we were walking out of a dream. That's what the bottle of bitters smelled like. Like walking out of a dream. I was almost floating. So much so that I didn't even hear Gilles.

"Thomas..." Jessica nudged me.

"What?" I blinked my eyes a couple of times. I almost forgot where I was.

"Gilles is asking about the bats," Jessica whispered.

"Oh, right. Makes sense here that it was Christophe," I said

"Damn crazy vampire, right?" Naberius gave an awkward chortle.

"And the owls came from Kill City? Marinette?" Jessica blurted.

I turned towards Murmur, "Do you think Marinette would send owls to attack someone?"

"To go after Christophe? I wouldn't put it past her," Murmur confirmed.

"So on top of everything else, Marinette and Christophe are fighting a turf war and we're in the thick of it."

Gilles pushed his thumb against the center of his forehead, right above his nose, as if trying to stave off a headache. It looked like it wasn't working. "Owls, bats and wolves, oh my..."

I took a deep breath, "There's something else, Gilles, or someone else."

Gilles gave me a look of annoyed impatience. "Spill it, Dante."

"Nick Noir," I said slowly, "He was at the house, left right before Dabriel went crazy."

Gilles said nothing, which said volumes.

"But I don't think it was him. He seems different. He made it clear he had no reason to harm me. And he had nothing to do with what happened to Jessica."

"I'm not about to take your word for it, but right now there's more pressing matters. We need to find the Intoxicantata and put an end to whatever's going on between Christophe and Marinette before it spills out into the rest of the city. It's already causing too much chaos and the Agentia is being spread way too thin."

I looked at Naberius, "You know where she is, don't you?"

Naberius closed his eyes for a second, then looked at me before leaning across the bar. For the first time I realized the scent I'd always smelled when he was around wasn't dog, but wolf. He gave me a half smile, "Yeah. I might. But you're not going to be able to take her on your own."

"Gilles?" I turned to him.

"Yeah, I can get some back-up. But you need to stay out of this one."

Murmur and Jessica silently watched us like we were some sort of soap opera.

"Because of the Alliance," I said softly.

"Yeah. Because of the Alliance," Gilles said. He placed a hand on my shoulder and gave it a small shake. "Look, we've known each other for ages, but you've always been a hard person to talk to. Did you know that I worked with your father?"

I looked at Gilles, "Wait. What?"

"You're a lot like him. He was a superb Mystixologist, and his library," Gilles shook his head, "It was the envy of the Alliance. He came in to consult on several cases, and most of them were ones I was working as well."

"He never told me."

"He didn't want you to know. He never wanted you involved with this side of things. He didn't want you working at the bar either, but there's only so much parents can do."

I could feel myself getting angry. "Did Jessica know?"

I looked over at her, she shook her head.

"No. Your dad was a little more on the CI side. We didn't want to jeopardize him, or his family. He was far too valuable as an informant."

"Who else knew," I asked and then paused. "Did Earnest know?"

Gilles nodded, "Yeah, Earnest. But listen, your dad did not get along with the Alliance, but thankfully he was okay with the Agentia. And he made me promise if anything happened to him, I'd look out for you, make sure you kept your nose clean."

"So that's why you've always been so hard on me?"

"Your dad…your parents. They were both so proud of you. But I had to keep you safe, and you weren't ready to follow in your father's footsteps. Still, I knew Trevor would make sure to keep an eye on you at the bar, and I knew you'd pick up a few things working here. Like your mom did."

"Trevor knew?"

"Yeah. He wasn't working with us, but he would do anything for your parents, and you. Then when everything went down with the fire and Nick Noir, the Alliance stepped in. The Alliance, with all their rules, made sure that if you stayed at the bar, you'd be okay, but step outside of that role and there would be trouble. And I was tasked to make sure you stayed in line," Gilles chuckled, "Which was not easy."

"Sorry," I shrugged.

"Your DarkWave dealings were to be limited to Mystixology. No elemental dabbling, no Dead Magic messing. I know you've got talents, but the only reason I was allowed to involve you was because of your affiliation with the bar. And Jessica put in a good word, lord knows why."

"So why are you telling me all of this now?" I asked. I knew about the conditions that had been laid down, but I'd had no idea that Gilles had been my secret guardian. DarkWavers generally don't talk about the DarkWave, but still…this seemed like important information. I'd known I was working in a DarkWave bar, of course, but I hadn't known which clans I'd been rubbing elbows with. I guess until now, I hadn't really cared.

“Now? Because I don’t like Earnest, and I’m not happy with the Alliance. Besides, you’ve proven yourself to be a good detective and an even better Mystixologist. Besides, with all these DarkWave shenanigans going on, I figure we are all in this together,” Gilles sighed, shook his head. “And let’s get another round of those Drunken Boats. It’s going to be a long night.”

17
FIREWATER

The long night turned into a slow morning. I opened my eyes and for a second, I had no idea where I was. Then I saw the gum stalactites covering the underside of the table and remembered I was at the Lost & Found. I sat up in my bedtime booth and stared at Naberius, who was sitting across from me. He was spinning a cigarette between his fingers with his eyes focused somewhere between the table and an alternate universe.

I gave him a concerned look. "You alright?"

Naberius looked startled, "Oh, right. Sorry. Little distracted."

I looked around, head pounding, Jessica was lying down in a booth with an arm crooked over her eyes, Gilles was in another booth, leaning against the wall, hat crooked over his head. There was a cough behind me. It was Murmur, sitting up and stretching in the booth behind me. She gave me a little smile. "I guess the sleepover's done?"

"Yeah," I said, echoing her stretch. "Last night was good, but we need to get back on it."

"Right" Jessica was up, standing and rubbing her eyes. "We need some fresh air. This bar is getting a little stale, and I need to clear my head, sort things out. Hangover ain't helping either."

Gilles gathered his stuff, "Jess, I can give you a ride home."

"Yeah. That works," She mumbled.

Naberius nodded towards Gilles, "You have the keys, right?"

"Yeah," he said, patting down his pockets to make sure.

"Good," Naberius said, "I'm going to try and track down my sister. Don't call this in yet. Let me talk to her."

"Are you sure?" Gilles asked.

Naberius nodded and left without another word.

"What's with him?" I asked.

"He's worried about Dabriel. You know better than anyone that family is complicated. Whatever's going on with her has got to have him a little freaked out," Gilles said, then looked at Murmur before looking back at me, "Look, why don't the three of us continue this talk. I'll drop Jessica off at home, and then we can meet somewhere?"

"The café?" I suggested.

Gilles gave the thumbs up, and I followed him to his parked Crown Vic. I said goodnight to Jessica and Gilles gave me a serious look, "What's up? You look kind of anxious."

"Well yeah, this case. It's starting to get a little too close to home. I don't just mean Trevor, but now it goes back to my parents. And I'm not sure I can handle it. My powers are still locked, Earnest seems to want my head, and we're getting caught in the middle of some voudou werewolf war? I don't know where it's all going, and I don't know if I want to," I shoved my hands into my pockets. "And then there's Nick. You're right. I shouldn't trust him. He's holding onto some secrets. And I can't prove he messed with my alcohol, but he was in my attic."

Gilles narrowed his eyes, "Yeah, we'll figure it out. Definitely. First, I need to get Jessica home. See you at the café."

"Sounds good."

I walked back to Murmur and looked at my car. It was covered with supernatural bat remnants, but it should be okay to drive. Unlike Jessica's car. The tires had melted, and the mystical bat guts had completely cooked and caked the front windshield.

"Need a ride?" I asked.

Murmur looked extremely irritated, her arms folded across her chest, "I do."

. . .

We pulled out of the parking lot, and even though Murmur was glaring out the window I allowed myself a small smile. Things weren't great, but Murmur seemed to be wanting to help, and Gilles was turning out to be an okay guy. I was getting glimpses of the side he never showed, and it wasn't all bad. And it also felt good to feel as if I wasn't alone in the world.

When we arrived at the café Mori was putting cups away behind the counter. She gave me a big smile as we walked in, "It's been ages, hasn't it," she joked.

"Ha ha. So how about a coffee?"

"The usual?" Mori asked.

I nodded just as Gilles arrived, sauntering into the café, "Make it three."

Mori started on the coffee and the three of us moved to a table. He looked a little uncomfortable. "What's going on, Deuxcoeurs?"

"Okay, so believe me, I never thought I'd be talking about this with you…" He started, fidgeting with the napkin in front of him.

"I'm really not that bad," I said.

"No, no you're not," he sighed, "it's, well, I guess I'm a little jealous."

"You mean Jessica? There's nothing there to be jealous of. Not anymore." Bonding time with Gilles Deuxcoeurs. Something I never thought would happen. And we weren't even drunk. Maybe we should have been. Mori interrupted with our Burnt Almond Mochas.

"Maybe we can make these a little more Irish?" I pleaded.

Mori agreed to break out her stash of whiskey if we didn't drink it all. I sat for a minute letting the warmth fill my chest before speaking.

"Gilles, I understand the jealousy thing. I feel it when I see you and Jessica working together. But it's more of a nostalgic jealousy. Jess and I are friends."

"I'm going to have a little chat with our barista and let you have your guy talk in private," Murmur said with a wink.

Gilles scratched the back of his head, "Sorry, this is kinda awkward, right? Awkward…guess with you it couldn't be any other way. One of these days you'll have to tell me about that nickname."

I grasped the steaming mug in front of me and stared down into it. Trying to find an answer in my caffeine. Jessica and I were old friends holding a broken heart between us, although I was pretty sure she'd let her half go a long time ago. I wasn't sure why I was still holding on to mine.

"Yeah, one of these days I might," I shrugged.

Gilles gave me a quick smile and continued, "I've been working with Jessica for a while now. We only started talking about a… different kind of relationship recently. We've been on a couple of dates, but she's really focused on her job."

"Some things never change," I said.

"I guess not, but when she's around you she seems so much more relaxed. I just wish I made her feel the same way you seem to."

"Listen Gilles, relaxed just means she knows me better. Doesn't mean she likes me better. The best advice I can give you is to just be yourself around her. Be honest, share things, talk to her about the crap that goes on outside of work."

Gilles stared down at the counter, looking slightly embarrassed, "Right, yeah…"

"So, just to randomly change the subject," I said. "What are we going to do about Christophe? Can you have the Agentia pick him up?"

"We'll get him, but it seems he's playing a little hard to get, for obvious reasons," Gilles said. "Look, I don't know exactly what's going on yet, but you're obviously in danger."

I laugh, "I'm not in danger, I'm in Vancouver."

"Don't take this lightly, Dante. Someone's playing with supernatural creatures and setting people on fire, and it seems as if now you've got a target on your back."

I agreed with Gilles, "I know, it's a little out of control. But listen. What if Christophe has the Intoxicantata, and Marinette obviously wants it – but I think now Dabriel is willing to kill for it…"

Gilles tilted his head and gave me a concerned look, "Then we need to find Christophe before she does."

"Yeah," I said. "That's probably a good idea. Do you know where he lives?"

"No. We know where he works, but we've had no luck finding a home address. It's not in the database," Gilles pulled a phone out of his jacket pocket. "We'll find it, though."

"Okay, great," I muttered. "What next?"

Gilles looked up at me after calling in a skip trace, "Team up and take 'em out."

I raised my coffee like a cheer. I was feeling a little freaked out, but thanks to the whiskey I was feeling a little devil-may-care as well.

"Right," he said, as Murmur came back to the table. "I'll follow up on our full moon friends. I'll send you Christophe's address as soon as we get it, and you can try to get some real answers from him."

"Sounds like a plan?" I shrugged.

Gilles finished the rest of his drink. "Alright. I'm going to go check in on Jessica. You okay here? You can't go home yet…"

"Yeah, I'll be fine," I nodded back towards Mori, "I think I might be able to crash at her place since my home's a bit of a mess."

Gilles and I stood outside of the café. Murmur had left in a cab for Kill City, and I felt as if I was still drenched in the scent of late-night bar life. My clothes were stained with alcohol, and my body hurt. I stood there for a second, letting a cool wind wash over me. I took a deep breath. It was going to rain again.

Gilles' phone started buzzing. He answered, "Deuxcoeurs here."

He listened for a couple of seconds, hung up, and turned to me.

"Dante," his tone was serious. "There's been another death."

"Who…"

"They haven't ID'd the body yet, but it's at Blundertown."

I tried to ask him for more information, but he ignored me and kept a grim expression locked on his face. The intensity of the silence made my head hurt.

My head had mellowed into a slow quiet rumble, which turned into a sharp static hiss as soon as we arrived at Blundertown Books.

We parked and got out of the car. Gilles striding ahead of me towards the door where agents waited.

THE WEATHER FOLLOWED me across the empty parking lot, a strange humidity thickening the sunlight. It left a taste of rain on my tongue. Yellow striped tape wrapped around the building and three cop cars were parked askew in front of it. Gilles' had parked on the other side of the street. One officer stood by the entrance, and another held a position closer to 4th Avenue, making sure any pedestrians kept moving. Otherwise, it seemed like a very tame crime scene.

I exhaled slowly and waited a second. I wasn't sure what to expect, but I had a feeling it wasn't going to be good. Last time I was here, Nick Noir had been squatting. The store wasn't open for business, so the list of possible victims was very small. I walked inside. Gilles was already in the middle of the store, talking to an officer. He glanced up as I entered. He looked worse than I felt.

"Dante," he nodded.

"Who is it?"

"Follow me."

We walked towards the back office. There were two other officers in the bookstore one of them searching the shelves, the other talking to a young woman. It was a young woman who looked to be barely in her twenties. She moved squirrel-like, shifting back and forth as the officer questioned her. She kind of looked like a squirrel too. Small, freckled face and chestnut hair pulled back into pigtails. She wore a mousy brown skirt, a yellow windbreaker, and dirty pink Nikes.

"Who's that?" I asked.

"Jules…something," Gilles shrugged. "My guy's talking to her. All I know is that she works with Christophe, part-time, but has no idea where he is."

I nodded, and moved towards Christophe's desk, "Okay…"

"Don't touch anything," Gilles said.

"Why would I?" I stopped, looked at Gilles. "You don't trust me? Am I still a suspect? I've been with you…"

"I know, just covering all the bases," he said. "Especially since the scene has a couple of similarities to what happened at the Lost & Found."

"But after last night…" I started.

Gilles rubbed his forehead, "I know. But this is my job. I've got people I need to answer to, and things are getting kind of complicated."

"What do you mean, kind of?" I asked, distracted by a leak in the ceiling near the door. It wasn't a leak, I realized, but a circle of condensation. "Can you start a fire using water?"

"What?" Gilles spun around and stopped me with a hand to my chest, "What did you say?"

I waited for a second as one of the officers led Jules out of the store. She looked nervous, I thought. Not guilty, but uncomfortable.

I didn't blame her – these officers had a way of making everyone feel like they were guilty. I gave Gilles a dirty look.

"What?"

"Nothing… anyhow, water, firewater…" I mumbled. "Not sure but it could be something to investigate. Rain can be a powerful addition to some recipes and water can be used as a magnifying lens."

"Why didn't you mention this earlier?" Gilles narrowed his eyes.

"I didn't think of it until now. Besides, I could be wrong," I pushed my hair back, trying to focus. On the night of the fire at the Lost & Found it had been raining. There had been rain when the bat-things appeared as well. If Dabriel is using her elemental heritage, and combining it with a strong knowledge of cocktails, things could get crazy. Or crazier. Especially here in rain-fall city. And if it was all connected to water, then the whole Fire elemental angle was a red herring. And if I could prove that? I'd be off the hook.

"So, who is it?" I asked.

Gilles walked into the office as he answered my question, "Kurtis."

I stopped in my tracks. "Kill City Kurtis?"

"Yeah," Gilles grumbled. "At least we know our friend Murmur didn't have time to do this. Not so sure about the innocence of her boss."

. . .

Not sure what to expect, I walked into the back. Torn books and ripped pages littered the floor, the pictures on the walls were all askew, the frames shattered. Splinters of wood, plastic, and glass were everywhere. The desk was bare, and every drawer had been emptied and flung across the room. I didn't notice the blood until I saw that the wall behind me was covered in splashes of red. All kinds of red: crimson and thick, drying brick brown, fleshy pink and chunky, splattered, and scrawled. It was as if someone had sprayed the wall down with someone's insides and then proceeded to work on an unfinished finger painting. And all along the bottom of the wall, across the floor, lay broken bottles.

I had no idea how many bottles. Fifty? A hundred? All of them empty, but the only stains were of flesh and blood. My legs shook a little, but I wasn't going to fall. I fought the urge to lean against the desk behind me and instead stepped closer to the blood-soaked wall. The markings weren't all random. I recognized some of them. "Vévés."

"Yeah," Gilles muttered, "I noticed that too. They show up somewhere else."

"Do you know what they mean?" I turned back to the wall and tried to not sound anxious.

Gilles scratched the back of his head, "These ones are usually used to call up the Loa and invite them in. Either into your presence, or into a body."

"Like a reverse exorcism?" I asked.

"Pretty much. It's the Voudou possession ritual. Only this doesn't make sense. The Invisibles are given much respect, and there are rules…" He explained.

"There always are and they're always broken," I interrupted.

"Yeah, but the Loa wouldn't possess the unwilling. Although they have been known to possess the dead. I think these markings were made for a summoning. Either to bring the Loa into the conjurer or one of their disciples. Kurtis's body is here, so he wasn't possessed, and if he did the summoning, they wouldn't have…"

The smell was getting to me. Feeling dizzy, I lifted my shirt to my mouth and tried to breathe through it. Slow breaths, not too deep. "All right. I need to see him."

Gilles gestured to behind the desk. It took me five steps to get close enough to see and three steps backwards to get away from it.

I wouldn't have been able to tell it was Kurtis if it hadn't been for the red suede shoes on his feet. I held back a choking sound, covering my mouth with the back of my fist. The body was sprawled, what was left of it, underneath the desk. His torso ended too soon, caving out into a hollow shell that emptied into a charcoaled mess shaped somewhat like a neck and a head. But there wasn't enough substance to make up a head. There were guts, though. Ribs splayed open to reveal a mess of innards; intestines, a soft bluish grey scooped over the liver, spleen, and indistinguishable segments of flesh. A Vévé was burned into the sickly mass like someone had used a laser beam to etch the design. I walked outside, and went around to the lot in the back, sat down, and didn't throw up. I needed a cigarette.

GILLES APPEARED a couple of minutes later. He didn't say anything. He sat next to me as I exhaled a thin stream of smoke. One cigarette left.

Kurtis had been disemboweled and burnt, his blood had been used to scribble symbols, and his heart had been taken. "Someone was very angry about something, I think," Gilles said quietly, eyes focused on the ground in front of him.

I examined the embers in my cigarette, and finally looked up at Gilles, "There's no way you could think I had anything to do with this."

"I know you're involved; I'm just not sure how. I realize this couldn't have been you; the timing puts you with me at the café, but I'm not in charge of this investigation. I'm here as part of the clean-up crew. This went straight to the Alliance."

"The Alliance?" I asked. "I thought they didn't deal with this side of things."

Gilles spat on the ground, "All I know is I got a call because there's too many DarkWaver bodies piling up, which means the Agentia is being pushed to the sidelines, and the Alliance is bringing in one of their heavy hitters."

"Fantastic…" I started.

Gilles held up a finger, "I'm supposed to work with the Vancouver police and keep this contained and quiet. Dabriel and Christophe are still unaccounted for. We're also going to talk to Marinette and Murmur."

What was going on? I kept my face stoic. The way Kurtis had died seemed to point towards Marinette, but at the same time, it felt way too obvious. And we had no proof Dabriel was involved, only suspicions. I needed a solid lead. "I need to go back inside."

Gilles led the way, giving tight salutes to the cops stationed outside the door. I looked towards the office, but I wasn't ready for that yet. I started walking around the room, taking quick mental notes of the scene. The cash register at the front counter was open and empty.

"How long has the bookstore been closed, officially?"

"According to the receipts, the last transaction was over a week ago," Gilles stood next to me. He looked tired. "So, it's been closed at least that long, although evidently not empty. Check this out."

Gilles led me around a corner rack overflowing with books. He stopped about a meter from the wall and reached over to hand me his flashlight. I peered behind the rack. More books, scattered, torn pages littering the floor. A few bottles of wine, unbroken. Someone had started using this place as their favorite bar before it had even become one. Three of the bottles were empty, one had been opened recently. And a sleeping bag.

"Nick was staying here," I said.

"Yeah," Gilles said. "As far as I can tell."

"Any news on where he is?" I asked.

"Not yet," Gilles said.

"And what about Earnest Caan?" I asked, wondering if Gilles had more info on the Alliance man than he'd let on.

"He wouldn't do this. If he was involved, it would not be hands on,"

Gilles said, eyebrows rising questioningly. "Do you really think he has something to do with what happened here?"

"Not sure. But something really feels wrong," I said, looking around. "Did you know he owns this place?"

Gilles shook his head slowly, "No. So that would mean he has a key."

"Yeah. I think you might want to check on his whereabouts, probably quietly."

"Yeah. Quiet would be a good idea. So where does that leave us now?" Gilles sighed and pulled a small black book out from his inside pocket and flipped through the pages, "Nick, and Trevor, were both working with Christophe in some capacity. Now Trevor's dead and Nick and Christophe are missing. Dabriel's involved but can't find her either. Naberius…"

"Naberius is good, as far as I'm concerned."

"And we've got drinks turning up at the Drunken Abbott," Gilles continued. "Presumably from the Intoxicantata, along with a dead DarkWaver. We know there's been a feud between Kill City and the Lost & Found, which points towards Marinette. Especially with the Vévés found here. I'm not sure how Blundertown, or Earnest Caan, fit into the picture, but it looks like between Marinette and Christophe, we've got two strong suspects."

"Add Dabriel as a possible third," I pointed out.

"Right, but there must be something else. A big missing piece. What if Christophe is trying to frame Marinette? I know there's no love between those two," I pointed out. "She was ready to rip my head off because she thought I was working with Nick."

Gilles was nodding and taking notes. He looked up at me without raising his head, "And you don't think she'd throw her Voudou around like this?"

"No, but I do think you should talk to her at Kill City," I suggested. "Just try to stay calm. You know she can get a bit emotional. And don't make any Voudou jokes."

"Those are the suspects I love talking to," Gilles said, still writing. "Crazy with no sense of humor."

"We should take another look around here first," I said, kneeling. I checked around the edges of the sleeping bag, finding nothing. I started thinking about Dabriel and Naberius, and the voice of the mystery man hidden in cloud and shadow, it had to be Christophe. I was so lost in thought I didn't realize the Alliance had arrived until a shadow loomed over me.

I stood and turned quickly.

Earnest Caan stood in front of the doorway, looking stylish and aloof as he surveyed the damage. His eyes passed over us without seeming to register our existence. I wanted to punch him. I didn't. He walked towards the back room. Gilles gave him a nod, and I just gave him a slight sneer, which he returned in kind.

Gilles gave a quiet laugh, "You sure know how to make friends, Dante."

"I don't need friends, I need answers," I mumbled.

"Thomas Dante," Earnest's voice boomed from the back room. He was in front of me in seconds, shaking a piece of paper in front of my face. "What have you been up to?"

I grabbed the paper out of his hand. It had been torn from a notebook. Mine. It was splattered with blood, but my name and number were still visible. Two thoughts raced through my mind. The first was *oh goddamn*.

Like I needed any more evidence linking me to dead bodies.

The second was a realization that the Agentia was not going to be able to examine this evidence. It was going straight to the Alliance. If I was going to hang for this crime, Earnest wanted to be the one holding the rope.

Gilles looked more disappointed than shocked. Earnest snatched the paper back and shoved it in a plastic bag. They were both waiting for answers, but for different reasons. Gilles wanted me to justify his trust, while Earnest wanted me to confess my guilt. Either way all I had was my word, and it was possible neither of them were going to accept that now.

"Gilles," I said, "I was with you all night – once you get official TOD it'll show I wasn't here. I'd say we need to find Nick."

"Yeah, but I wasn't awake all night, Dante," Gilles said.

"I know. But I know it wasn't me," I said.

"So, what do you suggest we do about this?" Earnest said, gesturing towards the back room.

"Look, here's what I know. Someone tried to frame Nick for the death of my parents, and he convinced me he wasn't involved," I said.

"But you were," Gilles added. "That's when the Alliance put you on probation. You were the one with the fire power."

"And that's why your elemental powers are supposedly useless," Earnest said quietly, "But like handcuffs, curses can be unlocked. Especially if you have something like the Intoxicantata to work with."

I was starting to get flustered. I had to keep cool, because it seemed as if I was the only one who knew I was innocent. "Gilles, I swear it wasn't me. I know you've got your politics involved here, and don't want to mix things up between the Alliance and the Agentia, but you know this clown is not interested in the truth. If we get Nick, he'll give us more answers, And I'd say Dabriel and Christophe have more to answer for than I do. I mean, Dabriel wants control of the Lost & Found. Maybe with her powers and Christophe's book, they're pulling all the strings..."

Gilles held up a hand as his phone rang, listened, said thanks, and hung up.

"We've got a lead on Rodrick, from Kill City. He's still a person of interest, but it looks like his alibi is solid. He's at the Drunken Abbott, and evidently Nick Noir was there as well. Three witnesses say they saw Nick leave the bar just before Rodrick got there."

"I think I'd like to talk to him," I said. "He might be able to lead us to Nick. But either way, you have to know I'm not the killer. Someone is working hard to set me up."

THE REMOVAL SERVICE HAD ARRIVED, and they were carting Kurtis's remains past me. The stench of death mixed with secondhand smoke wafted toward us and I almost retched.

Gilles turned and grabbed me by the coat lapels, pulling me until his nose was almost touching mine.

"If you are lying to me," he hissed through clenched teeth, "Or hiding anything from me, you will regret it. Someone brutally murdered this man, and if it was just the two of us on the case I wouldn't be as concerned, but Jessica is involved, and I don't want anything happening to her."

Gilles gave me a look that could rip the fire from a flame then pushed me away before storming outside. Earnest stood back watching, a big grin on his face.

"Shut up," I grumbled, brushing invisible dust off my coat. Earnest gave me a little salute and went to join Gilles. I followed.

Gilles stood in the parking lot, hands on his hips, studying the gathering storm clouds.

"Dante, I swear to god," He turned to look at me "You've got to give me more…hell, you've got to give me everything, or I can't help you."

I knew Gilles wanted to do his job, which was catching the bad guys, and I didn't want to get in his way. But this was getting personal, again. If Kurtis's murder was my fault, I'd have to live with the guilt, but I didn't want to pay for it as well. Someone else was responsible, and I was going to find out who.

"Gilles, I'm just as concerned as you are. Judging by the trail of dead, whoever did this won't think twice about killing any of us if we get in their way," I concluded. "And I know you can take care of yourself but there are some demons out there that could make both of us mincemeat."

Gilles didn't say anything, but he was upset. Angry upset. Then there was Earnest, standing beside him, looking as if nothing had happened. Heartless bastard. He had the strength of the Alliance behind him, which could be good, except he seemed to have his own agenda, which was not good. The Alliance had been known to sweep things under the DarkWaver carpet, so getting a couple of curious agents to vanish would be easy if it meant protecting a secret.

I watched as Kurtis's body was loaded into the ambulance and pictured the devastation inside the bookstore. I didn't want to; I couldn't help it. It was burned into my mind in vivid bloodstain red. I was not going to sleep easy anytime soon.

"GILLES, I wish I could give you more," my voice threatened to waver, crack, but I held it low and straight. "But I'm at a loss. We need to get everyone rounded up. I don't know how, exactly, but as far as I see it, there aren't any other options."

Gilles turned to Earnest. They walked away from me, talking out of earshot. Gilles gestured towards me angrily, Earnest ran a hand through his hair, glanced in my direction, and handed Gilles the bag containing the bloody piece of paper with my autograph.

Gilles started back towards me, and I could tell he trusted me about as much as a snake trusts a mongoose.

"Look, Dante," Gilles said when he reached me. His tone was cold and hard. "I'm going to need you to come down to the station and answer a few questions."

"Seriously?" I didn't have time for questions. I needed answers. "Gilles, I can't. Not now…"

"Earnest has agreed to let the Agentia take the evidence in. The page from your notebook," Gilles said, holding the evidence bag up in front of me. "We need to figure out how it got here."

"Let me go home, see if I can get a hold of Nick or Dabriel," I said. "You know I'm not going to run."

"Alright, but if you blow this off the Alliance can have you. I don't care," Gilles said.

"I get it," I replied and turned to leave.

Earnest moved in front of me and held up a finger, "I'm giving Agent Deuxcoeurs the evidence because I do not wish to aggravate the collaboration between the Alliance and the Agentia. But you don't deserve it."

"Just stay out of my way," I looked over at Gilles. "Thanks."

"Don't make me regret this," Gilles said. I could tell he was disappointed in me. I felt bad, but I had no choice. If I was a target, fine, but I didn't want anyone else getting caught in the crossfire.

"One more thing," Gilles said, "If you are behind this, or if this happened because of you, it won't matter where you go. You will be caught and made to answer for everything."

I knew Gilles wanted the killing to stop, as did I, but I also wanted to prove my innocence. And I needed more than my word to do that. I needed the other suspects, and some solid evidence. "I'm going to see what's salvageable at my place. And one last thing, you might want to watch the Lost & Found. If Dabriel can't have it, she might make sure no one else can. I don't think she'd hurt Naberius, but I'm not so sure about the building itself."

Gilles looked at me like I'd committed some supreme betrayal. I didn't even look at Earnest, though I knew his empty eyes were drilling holes into the back of my head. I felt like I was letting everyone down. Earnest, I didn't care about, but Jessica, Murmur, even Gilles.

I didn't like walking away from Gilles, but even worse was the feeling that I was walking away from Jessica. That was crushing. The hardest walk. I took a deep slow breath, prayed to the alcoholic gods of the gutters that I was making the right choice, and moved through the rain feeling more alone than I'd ever felt.

18
SOUL KISS

I left Blundertown as the rain shifted from a drizzle to a downpour. I couldn't focus on anything; I could only hold on to the regret and sorrow that surrounded me. I walked slowly to let the rain wash some of the sadness away. My car was still at the café, and my home was still a disaster. I didn't want to bother Mori, and Gilles... well, I was pretty sure he hated me now. I wasn't sure about Jess. Perhaps she hated me as well. My reasons for walking away, my reasons for not telling them the truth, meant nothing. Not right now. Right now, I wasn't really all that interested in proving my innocence. If I caught the person responsible, I might end up proving my guilt because I wasn't sure if I'd be able to let that person live. I needed to talk to Nick, find out more about who was behind the deaths of my parents. I might not want to give them to Gilles and find a way to take care of them myself. I probably needed to book a room at some lonely motel and gather my strength, my thoughts. My solidity.

I was so distracted by the weight of ruined relationships I barely registered the man walking towards me. When I sensed his presence, I stepped aside to let him pass, and he stepped aside in the same direction.

"Excuse me."

"No excuses," the man said. "Not for you."

"What?" I was suddenly on high alert. Considering the way things were going, if I was going to die, getting stabbed on the sidewalk while the rain came down seemed like a good way to go. I waited for the stab, but it never came.

"You're a little on edge, aren't you?"

I knew that voice… "Naberius?"

There was a quiet laugh, and he took a couple of steps back. "Yeah. Dante, I need your help."

"You can't sneak up on me like that, man…" I warned.

"Look, I know I'm a suspect. I can't take any chances, but I've gotta try to get Dabriel out of this."

I nodded, "Okay, but right now, I think I might be more of a suspect than you."

He moved closer, face coming out of the shadows, and I was facing the most pitiful version of Naberius I'd ever seen. He looked worse than I felt, and I felt like death warmed over.

"What happened to you?"

"After I left the bar, I tried to find my sister. She's not making this easy. I went to her place and found some demonic remains."

"What? Did you call the Agentia?"

"Are you kidding? I'm innocent, but I've got wolf written all over me, and judging by the bite marks, that corpse did as well."

"So, where is she?" I asked.

"Not sure. I lost track of her earlier, but I did overhear her talking to someone about being at the Lost & Found tomorrow night, and to get ready for a storm."

"Okay, I'm not ready to bring the Agentia into this yet either, but maybe if we can get to her before this storm, we can stop something bad from happening."

"Okay, so what now?"

I exhaled slowly, looking up at the night sky. The clouds were drifting, showing patches of stars floating in darkness.

"Do you have a car?"

He nodded.

"I need to go home. It's a little chaotic, thanks to your sister, but I need to recharge."

"Sorry," Naberius mumbled.

"It's fine," I shrugged, "Could have been worse, right?"

When we got back to my place, he sat on the couch as I tried to sort through a bit of the mess. "This is ridiculous," I muttered, giving up and sitting on a torn leather chair pushed against the window. I sat for a second, elbows on my knees, head between my hands.

"Dante?" Naberius said uncertainly.

"I'm fine," I stood up. "I just need a minute," I made my way to the bathroom.

I took off my jacket and studied my tired reflection a little unsteadily, thoughts spinning…and then I noticed something was missing.

"My amulet."

I placed my hands on the bathroom counter, I leant my head in and pressed it against my reflection in the mirror, took a deep breath and stared down at the empty sink. I feel stuck but part of me knew I could still figure this out.

"What?" Naberius called out from the living room.

I needed to remain calm. I splashed some water on my face, put my jacket back on, and walked out. "A necklace my mother gave me. It's gone."

We moved into the kitchen where I poured a couple of quick shots. Not the best weapon, but it'll do in a pinch, The Tequila Dead. I handed one to Naberius. "I want to check out the attic, but just in case…"

He nodded, and we slowly moved upstairs. I reached the top and was thankfully not met by someone who wanted to kill me.

"Well, it looks as if your home bar was spared," Naberius said, looking around.

I put the shot glass down with a sigh of relief. "Yeah, that's definitely a good thing."

"So, this amulet is important, right?" Naberius asked.

"Right," I moved to the bar set up and took stock of what I had to work with. "So, how do I find it…"

I absently pulled out my bar spoon and spun it between my fingers like a silver drumstick. I examined the bar as if answers would rise out of the marbled top. Instead, the answer came from Naberius.

"What about a Soul Kiss? I know it's not one of the good drinks, but it is a good bad drink."

He was right, a variation on it might work, and I didn't care which side of the coin this drink fell. I know where I'm going. I could knock back a row of Angel Hair shots and I'd still be a thousand miles from heaven.

If I used the Soul Kiss as a base, and added it to a Homecoming, I could possibly pinpoint the location of the amulet. Of course, that's if I had the right ingredients. I had the Amaretto, buried on the back of a shelf, but the Irish Cream I wasn't sure about. Hell, with the right alcohol I could probably whip up some reverse Voudou action and break the bastard's legs. But I was mad, not stupid. I needed to stay a little closer to the good guy side. The undiluted spray brings what is inside, out. The homecoming brings it home. And to tie it all together? I smiled to myself, the rain, and a drop of my blood.

"Alright, Naberius. Let's do this."

I grabbed a few things from the kitchen, including the last ounce of an old bottle of Bailey's and a needle from the sewing kit in the junk drawer. Then with a strength born of adrenalin and resolve; we moved outside.

"Which way?"

"Wait," I held a finger up.

I had to keep my measurements straight. I needed the rain, but I did not want to mix in it. A watered-down drink wasn't good for anyone. On the porch I pulled a few items out of my bag. A shot glass, a shaker, and the Soul Kiss mix. A hit of anise mixed with hints of lemon and rosemary. Add a dash of bitters, a splash of rainwater, a few shakes, the right words, and of course…the blood. A little jab with the needle, and that was that. Just a drop, needed to bind the ingredients and keep my special map quest moving in the right direction, and voila. Except what were the right words? I twirled the spoon like an alphabetical wheel, trying to hit the right letters.

"This is a different version," Naberius observed.

I gathered everything together and walked out into the rain, "This is the Soul Coming Home."

THE MIX WAS DONE; a few drops wouldn't change it now. I didn't have to get too tricky; this was more like making a toast.

Cheers to you, asshole, "Go n-éirí an bothar leat."

May your journey be a success.

I shot the drink back, the strange hint of citrus hidden in the sweet smoothness, and then the heat came, like a fever. Sweat on my forehead and goosebumps on my arms. There was a shimmer in the air like a mirage opening and unrolling. I turned in a circle, to orient the spell, and it stretched out ahead of me. A shimmering thread in the air, invisible to everyone but me.

"There we are…" I smiled.

Naberius squinted, "Nothing."

"My eyes only, but we've gotta move fast. One shot won't last long."

We got into the car and Naberius pulled out into the street. "Okay, we're moving. Just tell me where to go."

I nodded, "And what about Dabriel? Are you going to be okay if she doesn't want to be on our side?"

Naberius is a stoic wall of silence for a second, staring at the rain-soaked street in front of us, then he nodded.

"Yeah. Family is important, but this goes beyond that. We both owed Trevor so much, bringing us into the Lost & Found, taking care of us…" Naberius looked at me, and for the first time I saw the depth of the sadness he held inside.

"Where were you before you were at the Lost & Found?" I asked.

"That's a story for another time, Dante. Suffice it to say that we were being hunted. Trevor found us, hurt. He took us in and made sure we were safe," Naberius looked down at the ground, his voice softened. "If she had anything to do with his death, I would never forgive her."

"Look, I don't think Dabriel is that involved, she may be upset, and a little messed up, but I don't think she's the one using the Intoxicantata, and I'm pretty sure she's not the murdering type. She would have the knowledge on how to add something bad to the alcohol, and she's smart enough to work in some Voudou red herrings to throw everyone off track, but she's not the one sending evil animals after us," I tried to reassure Naberius.

"But the storm… I think she's tapping into the other side of her heritage. The wolf is moving into the rain."

"If that's true, it might make it easier to find her."

If Dabriel was somehow connected to the storm clouds gathering, it would be very draining. The more you create, the more that creation takes. It's true for mixing the drinks, it's especially true if you have elemental blood. Elementals are connected to nature, and nature is chaos. Chaos costs a lot of energy. Working with a storm would take a lot out of her, and if played right, that could give me an advantage.

"I think we might be heading for the Drunken Abbott," Naberius said, peering out at a passing street sign.

"I think you might be right."

The Abbott had been a central part of the punk scene in the '70s, but as it got dragged through the decades the clientele shifted more towards a local scene. That could have been good except the local scene at the Abbott consisted of criminals, rednecks, junkies, derelicts, and combinations thereof.

Perfect place to find a thief.

So, tracking down Dabriel might lead us to the book. It's also the last place Nick Noir was seen, which does not feel like a coincidence. And Rodrick, who might be double-crossing Marinette. So, find Dabriel, pull her from the dark side, get Nick to tell the truth, figure out if Marinette is involved, find Christophe, stop a storm, and wrap up all the loose ends like an innocence proving Christmas gift for Gilles. Easy. But first, my necklace.

I focused on the shimmer in front of me. It was still there, but it was going to fade soon. Didn't matter, we both knew where we were going.

The rain was slowing; the sun was starting to break through the clouds, low and ready to set. The clouds were stained with a vicious pink, and Naberius drove with the painted sky filling the rearview mirror.

19
DOUBLE SHOT DIABOLIQUE

The Drunken Abbott. A place usually inhabited by people you didn't want to be involved with; people you didn't want to know, people who you hoped didn't know you. We arrived just after sunset, but the approaching storm was making it seem even later. We parked a block away and tried to figure out the best way to approach the situation. As we got to the bar we noticed two small windows, both extremely dirty, on either side of the door. I attempted to peer through one. I made out the bar, a jukebox, and a small crowd of people milling about.

"What's the plan?" Naberius whispered next to me.

"We'll go around to the back patio," I replied, motioning for Naberius to follow, and we circled around to the small fenced off parking lot. We were still able to see through the wire gate and peered through the gaps. There were three empty tables, and one covered in pints. Four people sat around it, conversing between smoke and sips. I recognized Murmur and Rodrick immediately. Did Marinette know about this or was there some double-crossing going on? Then the other woman turned. It was the Bruxsa from the café. And next to her, one of those Asmodi demons. I ducked back behind the fence before they saw me. I was a little worried. If one of those demons was out there, there might be others inside. Naberius beckoned me over.

"I know Murmur and Rodrick, they both work for Marinette," Naberius whispered. "But the others?"

"They were at Four Calendar Cafe. The demon and the Bruxsa."

"The one looking for my sister?" Naberius asked.

"Yeah."

"I guess they haven't found her either"

I peered back around and watched for a second. The demon spawn was caught somewhere between its original form and the handsome human facade I'd seen earlier. The mix was not pretty to look at. The tiny horns twisting through slicked-back hair, the skin a strange shade caught between olive green and salmon pink. Almost a swirled skin tone. Walking up and saying hello wasn't the right thing to do, and jumping in guns blazing wouldn't go over well, especially with innocent bystanders inside.

"So, who took it?" Naberius asked.

I tried to remember the last time I'd seen the jewelry. "Someone from Kill City."

I pulled Naberius over to the side, behind a dumpster, and we crouched down to take stock of what we had. I wanted a big entrance, but not too big. I needed a distraction, and something that could keep the people inside from coming outside. I wanted these four alone.

"If you can take care of the people inside, I'll deal with the back porch crew," I suggested.

"Hardly seems fair, but I'm not going to argue."

I had the makings of a few special cocktails, my bar spoon, and a bottle of something awful smelling.

"Asafetida," I muttered, remembering.

But I should play it cool…or maybe not. I had a flash of memory hit the back of my head, and I knew what I could make for a weapon. The Double Shot Diabolique. Sometimes the garnish is everything. I emptied the small bottle of vodka into my shaker and topped it with Crown Royal and Butterscotch schnapps. Then something to represent a bullet. And I had a bullet. The one I'd dug out from the bar at Kill City. One bullet dropped into the shaker. Not to be swallowed, but to be held between the teeth as the alcohol flows past it and the power sits behind it. How did that song go? Anger's an energy? That's what I had to work with. There were a thousand things I could do, using my surroundings, but I didn't have time to figure any out. I had to trust my instincts.

First, the distraction; a stink bomb. I filled an empty bottle with a few drops of Asafetida, some rainwater, spit, and a couple of shakes of the Absenta bitters. The scent was so thick I could taste it on my tongue. I slowly swirled the mixture, blowing on it and muttering under my breath. Sometimes you don't need to know the exact language. If you have the basic meaning it all sorts itself out. That's part of the magic.

"Nolens foedo olet nobis," I breathed against the glass, calling for a big stink, and handed it to Naberius.

"What do I do with this?" He said, turning his face away from the stench.

"Get it inside and use it. I think if you make your way to the back door, you can pour it out. Pretty sure it'll create a wall of stink that nobody will walk through. Everyone inside will leave through the front, and these creeps will try and get out through this gate."

Naberius nodded and took the bottle, moving around to the front of the bar. I got my shot ready, shifted my position slightly, and waited.

I didn't have to wait long; I heard a few shouts and chairs being flung to the side. There was only one way out, and I was ready. Rodrick was first, thankfully. Gave me more time to figure out how to deal with the Bruxsa.

He fumbled with the lock and flung open the gate, placing his face right in the path of my swiftly moving fist. He fell backwards, more startled than hurt, right into the Asmodi, who yelped and stepped back, his heel coming down on the Bruxsa's foot.

I knocked back my makeshift shot, catching the bullet between my teeth then spit the liquid past it. It fire-balled through the air and hit the ground like a liquid grenade. Chunks of concrete flew up and knocked the Bruxsa backwards and off balance.

Everyone was down for the count, except for Murmur, who stood back at the far end of the patio, looking at me as if I had just crashed her birthday party. I strode in, hoping I'd have enough time to load another shot if I needed to.

The Bruxsa sat up and brushed dirt off her sleeves. She looked past me, towards the door, then slowly stood. She shifted her torso with a slow twist, and I could hear little cracks from her spine. She straightened up to her full height, and I suddenly felt very small.

Rodrick moved up and stood next to her with a look of disgust on his face due to thickness of odor. A line of blood dripped over his lip and down to his chin. The Asmodi just looked at me as if he was completely bored by my presence. Murmur started moving around the side of the patio, making her way towards me.

I could hear some shouting and yelling from inside the bar. Hopefully Naberius wasn't getting into too much trouble, and maybe he'd even join me. Might help even out the numbers a little. Still, I had to do this fast, as the fumes were already starting to dissipate.

"I'm sorry to barge in on your little gathering here," I gave everyone a big grin, hoping to add a little crazy to my stance. I kept my eyes on the Bruxsa, knowing her powers were probably greater than mine, and I spoke as steady as I could. "I'm here with my friend Naberius, who's keeping an eye on things inside. Neither of us want trouble. We just want to talk."

The Bruxsa raised an eyebrow and crossed her arms. It was like two snakes curling around each other, "What is it you wish to talk about."

"I believe that one of your friends here has something that belongs to me, and I would like it back."

The Bruxsa smiled slowly, "As long as you're being polite, we can talk. If, however, you could get this place smelling better, it might be more conducive to our conversation."

I nodded and shook up a quick little anti-odor mix. Vodka, vinegar, and cinnamon. Never use a potion you can't control. Something I learned a long time ago. I also learned that vinegar can be used for almost anything. I shot a quick mist into the foul doorway, muttered a quick "in aerem", and instant dissipation.

"I really don't have time for this," Rodrick said, exasperated, and strode back into the bar.

His voice echoed inside, reverberating through the small but crowded room, "As you can tell, the Drunken Abbott is experiencing a little problem of the more fragrant kind. We are closed until tomorrow. Your tabs have been taken care of, and we apologize for the inconvenience."

I stood nervously as the Bruxsa watched the crowd file out the front door. I saw Naberius move towards the patio. He walked out; nose covered by his hand. The Bruxsa looked at me expectantly.

"Yeah, he's with me."

The Bruxsa nodded, gestured for Rodrick to let him pass, and Naberius moved to take up a position across the patio from me.

Obviously the one in charge, the Bruxsa stood silent, as the others stood at the ready behind her. Rodrick gave me a snarl, while the Asmodi gave me nothing.

"What is it you want, Thomas Dante?"

"We're here for a necklace, holding a charm, that belongs to me," I said.

The Bruxsa laughed, a cold waterfall of a laugh. "You come in here like this, accusing without proof? If anything, you are the ones causing trouble. What can you say to stop me from calling the authorities and having you both arrested?"

Before I could answer, the pasty-faced demon whispered something in the Bruxsa's ear. He stretched up on his tiptoes to do so.

The Bruxsa tilted her head slightly, nodded then looked at me.

"According to Daggon here, you have something that belongs to me," The Bruxsa hissed, her voice thin and menacing, cutting through the weather like lightning. Daggon moved behind her and gave me a sick little smirk. Rodrick stood still, looking anxious, which made me feel a little more in control. They had the numbers, but maybe I still held some power.

"I have nothing of yours, lady," I said without breaking eye contact.

Raising a thin eyebrow the Bruxsa held up a long thin index finger, "My name is Aisha, and you will remember that. Now, Daggon tells me you have pages from the Intoxicantata, if not the whole book. Now, perhaps, I have something of yours. These things can be traded. You were at the vampire's bookstore, were you not?"

She looked angry. Obviously, someone who wasn't used to being challenged.

"Yes, I was at the bookstore, but the book we wanted wasn't there. Just a body..."

Aisha's eyes flashed, "Who?"

"I don't know if you know him, but Rodrick does. His name was Kurtis," I told her.

Aisha trained a hard dead stare towards Rodrick, and softly whispered, "Is this true?"

Rodrick shifted nervously. He looked scared. "He's making it up. Trying to get you against me. You got no proof, he's a goddamn bartender, not a psychic."

"What I am," I said, standing up straight, "Is a Mystixologist working for the Agentia Obscura. And Rodrick works with Marinette. As did Kurtis. You can call the Agentia, and they might take us, but they will take Rodrick as well."

Aisha glares, "Working with Marinette? He worked for me. And as I assume you've figured out, I need the book everyone seems to keep misplacing. As for Rodrick ..."

She turned and saw Rodrick surreptitiously inching backwards. Naberius noticed as well, and he and Murmur simultaneously moved to either side of him. Murmur shaking her head with a quiet little smile. Aisha stood, hands on her hips, waiting for him to come clean. Seems as if Marinette had no idea that Rodrick was playing for both sides. And it was clear that now both sides would have absolutely no use for him. Marinette would kill him if she found out, and Aisha demanded loyalty. Right now, she was not getting it. I realized I might be able to use that to divide and conquer.

. . .

I MOVED UP NEXT to Aisha, trying to let confidence cover my fear. "It looks as if both of us have ties to the death of Kurtis at Blundertown Books. But I do not have the Intoxicantata or any pages. The Agentia has one page as evidence, but other than that? I think Rodrick might be working for someone else entirely, and I'll bet this someone already has the Intoxicantata and hired Rodrick to pit the rest of us against each other."

"I suppose we should humor the liquor wizard, eh Rodrick?" Aisha muttered. "Daggon. Come here."

There was no response.

The pale skinned demon had disappeared. And with it, my amulet.

"My amulet…" I barked.

Aisha's entire body seemed to shimmer a little and then solidified. Must be some kind of Bruxsa magic, I thought.

"You will get your amulet back, and I will get my book, but right now…Rodrick?"

Her voice was soft, but sharp enough to slice.

"I ain't done nothing," Rodrick whimpered. "Please, Aisha."

"Come now," Aisha said, "If there's nothing to hide, there's no reason to worry."

Rodrick was worried, though. He jumped backwards, knocking Naberius against the wall. As he fell Rodrick moved behind a table while pulling a gun out from beneath his jacket. That took about half a second. I used the other half of the second to leap back over the outside bar, falling on to the sticky floor. I tried to think of some sort of protection mix but the crack thud of metal driving into wood distracted me.

I peered around the edge of the bar. Rodrick was standing behind the table, the gun in his hand. Naberius stood pressed back against the edge of the doorway, while Murmur had moved past him. But instead of hiding she leapt towards Aisha. At first it seemed like she was attacking, but instead she pushed Aisha out of harm's way and rolled with a few graceful somersaults towards me. In one swift motion she reached under the cash register, pulled out a small but deadly looking dagger, stood up, and threw it towards Rodrick. It hit Rodrick in the shoulder. With a look of disbelief, his mouth open in a soundless scream of pain, he took two quick steps backwards and fell to his knees. I got up, watching Murmur with a sort of fearful admiration. She walked towards Aisha, who had moved to stand above Rodrick. A look of distaste played on the curl of her lip.

This is not how I wanted things to play out. I hadn't wanted any more death, and now there's another to add to the pile. I steadied myself. Both hands on the bar in front of me. I was shaking. I realized if Murmur had wanted me dead, I wouldn't be here right now.

Naberius had moved back out to the patio and gave me a confused shrug. I replied with a wide-eyed shake of the head.

Aisha was the first one to break the thick silence. "You didn't have to do that, Murmur. He wasn't going anywhere."

Murmur sighed. She held another knife, dangling it lazily at her side. "Sorry. Reflex, you know?"

Aisha looked down with a fleeting look of sadness, then helped him up. "Oh Rodrick, you're not the smartest one, but you have your moments."

She turned her attention to me, her expression back to blank, "I assume the important part of this necklace is with Daggon. My apologies, Mister Dante. I will get it back, if you do not find him first. For his sake, I hope you do find him before me," Aisha gave me a humorless smile. "It seems you are correct. Someone is trying to pit us against each other."

Aisha turned her back to me and surveyed the damage to the bar. "We have some cleaning up to do, and I have a feeling your...smell, will not be easily erased. I thank you for showing me the weak link in my chain, but I do not want to be involved with you anymore. Now you and your friend should leave."

"We'll go, but what about Rodrick?"

"I will take care of him."

"And Murmur?" I motioned towards her.

"What about her?" She was still facing away from me, so I couldn't read her expression. she sounded tired, though.

"Will she be okay?"

"I'm fine, Thomas," Murmur said quietly.

Aisha smiled. And for the first time the smile showed warmth, "There's your answer. Now perhaps you should leave."

I glared at the Bruxsa, "Are you threatening me?"

"No," Aisha moved slightly and put her arm around Murmur. "I'm telling you. I am not your friend, and I have better things to do. You will come out of this alive, or dead. I don't care."

"Easier said than done. If I burst in to flames and end up charcoal who's to say you won't be next in line?" I asked.

"Let me worry about that," Aisha stopped and turned, "I've been taking care of myself for a long time. Longer than you can imagine. That being said, perhaps soon I will be able to take care of a few other things as well."

This was unexpected, but having a Bruxsa as an ally might be a good thing, and I could see Naberius was on the same page as me. So, we played nice.

"Mister Dante," Aisha said. I stopped but didn't look back. "I want the Intoxicantata for the recipes. To raise my power with knowledge and information. But we both know the book's concoctions can be used towards nefarious ends. You should look towards someone who isn't concerned with money, but of revenge."

I gave a nod but didn't turn around.

"One more thing..."

This time I turned around.

"I will not be this understanding the next time you get in my way."

I gave her a disarming smile, "Neither will I."

Aisha and Murmur exited into the bar, followed by Rodrick, while Naberius and I left through the back patio gate.

I was still upset, and a little angry. Maybe a little disappointed. I stood on the sidewalk, getting my bearings.

"What now?" Naberius asked.

What now indeed.

It was colder than it had been in a long time. And it was raining. I could see my breath as it floated into the air only to be destroyed by the scattershot cloud water. My stomach churned and I steadied myself for a second against a flash of the knife hitting Rodrick, the blood...

There was something about the blood.

I shook it off, "I'm going to call Gilles, let him know what happened. He's probably going to want to talk to Aisha and Murmur. Then I'm going to track down that little demon thief."

I put my hand up to my neck—it felt wrong without the necklace from my mother. It was an amulet that looked like a string attached to a dagger, but it was meant to represent a lamp with a flame emerging. My fire symbol, my lucky Khet. That was not a good thing.

I gave Naberius a concerned look, "If Daggon knows how it works or gives it to someone like Marinette or Christophe they could use it against me. It's a special talisman that's connected to me, but also to my element. It can help focus my powers inwards, but it can also pull that power out of me."

His eyes went wide, "Yeah. You need to get that back. So how do we find it?"

"I don't think the Asmodi would know how to use it, but Marinette would..."

"And there are definite connections between this place and hers," Naberius finished.

Whoever had my charm would have quite a bit of leverage, but regardless, it didn't really matter who held it. I needed it back. It was connected to me, so that means I'm connected to it. I just needed to find the right way to solidify that connection.

I called Gilles and filled him in on what had happened.

"Okay, I'm on my way over."

"And Jess? How's she doing?" I asked.

"She's feeling better," Gilles informed me. "She's out looking into leads regarding Christophe's whereabouts. I'm sending you the address we have now."

That was a bit worrisome, but I nodded, as the info hit my phone. "Thanks."

"She knows how to take care of herself, Dante," Gilles said. "Are you going to be at the Abbott?"

"I'm going to go back to Blundertown."

Naberius started walking towards the car, "I can drop you off."

"What are you going to do?"

"Find Dabriel."

HE DROPPED ME OFF, and I watched him drive away, heading off on his own personal wolf hunt. I hoped he would be careful.

"Good times, Awkward," I muttered to myself. "Good times."

I was in deep. The body count was climbing, and my luck was plummeting. It seemed as if the thin wisps of fog floating around me were the only friends I had left in the world. Fog never talks back, but it always leaves. I watched it leave as I stood in front of Blundertown Books. I knew the Agentia had gone through everything, but I also knew that it was very possible they might have overlooked something, especially if it was Intoxicantata related. Alcoholic secrets were well kept secrets. Blundertown Books was empty, locked, and barricaded with police tape and red cones. The surrounding streets were deserted. A shadow of a cat slipped against a parked car and vanished between the fence along the walkway and the wet silence of the hedge. I hoped Dr. Sax was alright. There was a skittering, and a rat shot out past me, heading for the alleyway behind the store. The shadow, now solid cat, chased after it. As far as I knew Dabriel was out there, gathering strength, and possibly planning a new way to kill me. I hoped Naberius could find her and work something out. I didn't know when she would try to strike, but now I knew how. It would be connected to either the earth, the air, the water, or the fire. Elementally, my dear.

Then, as if that wasn't enough, I still had Earnest Caan breathing down my neck, bringing the Triple Alliance together to vote me out of existence. I knew he wouldn't kill me, but he would use the Alliance to get me out of the way if he could. I peered through the dirt-streaked window. Couldn't see much other than a mess of books and papers. I couldn't get in through the main door, and I didn't want to break any of the police tape. I made my way around to a window on the far side of the building. There was a very small space between Blundertown and the neighboring establishment. If I could squeeze myself down the narrow corridor, I could make it inside. Once I got past that obstacle, I found another. I'd forgotten how bad it smelled, and now it smelled even worse. The store was thick with the stink of disinfectant, red wine, and blood.

The bloody scrawls had been covered up, and the books and papers had been pushed to the sides of the room. The crime scene was cleared, but the store was in total disarray. Christophe had obviously never returned to finish the cleaning job, but at least that meant I would be able to work undisturbed for the rest of the night.

It looked like the Agentia had cleared out the rest of the liquor, not that I needed a drink, but a shot of something would have helped bolster my spirit.

Later, I told myself. Right now, clues. I started at the front counter and methodically began working my way around the room. After an hour and a half of unsuccessful searching I slid down to the floor and leaning against a wall of books I fought the incoming crush of hopelessness. I threw up my last defense. Jessica. I tried to convince myself that we could be friends, but thoughts of her always appeared when I was feeling lost or helpless. I always thought she'd be the one I'd end up with, instead I ended up with nothing.

Everyone I allow myself to get close to leaves. That's why I held Jessica at a distance. That's why my friends weren't really friends. I mean, my relationship with Gilles consisted of sarcastic jibes, Mori gave me everything and got nothing in return, Naberius could easily take sides with his sister, Dabriel, who wanted to kill me. When I first started working with Jessica, she told me we'd go everywhere. We didn't. We never got to see Paris; we never made it to London. After my parents died, things got dark for me. Real dark. It was the closest I'd ever come to losing everything under the weight of depression. A thick numbness full of the deepest aches, and it flowed through my soul. I remember the funeral. It was the last time I felt close to Jessica. We were close enough to hold each other, cry on each other's shoulders. Close enough to drink until dawn and fall asleep against the noise of the morning rain.

Then she was gone. I pushed her away. I think that may have been a mistake. I hit the back of my head against the wall. I should probably just leave. I knew I should stay. I needed more light, though. It felt like the only light I had left in my life was a circle of dim amber spreading out from a slightly broken lampshade on the remains of a counter within a mutilated bookstore. This mess of light scraped through the dirty glass of the front door, only it wasn't dirt. It was blood. I groaned and grabbed one of the books next to me. I threw it at the door as if I could knock out the outside world. Annoyed it didn't work, I sat with my elbows on my knees, holding my head, staring at the chaos in front of me.

My eyes drifted over the scattered books on the floor, a couple of half empty bottles, torn pieces of paper, old potato chips, bits of broken glass …

"Wait, go back," I muttered. The paper. Recipes.

I sat up, got hit by a head rush, and almost fell over. I closed my eyes for a second, then crawled to the loose pages. These must have been left here after the agents had left the scene. Which meant someone had come back. There were five sheets of paper, one of them with torn edges, but none of them had any markings. No words, no illustrations. Blank. But just because you can't see something doesn't mean it's not there. You can use rubbing alcohol and turmeric to reveal invisible ink, but this was different. Most invisibility touched recipes were made with vodka or gin, but here, we needed heat. I had rum, pineapple juice, and I had the new bitters from Naberius. The Atmosphere Absenta had the anise, which could take the place of turmeric, and add just the slightest touch of heat. I mixed a shot, The Discerniblini, and using the edge of my sleeve I brushed it lightly over the pages.

I knew immediately they were from the Intoxicantata. Only it was one page that had been ripped from the book and copied four times. This is what Rodrick must have thought I already had. And now, I did. There was a title beneath an illustration, presumably the name of the drink, then a description written in flowing calligraphy. Difficult to read, but you needed to push up the flair for these drinks. It's part of the magic. Part of the show. The ingredients looked like a strange take on a Mai Tai even though the exact measurements were redacted. It was called a Dreamin' Tahitian and incorporated a blend of rums and added passion fruit liqueur to the Orgeat. It sounded like a full-on sweetness overload and according to what I could read you'd find yourself in a pleasant coma after a few sips. Anywhere from an hour to a day. I slid the pages into my bag, then stopped. On the back of one of the copies there was a note. The words were readable, and the writing was familiar. 'For the full recipe, $10,000.—NN.'

Nick Noir?

"Dammit!" I shouted into the empty store. I was one step closer to figuring everything out, and still too many steps to see the end. Maybe I could find out who he was selling them to.

I had a little running list scrolled in my mind; what were the drink recipes being used for, who was using them, where was Christophe, and what was the connection between him and Dabriel? Also, I needed my amulet. I'd check in with Gilles on that, but first, since these pages were important enough to kill for, I should probably get them somewhere away from me.

A shadow moved across the wall. I didn't have time to grab my bag from the other side of the office, but I managed to pick up one of the bottles on the floor. I ducked back into the little secret space behind the bookcase moments before the door opened. It could be the police; it could be something worse. The door opened.

It wasn't the police. Whoever it was had come in unconcerned about the police tape, they had keys, and they seemed to know where they were going. All I had was a bottle of whiskey and a few used books. Would have been perfect if I'd been a poet.

20
CRIMSON KISS

There was a soft scrape of metal on carpet as the door opened and shut. I stood between the wall and the bookshelf, holding my breath. Cautiously, I peered around the edge of the shelf. I couldn't really tell who it was, and then I noticed the shoes. Pink Nikes. She was obviously extremely distracted and probably wouldn't have noticed me if I'd been standing right in front of her. I watched silently as she started towards the office. She moved quickly but froze when she noticed the bloodstains. Most of the mess had been cleaned up, but the doorway and floor leading into the back room was still a hideous shade of reddish brown. Her eyes widened and she seemed to shrink back into herself, closing her eyes for a second. Then she took a deep breath and strode into the office. It sounded like she was rearranging the furniture. She was looking for something, and it wasn't the alcohol.

My bag was in the office. That wasn't good. I could wait until she was done, but I was tired of waiting. I was tired of running, not knowing, and hiding. I was tired of playing the good guy, and this might be the bad guy. Or girl. Although I knew if she could turn into a huge wolf, I'd be in big trouble. I stuck my bar spoon into my back pocket and rifled through my wallet for an appropriate piece of identification. I didn't have a badge, but I did have a faded press pass, a library card, something from the bartender's union, and an Agentia Obscura visitor's pass. It wasn't an official badge, but it had the Agentia's logo emblazoned on it, and a slightly unfocused photo of me in the corner. Even if you had no idea what the Agentia was, the badge still looked important, and governmental.

I brushed my clothes down, straightened out my shirt, and tried to not look like a homeless guy hanging out in an abandoned bookstore. I moved to the edge of the doorway, held my makeshift ID up, and cleared my throat. I expected her to be startled, but I didn't expect a scream. She ran backwards and hit the wall behind her. The impact caused her legs to give way beneath her and knock a book off the shelf above her. As she hit the ground, a volume of short stories hit her head. She gave me a dazed look.

I kept my jaw clenched so the laughter wouldn't slip out and stepped towards her. I gave her my best glare, "Returning to the scene of the crime, eh?"

"I didn't do this!" she cried, eyes wide in shock, "I work here."

"It's Jules, isn't it? You were here earlier, being questioned by one of my men," I said authoritatively. "It doesn't matter if you work here or not. The store's closed, and you aren't the owner. You're obviously looking for something specific. Maybe a cocktail recipe?"

"I don't know what you mean. Why would I be looking for that here?" She sounded scared, her voice almost a whisper. "Are you arresting me?"

"I don't have a reason not to," I said, pulling my phone out of my pocket.

"No, wait, I'll tell you," She said quickly, waving her hands frantically at me.

I sighed. Might as well play it a little nicer. I held out a hand to help her up, and she thanked me as she sat down at the desk.

"Well, Jules," I let her have a smile, "Why are you here?"

She looked at me, her head slightly tilting and her eyes narrowing.

"What?" I asked.

"You aren't a government agent," she said, "Not with those clothes. I did see you here earlier, but you're not one of the agents."

My coat had slipped open showing a stained and torn shirt. I no longer looked official or intimidating. I crouched down next to her. "You're right, but I work with Agentia. and I have officers on speed dial. And I'm not in a very good mood, so you probably don't want to try lying to me."

She gave me a defeated look, "Okay, but I didn't do any of this."

"I believe you, but you know more than you're telling me," I said, then took a chance with my next question. "Why are you looking for pages copied from a stolen book?"

"How did you know?" Jules was startled. "I swear I don't know what the pages are for. I was only supposed to get them."

"For who?" I demanded.

Her voice trembled, "Christophe."

"Listen, you have nothing to worry about. I'm not going to hurt you, and I'm not going to tell anyone I saw you here. I'm only trying to find out who killed Trevor, and what happened to the book these pages are from."

Jules sighed, "I've been working here, part-time, for about a year now. I'm just trying to get more hours, more responsibility. Christophe wanted me to bring him some books. Look, I'm not involved in any of the deaths, and I don't want to be involved in dying. I'm just doing what he asked me to do."

"I get it, Jules. But I'm here to help. I think Christophe is probably someone you don't want to be working for," I was using my best 'calming the savage beast' voice. I'd used it many times at the bar. You need a smooth voice to talk sense into the un-sobered. "If you really want to be a good journalist, then you want the truth. You don't want to start a career like this."

"Yeah, when I heard about the murder, I realized I might need to start thinking about a career change," she mused.

I placed the pages on the desk, "So, tell me, where are you supposed to take these, and why are people dying for them?"

Jules slumped down into a chair. She threw her arms across the desktop and let her head fall on top of them. "This was supposed to be a good day," she whined into her forearms. After a couple of seconds, she lifted her head and spoke quietly. "I'll tell you what you want to know, as much as I know. But you've got to keep me out of this."

"It's a deal."

"I get the recipe, you let me go, we never have to see each other again," she added.

I shook my head, "I let you go without the recipe, and you hope you never see me again."

Jules considered my proposition. "And you promise you won't mention me to the Agentia?"

"I promise."

"Deal," she whispered, sitting back in the chair. "Okay, I've had a few conversations with Christophe, trying to be a good employee, but also trying to, I don't know, work towards a promotion."

"Of course," I offered.

"He said he was thinking about bringing in a partner and expanding the store somehow. I wasn't sure if it was a bigger location, or what. Something about working with Kill City, the bar you know?"

I nodded.

"And maybe I could use the work, expand my horizons. Not just selling books, but alcohol as well. I was thinking like a bookstore wine bar, right?"

"Why not," I said and motioned for Jules to continue.

"Then last week he called me. Said he had the final bargaining chip, and I should meet him at the Lost & Found because it was gonna be good. He didn't say anything else."

"But something happened," I watched her expression, she looked nervous. Scared nervous.

"Who started the fire, Jules?" My voice was quiet, "Who else was there?"

Jules focused on the desk, eyes unmoving. "I got there right before the place closed. The door was open, but the bar was empty. I sat at a booth; it was in the corner, but I could see pretty much everything. The weather sucked that night: rain, lightning, thunder. Horror movie weather. I was about to get a drink when the owner, Trevor arrived. He was with Christophe."

"Then what?"

"It seemed as if nobody knew I was there, so I didn't move a muscle. I watched as the bartender brought out a big leather-bound book, placed it on the counter. The two men started arguing with her..."

"The bartender was female?" I asked.

"Yeah. She started getting angry, but calmed down when someone else walked in. A woman I didn't recognize."

"What did she look like?" I asked.

"I don't really remember. She stayed kind of in the shadows, dressed all in black and had very dark hair. She moved behind the bar, next to the bartender, and placed her hands on the book. Trevor started yelling, I mean like crazy yelling. He looked like he was going to hit her, and I just wanted to get out of there. I couldn't make the door without anyone seeing me, so I slipped under the booth. There was more shouting, then screams. Horrible screams," Jules shuddered, "That's when the fire started. I couldn't see it, but I felt the heat."

"Who started it?" I asked.

"I don't know. But Christophe ran out with the book. I waited a little longer, then the bartender ran out followed closely by the other woman. That was it. No Trevor. I called 911, but I was so freaked out I didn't wait around. I ran and didn't look back. I didn't mention anything to Christophe, told him I'd been running late, and I got to the bar after the fire department," Jules shook her head, "I know, crazy."

So, Christophe was part of this, Trevor got caught in the crossfire, and either this mystery woman or Dabriel had started the fire. I felt a bolt of energy, electric and sharp, filling me. I was going to get the person behind all of this. The person who had killed Trevor, and probably Kurtis. The person who'd threatened me and my loved ones. And it's possible, if the fires were connected, the person who might have killed my parents. It had been feeling as if everyone had been doing their best to keep me in the dark. Not anymore. Every piece was moving towards a disturbing picture. A goddamn alcoholic jigsaw puzzle of death. It had to be someone involved in as many areas as I was. Someone who'd led me in circles. Someone who had kept secrets from me and knew all the key players. Someone playing the part of the innocent victim, while she's about as innocent as a Crimson Kiss cocktail. And those are as sinful as it gets.

It all made sense—if I was right.

I HAD TOLD myself no more Mr. Nice Guy, now I meant it. It was white hot justice, and the scales were being balanced in blood. I had answers, but I needed proof. Still, I had more power than they thought I did and today was not the day I was going to die.

"Okay, listen. I'm not going to tell anyone I found you here, but you might want to go to Four Calendar Café. Ask for Mori. She can help you out," I told Jules.

She looked at me, relieved, "Thank you," She whispered and left without another word. I put the pages in my bag, added a couple of small bottles and two shot glasses, and smiled.

Now I was ready to pay Christophe a much-deserved visit. I called Jess, but straight to voicemail. Gilles answered, but he was on his way back to the office from the Drunken Abbott and hadn't heard from Jessica. Then it was taxi time. I made my way into the depths of Shaughnessy a nice neighborhood where all the sidewalks were lined with thick evergreen hedges and the streets, after being downtown, were so clean they made me feel uncomfortable.

I got out of the taxi and walked briskly towards the house, keeping close to the edge of the sidewalk. I didn't know what I was going to say, or do, but I had to do something. He held the answers I needed, and I was going to get them.

I stopped as I reached the entrance. This area of town was money, and the house fit in perfectly. I didn't even see the house until I'd made my way around the towering hedge wall.

It was extremely well hidden from the neighbors, and the iron gate, while not locked, was still intimidating. Then on the other side of the gate, the world completely changed.

It was a like the darkest, poisoned, and decrepit garden section of a fairytale. Weeds and strange flowers were everywhere, growing over the thin cobblestone path leading to the door. Vines threatened to strangle the twisted trees pushing their roots through the stone. Next to the house there was a rhododendron explosion. Glorious bursts of gold and purple mixed in with splashes of pure white and brilliant orange. All a surreal contrast amidst the piles of rotting flowers and dead leaves.

I thought about how to play it. I didn't want to spook the guy. And there was a chance he wasn't the killer. Although there was a chance he could be. I'd play it cool. Just checking a lead, working at the Lost & Found, friend of Trevor's.

There was a doorbell, but it didn't work. Flakes of dirty white paint fell to the ground as I pushed it. Nothing else happened. I tried knocking, rapping on the windows along the porch, which were all covered with grime and blocked by thick curtains that looked almost mold stained. No wonder Christophe never invited anyone over.

So. Choices. Wait for a killer or attempt to get inside.

I TRIED WALKING around to the back of the house but was blocked by a wall of tangled brambles and rose bushes. Back to the front door, and this time I tried the doorknob. It creaked open. An old and tired creak, not a haunted one. Christophe peered out at me, opening the door enough for me to tell that he wasn't happy. He was also not surprised. He was backlit by a sickly yellow glow emanating from an old lamp in the hallway behind him. The lighting, combined with his gaunt frame and tailored suit, gave Christophe a slightly supernatural appearance.

He smiled, which startled me more than it should have, and he raised a hand to a thin silver chain around his neck. I saw three charms, a key, a lightning bolt, and a shark's tooth. It made me wonder if there was a connection between Christophe and the Asmodi who'd taken my amulet. I took a step back.

"Why are you here?" He asked.

I was sure he already knew the answer.

"You know why," I said.

He tilted his head slightly, "There's nothing you can do here. You should leave."

"Not yet," I said, suddenly distracted. There was a slight hint of a familiar scent. White Musk. It wasn't Christophe, but there had to be something about this...

He peered at me curiously over his nose, "I'll call the Agentia."

"No, you won't."

I took a step towards him. I was taking a chance, but my gut was throwing down some heavy Morse code. Either that, or I really needed to eat something.

"If you do, I have a little story to tell them about Nick Noir," it was time to lay it all out and see what happened. His eyes narrowed, and he smiled. That was a little unnerving. He stepped back into the hallway. I used that step to move forwards. I held up my hands and attempted a reassuring look. I couldn't tell it was working or not, as Christophe's face was caught in a shadow.

"I just want to talk. I'm not going to do anything. I need answers."

But he wasn't listening to me, he was reaching for something that was on a table in the hallway. A gun? No, a sigil. An iron circle engraved with curled, floral, baroque patterns. It looked like a horned cross with two spirals near the bottom. Almost alchemical, but more elemental. I didn't know a lot about the sigils, but I knew they were very powerful, and very dangerous. Some could be used to summon the cursed, some could be used to repel them. I knew this one wasn't being used as an invitation. I barely had time to move out of the way as he leapt at me. I slid to the left, keeping my right leg out. As he tripped, I struck his wrist. The iron sigil flew out of his hands and across the hallway. Christophe stumbled out the open door behind me, trying to keep his balance. I gave him a quick little bow and darted further into the house. I moved slowly backwards down the hall as Christophe stomped back up towards me.

"Get out of my house," he growled.

Before I could say anything, he was running. Straight towards me. Arms up, hands in fists. He wasn't scared; he was furious. He was also not paying attention to any subtle movements I might make. With one swift motion I reached into my messenger bag for the little atomizer in the side pocket. It had about two ounces of the Soul Kiss. Used unfiltered and in your face, the effects are intense for all involved. I pulled it out and sprayed the mist between my outstretched fingers and towards his face. He moved through the mist before he realized what was happening.

The smell hit first, slowing him down. That thick aroma of anise and citrus. Then he stopped, our eyes locked, and thanks to the connection made I got hit with his thoughts. Not all of them, and not solid, but scattered and broken. Everything started moving in surreal motion. Tracers coming off Christophe's body as if it was drifting into the past, then forwards, towards me. Shifting like some bad 3-D film work. It felt like we were trapped in a pocket outside of time. He struggled to shake it, working against me. He was strong. But so was I. I reached out and grabbed his shoulders and got hit by a machine gun blast of images. Books, drinks, flames...

The fire at the Lost & Found, Jules, broken glass, splatters of blood. I saw Trevor, Naberius, the woman with black hair. Why was her face hidden from me? I couldn't tell if the images were from me or Christophe. I saw Dabriel. I saw Nick Noir but shifting towards a different face. I saw shadows of bats and owl feathers. I tried to push deeper.

"Don't," Christophe snarled, and swung at me, breaking out of the soul trance. Time sped up and he ran straight into me, his fists pounding at my chest. I tried to defend myself, but he was relentless. Hitting me hard, driving me back down the hallway. I tripped and fell backwards, and he fell over me. A fist connected with my face, and I saw a circle of stars.

I managed to grab his arms and twist myself up and over him.

Pinning his arms to his sides. The Soul Kiss isn't an easy thing to shake, but he was coming out of it. He stopped struggling, his eyes started to clear up from the glazed over sheen they had held earlier.

I did, however, still need answers.

I let him go, and he stood up swiftly, brushing off his suit and giving me a knife-edged glare. "Alright, Dante. Now what?"

"Now, answers," I said. "I want my charm, I want to know why Trevor is dead, why Nick Noir is back, and what Dabriel is up to. And I want to know who else you are working with..."

Christophe was behind me before I had finished my sentence, his hands on my shoulders, his breath on my neck. "And why should I answer to you?"

The front door, not fully closed, slammed against the wall. A gust of wind pushed through the house. There was no rain, but clouds whipped across the sky and gathered like soldiers waiting. A storm was coming. I was pretty sure it was coming for me. I started to answer him, but he interrupted, "You should leave, Thomas, now. Maybe you don't have to die. But if you stay, you won't get a choice."

"Christophe, right now, you're the only person who can help me figure this out. Maybe you can help me fight as well. You have the answers, so I can't leave. Not yet. I'm in danger regardless of where I am, and you're the only hope I have. I can fight this if I know what it is, otherwise, I'm probably going to end up like Trevor. I know you aren't an evil person. Not really."

Christophe threw his head back and let out a quick, sharp laugh. "You really have no idea what's going on."

"I have some ideas, but obviously I need more."

"I'll give you more, but you won't be able to stop what's happening," Christophe turned, letting his words stand solid and unbreakable between us. "You won't be able to save everyone."

21
ASK THE ANGELS

Christophe moved into the living room, which was almost exactly as I'd pictured it. Books everywhere. Along the walls, lined up on hardwood floors. They covered the coffee table and were piled up on the old square television. There were two huge bay windows looking out into the yard, but all I could see was a tangle of vines and thorns from the blackberry bushes. There was a large ornately woven carpet in the middle of the room, depicting some kind of Middle Eastern quest, and the long leather couch was sunken in and overflowing with mismatched throw pillows. The only thing out of place in the room was a computer on the corner of an almost presidential looking desk by the windows. Solid wood with a walnut stain and black and gold inlays. Probably what he used in his quest for his rare and obscure books. He sat down behind it and looked up at me. He seemed different. Maybe colder. The room smelled of old leather, whiskey, and musty paper.

I didn't say anything for a few minutes. I perused the shelves, looking at books of magic and history, mixology, and mystery. I'd never seen anything like it. I looked out the windows, peering between the shivering and scraping curtain of plants. The storm was moving faster, the sky, getting darker. I had a feeling I was running out of time.

Christophe turned in his chair. His back to me, looking out the window.

"When you live a long time, time can lose its meaning. Books helped keep me from losing myself. There is always something else to learn. With people, its different. For me, books last longer. But then I met someone who had the same passion for books as I did. I allowed him to become my friend, and later we became lovers. He was the one who told me about the Intoxicantata."

I'd never known Christophe to go on a date with anyone, let alone refer to someone as a lover. It was a little uncomfortable.

"You have a lover?"

"I had a lover," he said, without moving, then continued his story.

"He was always trying recipes out and looking for strange botanicals, different bottles. I studied that book. I read it cover to cover. Over and over. We connected on those pages, in those magics, and together we found there might be a way for him to live longer. Not as long as me, but longer than most mortals," Christopher faced me again. "Longer than you."

I had a strange feeling I was not going to like how this story ended. An ache of emptiness started to form in the pit of my stomach.

"We ended up selling that book to your father, who kept it at the Riddle House. He was the keeper of the book and had no problems sharing recipes with us when we asked. And then there was the fire, and he was gone," Christophe continued.

"The Lost & Found?" I asked.

"No," Christophe glared at me and slowly stood up. "It took me years to find out who killed him. The police wouldn't believe me, the Alliance tried to stop me, and the Agentia wouldn't help. Their only goal was to make sure none of the 'normal people' heard about anything. Their job isn't to solve crimes, it's to cover up the supernatural ones. Finally, I learned of a recipe that could help me figure it out. A recipe that was in the Intoxicantata. Which belonged to Trevor."

"Did you start the fire…" I stared at Christophe.

Christophe laughed, short and sharp, "Did I start the fire? You are asking me if I started the fire? I was willing to sell the bookstore, I have my own collection here, as you can see, but the Intoxicantata was to be returned to me. Dabriel had bound the book, but after a few attempts, I managed to break that binding. And that's how I learned it was you, Thomas Dante. You killed the only person I've ever loved."

I stared at him, shocked, silent. Then it dawned on me, "The shapeshifter. The one who looked like Nick?"

"And I was going to kill you."

"Well, I'm glad you changed your mind?" I asked, hopefully.

Christophe gave me a thin-lipped smile, "I haven't decided yet. Perhaps I can get more use out of you if you're left alive. At least until we have everything we need."

"And what do you need?" I asked.

"Power, of course. Combining the energy of the Lost & Found with the energy inherent within the DarkWave, and those born of it, we will be able to control this city. From there, who knows. Everything?" Christophe laughed. It seemed unhinged.

"And my amulet?" I asked.

"Dabriel has it. All parts of the puzzle, my friend. She's been a little unpredictable recently, but we have the same goals now," Christophe leaned back in his chair, "Personally, I wouldn't mind if you suffered a little more. Oh, and that annoying detective, Jessica…"

Our conversation was heading in a bad direction.

"Don't you dare," I moved closer, keeping my voice calm and quiet. "Where is Dabriel? And did you kill Trevor?"

The wind scraped the bushes outside against the glass. A few bottles on the windowsill shuddered together with quiet clinks. Christophe stood up and walked towards me. This time it was his voice moving quiet and dangerous. "Dabriel is getting a few things in order. As for Trevor? It was a shame, but he was trying to stop me."

"The storm…it's Dabriel, isn't it."

Christophe nodded.

"So, you stole the book, Trevor tried to stop you, and you just killed him?"

Christophe nodded, his eyes drilling through me. I knew I had to get somewhere safe, but if I left, I'd be heading into a storm that was decidedly unsafe. I kept talking, trying to buy some time.

"Okay, you wanted me dead, but you need me for something else. Power. Both you and Dabriel. Does it have something to do with being an Elemental?" I moved closer to the doorway. Christophe following me slowly. I wasn't sure if I should run or not. I looked at Christophe, who seemed to be more annoyed than angry.

That was it. The elemental connection.

"You know my powers aren't gone, they're inside me, and you want to use them?"

I was at a whisper, my words sliding out slow, my thoughts spinning fast.

"Who else is in on this, Christophe? Someone else must have been helping you set this up. You haven't been calling the shots from the start, have you?"

Christophe remained silent. His eyes narrowed, watching me. I was slowly realizing I might be standing in the worst place possible. Christophe smiled. It wasn't a good smile.

"You are a clever one, Thomas. But I have a problem you may be able to help me with. The Alliance, they are watching you. Therefore, if something happens to you, they will turn their meddling faces towards me. Earnest Caan, though, he's the one who could shift that balance. I wouldn't put it past him to attempt seducing Dabriel away from me. I don't suppose I could convince you could take care of him for me. Perhaps we could make some kind of arrangement?"

"You want me to take out a member of the Alliance?"

Christophe laughed, "Perhaps you can make it look like it was your friend Nick Noir? I cannot afford to tangle with the Alliance, but you already have. Besides, I have created some evidence you might be interested in. Proof that it was you who killed Trevor and that other one…Kurtis. Earnest will undoubtedly link those deaths to the death of my love. You are still a person of interest, I believe."

"How could you have proof?" I asked. "You know I didn't do anything."

Christophe closed his eyes, concentrating. For a second it was if the storm clouds from outside were flying across his skin. His body shook, but only his face was changing. Shifting, moving. Features distorting and twisting.

When his eyes opened, they were my eyes. "I have pictures, Thomas. I took some selfies of myself at the crime scene," His face was my face. He shook it and Christophe's face was once again in front of me.

"You aren't a Shifter, though. How…" I started.

"This is where books come in handy," Christophe's smile faded into something much less friendly. "I am learning how to take powers from others and pull them into myself. Nick Noir didn't need his DarkWave anymore, so I'm using it. We need your powers, Thomas, but if you don't help us, we might just have to take them from you."

"We? Dabriel doesn't need my powers," I took another step towards the door, "Who else is involved with this? Is it Naberius?"

Christophe just glared.

"I'm not going to do it, Christophe. I'm not going against Earnest, and I won't let you hurt anyone else."

"We'll see," he sighed, "I know someone else who might convince you to rethink your position. Now, I would love to stay and chat, but I have things I need to do. Be thankful I'm listening to Dabriel for the moment and letting you live."

He held his arm out; he was holding the iron sigil. He must have picked it up from the hallway. Without breaking eye contact, he put it to his lips, whispered something, then licked it. Slowly his body started to shift into a shadow of storms.

"What did you do?" I shuddered.

"With the power Dabriel has shared with me, and the abilities I ripped from Nick Noir, I can shift into the elements. I hope you stick with your decision to not help us," The storm cloud spun like a smile of hate and rain. "Because now that I have your charm, I will be able to drain you dry, and then I will kill you."

And with that he was gone, like a thundercloud vanishing into blue sky. My charm? He has my amulet…I fell back on to the couch and covered my eyes with the palms of my hands. "Think, Thomas. Use that tired brain."

I had to tell Gilles. He should believe me, but there was a chance he wouldn't. If the Agentia found anything suggesting Waver powers were being drained, Christophe would be sent to the Alliance for sure. If I could pull it off it might get the Alliance to take it easy on me. I might be able to get out of this a free man. But if there wasn't any proof, I'd look like a fool, and what if Gilles didn't believe me? Jess would, though. Earnest was not an option, but perhaps Marinette would help me, even if she didn't believe me. Enemy of my enemy, right?

I STARED OUT THE WINDOW, the trees were waving in the breeze, and leaves were spiraling down the street. This was something I hadn't dealt with before. This was something I don't think anyone had dealt with before. This was going to be me against something new. Lightning in a shapeshifting bottle. I'd thrown some strong mixes in my time, but never against someone like Christophe. And then on top of that, I had to take on the new queen of storms, Dabriel.

I had to figure out how to take both down without pushing myself deeper into the hole Earnest and the Alliance were busy digging for me. I had to fight fire with fire, only my fire had to play by the rules. You know, a nice polite fire against a malicious inferno. Easy.

I figured I was probably heading for an ending regardless. Screw it. I'll go out fighting. If I can get a good cup of coffee and a strong drink before the end, I'll be a happy dead man.

I started walking around the house. If I was alone here, I might as well take the opportunity to see if there was anything around that could help me: books, spells, alcohol. There had to be something in here. The place was like Dracula's castle, if Dracula had been a librarian.

What I needed, other than a drink, was an edge. For the first time I had a solid idea of who I was up against, and I needed to figure out something that could help me take them down. A little liquor up my sleeve, so to speak.

I knew Christophe was more powerful than I was, but he wasn't as careful, or as thoughtful. He was still going for spectacle at the expense of quality. Not that it wasn't impressive, or deadly. It was, but it also seemed to be lacking in sophistication. If only I had something I could use against him. Like… Like my amulet, but one belonging to Christophe. Something attached to him, spiritually. I felt the grin spreading slow. I had a page from the book. If I could use that to make a connection, and keep it under my control, I might be able to channel his power and use it against him. Or at least figure out a way to pull some sort of reversal mix in case I'd have to take back any power stolen from me. I'd need back up though. Gilles would take care of that. We had our differences, but I could trust him. He might not believe me, but he was on the right side. I stood at Christophe's bar, set up on a silver and mirrored table in the living room. I was impressed. And I noted, he had all the right ingredients for an Ask the Angels. Something I could use now, a little divine intervention. I made the drink, and I made a call. The drink was perfect, but the call went straight to voice mail.

"Hey, thought you might want to know. Christophe wants to kill me. I'm in his house right now. I think Jessica is in danger, and Dabriel has gone crazy. Call me if you get a chance."

I tried Jessica. She probably wouldn't answer, but I had to warn her.

"Thomas?" She answered.

"Jess, thank god," I said. "Where are you? We need to talk."

"Not now."

"It's important."

"Look, I'm at Christophe's house. Something's going on. I think there are people downstairs. You'd better not be involved with this," Jessica said. "I'm serious, Thomas."

She hung up on me and I stared at my phone in disbelief. "What the…"

Jessica was here. This was not good. I called her back.

"What do you want?" Jessica snapped.

"Don't hang up," I said. "I'm here too, in the house. Downstairs, it's just me."

There was a deep breath, a pause, another breath, "You're here? Why…never mind. You should go. This is way more dangerous than we were expecting and officially speaking you're still a civilian. I can't afford any mistakes."

"I'm ready for this, Jess," I said.

"I don't know. Can you call Gilles? I can't seem to get a hold of him…"

There was a pause.

"Jess?"

"Are you part of this?"

"Of course not."

I heard a drawer opening and paper being shuffled around.

"Be careful. I'm coming up. I didn't do anything Jessica," I said, anxiously. "Look, you've got to get out of here. We 've got to get out of here. It was Christophe…"

"What was Christophe?"

"He killed Trevor, Jess. We need to go. Dabriel's in on it and something big is going down right now. It's dangerous here."

"Right, dangerous," Jessica snorted. I heard her continue to open drawers, move around. She was right above me. I had to find the stairs.

"The only thing dangerous in here is the mess," Jessica said, continuing to rummage around, "A person could get lost and never be found. Listen Thomas, Christophe isn't here, right?"

"Right"

"But he was, so he could be back any minute. I'm not sure where Gilles is, but you are a civilian and I know you've got your recipes to fall back on, but if anything happens to you, the Agentia is going to be held responsible."

"Jessica," I said, running down the hallway looking for a way upstairs, "I understand, but trust me this once. I know he'll be back, but you're in just as much danger as I am. Maybe more. He'll use you to get at me, so you need to get out of this house."

She didn't say anything, but I could tell she had stopped moving. The silence echoed over the phone, static shake and still. Then, movement. I heard a muffled mumbling curse, and then a whisper of her voice. "Thomas? There's someone up here here…"

Over the phone and above me, I heard the floorboards creak, followed by a crash.

"Jessica!" There was the sound of glass breaking, the phone falling to the floor, a shout, and a gun firing.

I shouted at the phone. "Get downstairs!"

I ran through the house, looking for a way to get up. Nothing but a hallway of closed doors. Finally, through one of them, I found a way up.

22
THE SPLIT SKULL

"Jess!" I yelled out. No answer. After the delightful sound of shattering glass there had been nothing. I sped up the stairs, jumping over obstacles of fallen books, broken glass, and shards of wood. When I got to the top there were more broken bottles and bookshelves in splinters. Glass shards were scattered across the booze-stained floor. There were a couple of windows at the end of a hallway, broken, but the air was still thick with dust and a heady mix of conflicting and confusing scents rising from an assortment of herbs and spices strewn across the floor and mixing with alcohol fumes. The lights weren't working, but the outside glow cast a dull grey down a long hallway filled with bookshelves and old wooden display cabinets. There were a few doors, but none of them were open. I whispered Jessica's name, anxiously, and hoped nothing else would answer. I held my breath and strained to hear a sound that wasn't me.

"Where are you?" I muttered. The dust and stagnant fragrance stuck in my throat. There was a sound from behind a bookshelf about halfway down the hall. I slowly moved towards it. Then I heard something else, but I had no idea what it was. I waited to see if either sound would repeat. Slow seconds passed, then a I heard someone whisper my name.

"Jessica," I started to call out to her but fell silent when I heard the other sound. A scratching. Something behind, or inside, the wall.

"Jess?" I whispered; my face pressed against musty wallpaper. It seemed Christophe might have left something behind. I hoped it wasn't my old demonic snake friend. I could hear wind through the broken windows, rustling papers. A smell I couldn't place wafted up. It was acidic. There was something here, and I didn't care if it had clawed its way up from hell. If Jessica was hurt, I'd tear it apart. I moved across the floor towards where I'd heard my name slip out, wondering where the hell Gilles was. If the cavalry was going to arrive, right now would be a good time. I reached the bookshelf and swung around to the other side. There was about a meter between the back of the shelf and the wall. Nothing but a few old blankets. Then one of them shifted.

"Jessica," I moved towards the pile and the bottoms of a familiar pair of combat boots.

No answer. She was on her back. I cautiously moved closer, kneeling, saying her name and reaching my hand out to touch her legs. She responded with a whimper, and I pulled the blanket down towards me. She lay there; eyes closed, hair a tangled mess around her head. Nothing was ripped or torn, but there was something on her face. It was a thick viscous olive-green substance, and it smelled horrible. There was also some staining the carpet next to her head. A knife lay near the wall, just out of reach. It had the same sticky green on it. I moved towards Jessica first, reaching out to gently nudge her shoulder. Another whimper, graduating into a groan.

"Jessica," I knelt by her head. Her lips moved slightly, but there wasn't any sound. "It's okay," I said quietly. "You're okay."

I sat next to her, taking her hands in mine. I kept my eyes on the entrance to our little secret space. If there was something out there, it either didn't know I was here, or it didn't care. I slowly lifted her head.

"Tommy?" Jessica whispered, barely a breath of sound.

"Yeah, I'm here. You're alright," I reassured her. "I'm going to look around, and call Gilles again," I crept to the edge of the bookshelf and peered around.

"They're still here," Jessica muttered behind me. I turned to see her trying to sit up, her eyes half shut, her arms shaky. "Don't know where."

I stopped, "Who, Jess?"

"They were waiting for me," she mumbled and lay down again.

I called the emergency Agentia number, told them to get Gilles to this address, and that they should send an ambulance for Jessica. That's when I heard the noise, the scratch, the shuffle. The sound from behind the walls was getting closer. Like it was scratching through the wood. I hung up and tried to get a bead on the sound, but I knew my priority was Jessica. I had to get her outside before I could figure out what was lurking in the walls and not get killed. I knelt, and she grabbed my arm, trying to steady herself as she sat up.

"Jess, what happened?"

She ignored my question, "Gilles. Get him."

"I'm trying. Agents are on their way, but we've got to get out of the house. Now."

She stared at me, her eyes were bloodstained, and she wasn't blinking. Maybe the green slime. It was on her lips. If she ingested some kind of demon or DarkWaver blood, she could be in a lot of trouble.

Jessica tightened her grip, "Spells. Don't know which ones. Couldn't tell."

I lifted her to her feet, "Jessica, c'mon, get up. If we're in danger, we need to move."

Then there was a crash and the sound of wood splitting from behind the bookshelf. Whatever was in the walls had decided to come out. Jessica and I turned to look as a thin green wing slowly unfurled and twisted around the corner. Like a bat's wing, but thicker, far longer, and with talons that curved like obsidian scythes. Adrenalin allowed me to move fast. In one swift motion I pushed Jessica behind me and grabbed the knife on the floor before running past the creature into the hallway. I was hoping to draw its attention away from Jessica, although I probably should have thought of a better distraction than myself. The thin wiry creature was faster and sharper than the blade in my hand, and as I passed the creature its tongue whipped cobra quick from between emerald scaled lips and it sliced at me with its wing, catching the side of my leg, cutting through my jeans, and drawing blood. I fell forwards, hitting the wall, and the knife flew across the room.

Attempting to ignore the pain, I grabbed my bar spoon as talons scraped behind me across hardwood floors. I turned on to my back, holding the spoon in front of me only to have it knocked out of my hand by a whip of a green tail. The thing's head was turned away from me and focused on Jessica. She was sitting on the floor, caught in shock. She looked like a little girl watching cartoons. Her hands clasped together; her eyes wide with excitement, only this cartoon could kill. I didn't have time to mix anything, but I had a few more tricks, or in this case, sticks. I reached up to a shelf above me where I'd seen a jar full of multicolored swizzle sticks, the kind used for holding garnishes in cocktails. I knocked it over and they fell on me. I grabbed six of them and slid them along the floor until they were wet with spilled alcohol. I whispered to them in my hand, a quiet recipe of sharpness and speed, and let them fly like liquored up darts.

Four of them glanced ineffectually off the thing's skin but one hit and stuck above a crawling leg, and another found its mark on the side of its left eye. A sharp whine and a hiss of pain came from the creature, and it tried to dislodge the offending spikes from its hide. But as it struggled, its wings, twice as long as the body it was attached to, flailed about, stabbing through the air. I stepped back, but not far enough, as an edge of a wing sliced across my shin. I screamed, feeling like I'd been cut to the bone.

"Jessica," I groaned as I put too much weight on my injured leg, "Can you get up?"

I hobbled over to her and pulled one of her arms around my waist so we could help each other limp down the stairs. I had no idea what was wrong with her. Until I knew I didn't want to chance using the wrong mix.

"What is it? Do you know?"

"Some kind of demon..." she mumbled and then tried to say something else. "Twisted. Zombie witch Asmodi...bunch of 'em."

We walked towards the stairs, slowly. "Asmodi? The Bruxsa did this?"

She nodded weakly. It had to have been Aisha who did this. One of these things might be the Asmodi from the Drunken Abbott, Daggon. The one who had my amulet, only now without any semblance of humanity. That must have been how Christophe had gotten his hands on it. I was starting to feel my leg again, which was good, but it was electric lightning bolt of pain. I was also leaving a trail of blood behind us.

"Stopped three of them," Jessica asked. There was a tremble in her tone I'd never heard before. "Tommy? I think I'm dying. Am I dying? I'm not dying, am I?"

"I don't think so. I think it's this green stuff on you. Where did it come from?"

"Asmodi. Dead one. Blood's not red, you know?" She faltered, her speech slurring, and almost fell again. The ambulance needed to show up. Soon. The creature wasn't moving but its body covered the knife and my swizzle sticks. I managed to get my bar spoon back, not that I could do anything while holding up Jessica. I felt like we were two thirds of the Three Stooges, shuffling like awkward drunks down to the main floor.

"How many left?"

"Three."

"Where'd the other two go," I said tautly.

"Tommy," Jessica mumbled, stopping halfway down the stairs, "You can't leave me here."

"I'm not leaving you," I grunted. "You stopped. C'mon. Work with me."

We were heading for the front door when there was a shuffle from upstairs and then a hiss. It didn't sound like the thing I'd just fought but I didn't look, I moved. Ignoring the pain in my leg, I sped up my limp, pulling Jessica along with me. Of course, Christophe had sealed the front door. We weren't getting out that way. I swung around. Back door. But to get there we had to pass the staircase. I'd been right. The hissing thing wasn't the bat-winged creature, which was hopefully dead, but one of the demons from the café. The human side of it had all but vanished, leaving a mottled olive-green skinned creature with protruding teeth, but I recognized the horns. It was wounded but making its way down the stairs. It's hand dragging against the wall, leaving a trail of green blood behind it. It seemed a little dazed, but it was still moving too fast for my liking. Thankfully the back door wasn't magically sealed like the front door. One of the other demons crawled into view. I had to pull Jessica out onto the back porch. I shut the back door, and as we got down to the yard there was a hard sharp thud against it, shaking the hinges.

"We gotta move, Jess," I insisted, pulling her up. She seemed to barely be able to open her eyes, let alone hurry. The path around to the front of the house was a mess of old furniture, big thorny bushes, and weeds. If we could make it through, we should be okay. There was a shed at the far end of the yard. It was easier to get to, and there might be something I could use for a weapon in there.

"C'mon, please," I begged, trying to pull Jessica with me.

"That's not my house," Jessica said. She was fading fast, and we were running out of time. The kitchen door was hit again, a crack appearing in the center.

"Jess, can you walk?"

Jessica nodded loosely. She dragged a bit, but when the door behind us split with a sound like a gunshot, she turned. Her face froze in shock. The thing's green head peeked through the split like a demonic Jack Torrance. And it was changing, elongating. It's face getting thinner, pushing out and becoming more reptilian. And then its legs pushed through, scratching, and clawing chunks out of the wood. Burning red eyes were locked on us, unblinking.

"What is it?" I whispered.

Jessica couldn't tell me, even if she knew. I gave her a little push, and she started moving ahead of me towards the shed. I checked my pockets and bag for anything I could use. I had the knife, but I really didn't want to get that close. I needed protection more than a weapon. Wait, that was it. This thing wasn't your normal everyday Asmodi, but something with much more of a reptilian side. I needed protection from snakes, by snakes. Maybe I could fight fire with fire. Fire, in this case, being evil reptiles. The other fire had to be some kind of cocktail with fangs.

I had the bitters from Naberius and a couple of small bottles of alcohol. I looked up, Jessica was almost at the shed. I frantically tried to remember the right mix. Snakebite? No cider. Snake in the Grass? I was a little short on mixers. I glanced up. The creature was through the door and heading for the porch. And it wasn't alone. The other was behind it, also shifting into some snake skinned creature of doom. Reptilian, but more menacing. Closer to a dragon than a lizard. They were moving fast, and I was out of time. I had to improvise.

Black pepper bitters, check. Gin, check. Then a few blades of grass, and some lemon juice. If I could use the bar spoon to stir up the potency, I might have something good. The grass would ground it, the lemon would elevate it, and the right words could help create a makeshift barrier. The things were closer. Claws digging into ground, tails flailing wildly and kicking up chunks of dirt. The one in the lead stopped in its tracks, pushing back on its hind legs. Was it going to jump? I was facing off against a real live leaping lizard and the only defense I had managed to create was a shot of Pepper Spray?

"No ver el mal!" I yelled at the drink I'd made. I didn't have time to think of anything else. It came at me, surprisingly fast. See No Evil.

I DID NOT WANT to see this evil anymore.

Its tail stretched out like a razor; its claws moved towards me in some slow-motion death crawl. I poured the shot into my mouth then sent out a fine spray. It shimmered in the light for a second before it got caught in the breeze, the fine mist falling over the creatures, and I realized I'd made a mistake. Perhaps the evil couldn't see us anymore, but it was hard to tell because I could no longer see them. I'd made our monsters invisible. There hadn't been much spray, so the effects would wear off soon, but for the moment it seemed we were all flying blind.

I could see the grass getting flattened under invisible feet, and I could hear guttural, almost retching noises mixing with the sharp hissing, but thankfully it seemed like the creatures couldn't see where I was either.

I needed something else. If not a way to see them, at least a way to stop them. I turned and ran towards the shed. Jessica had collapsed near the door. I pulled her up and pushed inside, dragging her with me. As I slammed the door shut, Jessica slid back down and slowly crawled towards the corner. Looking around it seemed hiding in the shed might have been a bad idea.

Jessica sat in the corner, shaking, against a broken washing machine and a cracked sink. I pushed a large chest full of old books in front of the door and stacked as many boxes as I could on top of it. I jammed a mop handle tightly between the doorknob and the floor and reinforced it with more boxes. I pulled my phone out of my pocket, and…nothing. No service, and the battery close to dead. Just like me. Right. On my own it was. I looked around the shed for something useful: wine, champagne, party supplies…

"Party supplies," I said out loud. There were bags of plastic cups, straws, and more swizzle sticks, ice cube trays, and some cocktail umbrellas. I tried to remember some wine cocktails but was distracted as the things outside slammed into the door. They wanted us, to eat or destroy, and neither of those options worked for me. Scanning the shed, I saw one window. It was protected with metal bars. They couldn't get through there, but we couldn't get out either. I needed a weapon. I rummaged through the boxes on the floor and through my memory. Anti-dragon drinks and wine cocktails? Maybe something tiki touched? I twirled a broken paper umbrella between my fingers, mind racing. I'd never had to get rid of things like this before.

"Jessica? You still with me?"

She'd moved away from the sink and sat slumped against the beat up and unplugged fridge.

"Barely," She mumbled.

"Do you know what the hell we're dealing with? These things are not your everyday Asmodi," I glanced at the door. The banging had stopped, but the clawing had started.

"Not natural," Jessica shook her head slowly, and then sat up, clutching her knees to her chest. "Some kind of hybrid. Christophe was working with some strange witch creature. Mixing demon genes."

"Aisha," I muttered.

What if that's why Aisha had been looking for Dabriel? Something to do with the Lycan / Elemental blood she carried. I hoped I was being paranoid, but I still filed the information away and concentrated on what I needed to do to get us out of this current mess. I spun cocktails through my mind. The Screaming Lizard needed Green Chartreuse, while it was grapefruit juice for a White Dragon. Maybe a twist on the Lounge Lizard? Amaretto, Rum, Cola. There was an old, flat bottle of coke in the broken fridge. It might slow it down long enough for us to get to the front of the house.

"Eggshells," Jessica proclaimed from behind me.

"What?"

Jessica looked at me as if I was stupid. "Eggshells make lizards think there's other creatures around. Maybe it works with these things?"

"Great, but we don't have any eggs."

Jessica stood up slowly and steadying herself against the fridge with a look of extreme concentration on her face.

"Other things lizards hate," She took a deep breath and started counting items off on her fingers, "Peacock feathers, pepper spray, coffee, tobacco, garlic, onion, cold water."

I stared at her, "How do you know all this?"

"Gilles hates reptiles," she nodded weakly, and repeated, "Cold water."

"Wait, you're right," I spun around, "The sink."

Jessica gave me a slow nod and closed her eyes. I was impressed; she was not well but still managing to push through. Alright, cold-blooded. If I could cool it, I could slow it. The sink was broken, but the pipes were still connected. If I could get at them, I could get some water.

While I was struggling with the plumbing, the scratching had intensified and had also graduated to climbing. One of them was scaling the wall to get on the roof. "Fantastic," I muttered. The ceiling looked solid but looks can be deceiving. I pounded at the pipes while the demon tried to claw through the tiles. Shards of wood and too much dust started raining down on us, but I was determined to get to the drainpipe.

I got the water going. It was a slow trickle and not the geyser I was hoping for, but it was cold. I found a bucket and started on the drinks. First, a Lounge Lizard, with a hit of garlic from the rack of stale spices shoved in a cupboard alongside empty cleaning bottles and molding sponges.

"This, along with cold water, will start some slowing," I told Jessica, "But we need more. If I could use the champagne, or the wine…" There was a thud behind me. I turned, and Jessica had fallen to the floor, eyes closed. "Jess?"

I was pretty sure this was because of her contact with the demon's blood. All the strength she had mustered up earlier had faded. I started towards her when a large chunk of the ceiling fell to the ground in front of me. I looked up and saw the pale green belly of one of the raging reptiles. The wood at the door was also splintering. That one was halfway through, its head and long tongue flailing back and forth. Meanwhile in the space above me the hole was still too tight to let its full body come through. This whole mess was making my head hurt. There was a drink, Sudden Headache. But I needed it to hit harder. I could give this monster a migraine. A real skull splitter if I mixed it right. I'd need some triple sec, something to use instead of mango, and lime juice. Champagne, it's not just for breakfast.

I poured some water into an old cleaning bottle, turned the nozzle from spray to stream, and started spraying the thing in the doorway down. It seemed to work. The lizards spastic head started to slow a little. I ran to the fridge and flung the door open. I instantly closed it after being hit by a foul stench of old milk and molding cheese.

I steeled myself and opened it again. Maraschino cherries and an almost empty bottle of Rose's Lime Juice. I grabbed a bottle of champagne and poured it into a red plastic cup. In another cup I combined a couple of ounces of Triple Sec from a mini bottle with the cherry and lime and then looked around for some tequila. I dumped the contents of my bag out on the floor. I had a little simple syrup and maybe an ounce of tequila, but it might work. I shook the mix while thinking about description and language. A skull splitter, a split skull. Yeah, that's the cherry. I'd make a cherry bomb. And not French, but maybe Greek. I didn't know head, but I remembered 'Skull'.

The other lizard was still moving, writhing through the ceiling. I cleared a path and pulled Jessica to her feet, positioning her next to the door. I got the bucket of water ready, mixing in the Lounge Lizard portion. Shards and splinters rained down on the floor, and along with them, an extremely large reptile. At the doorway the water spray was wearing off and the creature was starting to move at its regular speed. Its tongue curled out like slick wire towards us. I kicked backwards, the door fell apart over the creature, and I threw half of the bucket of alcoholic water at the approaching beast and dumped the remainder over the one in the doorway. They didn't stop but slowed until they seemed to be treading through air made of molasses.

Jessica and I stepped carefully over the one between us and the back yard. I had a champagne cup in one hand, Triple sec mix in the other. The timing had to be right, especially since the champagne was flat.

This was the knockout drink. I'd made champagne cocktails many times, but never as a weapon. I'd have to make it hard and strong, and I'd have to focus everything on the description.

I waited, resisting the urge to run. Jessica moved towards the house. I heard sirens approaching. This had to work. One of the demon dragons was halfway out of the shed, eyes on me like hooks. The other close behind it. I had to try to get both with this one.

I pulled the small shaker from my bag, poured the liquids in, and gave it a few hard jerks over my shoulder. I cracked it open, poured the liquid into a cup, and threw it at the creatures.

"Spasméno kranío!" I yelled, focusing all my thoughts on the rough translation of a split skull, and my emotions. My fear and anger, and my desire to get out alive. I pushed it all through the liquid flying. It caught my words and wrapped around them. Droplets shook into silver—like Mercury. It swirled in slow motion, covering the closest creature, which squealed and writhed underneath, as if being burned. It was a horrible sound but thankfully ended quickly.

One down, one to go, but I had nothing left to throw, except possibly some fire. Three matches left. The alcohol wouldn't catch unless I helped it out.

What was that drink...Lava Flow. But I needed a bigger fire. I needed Volcano big. I lit the umbrella on the third try. It drifted, burning, towards the monster. "Mana Lua Pele. Mana Lua Pele," I chanted, hoping to focus the divine power of the Volcano. It worked, but too well. The remaining Asmodi burst into flames, writhing and crackling. It sounded like a huge bag of Pop Rocks bursting with lizard flavor. I felt the heat on my face and started moving towards the side of the house while the burning reptile was shuddering back to the shed.

As the flames hit the shed and started to curl up and over the entire structure, I remembered I'd seen a couple of old propane tanks in there. I caught up to Jessica and pulled her along with me. We made it to the corner of the house right as there was a deafening explosion. Chunks of wood, glass, and pieces of reptile showered the back yard. The shed was gone. I threw Jessica down and covered her with my body.

Her eyes were closed, and her skin still held a sickly pallor, but her breathing felt regular. My leg still hurt, but I barely registered the pain. All I wanted was to close my eyes and sleep, and the only thing going through my head were thoughts of barbecued iguana. I turned and watched the burning shed. The neighbors would be talking about this one. My head tried to match the throbbing in my leg with a pounding of its own, but the count was off, and I was caught like a seasick rhythm between the beats. Using this kind of magic always left me with a bad hangover. Still, we were alive. Now I had to deliver Jessica to help. I sat down next to Jessica. This wasn't going to be easy. There was a crash and a shout, as two EMTs came crawling through the haunted yard sale growing at the side of the house. I waved my hand, tried to shout, and that was as much as I could handle. The black dots won, and I feel back onto the lizard gut grass.

23
DEUX AND D'EUX

When I came to, I was on a stretcher in the front yard. Jessica was beside me. There was an ambulance, a fire engine, and a small crowd of people taking pictures and pointing. Gilles was going to be pissed, but at least we weren't dead. I looked over at Jessica who had started to sit up as well; bats and elementals and murderous fools draped in bad weather be damned.

"We're alive!" I yelled up to the swiftly darkening skies. I knew Dabriel was still out there, and whatever her plans were, she wasn't done, but neither was I. The EMTs pushed us towards the ambulance and got Jessica inside. When they came for me, I shook my head.

"I'm good. Let me sit for a bit. But could you do something about this?" I lifted my leg and showed them a horrible looking purple and black bruise. It was almost big enough to start breathing on its own. It looked like the swelling pushed the cut closed which stopped the bleeding. I laughed more out of shock than there being anything funny about it, which I probably shouldn't have done. I'd get hit by some kind of sedation if I wasn't careful.

I gave the EMT a totally serious look, "I'm not crazy."

He didn't look convinced. I was feeling the high of having won this battle. Nothing was going to stop me now. A few drops of rain fell, then a light drizzle. Nothing I couldn't handle. I lifted my face and let the water lightly wash over it. Felt like springtime. I laughed again.

"You've had your turn, Dabriel. Now it's mine. And I don't care how many elements you can throw at me."

I stood up and stretched my arms out. The rain washed over me like victory. I looked at Jessica, there couldn't be any more casualties on my side. I wouldn't allow it. I should get some more liquids, and gather anything else I could, before I faced Dabriel. And Christophe, who had something belonging to me; something I needed back. They'd hurt Jessica and they were going to pay for it. There was a flash of lightning, then a thick silence. I counted five seconds before the thunder hit, and all the windows of the house behind me shook. The wind picked up and the rain fell heavier, like wet bullets driving down. Another fork of lightning danced across the horizon, between clouds, while the sky shifted from a hideous grey to an ominous orangey green. I didn't care. My best bet was probably to make it to my house or the Lost & Found. My bag, I was sure, had been destroyed by the fire, but I had some replacements in my attic. I figured it would be safe to go home, but I didn't want company. I'd make sure Jessica was taken care of, then I'd go. Jessica wasn't going to like me leaving, especially if she was still under the influence of whatever evil substance Christophe's bats had filled her with. But I couldn't stay.

I could hear police sirens, and I knew the Agentia was on their way as well. I hoped Gilles was with them. He'd make sure Jessica was okay. I took stock of my surroundings; one of the EMTs was on the radio in the front of the ambulance, while the other was with Jessica in the back. What a mess. The wind was whipping the smoke from the back in quick spiral curls around the edges of the house. I hoped Dabriel wasn't going to mount another attack right here. I didn't know the full extent of her powers, but this wind did not feel natural. I took a step towards the street and almost fell over. I looked down and there was a fresh stain of wet red on my jeans.

"Dammit."

I gingerly pulled up my pant leg, which made it hurt even more. It wasn't a cut; it was a long gash stretching from my ankle to a few inches below my knee. It was worse than I'd thought. I stood, taking a few slow breaths, and watched as two firemen walked around the corner of the house. It looked like they had the fire contained. I wondered how much of the monster had remained, and how many questions it would raise.

I LIMPED BACK to the ambulance. Jessica had an oxygen mask over her face, and her skin was almost devoid of color. Her breathing was steady, though, and there was a slight quiver on her lips as I brushed a wisp of red hair back from her eyes. I was angry Jessica, and I had almost been burnt to a crisp. I was angry about evil creatures and elemental powers. I was angry I'd been lied to and used, and I hated how every time I closed my eyes, I could see dead bodies. And they were all pointing burned and mangled fingers at me. And I was angry Trevor had died, and I had not yet avenged him. Christophe had a few things to answer for. And if Dabriel was a part of this, where did Naberius stand? But Christophe. There was a good reason he'd left without finishing me at the house, and by good, I mean evil. Judging by the gathering winds, Dabriel was getting angry about something as well. I had no idea she was so powerful, and if she was being led or used by Christophe, I had a fight in front of me.

I had to reign in my anger. Focus. I didn't know where Christophe had gone, but I could figure it out. I had a feeling he'd gone to join Dabriel. That meant the center of the storm. I couldn't use my elemental powers, but they were still in my blood. I could feel the difference between a natural storm, and one created or coaxed into being. It was like a taste on the tongue, a pulling of the skin, a tingle in the veins.

FOLLOW THE WIND, read the weather, watch the movement of the clouds. They were thick and starting to glow with the first strokes of sunset shadows. It would be dark soon, but I still had some light left.

The clouds were moving fast in a northeast direction. They could be anywhere, maybe downtown, but if Christophe and Dabriel were going after people I cared about, I'd place my bets on the Lost & Found. I needed a car, and alcohol. I looked around to see if I'd be able to make it to the Continental, but it was parked pretty much between the fire engine and the ambulance, not a good place for a quiet getaway. I took stock of my belongings. Other than two cocktail umbrellas and a swizzle stick, I was weaponless. I had a cigarette, which I was tempted to smoke, but nothing to light it with, and one unopened mini bottle of rum. That wouldn't do much unless I could find something to mix it with. Anger lends power to everything, but one spirit on its own was about as good as nothing.

This was it, the end, but not mine. I could turn the fear into strength, and the hurt into useable energy. I could feel it all rolling and boiling and mixing up inside me, as if I was full of lightning, as if I was breathing fire, as if my blood was running mercury. My wrist pulsed; my birthmark was almost glowing. That was the power I needed—elemental power—if I could push it past the confines of my skin. Christophe was going to answer for what he'd done. Triple Alliance be damned; I wasn't going down without a fight. Even if it meant I'd have to own up to the Alliance and take my punishment. This wasn't the time to play by their rules. I had to play by mine. I was a few blocks away when I realized there was no way I could walk to the Lost & Found, even with my newfound lightning fever, and I was in no mood for public transportation. My phone was dead, and my wallet was empty. I could walk to Four Calendar, though. Hopefully Mori would be working.

As soon as I walked through the door I felt as if I'd made it home. Sometimes there's nothing better than the warm orange glow of a comfortable and familiar café. There was a smell of freshly grated cinnamon hanging in the air, and the music flowed smooth and shimmering around me. It felt like winter outside, but as the door closed behind me, the café surrounded me, and Mori came running up to me.

Mori led me to a seat at the bar then left me to start on a double espresso. "Be right back," she said over her shoulder. I nodded and spun around on the stool to face the rest of the café. I knew I looked a little worse for the wear, but at least I'd stopped bleeding. Nobody was talking, everybody was looking at me.

I smiled awkwardly and turned back around towards Mori. The people here weren't like me. The people here were living their lives, letting the magic happen around them. And here I was, burning down buildings and fighting Satanic Salamanders in the middle of Shaughnessy.

"I, ah...I probably shouldn't be here," I said as Mori returned.

She smiled and placed the Deux and D'eux in front of me. The café's take on the Double Double. Mori leant slightly over the counter.

"Just drink. You can stay as long as you need to."

These people weren't here to take sides; they were just people who wanted a good cup of coffee. All I wanted was to gather some strength, some resources, and if I was lucky, a car. Then I'd be on my way.

"Could I borrow your car?"

Mori sighed and put her keys on the counter.

I gave her a sheepish smile, "Thanks."

"You need help? I can close..."

"You've helped enough. Believe me. Besides, if I made you kick all these people out on a night like this, they'd hang me from the heavens."

Mori nodded. "Hope you find what you're looking for," she gave me a hug. Then she stiffened and stared past me, over my shoulder.

"Mori?" I asked, as the café door slammed open.

I turned sharply, and even though he was standing in shadow, I knew who it was. "Earnest," I growled.

He stepped into the light, his face expressionless, lips a tight line. He looked as if the rain hadn't touched him. Hair unmussed and clothes dry. He unbuttoned his jacket and twirled a thin cane around in his hand. He gave Mori a quick nod and sat next to me at the bar.

"One extra hot cappuccino, please," Earnest said, and turned to me.

"Well now, Dante. I knew you were going to be a problem, but I had no idea you were going to be so dangerous. Channeling the elements against your enemies in this city? Stupid, foolish, and dangerous, and that's a bad combination. You do realize this will just give me more ammunition to use against you."

"You think this is me?" I asked, gesturing towards the outside storm, incredulous.

Earnest looked at me with a smirk, "It doesn't really matter what I think, Dante. Everyone loves a good scapegoat, and you fit the bill. The Alliance wants an elemental, and you fit the bill. Everyone goes home happy. Except for you, but that's fine by me. You and your little alcohol stain of a life can just sit here quietly until the Agentia arrives. My word against yours, right?"

I WASN'T sure what to say.

No, I knew what I wanted to say. With a few words and a hit of coffee and rum I could throw a reverse Carajillo in his face and he'd be too scared to move. I held on to my anger though and exhaled slowly.

I made direct eye contact. "Earnest, I don't know what you are talking about, and right now I really don't care. There's a killer out there, not in here, and I'm next on the list. So, you can hold on to all your misaligned conspiracies and go whine about it to your holy Triple Alliance, but I need to stop this, or I'm dead."

"Don't tempt me, Dante."

My buttons had all been pushed. I leaned back a little further, my hands resting on the edge of the counter, and slowly nodded. Earnest relaxed slightly; his guard lowered. I made my move. Wrapping my legs around the bar stool and leaning back even further, I swung down, almost falling over, but managed to grab his cane as I went. I caught myself, holding on to the counter for a second, but I'd put too much strain on my bad leg. With a pained yelp I fell to the floor. I still had the cane, though. I was on my knees and brandishing it like a sword when Earnest got up and took a few steps back, arms raised.

"You don't want to do this," he said tightly.

I smiled and slowly stood up, "Yes. I. Do."

I swung the cane back, and with all the strength I could muster I brought it forward and across Earnest's legs at the knees. His legs buckled underneath him, and he fell forward. He caught himself with his arms out, and I heard a quiet grunt of pain. I took advantage of the situation and gave the cane a quick spin, sliding it up so my hand was wrapped around the thinner end, and promptly hit him hard across the back of the head. I stepped back panting and shaking from the adrenalin rush. Earnest lay still but breathing. He was going to come too with a bad headache and a renewed hatred for me, but I couldn't worry about that. I looked around at the few people who had been brave enough to stay. They were all staring at me as if I was insane. Nobody expects the Triple Alliance, I thought to myself. I giggled. Not everyone there knew what I'd done, but a couple of people stared at me with such horror, I knew I wasn't the only Waver in there. I'm sure some of them were already trying to figure out what they were going to wear to my funeral.

"I know, it looks bad," I said to my nervous audience. "But I assure you it could have been worse," I shrugged and turned towards Mori, who was shaking her head.

She walked over to Earnest, who was still lying, softly breathing, on the floor. She gave me a concerned look, "Not bleeding, but there's some swelling. I hope you know what you're doing, Thomas."

"Kind of. But yeah...he's gonna be pissed," I was hoping if I made it through this alive, and brought the Alliance the true evildoer, I'd be somewhat forgiven.

Mori held her keys out to me.

"Thanks."

"You know the cops are gonna come, and they are not going to be happy about this," Mori said. "What should I tell them?"

"Tell them you get some annoying customers," I nodded, looked around the room, and gave the remaining customers a salute, "As you were, my friends," And swinging the keys around my finger, I left the warmth and comfort of the café.

I made a beeline for my mess of a house, where I gathered up a few things. Grabbing a black knapsack covered in various skull-shaped patches. I added two small cans, one grapefruit, one tomato. A Ziploc bag full of ground coffee, a barspoon, two clear plastic cups, a can of sprite, a small plastic bottle of Orgeat, a bottle of bitters. Add to that a book of matches off the counter, and some lighter fluid. Oh yeah, and of course, five mini-liquors.

24
LOST & FOUND

I prayed to the Goddess of the highway and touched the roof of Mori's car as I passed through yellow light after yellow light. My thoughts spun faster than the wheels. I had to focus, but the more I tried, the blurrier everything seemed. I rolled down the window, let the rain and cold air come in. The clouds were rolling in hard and fast, but the rain was starting to let up. The wind pushed leaves and branches across the road and threatened to throw even more debris in my way. This weather was getting weird. The lightning never stopped. I waited a few seconds, a thin wire fork split the sky above me. There was no thunder.

Sometimes magic freaks me out.

The flashes of lightning left everything in a surreal strobe glow, even when the blue silver light faded. The edges of the sidewalk jutted out in sharp contrast to the street, the city trees stretched nightmarish branches between razor edged telephone lines. Thankfully I was on side streets. The main roads would be a mess. The streetlights flickered like some horror film flashback, and the traffic lights weren't faring much better. I heard tires squeal, brakes scream, and metal crunch not once, but three times before I hit East Van, sirens moving in every direction. I assumed some of them were meant for me, but there were other distractions on the road. I drove fast, but not 'Hey look at me' fast.

When I neared my destination, I turned the headlights off and drove slowly past the bar. The wind was shaking the street signs and filling the air with paper and leaves, but other than that, there was no movement. There was one yellow light, hanging, swinging, above the front entrance. I knew someone was inside, though. I could sense the energy and feel the storm focusing, coming together around me. I needed to be careful. Most likely she'd be expecting me.

A whirlwind formed around the perimeter, touching down on the rooftop briefly and lifting again. It didn't seem to do any damage. I drove a block away and turned the corner, pausing at a deserted fast-food joint. Thankfully it wasn't a residential neighborhood, and the few businesses here were closed because of the storm. I drove around the empty restaurant, parking the Fiat in the back. I seemed to have bad luck with cars, and I wanted to keep this little getaway safe. Besides, having a still-in-one-piece car to hand back to Mori would probably be a good idea. I had to duck as large broken branches made their way through the air, and to push against the wind as I crossed the street. There wasn't much rain anymore, but the few drops hitting hurt. I held my hand out. It wasn't rain at all. It had started to hail. I fell into a fast, painful limp. I wasn't sure if it was the source or the actual storm causing it, but every injury I had was all anxious and eager again. I felt every bruise and cut.

I MADE it to the bar without seeing another living soul, which made me think about the non-living ones. Dabriel would have some safeguards up. If I didn't have to deal with those creepy bat things again… I shuddered. The storm was focused on the Lost & Found. Under the shifting clouds and peppered by hail, a wet fog seemed to be undulating, wrapping around the exterior of the bar like a wet defense. On my side, however, was a bar stocked full of alcohol, provided I could get to it. There were several ways to see what couldn't be seen. Most of them connected to other forms of magic. All that Third Eye stuff.

Realms I didn't want to dabble in. No thank you, Chakra Khan. Thankfully not everything had gone up in flames at the shed, and I had a hit of the Soul Kiss left. It was a powerful base for so many mixes, but here I needed it straight. No chaser. A couple of drops and it burns the veil between worlds. This is not always a good thing, but sometimes it's necessary. I let it slide down the back of my throat. There was a slight stain of sweet followed by a soft burn. I closed my eyes for a second and let the warmth spread. When I opened them, it was a new world.

I could taste the fumes from the cheap pumps at a nearby gas station. A car radio played a few blocks away, and there was a train heading towards downtown. I felt the rain pushing through the air around me, and a shiver of anticipation surging through the atmosphere seconds before another sliver of lightning flickered across the sky. I could see oil and water swirling towards the drain on the slick concrete, and I'd never seen it look so brilliant before. I lifted my face to the sky and caught raindrops on my skin, ecstatic. Water slipped into my mouth, and I tasted a hint of winter. It waited, slightly shivering, behind this last fling of autumn glow.

Even the Lost & Found stood out, irradiated in some strange light. The storm building around the structure wasn't touching it. The ground was soaked, but the walls were dry. I moved closer, letting the Soul Kiss wash over me. It hit my nervous system, touched my blood. The world behind our world is an exact duplicate, but without the structure of time holding it in place. Memories, of what has happened and of what might never happen, float around us. There are ghosts in everything. I reached out to touch the corner of the Lost & Found. Cold brick, but more. In an instant I saw the past, the bricks being placed, the paint going on. I saw, what, the future? A possible future? The bricks crumbling, flames rising. I stepped back, and I saw a shimmer over the entire bar like a projection of itself playing on the walls. A flash of a stripped-down skeleton of a building; all wood beams and concrete base. The image flickered and the vision changed until the whole wall was engulfed in fire. A hole opened on the corner. Flames shot out, a flicker of movement inside, and it was gone. Only the solid wall of the present remained. Probably not a good sign.

It wasn't only who was in the bar. The entire building held power. Something had changed at the Crossroads. There was a light missing. The balance was off. The Lost & Found had always been a place of power, but it had always been a balanced power. Trevor had always switched his drinks. To keep the dark and light in play. But now there were only shadows. Shadows of alcohol-fueled nights and lost mornings, the emptiness of desire, the sharpness of revenge, the stupid anger of drunkenness. And over it all, a spiraling weave of hatred. All these negative emotions and feelings hung down the walls. They crawled over the roof like twisted Christmas decorations. Ghost lights attracting ghost things. I saw some of them, shifting like visions at the corner of my eye; moving every time I looked.

I also saw symbols. Scrawled and carved everywhere. Some were Vévés. But there were others. Newer ones, older ones. Astrological, elemental, and even Satanic. Great. Voudou I could deal with. There was a natural belief there. A tie to the real world I understood. But Black Magic was different. Black Magic was used for only one reason: to cause suffering to others. It was selfish, it was corrupt, it was evil. It was used by a very select few, usually NewWavers. Most of the other Wavers wouldn't touch it, and the Triple Alliance had all but forbidden it. They can't completely abolish any kind of magic, but they can dissuade you from using it.

I was up against a big bad, and I'd already seen the bar collapse into flames. I didn't know if it was something I could change, but I had to try. The future has not been written in stone. I pulled my jacket closed and my knapsack tight against my back. The wind was crazy. It howled down gutters and through storm drains like a banshee lost and looking for a way home. I slowly walked around the bar, trying to figure out the best way to approach. The energy was affecting me, though. Combined with the Soul Kiss I started feeling light-headed and seasick at the same time. I reached the back, a dumpster full and pushed against the back door, the parking lot empty. I braced myself against the wind and took a few deep breaths and tried to focus on the reality of the night around me. Take energy from the true nature of the storm and use it.

THE RAIN HAD STARTED UP, harder than before. I was getting drenched, but I was loving it. Tonight, there were two forces at work: Dabriel's storm, and true nature. Real wild magic. I felt alive. The energy, the Soul Kiss, the night, the rain. Electricity pulsated inside of me as if I'd found the energy I'd been fighting. In this exhilarating night, it could all be mine. I'd felt this before. The night I killed the shapeshifter. The surge of power, the temptation, this wire-edged drug quivering against my skin. I tasted lightning; I felt the night tangling up like webs between my fingertips. I could use this, even without the alcohol. I could shape the world and pull this energy into me. I stood before the door of the Lost & Found knowing with one breath I could tear it apart. I could do so much more. I wouldn't have to worry about Earnest. I wouldn't even have to worry about the Triple Alliance. I could tell them all to go to hell. I could do whatever I wanted. I walked to the front of the bar, soaked through to the skin but feeling nothing but heat. I touched the front door, and knew I had the strength. I placed the palm of one hand against it and lifted the other to the sky. I could feel the night and the lightning running through me. The elements in the storm. I could hold them, control them.

I could see the green-orange light of the sky creeping down and slipping inside the bar, through the cracks, through the gutters. The painted-over windows pulsed with an ultraviolet light, and it was flashing in time with my soul. Pulling, calling, hating, loving, wanting. This place was overflowing with a flammable desire. Dabriel was inside, but this wasn't just her doing. There had to be someone else in there, and somehow, they were orchestrating the same storm I was wrapping around my fist. They were calling it down to use against me, so why shouldn't I use it first? I couldn't remember the last time I'd felt this angry. Or this powerful. I took two steps backwards and stretched my arms out against the circling wind, as if I was being crucified by unholy weather. I heard Earnest's words replaying in the back of my mind, "Even if you don't know who you are, or what you can do, I do," My jaw tightened, and I arched my back. My arms taut, my fingers splayed. I knew now. I let the lightning play between my fingers like spinning electric quarters around my knuckles.

I was elemental, and fire was my life. No. It was life…and it was in everything.

I don't know how Earnest figured it out. I had too much in front of me, and a new world within me. I could destroy this building and everyone in it. Maybe then I'd go and ask my questions. What could they do against me? Everything working against me, everything standing in my way, everyone who was trying to hurt me. I could burn them all down before they knew what was happening. I could burn them like…like …

Like Trevor.

I stopped and dropped my arms to my sides. I couldn't breathe, and I felt a burning, a heat twisting out from my throat. It started out warm and almost comforting, but quickly shot into my limbs, spread out across my chest, pulled me down in pain. I was on my knees, on the ground. Steam rose from my hands as they pressed against wet asphalt, and I knew the hissing sound I heard was the falling rain evaporating off my back. I felt a sharp tight blue burning fire at my throat. I rolled on to my back. I reached up and grabbed at the source. It was the amulet Dabriel had given me. The silver charm shaped like the chemical symbol for alcohol. It burned like frostbite. I tried to let go, but my fingers were frozen to the metal. I used both hands, pulling, but it wasn't working. I closed my eyes. This might be the end. Quietly burning and freezing to death on a dirty downtown sidewalk. Could've been worse, I guess. I caught a whiff, a familiar scent under that of asphalt and rain. Soft and floral, powdery…

White Musk. Dabriel.

Then I felt a breath, a warmth on my wrist, and it moved up towards my hand. Like soft lips touching the back of my hand. Like a whisper against my skin.

"Mom?" I whispered.

I opened my eyes, saw nothing but the rain. Dark clouds. The storm pushed down on me. It felt like my hands had thawed, like my body was healing. I still held the medallion in my hand, but the silver was starting to glow with a warm light, the blue fading to yellow. I sat up, still holding the silver, and the symbol on my wrist, my birthmark, my elemental mark was glowing, and behind it, as if traced beneath my skin and above my bones, was a small shape of lines. Like a Vévé, but for me, of me. Of my family. A Vévé used to indicate alcohol, or a wine spirit. These were the spirits I needed to call on. It felt like home. It felt like a place I'd always wanted to remember. The rule of threes, and I was the tip of the triangle. My fire, my alcohol, my soul. This was the thing I had that raised me above those who wanted to hurt me. I was whole.

I stood up, the anger clearing. Thoughts of revenge and destruction faded away. This hatred wasn't me. I could take this power and use it in the right way. I had to stay on the path I had chosen. Use the energy instead of letting it use me. Perhaps I would be judged; perhaps I would stand in front of the Triple Alliance, and they would find me guilty. But I was not going to be found guilty of doing the wrong thing.

I am not cold-blooded, I am not heartless, I am not the people I am fighting against. I have good inside of me, people I love and people who love me. My powers, my reason for being here, for living, for breathing, is to make things around me better. I am here to create, I am here to find truth, I am here to win. All the hate I held inside left like a breath of fog into the cold night air. I felt the rain falling again, hard, refreshing. I felt the pain in my leg, reaching through my whole body, but it wasn't going to stop me. Like anger, pain can be focused and transformed. I had a few weapons available to me, I had a few mixes up my wet sleeves, and I had the strength of my past, and the hopes of my future. And I had a brand-new fire burning inside. I was on my own, like it should be. The burn from my silver charm had changed. It felt different. It felt warm.

I opened the door and walked into an empty bar.

The storm pushed in like a wall behind me, throwing leaves and debris into the red lit room. I felt evil staining the walls. Things had changed. The floors were a solid, but slightly shimmering black. A very recent development. My feet made little clicks as they stuck and unstuck to the sticky paint. The walls were etched with strange words and scribbled designs; the atmosphere had shifted into some thick malignant funk. The music was foreboding and ominous. "Typical evil," I muttered, but I didn't feel any better. Where was everybody? I could understand how the force of the storm around the building would keep most of the customers, and even the regulars, from venturing inside, but still…empty?

A glow flickered on the other side of the room, from under the door to the office. Maybe not so empty. It was time to face what was coming, holding only a power I wasn't quite in control of against a woman who seemed to have hijacked the energy of an entire building. I wasn't sure what my plan was, but I knew it was going to involve a fight.

And I couldn't wait.

25
INVISIBLE MAN

The sharp acidic fumes of paint were mixing with a thick earthy mossy stench. It filled the air and my nostrils until I was almost choking. I stood in front of the door, the wind outside pushing against it, surveying the bar. Other than the walls and the floors, it didn't look different, it felt different. The effects of the Spiked Soul Kiss were still lingering. All the emotions, all the hurtful and dark thoughts I'd been wrestling with outside were here, practically dripping off the walls, through the dust and grime caked on the ceiling, through the slick surface of the midnight floors. And then I saw the shadows. Only they weren't shadows. They were thicker and greyer. Strange ethereal beings emanating vicious fumes of fear and hatred. Crawling around corners, hanging like putrid bats from the bottoms of tables and chairs.

I took a step towards a corner booth covered with these strange shifting grey creatures. They were like slimed over gremlins. A dozen misshapen heads turned towards me; dull eye sockets focused upon my movements. Thick tongues licked slippery lizard-like lips. They could see me, so they could probably do more, but they didn't seem threatened by my presence, only slightly interested. They were busy soaking up, sucking in, feeding upon the evil covering the bar like a second skin. It wasn't paint sticking to my shoes, it was the slime of the repugnant.

I took a step back, and the slime heads went back to licking the gelatinous membrane of repulsion. The stench was still surrounding me, but like living in a barn full of manure I was acclimating to it. I walked slowly towards the bar. There should be some kind of trap. Some kind of alarm. I couldn't let my guard down. Dabriel may have more power than me now, but I'd had more experience. If I didn't succumb to the potency of my surroundings, the electrical sharpness of the elements and the rage that grew inside me, I might be able to walk out of this bar alive.

But still, where were they? I had my eye on the office, but then I remembered the Speakeasy. The Blind Pig. I slowly walked towards the secret entrance, feeling a little unnerved by the silence and the emptiness. All I could hear were my footsteps and the rain outside. It was the last table at the end of the back wall; you sit down and press a lever in the floor, and a panel opens. I had to crouch slightly to go through, which didn't exactly feel safe, so I ended up stopping halfway between the entrance and the exit. Listening. Letting my eyes adjust to the dim blue light. There were more shade creatures in the tiny hallway, all of them almost translucent, showing nothing inside except a constant swirl of mucus. Not pleasant. They were slinking along the edges of the floor, as well as the low ceiling. Empty eyes dead and haunted, following me, watching, possibly waiting. I didn't want to know what they were waiting for.

I rummaged through my knapsack looking for something I could use in case they wanted to do more than watch me. I stuck the bar spoon in my back pocket, and realized I could make a variation of the Invisible Man. It wouldn't be perfect, but it might help me get closer and remain unseen. And then it hit me…I was in a bar. Idiot.

I moved fast and quick, ignoring the little things at my feet, above my head. If they weren't bothering me, I'd refrain, for the moment, from bothering them. I went back behind the bar, wanting to move fast and get this over with. Or at least get it started.

Gin, triple sec, cognac, orange juice, ginger ale. And then the power to make it do what it says on the label. I didn't have the right ingredients for the full effect, but with an eyelash plucked, touched with the tongue, and whispered against, I could make those evil little things look solid compared to me. I took the shot and moved back into the secret passage. It was working. My arms, my legs, were turning transparent. Not fully invisible, but well camouflaged. This one went quick, so I had to keep moving forwards if it was going to be of any use. I could see a flickering sickly glow up ahead, and I heard chanting. It wasn't English, it was German.

Not good.

I knew some German, mostly beer related. But I knew how to read the tone as much as the language being used. I continued moving forwards. There was a sharp turn in the passage, and then it opened into the Speakeasy. I stopped at the corner and held my breath, concentrating on the chant. It was a man and a woman both speaking at almost the same pitch and level. There were only two reasons for working this kind of magic: one was for a possession, the other for a weapon. The repeating words circled around and built up an energy to use against someone. In this case, me. I paused. One of the voices was familiar, but I still couldn't place the other. The language had been throwing me off, but it was Dabriel and someone else. Not Naberius… then, in time with a pause in the chant, the building shook. The first hit of thunder in hours. The rumble spurred the chanters on. The voices began again only this time harsher and more intense than before. I turned the corner. The room was bigger than I remembered, a maze of shelves leading to the bar at the far end, but I couldn't tell where the people were. Most of the shelves were full of books. Old leather-bound volumes with ornately decorated spines. The voices were carrying from somewhere within the maze of books. And there was music again, very low. Instrumental and bass heavy, pulsating like an undercurrent to the chant. The sick tiny creatures were everywhere, and they were slowly making their way through the maze, stopping occasionally to feed on some sort of energy trail covering the ground like a mercurial sickness.

. . .

I QUIETLY ENTERED THE MAZE. The ethereal slugs, as they were starting to become, were no longer concerned by my presence, but focused on finding their way to the source of the incantation too. I was wrong. It was a summoning. They moved like a pestilential parade between the storm building outside and the evil inside. The speakeasy had a line of thin windows near the ceiling, and the beat of the rain mixed with quick flashes of electricity. The thunder was back with a vengeance and each electric dazzle was followed by an almost instantaneous cold crack and rumble. As I moved, I passed more boxes like the ones from Blundertown Books, but these boxes weren't holding alcohol. It looked like bitters. The sizes moved from 16 to 6.7 to 4-ounce bottles. All labelled with a black logo of a familiar symbol. The horned cross with two spirals. The one from Christophe's iron sigil. And they were all empty, ready to be filled.

THERE WERE OTHER BOXES, piled almost to the tops of the shelves surrounding me. Some of them full of empty beer bottles made from emerald-green glass. In others there were bags full of what looked like chocolate but mixed with strange brownish red berries. It smelled like cinnamon and chamomile, mixed with vinegar. I closed a box in disgust and moved to the next stack. It was even worse. Ice cube trays were sealed in plastic and filled with a thick yellow liquid, gelatinous and smelling like fish oil and licorice. I recoiled but continued, opening boxes along the way. Boxes full of slightly off-white rock salt; one with vials full of a thick silver liquid. Mercury. Others were filled with Sulfur. The three primes of Paracelsus. This was hardcore elemental alchemy. I found black powdered coal and metal scrapings: Iron, copper, silver. Containers full of strange things, some recognizable, some not. Bags of reptilian scales, glass jars full of Vermilion—the brilliant red turned an unnatural hue by the blue light. There was wormwood, honey, lead, and something smelling an awful lot like manure. This was shaping up to be either a Mystixologist's dream, or worst nightmare. Considering who was involved, I figured it was moving towards the horrific side of things. Dabriel must be using the

Intoxicantata. It looked like the plan was to mass market some of the recipes. She was playing with fire and not your normal kind of burn the skin fire. This was literally playing with Hellfire. DarkWavers messing with drinks is one thing, but if the NoWavers started drinking these mixed magiks there'd be an exchange of energy, a corruption of innocent souls.

But there had to be something tying it all together.

I wouldn't have figured it out if all my senses weren't spinning on heightened waves. She was using the creatures. What tied everything together was the Lost & Found. Remnants of souls, desires, hatreds, memories, dreams, pain, and suffering. All those feelings lingered within the building. They worked together, spiraling like an invisible whirlwind around the eternal gravity of the Crossroads. Was this the energy Earnest Caan had been talking about using? Was he involved in this? Maybe all his talk about throwing me to the Alliance was a way to shift the blame. I was the scapegoat, and he was working with Dabriel. Who else would be able to move unnoticed through all the Waver bars? The man behind the curtain, staying out of the spotlight, was a member of the Triple Alliance.

I felt sick, weak, unsteady. I needed something to balance out the sickness of combining the Soul Kiss and the Invisible Man. As the voices undulated in waves against the fury of the weather, I quickly mixed myself a Vadász. It means 'hunter' in Hungarian and consists of red wine and cola. I added a dash of Orgeat to make it stronger. The almond syrup gave it an edge of watchfulness and clarity, the rose water for its healing properties, and the orange for its calming properties. I downed the shot and immediately stopped shaking, but I could still feel the evil undertones of the chant. It lit a glimmer of fear within me, but I had to ignore it. The words sounded thick and dark. I understood the meaning more than the exact translation. This language was meant to weaken and harm the enemy. A vocabulary that could kill. Umbrnigen, töten, blut und hass. And then a phrase one could apply to many things, but here it had to be for a special mix. "Aller guten Dinge sind drei."

Or "All good things come in threes".

Like cocktails. But using this phrase with darker powers leads to something you really don't want to drink. I had to come up with a plan, but it had to be the right one. What good is smart when you're up against a clenched fist? I thought about Jessica. I thought about Mori. I thought about how the Lost & Found was my home. I had to do this. Nobody else would.

The voices were getting drowned out behind the constant drum roll of thunder. It was time to move my energies in a new direction. I put a hand up to my neck and held the silver charm, trying to feel the same energy I'd felt before. I knew it wasn't in the necklace, it was in me, but I also knew I needed a way to channel it. That's why wizards had wands. I pulled the bar spoon out and pointed it towards a speaker in the corner. Concentrate. This wasn't alcohol, it was deeper. It's inside of me. Blood is thicker than vodka. A warmth of heat flowed inside and outside of my fingers, prickling and tingling. I didn't have a strong knowledge of German, but I could work a more traditional spin.

"Tace atque abi!" There's power in insults. This wasn't the best one, "Shut up and go away", but it was the first one I thought of. A flourish of orange flame spun from the end of the silver spoon to the edge of a speaker hanging on the wall. I didn't know how I was doing it, but I knew how to do it. The slick lick of fire wrapped around it, causing the plastic to start bubbling and melting. A thick black sludge filling the room with an acrid stench.

I spread my arms out and lifted my head "flammidemmia!" A bit overdramatic, but I didn't have time for subtlety. My opponents couldn't see me, but after this, they'd know I was here. An inverted whirlwind of soft flame formed in front of my forehead. A burning cone that held no heat. It was a twisting shell containing a storm of fire. I sent it up and over the maze. I pushed it towards the farthest wall. It hit and burst. A soundless explosion of liquid blue sprayed out of a shattered orange glass. The music and the chanting stopped, broken by a shout and a loud surprised swear. I ran as fast as I could between the walls of books, hoping to take advantage of the confusion. There was a man lying flat on his back across the marbled bar.

He was wearing a long black robe, arms crossed over his chest. It was Nick Noir. His eyes were closed. I couldn't tell if he was alive or not.

Christophe and Dabriel stood on opposite sides of the bar, and two women stood between them. Aisha and Murmur. Dammit.

Murmur stood about a foot behind Aisha, who was furiously pouring a variety of liquids from strangely shaped bottles into a large silver shaker and made strange flourishes with his hands over the container. Christophe and Dabriel both stared up at the dripping blue flame silently climbing over the walls. The light and shadows crawled across their faces. Dabriel's beauty became a venomous glamor while Christophe's profile was already sinister enough.

Surrounding the cocktail shaker were three long golden candles, burning a black flame. Thin tendrils of smoke spiraled up into the air above them. I didn't know what sort of mix they were working on, only that it was probably meant for me. I hoped I had enough within to stand against it. Dabriel held a spoon, like mine only more twisted and copper, between two fingers. A line of mason jars lined the counter between Nick's body and five crystal glasses. Each one already held what looked like a thin layer of deep red, glistening blood.

I noticed something around Nick's neck: my Egyptian amulet. And something was carved into the bar underneath his head. The same elemental symbol I'd seen earlier. Perhaps it was being used to draw out the power inherent in the necklace. Meanwhile all the little creatures were still moving, crawling, slithering around the floor, up the sides of the bar, and they were stretching as they got closer to Nick. Turning into more wormlike shapes. Their colors were shifting, moving from the vomitus green to a more dayglow chartreuse, like that viscous squishy slime I got in a little plastic trash can as a kid. I shifted just a little, trying to see more.

I shouldn't have. Christophe pointed in my direction and gave a shout. I knew he couldn't see me clearly, but he knew I was there.

"Dante," he called out, "Good of you to join us."

"Of course," I laughed, trying to throw them a little off guard. "Thanks for the invitation."

Dabriel shielded her eyes and squinted, trying to see more clearly, but I'd moved back against a shelf, hiding in plain sight. The camouflage would wear off any second, so I had to figure out my next move quick. Her expression shifted into hatred, and she pointed her bar spoon at the place where my voice had come from.

"Phainó!" The word echoed strangely in the room and with it a bright blast of the whitest light emanated from the tip of her makeshift wand. I was stunned, blinded. As the pulsating black spots that filled my vision cleared, I realized I was visible again. Aisha made a motion and Murmur left her position and started moving towards me.

"Bring him to me," Aisha commanded with a sneer.

Murmur started running towards me, and even without magic I knew she could probably do some damage if I let her.

I didn't let her.

I grabbed matches and the lighter fluid, then shot a stream towards Murmur. Lighting my end of the trail, the liquid burned towards her. But when it reached her, it didn't seem to burn.

In fact, it seemed to make her happy. He stopped and took a deep breath. And with the breath she started to suck in all the flames I'd sent at him.

"You're a demon?" I whispered, incredulous.

"Part demon," she hissed.

My hand touched the floor, index finger touching the burning liquid. I had to try again, harder.

"Ignis in flore," A wall of flame shot up, almost hitting the ceiling before falling towards the demon, although I still wasn't sure what kind of demon it was. She cowered for a second, stepped back, and then muttered a phrase against the fire, *"Kánei krýo. Échei aéra."*

It was her Greek against my Latin, and the results were unexpected. Murmur looked as surprised as I did. A wind, touched with an Arctic bite, came from his outstretched hands. It pushed against the fiery stream, enveloped it, and changed it into a perfect ice sculpture of fire.

The flame still burned inside the iced shell, and without warning the two forces exploded and both Murmur and I were thrown backwards. Even the two remaining behind the bar had been hit by a flurry of fire and ice. And they looked pissed.

I wanted to turn them all over to the Alliance and clear my name, so I wanted to make sure they lived through this fight. Besides, I wasn't quite sure how to kill an immortal. What I was sure of was they probably didn't have the same desire to keep me alive.

We all felt the power flowing through the room, pulling from the energy between us. It was thick and tangible. It was wild and uncontrolled in the speakeasy with the slime snake worms, the blue fire still lingering on the walls, the storm outside, the alcohol and amulets. It was like a supernatural twister caught reckless within the confines of the bar. Books fell to the floor, bottles shattered, and cracks appeared on the ceiling and the floor.

The storm was raging harder inside than it was outside. Books were starting to burn, and so was my knapsack. I grabbed what I could before throwing the burning leather bag towards the bar. I traced my steps quickly back to the speakeasy entrance, holding onto the shelves to help me keep my feet on the floor. I needed to take this into the main room, and hopefully outside. The power building up could destroy us all. And I needed to get them away from Nick. I couldn't tell if he was alive, but if he was, this could be his only chance to escape.

Christophe was looking a little confused, as if he wasn't sure where he should go. He gave me a look that reminded me of a deer caught in a blinding light. Dabriel struggled to keep her balance, both hands on the bar as she yelled obscenities at me. Christophe picked up one of the cups on the bar, and muttering something in Greek, flung it towards me as I backed away.

I ducked out of the way as it hit and shattered above my head. It was full of something extremely flammable. The blood, mixed with whatever else had been poured into it, burst into burning droplets. Thick like ink but smelling like burning leaves.

"There's nowhere for you to go," Murmur shouted, her words blowing past me on waves of ice-cold wind. "No way out now."

Christophe picked up another glass and moved towards me as I turned a corner. All I could hear was the crackling of the fire, and quietly underneath, Dabriel's laughter.

Heat rose from the silver charm around my neck. I reached up to hold it and an electric shock ran through my body. I wondered if I could use it to go back through the maelstrom and get Nick and my amulet, but now there was really no point. Even if I figured out how to channel this electricity it was still four against one. I needed to even those odds. I ran back towards the secret door, hearing shouts and the crack of fire behind me.

The hallway back to the main bar was thick with strange bluish smoke. The air glimmered with remnants of energy. I looked back and Murmur was heading towards me, Christophe and Dabriel following close behind. I had lost sight of Aisha, who was most likely still standing over Nick. Murmur stopped suddenly, waiting for something. I didn't want to find out what it was. I noticed while she was avoiding the tight licks of flame shooting out between the shelves, Christophe ignored them completely and moved closer, a tight smile on his face, his eyes locked on mine. Then his arm shot up into the air, his hand holding something. My amulet.

He started saying something. I couldn't hear the words, but his lips were moving fast. He lowered his arm, moving the fire symbol to his chest, and started walking in my direction. Murmur and Dabriel flanked him like officers of the damned. I hurriedly turned the corner as the trio continued determinedly towards me. What was he up to? I needed that amulet back. Soon.

Murmur arrived first, but she wasn't expecting me either. I pushed up and towards her, slamming my head into her chest. She pounded a fist between my shoulder blades, and we tumbled back down towards the fiery room past Christophe and Dabriel, who stepped aside to let us flail past them. We somersaulted over each other and came to a stop against the wall.

I scrambled to my feet and leapt on Murmur, but she was not about to give up easily. I grabbed her head and slammed it down on the floor while her knee ended up between my legs. I howled in pain, eyes watering, as she frantically tried to push me off.

Her hands grabbed at my hair and pulled at my ears. I could see her eyes start to turn red. Fire red. I needed to do something. I let her kick me off and used the momentum to move backwards so I had time to reach my Soul Kiss spray. I only had one hit left, and I didn't know how this would affect her, but it was worth a shot.

It hit her full in the face, and she went rigid. Full stop, eyes glazed, her face caught somewhere between human and demon. I reeled back and hit her as hard as I could in the stomach. She went limp. All the breath knocked out of her. I started to get up, turning, and found myself staring into the barrel of a gun. It was Dabriel. "Magic's too good for you," She spat.

I tried to hide my shock, but it didn't work. She threw her head back and laughed. Mistake. I swung my arm and knocked the gun out of her hand. It hit the ground and went off, echoing loud and sharp. The bullet vanished harmlessly into the wall, but as I turned to go after the weapon an excruciating pain erupted along the back of my thigh. I yelled out, my hands going to my leg, and I fell. Christophe stood silently in the corridor between the main bar and the speakeasy behind him. He was holding a long thin dagger, dripping with my blood. I pushed backwards, ramming into Dabriel, and knocking her against the wall. Gritting my teeth, I turned and ran towards the main bar as behind me the three regrouped. Dabriel picked up the gun, while Christophe helped Murmur to her feet.

"Just shoot him," Christophe yelled.

There was an empty click, then another. Dabriel swore, and the gun flew past me, bouncing off the wall and spinning to a stop a meter away. I leapt through the open panel into the main room of the Lost & Found and quickly moved to close the small doorway behind me. I saw Christophe touch the edge of his blade and then place a blood-stained finger on the tip of his tongue. He kept his eyes on me as he pulled a thin vial from a pocket. It was filled with a clear liquid. He spit a mix of saliva and blood into the tube and shook it while repeating a word over and over. Ouroboros. He chanted until it sounded like one long undulating chain of sound.

"Ouroboros, Ouroboros, Ouroborosouroborosouroborosouro..."

His eyes were closed, head tilted back, and he slowly poured the liquid on to the floor. It bubbled, steam rising, moving towards me like a tiny living rivulet. It was growing bigger at the head as it moved closer. The back end was still liquid, but eyes and a definite serpentine shaped snout was forming at the front. This was some powerful magic, and I was in its path.

"Where's Murmur?" I heard Dabriel ask.

"Dammit," Christophe spat back at Dabriel, "Find her!"

I tried to stand. Unfortunately, the wound I'd sustained wouldn't let me. I used my good leg to push backwards towards the bar, but the spit-snake was already coming through. I could hear it hissing above the distant crackle of fire. Dabriel took a step towards me, her eyes wild.

Behind her, Christophe was letting the growing snake through, and as it passed him, he stomped on it. For a second, I thought he was helping me, but no. He wasn't killing it; he was separating it. Into two, then three, and finally there were seven liquidized serpents. All of them singularly focused on me. They were growing, solidifying, and starting to move faster.

Dabriel grinned maniacally and moved closer. Her face was shining with sweat, her eyes filled with excitement and hate. She had picked up the gun and was pointing it at me. Probably this time with bullets included.

"Dabriel. Find Murmur, now," Christophe hissed. She turned and went back into the Speakeasy. Interesting. Since Christophe was the one in control here, maybe there was a way for me to create a divide between them. I knew Dabriel was not happy about taking orders, maybe I could make her even more unhappy about it.

She came back, looking slightly nervous. "She's not there. There must be another way out of the Speakeasy..."

This was an interesting turn, I thought.

"How could you do this, Dabriel? What did I do?" I asked her, as I stood shakily. As soon as I put weight on my bad leg I stumbled and grabbed at the counter.

"You ruined everything," Dabriel said. "And your death will make it better."

Before I had a chance to ask her what she was talking about, she raised her arm and fired. The bullet grazed my shoulder, and I fell backwards, knocking over glasses and random containers. My head hit the floor, and before I could get out of the way I was hit by a falling metal fruit tray. I lay still for a second, covered in wedges of lemon and lime, cherries, and sliced cucumber. I was trapped in a burning bar swimming with soulless supernatural creatures and enough Mystixology ingredients to intoxicate an army. And all I had was some lighter fluid, a bar spoon and a handful of fruit.

Who says I don't know how to party?

I picked a piece of lemon off my throat, and as my hand touched my alcohol charm, I got another shock of electricity and a whiff of burning citrus. I smiled. Reptiles don't like citrus.

26
BOILERMAKER

I was stuck behind the counter, but I kept quiet. I had a feeling my enemies thought I was dead. I was also within reach of a few dozen bottles of alcohol, which would've been great if they weren't locked in the cabinets behind me. I could see them all, right there, through extremely thick glass. Liquor, liquor everywhere, but…

I started to quietly pull myself up but slipped on maraschino cherry juice and fell back onto a pile of limes. I swore under my breath. I knew the fire was still burning in the Speakeasy and would find its way into the main room soon. I needed a weapon. I had smoke, and I had the inherent force of the crossroads rising like invisible fumes through the conflict. Chaotic magics seeping into the bar and filling the room. Good or evil, it was a vitality I might be able to tap into.

I grabbed a glass from the floor, and some limes. I had vinegar and sodium, both found in pickles, and they were great against pests. The pickles were right above me. Part one: squeeze the lemon juice, add some brine and spit, and cut it with club soda. Luckily, for parts two and three, I'd managed to keep a couple of small bottles from the knapsack, vermouth, and gin. It was like a Negroni, but with my own makeshift citrus pickle juice in place of the Campari.

The important thing here was to make sure the measurements were on point. I made the mix in the glass, covered it with the bottom half of a shaker, and shook. I took slow deep breaths, trying to let the mystical atmosphere fill and flow into my lungs. Mixing within, mixing without. Find the flavor, find the words, tie it all up with power and a little added reverse twist. Add the pickle into the container and shake with the cocktail before I poured.

Now, phrasing. I knew 'snake in the grass', but I wanted these snakes out of the grass. I wanted them dead or gone. I wanted them to burn themselves back to hell.

"Fututus et mori in igni!" I cried. Go die in the fire, you bastards.

I stood up, surprising Dabriel, and shouted it again, while scanning the room for Christophe. He was nowhere to be seen. I raised the cocktail mix in one hand, did a long pour into an empty glass while shouting out the phrase again. "Fututus et mori in igni!"

I poured half into my mouth before spitting it on the ground in front of the closest snake. The liquid splattered out mixing with the broken glass and splashing the head of the snake creature. It hissed and turned away, scars forming in the skin, which was still hardening. The droplets on the floor had turned into small globules mercury mixed with charcoal. Each droplet focused on a different snake. Seven silver balls of water, pulling in bits of splintered glass, spun like razor-blade wheels towards the creatures. The snakes, magical but not stupid, seemed aware of the danger they faced, and they all began slithering away.

Now, with each move the creatures made, the water balls followed. It was like watching a strange video game. Push the snakes into the fire. Dabriel's whole-body shook, and she yelled at me, hands flailing over her head like a temper tantrum. Christophe reappeared, coming out of the entrance to the Speakeasy holding three shot glasses, each overflowing with silver glittering liquid. He handed one to Dabriel. She calmed down a bit, which worried me, and then smiled. That worried me even more.

"Shotgun Cocktails. Time to bite the bullets, Dante," Dabriel shouted, throwing her glass. It flew with surprising speed and force towards me and thudded into the cabinet directly above my head. It didn't break but lodged into the wood. I dropped, shouting out in anguish as my shoulder hit the edge of the counter. Gritting my teeth, I crawled to the far end of the bar and slipped around the corner. At least there were only two left. Another hole appeared in the wood, this one shattering the glass of the cabinet and a bottle or two. A little river of whiskey started flowing out. That was two. I poked my head up…and there was the third, narrowly missing an ear. My leg was hurting like hell, and it was bleeding. More smoke pushed in from the speakeasy and a thin tongue of orange red flame licked out of the doorway. Once that fire got in here, we'd have a nice flaming cocktail going. Enough for everyone.

"Enough," Aisha shouted from the doorway. "Thomas Dante, show yourself."

I slowly pulled myself across the floor, my legs dragging, and peered around the corner. The snakes had all been driven back into the speakeasy, and Aisha stood holding the dagger and my amulet. Dabriel and Christophe stood on either side of her, glaring at me. My mind was spinning. I had assumed Christophe was the one in charge, calling the shots.

"You think you're pretty smart, don't you?" Christophe sneered, "But you're no match for us. Stop fighting and let this end."

"Or you could make this more difficult, which I think I might enjoy…" Dabriel added.

Aisha shot a look towards her, and she quickly lowered her head. Interesting. I guess I had been wrong about Christophe.

"Right, good plan," I clenched my jaw and took a deep breath. Ignore the pain. "Dabriel? I thought things were good between us. I thought we were friends…"

"We were…acquaintances. You couldn't see how envious I was? Of your powers? You're an elemental, and you wasted that on petty revenge. And then instead of making atonements, or doing your penance for the high and mighty, you hid away behind your bottles,"

Dabriel said, "And even that came so easy to you. I studied for years to understand the powers that the drinks held, how to use different ingredients, but you get your mixes right without even really trying. We need what you have, and the only way to do get it is with your blood. You might as well give up now. It's not going to be hard keeping you in here while the place burns down around you."

"Around us, you mean," I said. "And what about all the equipment and the ingredients you've has been stocking up on. It's all going to go if you do this. A blaze of goddamned glory. Line up the shots, my friends. Let's drink to our demise."

"Fool," Dabriel snarled, before whispering something into a clenched fist. "This energy, my friend, I took from you. From that charm you wear. Somehow, you've managed to stop the drain, but before the night is over, I will take what should be mine."

She stepped back and hurled a small ball of fire at the bar. It hit and exploded on the countertop harmlessly, but I knew if one hit a shelf of liquor, things would get very hot very fast. But now I had an advantage. I knew how to upset Dabriel, and that would either make her careless or just angry. Maybe not really an advantage, but...

"So clever. We've been making fiery cocktails for ages, and that's all you've got? We covered all this Blue Blazer stuff in high school," I snickered. "All this alcohol around, and you're playing with fire? How amateurish is that? Move onto something worth your time. Hell, move onto something worth my time."

I looked around the bar, back at the cabinets, searching for something I could use as a weapon. Christophe took a step forward, but Aisha pulled him back.

"Remember, we need him alive."

"Yeah," I agreed. "You do...wait, you do?"

"Don't start, Dante," Dabriel said between clenched teeth, her voice low and menacing. "One of us is holding fire between their fingers and the other is bleeding to death in a pool of well drinks. You're a stuck-up pretentious know-it-all who doesn't deserve anything, but since Trevor is dead, we need you, or at least what's inside of you."

"That's not much," I said. "Not anymore. Maybe I could give you something else?"

Dabriel laughed, then stopped as if a brick wall had fallen on humor. "You're not getting out of this, Thomas Dante. You can't see it, can you. Both you and Trevor, so blind to all you could've had. All those years watching him waste his talents, all those years pretending to be impressed by your little mixed drinks. You fly all high and mighty, but you've squandered every gift you've been given, every lesson I've tried to teach you. No more, Dante. What I took from Nick Noir is still attached to him. Once I can sever that tie, it will be mine, and he can die. And I will do the same with you. Your power will be mine. And when this is over there won't be enough of your blood left to make a Celebratory Caesar."

"You know I'm not alone, right? Gilles and Jessica are still out there, and Dabriel, what about your brother? Naberius doesn't want this for you. You must know that."

"What I know is that the Agentia has nothing on me, but once we're through with you, all the evidence will point to you. I'm going to be the victim, and you're going to be dead. A fire spell gone wrong, with you in the middle of it. I'll get the bar, and you'll be forgotten," Dabriel sighed, "And my brother? He's not going to stand in my way. He doesn't get involved. You should know that by now."

"Sorry to rain on your boring parade," I retorted. I needed to distract. I needed to lie… "But the Alliance and the Agentia know all about this. I'm willing to bet agents are on their way right now. A burning bar is not something that goes unnoticed. Once our favorite Wavers come and find your soul sucking spells and your plans to mass market the mystic juice, it'll be all over. You know how hard they come down on abusers of magic, right? It isn't pretty."

Dabriel's mouth twitched and creased into a crooked grin. "I don't believe you. You're trying to distract me, Dante."

"I'm trapped in a burning bar, no escape and all that. Why would I lie to you now?" I said. "If I was lying, I'd be telling better stories than these. Oh, and I have one more for you, Dabriel. You tell me if I'm lying. One of your partners here is playing you. You aren't the only one who can lie and scheme."

Dabriel's eyes narrowed. I got her. Now I just had to prove it. It was starting to kind of make sense, though.

"This is obviously about more than the bar for you, but what about them? Christophe has his dreams, his plans, and your Bruxsa friend? This is personal for you, but Aisha doesn't care about any of this. They are using you to get what they want. Sure, maybe you all want me dead and drained of all my powers, but then what?" I laughed quietly, "And you thought I was the stupid one?"

I stopped to cough. It was getting harder to breathe. Smoke and strange fumes were pouring in from the Speakeasy, and the flames were slowly climbing the walls, going for the ceiling. Aisha turned to Dabriel, saying something, her hands gesturing wildly. It looked like she was failing to be convincing. Behind them, I could see the entrance to the speakeasy was engulfed in flames, only they weren't normal flames. I felt the heat, and the walls were burning. The flocked wallpaper curled up and disintegrated, but the fire was tinged blue and green. A supernatural glow shone through the orange and yellow burn. It was filling the room, but it didn't seem to be moving outside. It was like it was controlled, or aware.

"And don't forget about Marinette, Dabriel. She's not going to let you take over the Crossroads."

"Shut up. You have no idea," Dabriel yelled. "You know nothing."

"I always thought you were the good one, Dabriel. I never trusted Naberius, but now I know. You're the weak one. You're the one who's lost."

I had to keep her distracted, keep her on the defense. She didn't seem to be as confident when she was flustered. This might give me an opening, for something…

"Enough with this talk," Christophe said. "You know what happens when you sit around and explain everything. We can do this without him. Let me kill him. There are other elementals, and we need to get out before it all goes up in flames, and if we go now, we might be able to get Naberius back on our side."

"It won't be easy," I said. "I've got some tricks left that'll blow your mind. I may die, but there's no way I'm going to die alone. Not here, and not today. All this fire, all this power? Are you kidding me? I'll bring the whole bar down on top of us."

"Quit babbling, you idiot," Aisha yelled. "Stop trying to confuse her. The Alliance wants to lock you up, the Agentia won't help you, and Christophe wants to kill you right now. Give up."

I knew if I didn't stop them, Jessica would be in jeopardy as well. Everyone connected to me was in danger at this point. If I died, I had to make sure I didn't put a target on anyone else.

"Go to hell, Aisha. I'm giving you nothing."

I knew I couldn't make it out without a fight, but I didn't know if I had any fight left in me. The fire was spreading, the smoke was obscuring my vision, and somehow Aisha had managed to create a thick wall of fire that was moving between us, blocking the back of the bar.

She stood behind the flaming obstacle making gestures and mouthing words. I couldn't make them out, but I could see the hate emanating off her.

"Dabriel, Christophe. Leave, now," Aisha said. "I'll finish this."

They started towards the back office, but just before they moved out of sight, I swear I caught Aishas looking back with a worried glance, but when she turned back to me it was all anger.

"It's closing time, my dear," Aisha sneered. She ran a hand through the flames, caressing them, and they seemed to caress her back, "But please, don't worry. I'm not going to let you die here all alone. You're going to have company."

That didn't sound good.

"This little trick I learned from Trevor. He taught me a lot about fire," Aisha held my amulet directly over the fire while spinning her other hand in a tight figure eight motion, drawing the flame towards the amulet in a small burning whirlwind. "Of course, he told me this was never to be used in public, and I should be careful if it's around anything larger than a candle flame."

The fire pulsated as she traced a line of symbols in the air, the letters burned and floated above the wall of flame. δράκους.

"Let's find out why..." She raised her eyes slightly to catch mine, making sure I was watching.

The air solidified around the burning incantation. "Drakon," Aisha chanted, "Drakon fotyá. Drakon."

She moved slowly back towards the office door while continuing to repeat those words. The symbols in the air spiraled and formed a burning globe. Aisha raised her hands to the ceiling, and one last time, completing whatever curse she'd been casting, she yelled, "Drakon!"

The lightning outside hit. The thunder rattled, but it was a quiet and rolling explosion, muffled by the smoke and fire, followed by the stink of burning flesh and death. Aisha crouched by the office door watching me as the light played through the room. Oranges and greens and flashes of electric white from outside mixed with rolling grey smoke. I was in a bar in Vancouver, but it might as well have been one of the circles of Hell. The fiery globe between us was spinning and shifting. Morphing into something else. A fiery snake, a lizard...no, a full-on fire breathing creature of darkness. The power Aisha must have used to call it forth is what really shocked me. Being able to create living forms from the elements was not an easy trick, and it never ended well for anyone.

The power drain usually killed the summoner as well as the intended victim. Aisha was struggling to stand but kept falling back against the wall. The burning Dragon shuddered like a flame caught in the wind and moved slowly towards me. It stopped and reared up on two scale covered hind legs, thick and golden green. That's when I noticed it had two heads. One of them was peering around the bar, but the other watched me with electric red eyes. Something was amiss, though. Aisha was finally standing, although shaking from the drain of energy, and I wasn't the only one picking up on it. Dragons hate people. Dragons also eat people. And if you've recently called a dragon into existence, or worse, pulled it from some alternate dimension or universe, you are not the creature's favorite being.

Aisha's eyes darted from me to the dragon, to the exit behind her.

She pointed three fingers at me and hissed something at the dragon's head closest to him. It swayed slightly but didn't turn. She lifted my amulet, spat on it, and threw it at the dragon. Its mouth opened, exposing huge teeth dripping some kind of thick foaming spittle.

Now, thanks to the taste of my special token, both creature's heads were watching me. It gave a double split tongue flick and steam-filled hiss and started moving slowly closer. It was half engulfed in flame, but it wasn't burning. It was part of the fire, and I realized it was soaking up the fire around it. Give thanks for small mercies. Aisha moved to the exit, giving me an almost apologetic smile. She was standing taller, stronger.

"You have nowhere to go, Dante. I am sorry. You should have agreed to help me when you had the chance. Now it's too late. You see before you the jaws of defeat," She spread her arms out wide, crucifix style, and cried out towards the dragon-demon, "Finish it, now."

I pulled myself up, barely able to stand, but I wasn't going to face death lying down. I steadied myself and tried to send a withering look at Aisha. I took a step forward as the creature continued sucking in flames, growing larger.

"Jaws of defeat?" I laughed. "That's what you came up with?"

Aisha faltered a little, her proud stance slightly deflating. I could see a seed of doubt growing behind her certainty. I didn't have my amulet, but now I knew exactly where it was. I took another step forwards, raised my arms, then lowered them until both hands were pointing at the dragon's heads.

"Here's something you might not know. When you let go of something that holds power, you lose that power. Even if you place it somewhere like, oh, I don't know, inside a dragon" I smiled. "As long as you held the amulet, you held a part of me. Now you don't. I can now literally snatch victory from your so-called jaws of defeat."

I closed my eyes and found the connection to that which belonged to me. Like a thread in the air. And I spoke the words inscribed on the back of the amulet, solid and steady. "Kulle muškila wa-liiha Hall."

Something both my parents had taught me, forever written on the back of my amulet in Egyptian Arabic; every problem has a solution.

The reptilian creature paused; confused and sucking in smoke and fire. Its heads moved back and forth; a hideous guttural hacking noise emanated from its throats. I repeated the phrase while focusing on pulling an invisible line towards me. I took a step backwards, feeling like I was fishing in the wrong ocean.

"Gonna need a bigger bar," I muttered to myself, and gave a hard psychic tug.

The creature was resisting, and it felt like my forehead was being pulled outwards. My temples pounded and I started to see a mandala of black spots. Midnight shadows were closing in like a collapsing tunnel around my vision. I faltered and fell as Aisha let out a delighted laugh.

"You have something of mine, monster. I need it back," I choked, having trouble finding the strength to speak. The summoning spell caught in my throat; sharp, burning. I barely held on and felt as if my skin would split down the center of my face. Any second I'd have to let go, which would release the tenuous hold I had, and I'd be nothing but dragon food. Its tongues flicked back and forth; its sharp tail rose up and sliced down, splintering the hardwood floor.

I COLLAPSED. Images were flashing behind my clouded eyes: Jessica, lying in the ambulance, my parents showing me how to mix a simple Manhattan, and Trevor sharing his secrets with me. They were all there and they were waiting for me. I could go right now.

But there was a shimmer, a glow around my visions. They weren't waiting—they weren't beckoning. They were pushing. All of them. The vision was telling me to stand, to fight. This was not the end of the story. Gathering every bit of strength I had, I stood up. I subconsciously grabbed for the amulet that used to be around my neck, but my fingers wrapped around the alcohol charm from Dabriel instead. It was if I'd grabbed a live wire. That *is* how she did it. Draining my power, somehow, through the charm I'd been wearing ever since I got it.

"No more," My breath stung my throat, and my voice cracked. I ripped the chain off my neck and threw it to the side. I stood as straight as I could, staring at the fires in front of me. I was not going to die lying down. I was going to look death in the face and let it take me where it would. I spoke the phrase that was inscribed on the back of my amulet one last time. I couldn't even tell if I said it right. The fiery creature's eyes flickered like a bad lightbulb, and it took two unsteady paces back. It released a scraping cry. A high-pitched shriek cutting through the air like metal against metal. The dragon's heads smashed into each other. Limbs, heads, and tail thrashed against the floor. Huge chunks of wood flew up from the onslaught. Even though I might have been watching its death throes, my resolve weakened, my strength left me, and a blackness came over me like a blanket of finality. I lay on the floor, staring at the ceiling, while only a few feet away the monster convulsed.

"Thomas!" I heard Aisha shouting, but I couldn't see her. The fire burned like a low gas flame, but the smoke choked the room. Her voice was panicked, "What's happening?"

I shook my head, got to my knees, and pulled myself up using a nearby chair for support. Aisha stood shouting behind the shuddering dragon, "Drakon! Get up, Burn it all! Burn him! I brought you here, you are mine. Drakon! Fotyá!"

The creature gave a spasm and turned one of its heads towards Dabriel, the other towards me. It looked like it was trying to decide, but then with a sick tearing sound the scaled skin at the crux of the two necks split open and the amulet burst out as if shot from a slingshot and flew straight into my hands. I collapsed on to the floor, drained, but filled with a huge sense of relief; however, there was no time to relax into it. Both Aisha and the beast howled. The creature had come to a decision. All four of its eyes, both heads, turned as a thick obsidian blood poured from the gaping wound in its neck and pooled on the ground beneath it. Slowly, but with obvious determination, it moved towards Aisha.

"Damn it," I couldn't let it end like this. I had one last chance, and hopefully enough strength to pull it off. It was like taking a last breath. I couldn't feel my body anymore, except for the ball of pain in the shape of my head, but I pushed against it and called up all the elemental blood I might have in my veins. I felt a burning, a heat under my skin, then a lifting sensation. It wasn't like anything I'd felt before, but it was part of me. It felt like wind, but softer. It felt like air. Warm air. The softest, gentlest flame. Fire didn't need to be harsh and destructive.

I smiled weakly, hoping I was right. If there was somewhere that held the things I'd need to break the Alliance's hold on me, it would be here, and now. All the unbridled power, the alcohol, the fire, the adrenalin. I had to try.

Or I would die.

"Alis grave nil," I whispered. Nothing is heavy to those who have wings. I felt myself rising. And the heated air lifted me in gentle hands and then not so gently threw me past Aisha. Spinning, somersaulting across the bar, I hit the office door hard. It slammed open, almost off the hinges, and I landed in a heap by the exit to the alleyway.

"That didn't quite work out like I thought it would," I groaned. I rolled over onto my hands and knees. The monster was still heading for Aisha, who was moving towards me. The warmth flowed around me like waves parting around a rock. The dragon and Aisha were being pushed against their will into a sideways hurricane, and I was in the eye of it. A heatwave tornado created by a broken elemental. I scrambled backwards, through the back door into the dark alley. I'd expected to find myself outside a war-torn building ravaged by flames, but there was nothing. Not a wisp of smoke, not a lick of fire. Somehow all the energy was staying inside. As if the walls had been built specifically to hold magic. The city remained oblivious.

What I did find was a full-blown storm. The air from the Lost & Found pushed out into the world, mixing with the weather, and Aisha and the dragon were coming with it. I scuttled backwards, trying to stop the wind I'd created, but it swept me up as well. The three of us spun out of control and up into the air. Aisha screamed; I heard a stuttered pained screech from the dying dragon, but I was too weak to make a sound. I don't know how high we went. Too high. I imagined falling, smashing to my death on city streets.

And then down. The rush hit hard. My entire body tensed up, ready for impact. It didn't happen, but Aisha wasn't as lucky. She slammed on to the rooftop while the creature plummeted past her, straight through. I was the only one spared, held by a heatwave with feathered hands and lowered like a mother placing a baby into a crib. On the other side of the hole created by the fallen dragon, Aisha moaned in pain. She wasn't fully transformed yet. The Bruxsa was still developing, but not yet undead.

"You can still save yourself, Aisha. You don't have to die…"

She turned and looked over at me. I could feel heat rising beneath me. Smoke was coming up, but it didn't rise into the air above, but crawled along the roof, covering everything in a thick charcoal fog. I sat up, then screamed at the pain in my leg. The throbbing in my head had escalated into full blown blinding migraine razorblades. I crawled towards the gaping hole and peered through. My eyes watered from the billowing smoke. I was directly above the speakeasy. The dragon was still alive, though badly hurt. It wasn't moving, not much, but its twin set of jaws opened and closed, its tail snapping against the walls and floor.

"I will not die like this," Aisha yelled at me. "You will."

She got to her feet, swaying slightly, and took a step forward, moving slowly towards the edge of the hole in the ceiling. She looked down, raised her head, glared at me, and before I knew what was happening, she'd leapt across the smoke- filled chasm towards me.

She landed close to the edge of the shattered ceiling, and I stepped backwards as she slowly moved towards me.

"What did you do?" she demanded.

"Waver law. You should have known."

"What do you mean?"

I smiled, and it hurt.

My voice was cracking, my words hurt my throat, but I continued, "You know power, but you weren't born with it. You don't understand it."

"But I'm going to take it…"

"No," I said quietly, taking another step backwards. "You never learned the meanings, did you? You just wanted the result without having to deal with any of the consequences."

Aisha's lip curled up, "Right now, I just want you dead."

I ignored her, "Any binding used on a summoned creature only lasts if the binding holds. You lost the amulet," I said, "Which means the creature is free. Bound to no-one."

"But it will still kill you," Aisha growled.

"Yes, but it'll happily take you as well. You know natural law doesn't really apply to these otherworldly creatures, right?"

"What law?" Aisha asked.

"You know, like the way our universe works. These things heal fast, especially when they eat fire the way this one does. Like the way wolves and Elementals heal faster than humans," I managed to nod towards the pit. The creature was on its feet, blood seeping from the V of its neck, but the wound was almost gone. Aisha turned to look and then looked back at me. I could see her certainty had been replaced by fear.

"Can you stop it."

"Not like this. But it's fine, I'm ready to die. You'll keep me company, right?"

Aisha looked at me, and then before I could react, she leapt towards me, grabbing my shoulders.

"No," She pulled me close, her face right in front of mine, "It wasn't supposed to go like this. But if I'm going down, you're going down with me, and I'll deal with you in hell."

I MIGHT BE able to get out of this alive, I thought to myself, but if I used my magic directly on Aisha, even in self-defense, the Alliance would have a field day. There was still humanity left within her. I knew I was going to be in trouble as it was if I survived.

I gave her a soft smile and shook my head, "I don't think so."

"Then you can go without me. I'll get away while it's busy chewing on your bones," She spun around so now I was on the edge. I struggled, but Aisha was exceptionally strong. She was also working with fewer wounds than I was. The smoke was up to our knees; the fire burned slowly and patiently, still being pulled through the dragon's hide, healing it below as we fought above. The commotion attracted the creature's attention, and it slowly moved beneath us. Its eyes were flaring up into a horrible red again; its mouths salivating, waiting.

I managed to kick her legs out from under her and we both fell, practically balancing on the edge of the opening. She yelled and tore at my arms as I tried to pull myself over her and away from the chaos below. Then there was a commotion down below, something moving behind the creature. I managed to scramble back, away from Aisha, but before I got too far, she pushed out with her leg and gave me a shove. With a shout I started rolling over the edge. Suddenly, a shape flew past me from below and landed on the roof top. I was grabbed by a clawed hand, talons jabbing my skin, but it was better than falling to my death.

I was tossed like a doll across the roof, and as I rolled to a stop I looked up and saw a familiar shape. It was Dabriel. Wolf Dabriel. She was almost completely transformed, but the human in her was still visible. She stood on her hind legs, towering above Aisha, and threw her arms back while letting loose a bloodcurdling howl into the storm and night above her.

Then too fast to react to, Dabriel grabbed Aisha's leg and unbalanced by the weight, they both started to slide over the jagged opening of the roof. Aisha caught a vent pipe, while Dabriel stuck claws into a wood beam jutting out from the wall. I started crawling towards them, trying to avoid holes starting to burn through the structure. Aisha hung on, glaring at the beast beneath her with a mix of horror, revulsion, and hostility. I could see her close her eyes and her lips start to move. She was trying to conjure something.

She held on to the vent with one hand to start an incantation in the air. I didn't know if she was going to work it against me, Dabriel, or the creature below, but I knew I couldn't let her finish. Dabriel knew as well. She let loose another howl and clawed at the beam. It looked as if she was trying to pull herself up, but she wasn't. She was swinging herself, shifting her weight back and forth, trying to get closer to Aisha.

If she missed, she'd fall to her death.

"Dabriel," I yelled. "I don't know if you understand this, but don't do this. We can fix this. Think about Naberius. Your family. Think about the bar, we can make this work. Climb back up..."

Dabriel, almost all wolf by this point, looked up at me and I saw a glimpse of something. More than pain, there was a depth of sadness in her eyes. The shape of a broken heart.

She hung motionless for a second.

"Dabriel," I pleaded. "don't..."

Behind her, Aisha continued to make gestures in the air and the dragon circled below. Dabriel swung one last time and let go of the beam. Her body sleek and sinewy, curved toward Aisha, and with a sharp growl, caught on to the same vent. She was hanging by one hand and used the other to swipe at Aisha. Claws met flesh, and Aisha screamed in pain. She retaliated by using her free arm to grab at Dabriel's snout, scratching and drawing blood, and then maneuvering herself to get at the wolf's eyes.

Dabriel, in pain, was starting to change back into human form, but something else was happening beneath her. The fire was being pushed away by a sudden wind. A controlled wind that circled beneath her. I realized that as the wolf faded, the elemental side grew stronger. And just in time. Aisha lifted her leg, kneeing Dabriel in the ribs, and she lost her grip.

Falling, Dabriel reached up and grabbed Aisha's foot, and they both dropped. Straight towards two wide open fire dragon mouths. Seconds before they were caught upon daggers of teeth, Dabriel's wind swirled and lifted both just above the beasts reach. Aisha shouted in rage and attacked Dabriel in midair. Punching, grabbing, biting, and scratching in a frenzy of anger and destruction. The wind beneath them lost some power as Dabriel struggled and then vanished. The two of them both screamed as they fell towards the waiting creature.

. . .

Dabriel's shoulders and chest were caught by one set of jaws, while the other grabbed at Aisha's legs. Aisha pulled herself free, screaming as teeth tore flesh, and fell to the ground below. Losing its meal, the second head turned its attention on Dabriel, and made a toothy grab for her limbs. Dabriel screamed in pain as the beast held her stretched between its heads. Teeth slowly pushing down, breaking skin. Beneath her Aisha crawled slowly towards the exit.

The fire was pushing up stronger, flames getting closer to me, and I had to pull away from whatever was going on below. Now that Dabriel's wind had dissipated, I could feel the heat and fear turning into sweat. I wasn't going to make it. But at least I knew that Gilles would make sure that I wouldn't die in vain. I had faith in him, and in Jessica.

Jess...I wished I could have said good-bye.

I'd managed to destroy a large part of Aisha's plans, and Dabriel had sacrificed herself to help me. I rolled on to my back, stared up at the sky. I didn't think Dabriel was going to survive, and I was pretty sure I wouldn't either. Perhaps Naberius would be able to rebuild the Lost & Found. I knew I owed Naberius a huge apology. I'd spent so many years trusting the wrong person, I felt a little stupid. Stupid and ready to die. There's an epitaph.

I took a deep and slow breath against the smoke and the heat of the fire and crawled to the edge of the roof where I could see what was happening below. Aisha was trapped under the foot of the demon dragon, screaming and cursing, and Dabriel hung limp from the dragon's jaws.

The rain had stopped, but the thunder came down hard. I stared at the carnage and destruction below, and then the rooftop cracked beneath me, and I lost my balance, barely managing to grab the edge. I was going to die. My mind raced.

Final wishes, last words, last meal, last cigarette...

I did have one smoke left; I laughed to myself.

Wait. What if I could use my last cigarette for a final mix? If I could get to the bar without dying, I might be able to give living longer a chance. The cigarette was tucked away with a book of matches in my little silver tin. Inside jacket, zipped up pocket.

"Dabriel! Can you hear me? Your wind, bring it back. Help me down!"

I saw her head move slightly; her eyes open. She tried to say something, but I couldn't tell what it was.

"The wind!"

Her arm moved slightly, slipping out of the creature's mouth, her fingers twisting in the air, and I felt the air pushing up against me. It was weak, but it felt strong enough to cushion my fall. I hoped. I let go, fell…and didn't hit the ground.

I hit the beast, and it threw its head up, startled. Dabriel screamed in pain, but one of its mouths opened, partially releasing her. I tried to pull its other mouth open, jumping and grabbing on to its other head, but those jaws were too tight. A death grip that would not release. Streams of blood ran down the length of Dabriel's body, pooling on the floor. The creature shifted its stance, pulling its heads farther apart so one could get a better look at me. Dabriel shifted, raising her head slightly. There were long gashes like jagged train tracks along her skin where flesh had been divided by tooth. Then as the dragon moved one head towards me Dabriel grabbed my hand and pulled me off the other. She growled as she held me, swinging me towards the other side of the bar that had not been hit as hard by the fire. She was changing again, shifting back into wolf form. It was not a fast transformation, and I could tell she was fading fast.

I yelled out in pain as she swung me. It felt like my arm was going to tear off. I screamed up towards the thundering sky and all I got in response was a weak laugh.

"It's been fun, Thomas. I'll buy you a drink in hell," she muttered. I felt her grip loosen.

"Dabriel, what are you doing?" I yelled.

"Making it right…" She wheezed as she released me on the upswing. The strain got her as well, pulling her against teeth. Her leg was still caught in one of the demon's jaws. As I flew the sudden shift of weight surprised the creature. With a supreme effort, Dabriel wrenched her leg free and crashed into the scorched floor of the speakeasy while I slammed into the top of the bar with a sickening thud. A shower of sparks swirled up, caught on an updraft, and I held a brief instant of wonder as a miniature flurry of tiny shooting stars spiraled up into the night, burning into the sky. I tried to get up, but slipped and feel to the floor, dazed.

A horrendous screams engulfed the room, and I turned to see the creature tearing into Dabriel. There were horrific sounds of mangled flesh and breaking bones, and scraping and slurping noises from the dragon, and finally, a last strangled scream. I turned my head, fighting back the urge to vomit. I couldn't look, but I knew I was going to be next if I didn't do something. Every bone in my body hurt, but I managed to crawl behind the bar looking for alcohol. I was having trouble breathing in all the smoke and only had enough energy for one drink. I hoped it would be strong enough. I got my tin and scanned the bottles, grateful the bar in the speakeasy wasn't locked. It had to be rye. Not gin, not vodka, not rum, not tequila, not crème de menthe…I threw half a dozen bottles over the bar towards the dragon, hoping some of them might catch fire and give me some time. Finally, I found the liquid I was looking for. I crawled towards the end of the bar and spotted a tumbler on the ground. That would have to do. I focused on the recipe. All four Elements coming together as one. I rolled over again and saw what was left of Dabriel. The monster was simultaneously chewing through her torso and trying to find something. Me. There was a flurry of blood and flame, smoke, and guttural growls.

I moved to a sitting position, trying to catch a breath, and my eyes got stuck on the view above me. The storm was clearing, Aisha had scurried away, Dabriel was no more, so all the power brought forth had been freed into the world. The hole in the ceiling had opened into a makeshift spotlight on the stars, visible thanks to the surrounding power outage.

The city sleeps, the stars play in its darkness. This was it. The perfect moment to do or die…or both. I wasn't expecting to survive, I was expecting a death worthy of a hero I'd never been. I took the last cigarette out of my tin, slid it between my lips, lit a match, closed my eyes, and inhaled. Head rush, head spin. I felt myself drift up towards the ceiling before crashing back down into my body as I exhaled, like some brute force astral projection. Even my soul ached. I held the cigarette between my fingers, blew a thin stream of smoke onto the glowing eye at the tip, and realized this was my wish smoke. The last one from the pack. The one saved for a rainy day or a day of death. All I wished for was forgiveness from Jessica.

I held that thought behind closed eyes for a second, took another drag, and started on the mix. Two shots of Rye for the spirit and a dash of bitters for the soul. The last dance of a dying chance. Earth came from the tobacco, fire from the cherry tip, put out by water, which was my spit. All I needed was the wind, and I had a breath, stained with smoke. Not enough for a story, and barely enough for a joke.

I stirred the tobacco-stained cocktail in the glass with my finger, covered it with my palm to give it a few quick shakes. The Catcher in the Rye. Not a pleasant aroma, but it wasn't meant for a nightcap, it was meant for an ending. I poured as much of the drink as I could into my mouth, not swallowing, but swirling and tasting. I let the elements inherent in the mix fill my head. I moved to the edge of the bar and saw the monster had figured out where I was. It looked as if only one of the heads was working, but still…one too many heads for me. I held the liquid in my mouth, knowing I needed to be closer. I needed to be too close. I never thought I'd be going out this way. Dinner for a demon. C'est la vie.

As the thing slithered towards me, half blind, all anger, I pulled myself towards it. When we were about four meters apart, I spat the drink out in a fine spray. It showered out in front of me, spreading into a burning web of alcohol and fire. It held all the elements within it, and it shimmered as I blew it forward, floating like a net of tinsel towards the fiery demon. It screamed then, not a human scream, but a high-pitched and horrible wailing whining scream. I watched as long as I could, fighting the haze that was trying to shove my consciousness aside. I slipped back and down onto the floor as the creature became engulfed in a fire stronger than its own. But it still, slowly, moved closer. I started pushing myself backwards, trying to get away from the thing, but I knew I wasn't going to make it far.

Thankfully I'd be unconscious by the time it arrived. My eyes were stinging, my ears were ringing, and I thought I saw a movement from the far end of the bar. A shadow, something…a wolf. Not Dabriel, but larger, darker. I couldn't focus and forced my eyes to stay open for as long as possible, viewing the scene through a blurred squint. I saw a flash of bone white claws, then a spurt of blood from the demon's one good head. It turned and snarled, crimson-stained teeth bared towards something, and then shuddered to the ground.

"Naberius," I coughed, hoping I was right.

And as my eyes closed, I saw the wolf nod slightly towards the fallen creature, as if honoring it, then it turned towards me with a sharp-toothed smile. It fell to the ground on all fours before effortlessly leaping to my side.

I didn't know what this wolf-thing had in store for me, but I had a feeling the dragon might have had a more pleasant experience.

And then everything went dark.

27
LAST CALL

"You don't have to go home, but you can't die here," a man said.

I opened my eyes slowly. For a moment I thought I'd died, and heaven was a bar. I tried to move, sit up, but pain stopped me.

I could move my eyes though and as the blurred world around me shook into focus I realized two things: I was lying in a booth at Kill City, and I could taste lipstick.

"He's coming around," the man who'd spoken earlier leaned over me and his voice and his face fell into solidity. It was Earnest Caan. And he was smiling. And thankfully he wasn't wearing lipstick.

"It's about time," a much nicer voice and face, with lipstick, came into view.

"Jessica?"

She nodded, before giving me a long hug. It felt nice. "You're okay. Thank the gods."

"Barely, I think, but yeah. And why is Earnest here? And, more importantly, why am I alive?" I asked, sitting up, slightly bewildered, "And why do I taste lipstick?"

"Gilles called Earnest in. Don't worry about it. And as for the lipstick, I had to kind of revive you," She grinned, "You didn't seem to mind."

I blushed so hard I almost passed out again.

"Where's Naberius, is he alright?" I asked.

"He's fine. He's right here," Jessica sat next to me as Naberius appeared with a large glass, filled to overflowing.

"I managed to get out of the bar with you before it collapsed," he said, handing me the drink. "Corpse reviver number 99. On the house."

"I don't know if I can stomach this," I said, although all I wanted was to drink the whole thing in one gulp. Drown myself in it. I sat up slowly and took a sip.

"Your basic recipe, with a twist: a little Valerian flower, some Arnica root, and a drop of chocolate bitters. It does a body good," Naberius said.

"Thank you…look…what happened in there, with Dabriel…"

Naberius waved my sentence aside abruptly, "Not right now, Dante. Later. It's done," and he moved back to the bar.

I looked over at Earnest, "And you, Mister Alliance? Are you here to take me in?"

"I had planned to, yes. I was on my way to pick you up when I received a call from the Agentia. Your friend Gilles had been in contact with Naberius. Gilles told me to get to the Lost & Found. To meet him and Naberius. I assumed I'd be able to catch you in the act, but no. I arrived in time to witness Aisha escaping and Gilles in pursuit. Naberius, without hesitating, went in to help you. I saw enough, Dante."

I gave a wry smile, "Well, I didn't want to die. I'm surprised you didn't let the building fall on me."

Earnest gave me a dead stare before bursting out laughing. "You really don't think much of me, do you? You should not take me or the things I do lightly."

He took a few steps towards me, twirled his walking stick, and then pointed it at my chest, "I am a member of the Triple Alliance, but

I don't blindly follow their archaic book of rules, Mister Dante. You are, at the moment, far more important to me alive."

"Good news for me, then. I still don't think I should work with you, though."

Earnest shrugged and twirled his walking stick like some crazed Charlie Chaplin, "No decisions need to be made right now. Maybe we can all come to some sort of agreement. I am not hell bent on having everyone killed," a quick wink, "though that is always an option."

I sat up, head pounding. "Now is definitely not the right time, Earnest."

"We'll talk later, but I'm not talking about what Dabriel was trying to do, or Aisha. That was never my intent. I say we rebuild, keep the Lost & Found open. You and Naberius would be in charge."

"In the shadows where you belong, right?"

Earnest nodded, "I'll take my share of the profits, and I'll still deal with the souls and the spirits, but never at the expense of innocent lives. My plan was always to cater towards the high-end cocktail experience. Special drinks for special occasions and treats for the high rollers willing to put dents in their souls for a taste of the forbidden. We would always make sure to keep balance. That's where Dabriel failed. Besides, it wouldn't hurt to have the Alliance on your side for once."

If I could have laughed without it hurting, I would have. "Do we really need Alliance sponsorship? The Lost & Found should stay non-denominational. All souls welcome."

"Just think about it, Dante," Earnest said quietly. "The Alliance will still be watching you. It might be worth your while to have me there to keep things copacetic."

"I'm not going to agree to anything without talking to Naberius."

Earnest stood up and pointed at me, "This conversation is not over."

"It is for now."

Earnest's upper lip slightly twitched, but he turned without saying anything else and walked out the door.

"That man needs to relax," I said, leaning back against the cushioned booth. "So. What I miss?"

JESSICA FILLED ME IN. The VPD had arrived on the scene, along with the Fire Department. Gilles came back to smooth things over with the police, and I'm not sure what sort of deal the Agentia made, but it had to have been impressive. I knew I'd never have been able to explain Earnest's presence, a two-headed demon corpse, multiple mounds of ashes, and one chewed-up body. Gilles evidently knew better magic. Aisha, unfortunately, got away with the Intoxicantata and Christophe had vanished as well, with Murmur.

"If Aisha's smart, she'll get her vindictive ass out of town before Marinette goes looking for her," Jessica grumbled.

"Marinette? Why..." I asked.

"Kill City was next on the list for Dabriel and Christophe, with Aisha calling the shots. Turns out Murmur had been sharing Marinette's secrets with them," Jessica said. "And there's also Trevor. He and Marinette were a little more than friends, and Marinette doesn't forgive or forget."

"And Nick?" I asked, "He was there, but I couldn't tell if he was dead or not."

"No sign of Nick, but the Agentia and Alliance are out in full force trying to track him down."

"Is the Lost & Found still standing?" I asked as Gilles walked into the bar.

"Barely," Gilles said, sitting down across from me, "I just came from there, the fire took most of it."

I was lucky Naberius got there when he did. The alcohol mixing with the remaining magics provided some more fuel, and the last breath of the storm fanned the flames. The Lost & Found wasn't the only place to burn. Blundertown Books had hosted a thorough fire-party. Turns out Aisha had seen to that before she left town.

"She's trying to cover all her tracks," I said, attempting to stand. I couldn't and grimaced at the pain.

"Dude, I'm taking you to the hospital," Jessica said, helping me to my feet.

I didn't argue.

As we drove, I thought about what had unfolded. So much. I didn't trust Mister Caan, even though he saved my life, but it did feel like the constant threat of the Triple Alliance was going to be a thing of the past. Another positive thing to come out of this were the stories from the rumor mill: tales of how Thomas Dante was back in action, stories of me battling vampires and demons and holding my own against elemental fury and ancient Voudou curses. All greatly exaggerated, of course, but who was I to dissuade anyone of their notions of my abilities?

I told Jessica to start letting people know I'd be available for hire: ready to help the helpless, battle injustice, and as soon as the Lost & Found was up and running again, I'd be making drinks worth dying for. It also helped when Marinette said she had my back, and any one foolish enough to take me on would have to answer to her as well.

I did have to deal with the Triple Alliance one last time, but surprisingly, Gilles and Jessica stood by me. The powers that be recognized I had done battle with, and triumphed over, evil. And I did it while remaining within the bounds of the DarkWaver Commandments. I was found not guilty, and they even removed the Reoite Corraich. I needed to learn how to control and focus my elemental energies, but Naberius promised to help. As did Gilles. I'm pretty sure whatever happened, he would be on my side often. He had proven himself to be someone I could call on in a pinch, and if what had happened was a taste of things brewing in Terminal City, then there would be plenty of pinches.

I was laid up in the hospital for a few days, and Jessica came to see me once. It was slightly uncomfortable, but I think she finally forgave me. Maybe not for everything, but for the important things. She was getting more serious with Gilles but was still willing to work with me if I could suck it up and be decent to him. I could. I knew my career as a Mystixologist at the Lost & Found would continue, but perhaps I could play another angle as well. It felt good, it almost felt right. Once again, I could be out there, solving the supernatural crimes. Maybe a new business card was in order.

Thomas Dante, DarkWave Detective.

Not as Awkward anymore, even though I had a cast on one leg, a strange metal sling on one arm, and two fractured ribs which kept me calling for extra hits of whatever painkilling concoctions I could get. I knew this because Murmur came to visit me. I was surprised, but still, it made me smile. It hurt when I smiled. It really hurt when Murmur gently lay down next to me on the bed, but I didn't let her know. I smiled, closed my eyes, and pretended we were lying on a beach somewhere far away where it didn't rain so much.

Nick had saved her from the Lost & Found, but knew he'd be in trouble, so he was once again shapeshifting in the wind. On a positive note, Gilles, maybe trying to get on my good side because of Jessica, had gotten in touch with a miracle-working mechanic who could return my Corona to its almost original splendor. Black Sunshine was coming back. I wasn't a big fan of flowers, but everything was coming up roses. It felt good to have friends again.

As for me, when I got out of the hospital, I felt like part of my past had been put to rest. Tortuous memories had been placated and tucked in. My future was clear and clean, although I had a suspicion that the Triple Alliance were going to keep their beady little Waver eyes on me. It didn't matter how careful I was or said I was going to be, I'd found a new power inside. A new way to incorporate the elements and the elixirs. Still, part of me wasn't sure I still wanted to be involved in this anymore. Watching the Wavers play their little games while everyone else went blindly on about their lives as if losing their soul was business as usual.

Reality is what you make it, right? It would be nice to find a place where curses stayed in books and drinks only got you drunk. A place where you could find monsters in the movies and not worry about them waiting for you somewhere after the credits rolled. Somewhere where the dead stayed dead and only their memories lived on. I laughed to myself. Even with all my complaints, nowhere else was for me. I couldn't be anyone else, and I couldn't unsee the things I'd seen. My elemental powers were coming back, and with them a knowledge of the world around me. The connections between the seen and the unseen and how I could work between them, and through them.

Not everyone deserved help, but some people needed help. The Lost & Found was a place where I could help them. It was time to shift the scales in a better direction. I ordered an Amor Fati from Naberius. He smiled and added a little twist to an old recipe originally concocted in a favorite New Orleans bar. The warmth hit just right.

So yeah, come on by. If I'm not here, Naberius will hook you up. If you're looking to drown your sorrows, or your ghosts, this is a great place to do it. If you're looking for someone to talk to, share a story with, we've got you covered. If you're looking for someone to help with a haunting, tear apart a curse, or give a demon a ticket out of town, well, we can help you there too. Pull up a chair, find an empty seat. Mister Naberius is behind the bar, and I'm your host for the evening. Tell me a story. Make it a good one, and I'll buy you a drink.

My name's Thomas Dante. I own the place.

LOST & FOUND

COCKTAIL MENU

Monk's Dream

Coffee Liqueur, Frangelico, Irish Cream

Take this one as a shot for a quick benediction, or in a larger glass for a slower service. Your choice, either way you will feel as if your prayers are being heard. They might not be answered, but you'll know that at least someone is listening.

Mephisto's Waltz

Gin, Vermouth, Whiskey, Absinthe, Simple Syrup, Orange Bitters

Shaken until everything is dancing, swirled into a martini glass, and the music hits as you take your first sip.

Lucifer's Friend

Jagermeister, Cinnamon Schnapps, Whiskey (Irish and Bourbon)

A layered journey for friends of the fallen angel. This could bring you up or it could take you down. It's recommended that you know which way you want to go before trying this drink.

VouDou Daze

Amaretto, Rum, Tequila

Trip into a slow trance with this little mix. Just don't make any promises you can't keep.

Courting The Lord

Absinthe, Peach Schnapps, Pomegranate, Lemonade

While giving off a devilish look, this drink leads you a little closer to the angels. The soul is opened, the flavors smooth the way, the music plays against the taste and you sing along with every sip.

Lillith's Kiss

Gin, Absinthe, Cointreau, Vermouth, Orange accents

Chilled, mixed, stirred, strained and garnished. The subtle sweetness of a floral enchantment coupled with a crisp cucumber gin and a twist of sharpness, a perfect compliment to slide across the bar towards someone you love.

Brimstone Rock

Gin, Pomegranate Juice, Grenadine, Lime Juice, Bitters

Open this box of flavor and you may not be able to close it again. That might not necessarily be a bad thing.

Ask The Angels

Gin, White Crème De Menthe, Lemon Juice, Bitters

The question is up to you, the answer is in the glass. An unfinished drink is like an unanswered question.

Illuminati

Bourbon, Peach Schnapps, White Crème De Menthe

It's sort of like a whiskey conspiracy. You know that you are drinking the Bourbon, but it's all cunningly covered up by a soft swish of mint. A snowfall, with fire.

Skating The Abyss

Absinthe, Champagne, Mandarin Juice

This is our slight twist on the Hemingway standard. A death in the afternoon is always an occasion, but being loved to death is a little more special.

Paradisiac

Prosseco, St-Germain, Crème De Violette, Citrus

A little bit Paris, a little bit New Orleans, a little floral, and a sweetness that is cut by the citrus. It's a little hard to describe... Perhaps like this; after the storm, before the sun comes out again, there is a moment like no other. Like fresh cut grass, like falling in love, like springtime. Like this drink.

Soft As Snow

Cinnamon Liqueur, Crème De Menthe, Milk, White Crème De Cacao

A slinky little mixture that hides the heat underneath a minty kiss of dream.

Stagger Lee

Irish Whiskey, Cherry Liqueur, Orange Juice, Sweet Vermouth

The tale has been told that back in the winter of '32 the last cocktail made by the bartender at the Bucket of Blood was this one, requested by a man who wouldn't think twice about shooting you over a poorly mixed drink. The details are vague, and change with each telling of the story, but one thing stays the same. This is one mean mother of a cocktail; and its name is Stagger Lee.

Sante Sangre

Gin, Cointreau, St. George Absinthe, Applejack, Sugar, Lemon

You don't want to take this one lying down, unless you're dead. Hangover remover is an understatement. This swirls somewhere between a Bloody Mary and a Corpse Reviver and can also help in an exorcism if you are running out of Holy water.

ACKNOWLEDGMENTS

I raise a glass or few to all at Dead Sky Publishing for believing in my words and helping me push them forwards; Thank you Steve Wands & Jeremy Wagner. I'm grateful for Megan Yundt's insightful edits, and so appreciative of the work Reiko Murakami did for the cover. Much gratitude to Anna Kubik and her awesome edits. — A Votre Sante!

To Meredith, Andrew & Soma. Always my family. — Egészségére!

To Legion, my bar-hopping companion in Vancouver when the idea for this story hit, & Elsie who joined in on a few rounds. Also, to Scott Chernoff, who taught me long ago that you should never leave a drink unfinished…even if it meant leaving the bar after last call with half a pint tucked away in your coat — Skol!

And to those who helped influence, edit, and spark, stir, and stir the earliest mixes of this book. Friends both old and new — You are all way more inspiring than alcohol! — Kampai!

I also want to thank every bar that's served me a well-made cocktail. I should probably thank the bars that I didn't enjoy so much, because without the bad you really have no way to appreciate the good. I just don't have the space to name them all. That being said, I would like to raise a glass to the Lava Lounge in Seattle, where I spent many of my formative alcoholic years, and to Bar Leather Apron in Oahu, where Justin pours magic into each cocktail without even trying. — Okole Maluna!

And to all my readers — Sláinte!

Yours, in whiskey and words—
Marcel Feldmar

ABOUT THE AUTHOR

Marcel Feldmar grew up in Canada, and then left.

He spent some time in Denver and Seattle but ended up living in Los Angeles, where his words get caught in traffic. He has been a regular contributor to The Big Takeover Magazine since the mid 90's and has also been working on some spoken word / music collaborations, which can be found under the name *Blue Discordant Way* on Bandcamp. Feldmar has contributed poetry to the Curious Nothing, 7th-Circle Pyrite, Rabbit's Foot, Low Life Press, and Pulp. He has a short story in Absolute Zero, the anthology from Dead Sky Publishing, and his work can also be found online on Reddit's nosleep forum, as the six-part serial "I Have To Get Rid Of This Guitar I Found" co-written with musician Kirk Hammett.